THE DEADLIEST BOUQUET

ERICA SCHULTZ
SCRIPT/LETTERS

CAROLA BORELL
ART

GAB CONTRERAS (#1–3)
TOM CHU (#4–5)
COLORS

JAMES EMMETT
EDITS

ADRIANA MELO
& CRIS PETER
COVER ART

LIANA KANGAS
NATASHA ALTERICI
INTERIOR COVER ART

D1378454

THE DEADLIEST BOUQUET. First printing. April 2023. Published by Image Comics, Inc. Office of publication: PO BOX 14457, Portland, OR 97293. Copyright © 2023 Fenix Works, Inc. All rights reserved. Contains material originally published in single magazine form as THE DEADLIEST BOUQUET #1-5. "The Deadliest Bouquet," its logos, and the likenesses of all characters herein are trademarks of Fenix Works, Inc., unless otherwise noted. "Image" and the Image Comics logos are registered trademarks of Image Comics, Inc. No part of this publication may be reproduced or transmitted, in any form or by any means (except for short excerpts for journalistic or review purposes), without the express written permission of Fenix Works, Inc. or Image Comics, Inc. All names, characters, events, and locales in this publication are entirely fictional. Any resemblance to actual persons (living or dead), events, or places, without satirical intent, is coincidental. Printed in the USA. For international rights, contact: foreignlicensing@imagecomics.com. ISBN: 978-1-5343-2489-3.

IMAGE COMICS, INC. • **Robert Kirkman:** Chief Operating Officer • **Erik Larsen:** Chief Financial Officer • **Todd McFarlane:** President • **Marc Silvestri:** Chief Executive Officer • **Jim Valentino:** Vice President • **Eric Stephenson:** Publisher / Chief Creative Officer • **Nicole Lapalme:** Vice President of Finance • **Leanna Caunter:** Accounting Analyst • **Sue Korpela:** Accounting & HR Manager • **Matt Parkinson:** Vice President of Sales & Publishing Planning • **Lorelei Bunjes:** Vice President of Digital Strategy • **Dirk Wood:** Vice President of International Sales & Licensing • **Ryan Brewer:** International Sales & Licensing Manager • **Alex Cox:** Director of Direct Market Sales • **Chloe Ramos:** Book Market & Library Sales Manager • **Emilio Bautista:** Digital Sales Coordinator • **Jon Schlaffman:** Specialty Sales Coordinator • **Kat Salazar:** Vice President of PR & Marketing • **Deanna Phelps:** Marketing Design Manager • **Drew Fitzgerald:** Marketing Content Associate • **Heather Doornink:** Vice President of Production • **Drew Gill:** Art Director • **Hilary DiLoreto:** Print Manager • **Tricia Ramos:** Traffic Manager • **Melissa Gifford:** Content Manager • **Erika Schnatz:** Senior Production Artist • **Wesley Griffith:** Production Artist • **Rich Fowlks:** Production Artist • IMAGECOMICS.COM

CHAPTER One

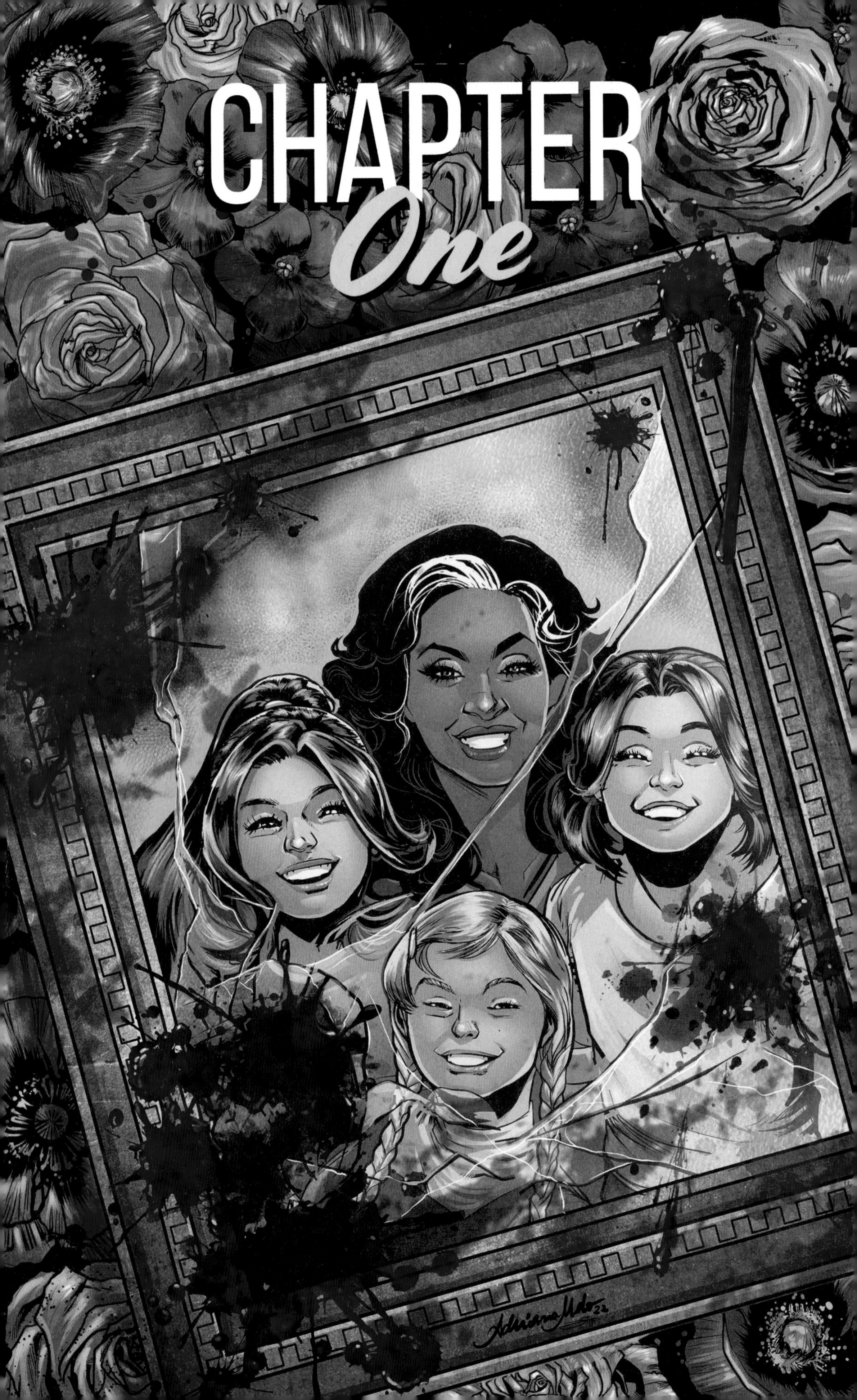

NORTH JERSEY
FEBRUARY 15, 1998
EARLY MORNING
911, WHAT'S YOUR EMERGENCY?
...
HELLO?
KLIK
Employees only
WHY...?
RING
RING
RING
C'MON, POPPY... PICK UP.

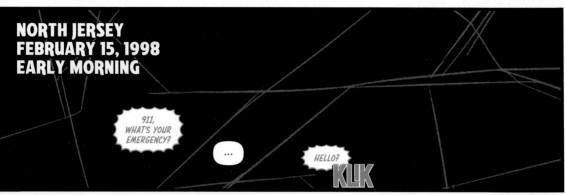

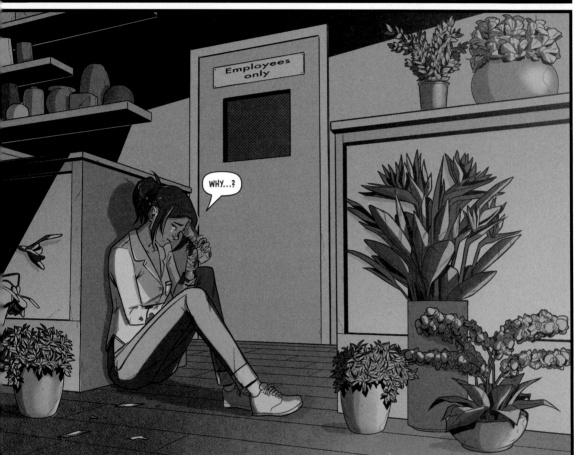

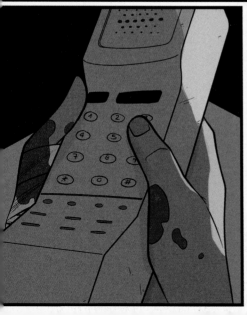

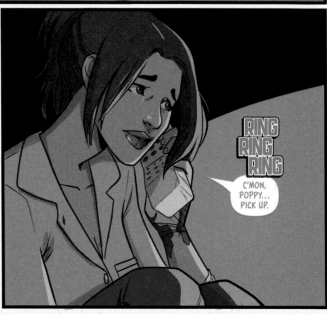

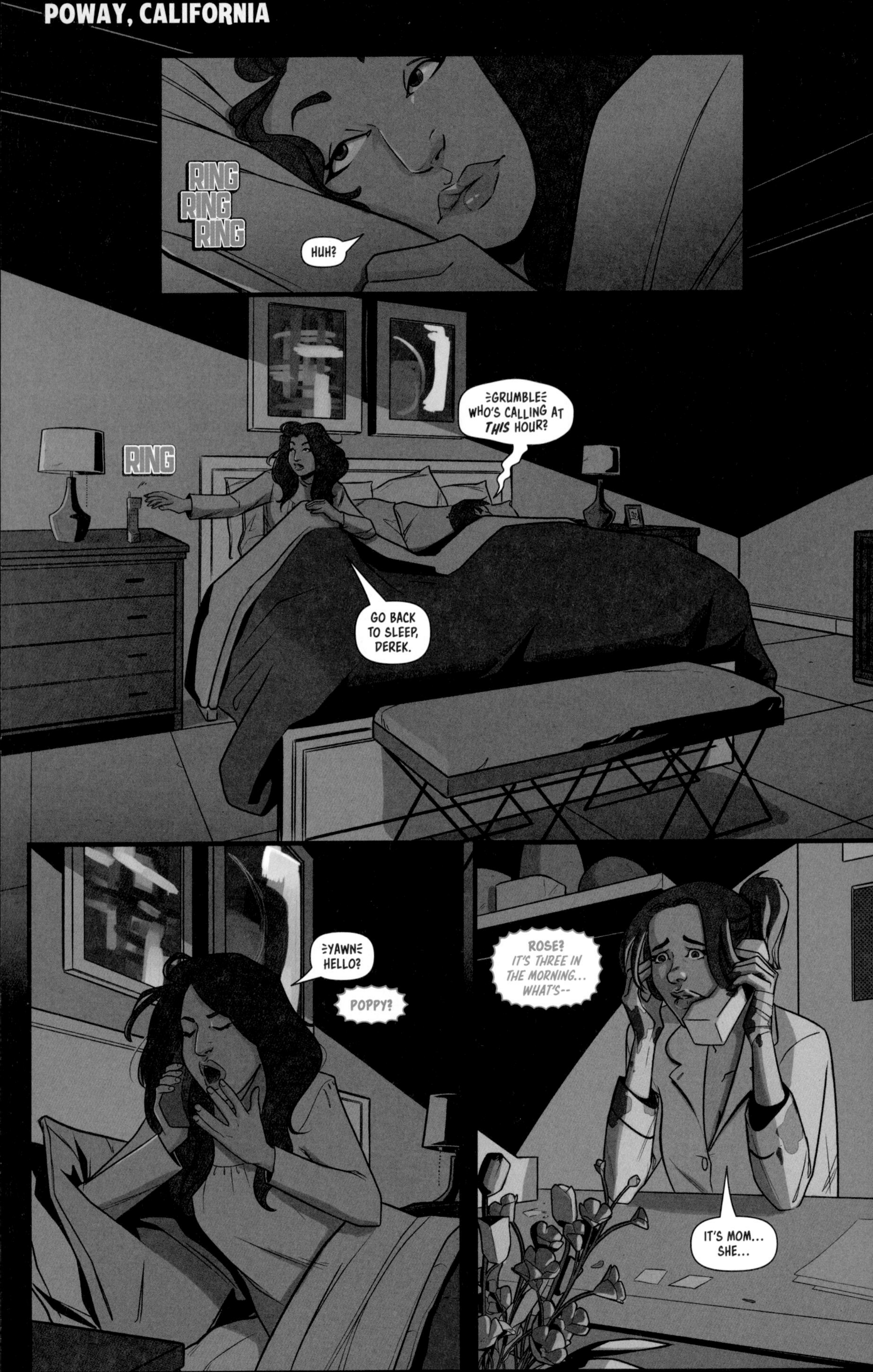
POWAY, CALIFORNIA
RING
RING
RING
HUH?
RING
≡GRUMBLE≡ WHO'S CALLING AT THIS HOUR?
GO BACK TO SLEEP, DEREK.
≡YAWN≡ HELLO?
POPPY?
ROSE? IT'S THREE IN THE MORNING... WHAT'S--
IT'S MOM... SHE...

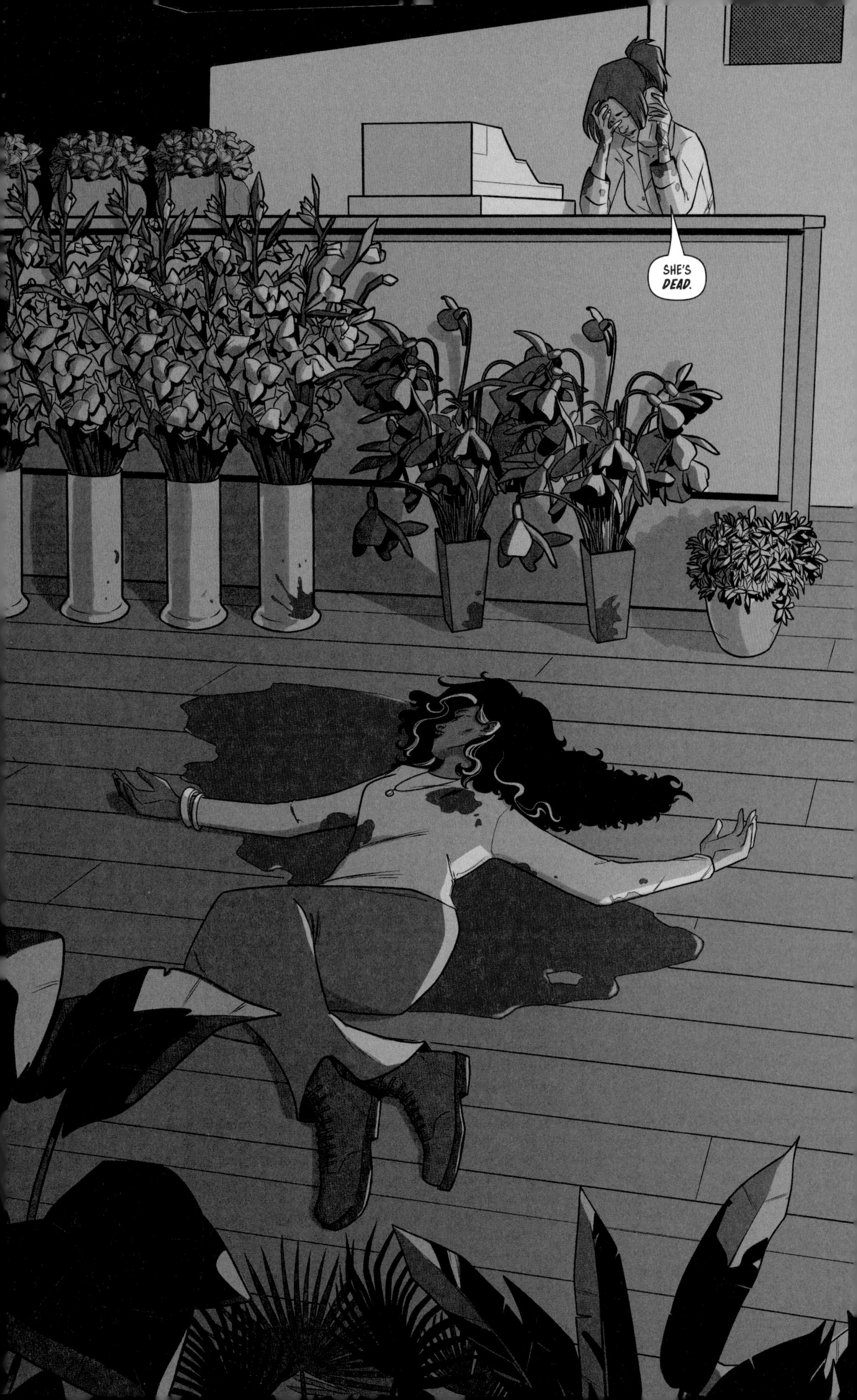
SHE'S DEAD.

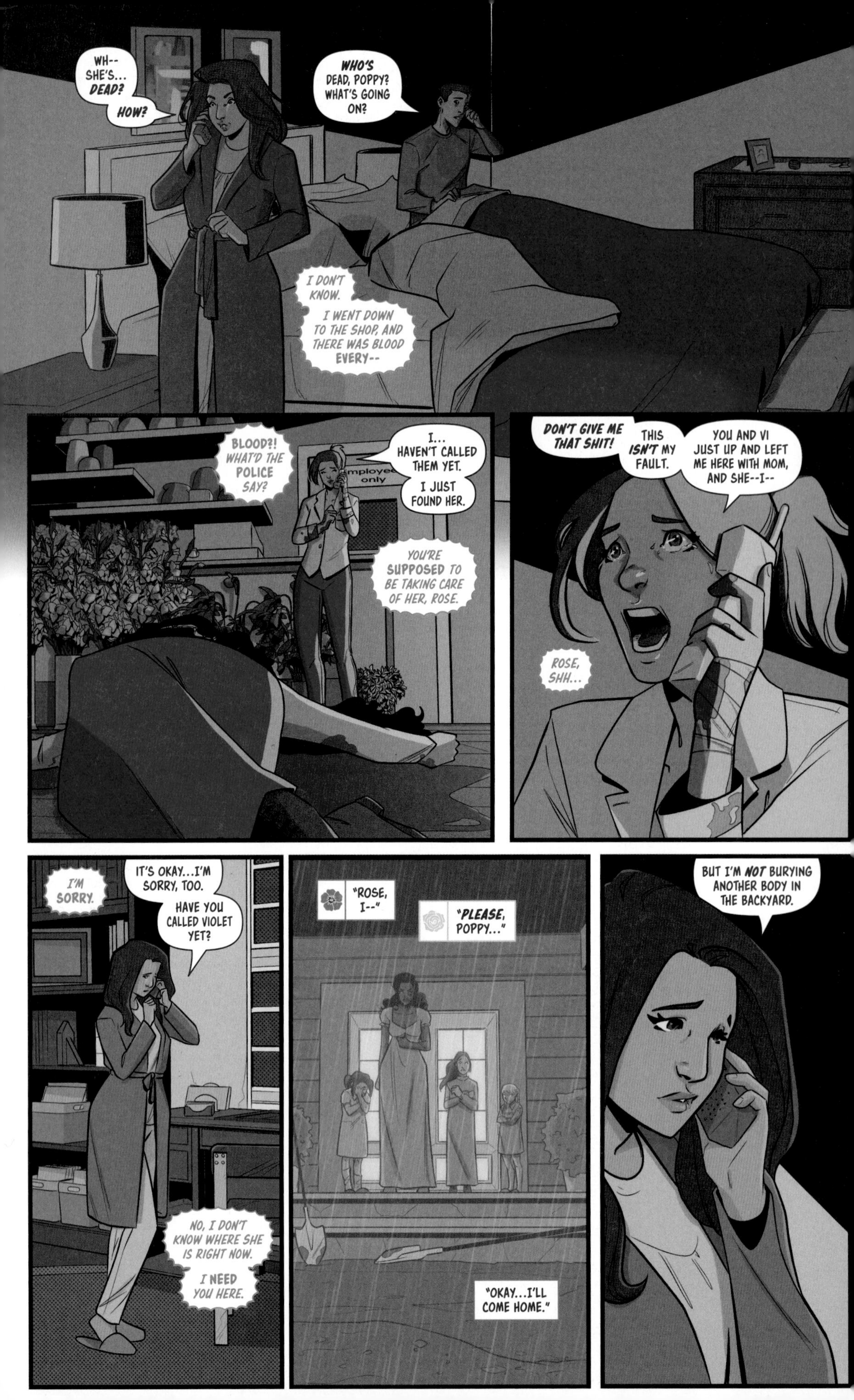

WH-- SHE'S... DEAD?
HOW?
WHO'S DEAD, POPPY? WHAT'S GOING ON?
I DON'T KNOW.
I WENT DOWN TO THE SHOP, AND THERE WAS BLOOD EVERY--
BLOOD?! WHAT'D THE POLICE SAY?
I... HAVEN'T CALLED THEM YET.
I JUST FOUND HER.
Employees only
YOU'RE SUPPOSED TO BE TAKING CARE OF HER, ROSE.
DON'T GIVE ME THAT SHIT!
THIS ISN'T MY FAULT.
YOU AND VI JUST UP AND LEFT ME HERE WITH MOM, AND SHE--I--
ROSE, SHH...
I'M SORRY.
IT'S OKAY...I'M SORRY, TOO.
HAVE YOU CALLED VIOLET YET?
NO, I DON'T KNOW WHERE SHE IS RIGHT NOW.
I NEED YOU HERE.
"ROSE, I--"
"PLEASE, POPPY..."
"OKAY...I'LL COME HOME."
BUT I'M NOT BURYING ANOTHER BODY IN THE BACKYARD.

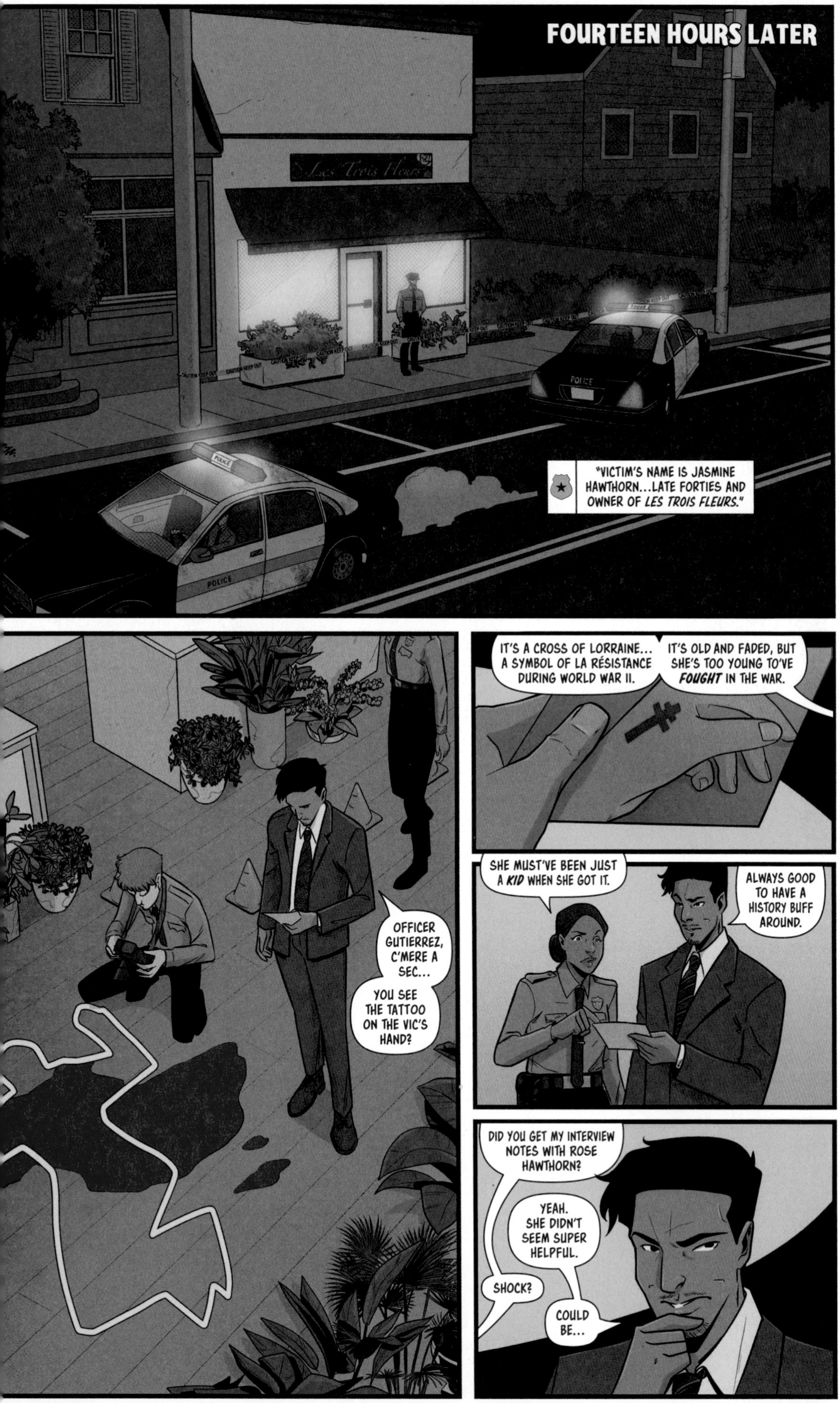
FOURTEEN HOURS LATER
Les Trois Fleurs
"VICTIM'S NAME IS JASMINE HAWTHORN...LATE FORTIES AND OWNER OF *LES TROIS FLEURS*."
OFFICER GUTIERREZ, C'MERE A SEC...
YOU SEE THE TATTOO ON THE VIC'S HAND?
IT'S A CROSS OF LORRAINE... A SYMBOL OF LA RÉSISTANCE DURING WORLD WAR II.
IT'S OLD AND FADED, BUT SHE'S TOO YOUNG TO'VE *FOUGHT* IN THE WAR.
SHE MUST'VE BEEN JUST A *KID* WHEN SHE GOT IT.
ALWAYS GOOD TO HAVE A HISTORY BUFF AROUND.
DID YOU GET MY INTERVIEW NOTES WITH ROSE HAWTHORN?
YEAH. SHE DIDN'T SEEM SUPER HELPFUL.
SHOCK?
COULD BE...

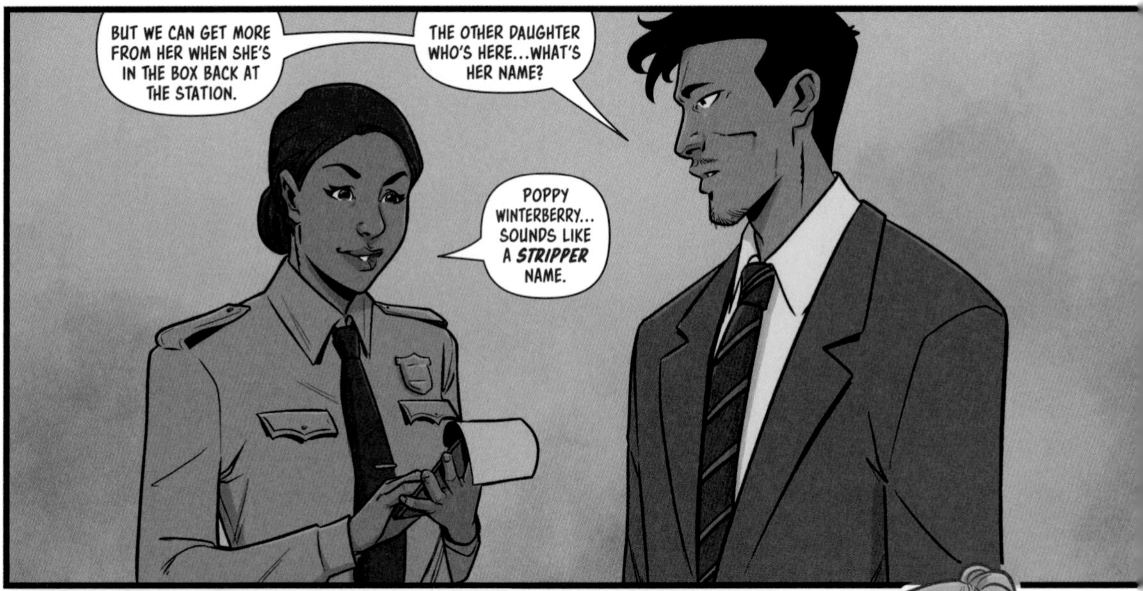
BUT WE CAN GET MORE FROM HER WHEN SHE'S IN THE BOX BACK AT THE STATION.
THE OTHER DAUGHTER WHO'S HERE...WHAT'S HER NAME?
POPPY WINTERBERRY... SOUNDS LIKE A STRIPPER NAME.
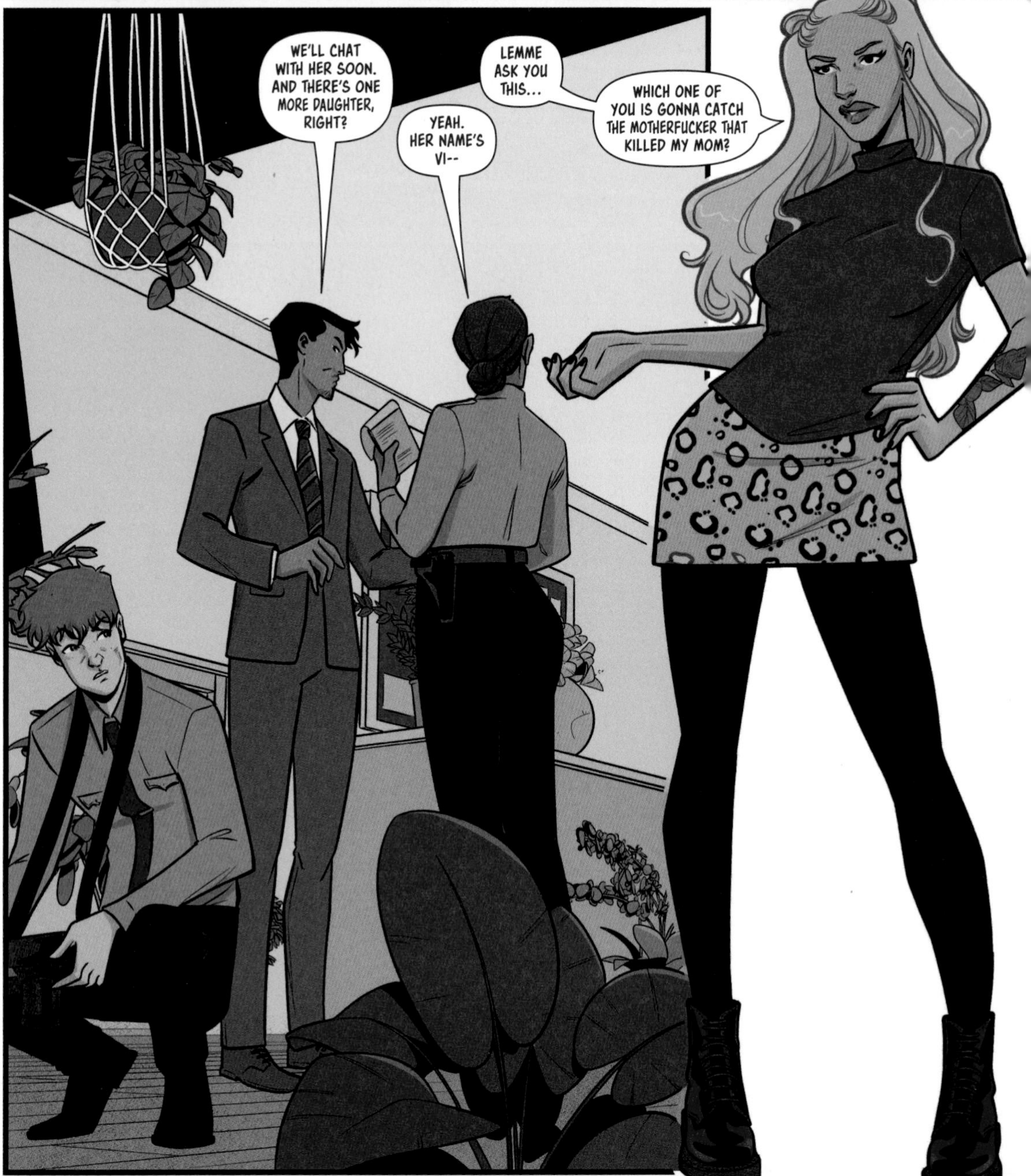
WE'LL CHAT WITH HER SOON. AND THERE'S ONE MORE DAUGHTER, RIGHT?
YEAH. HER NAME'S VI--
LEMME ASK YOU THIS...
WHICH ONE OF YOU IS GONNA CATCH THE MOTHERFUCKER THAT KILLED MY MOM?

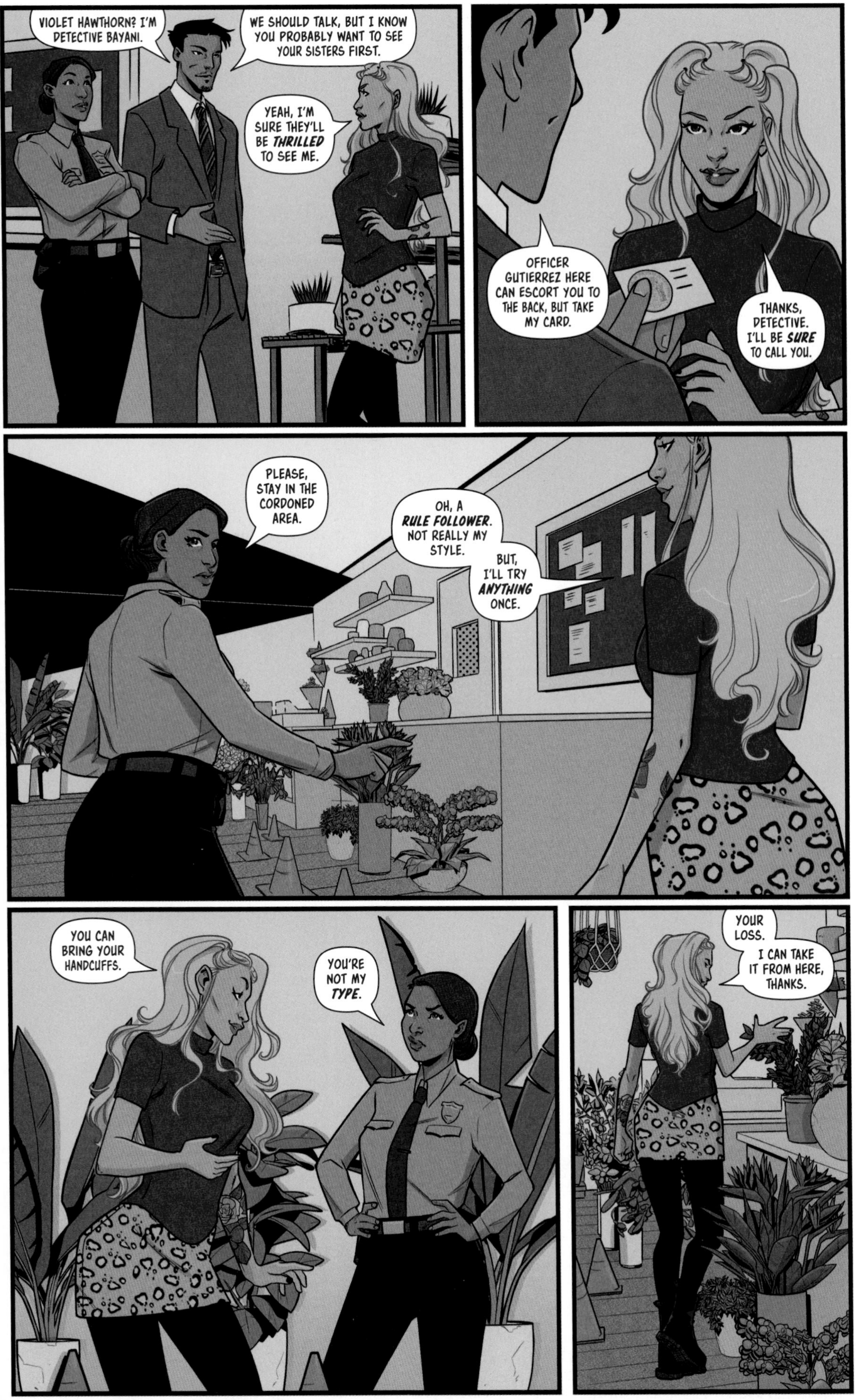
VIOLET HAWTHORN? I'M DETECTIVE BAYANI.
WE SHOULD TALK, BUT I KNOW YOU PROBABLY WANT TO SEE YOUR SISTERS FIRST.
YEAH, I'M SURE THEY'LL BE ***THRILLED*** TO SEE ME.
OFFICER GUTIERREZ HERE CAN ESCORT YOU TO THE BACK, BUT TAKE MY CARD.
THANKS, DETECTIVE. I'LL BE ***SURE*** TO CALL YOU.
PLEASE, STAY IN THE CORDONED AREA.
OH, A ***RULE FOLLOWER***. NOT REALLY MY STYLE.
BUT, I'LL TRY ***ANYTHING*** ONCE.
YOU CAN BRING YOUR HANDCUFFS.
YOU'RE NOT MY ***TYPE***.
YOUR LOSS.
I CAN TAKE IT FROM HERE, THANKS.

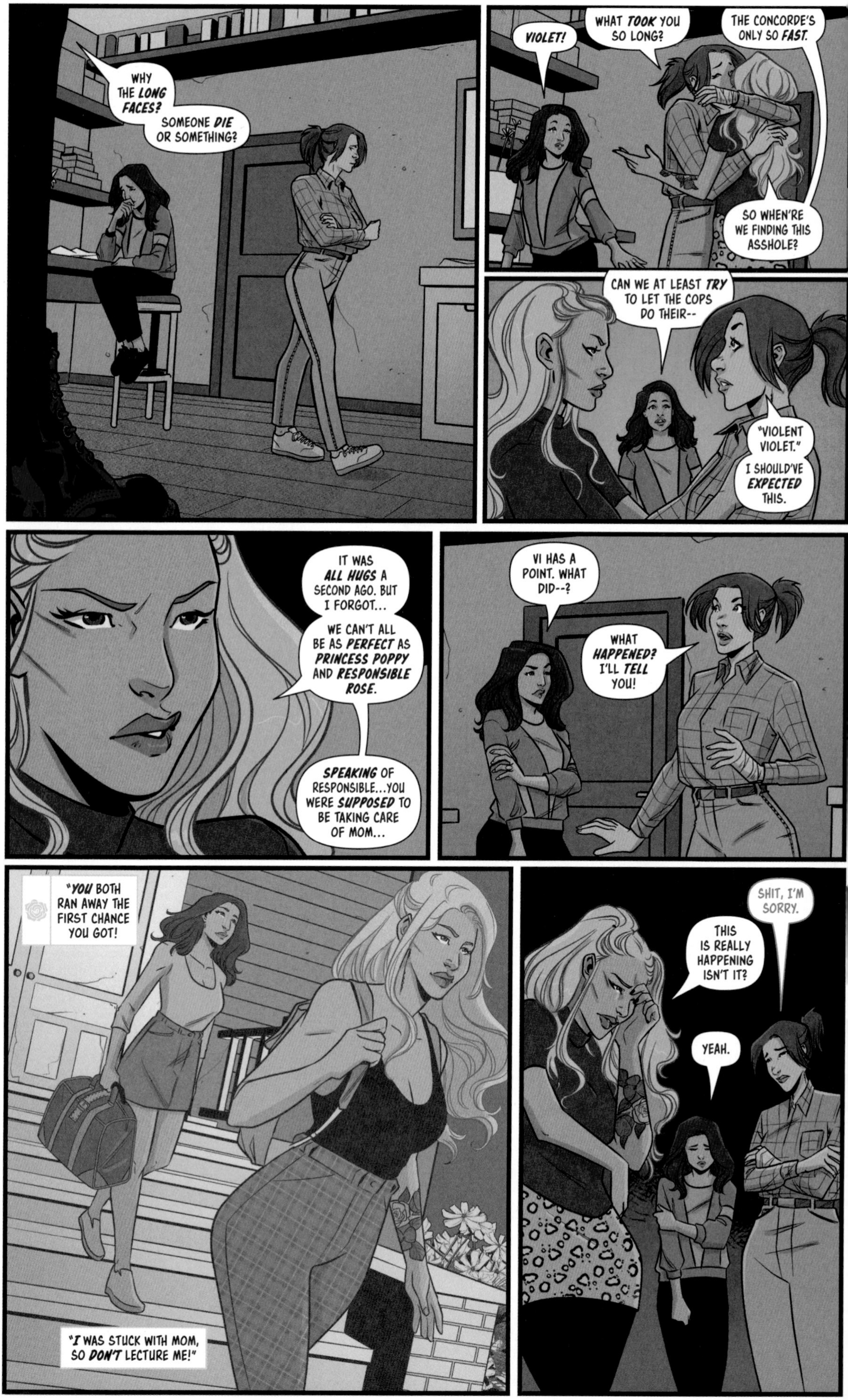

WHY THE LONG FACES?
SOMEONE DIE OR SOMETHING?
VIOLET!
WHAT TOOK YOU SO LONG?
THE CONCORDE'S ONLY SO FAST.
SO WHEN'RE WE FINDING THIS ASSHOLE?
CAN WE AT LEAST TRY TO LET THE COPS DO THEIR--
"VIOLENT VIOLET." I SHOULD'VE EXPECTED THIS.
IT WAS ALL HUGS A SECOND AGO. BUT I FORGOT...
WE CAN'T ALL BE AS PERFECT AS PRINCESS POPPY AND RESPONSIBLE ROSE.
SPEAKING OF RESPONSIBLE...YOU WERE SUPPOSED TO BE TAKING CARE OF MOM...
VI HAS A POINT. WHAT DID--?
WHAT HAPPENED? I'LL TELL YOU!
"YOU BOTH RAN AWAY THE FIRST CHANCE YOU GOT!
"I WAS STUCK WITH MOM, SO DON'T LECTURE ME!"
SHIT, I'M SORRY.
THIS IS REALLY HAPPENING ISN'T IT?
YEAH.

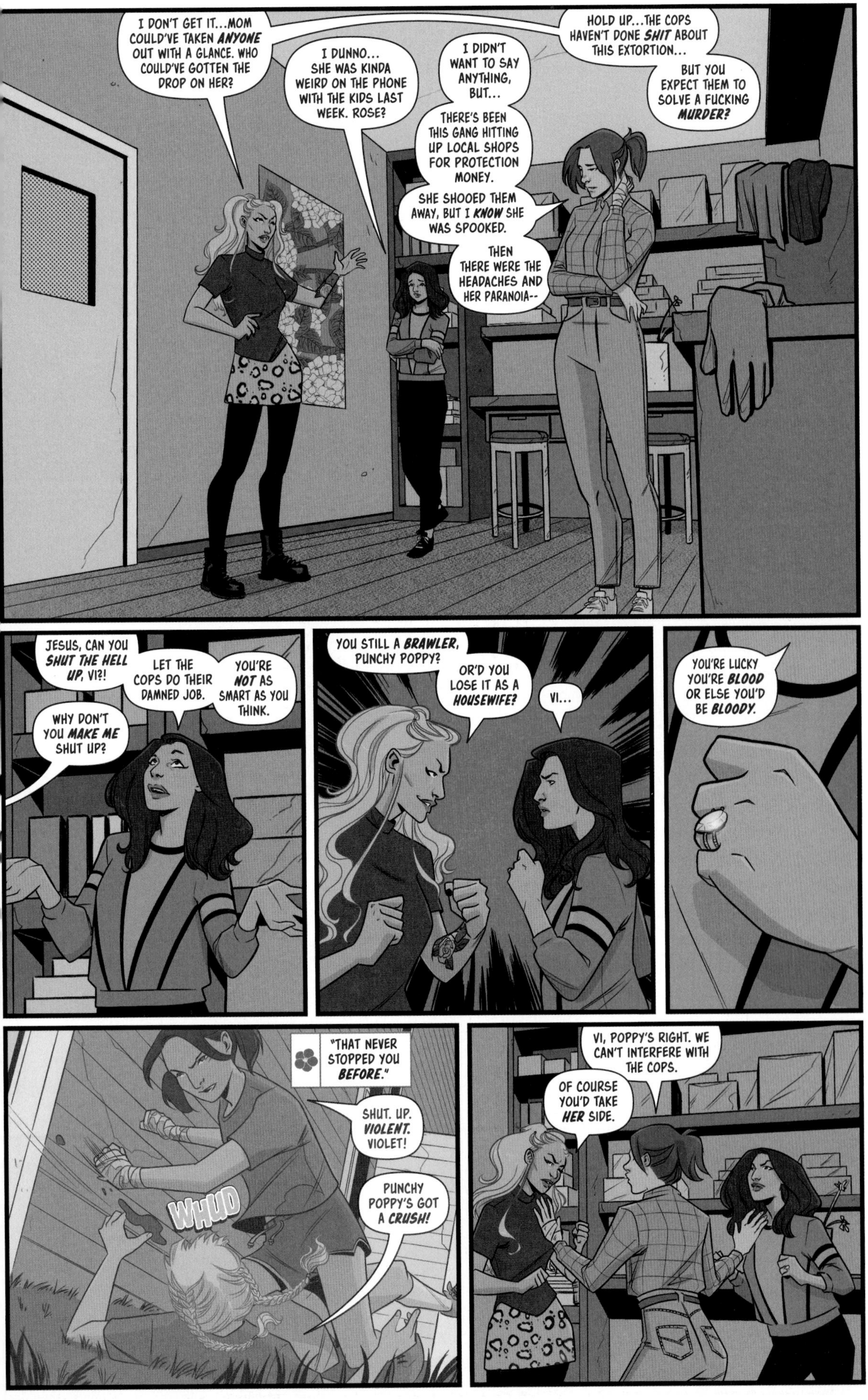
I DON'T GET IT...MOM COULD'VE TAKEN ANYONE OUT WITH A GLANCE. WHO COULD'VE GOTTEN THE DROP ON HER?
I DUNNO... SHE WAS KINDA WEIRD ON THE PHONE WITH THE KIDS LAST WEEK. ROSE?
I DIDN'T WANT TO SAY ANYTHING, BUT...
THERE'S BEEN THIS GANG HITTING UP LOCAL SHOPS FOR PROTECTION MONEY.
SHE SHOOED THEM AWAY, BUT I KNOW SHE WAS SPOOKED.
THEN THERE WERE THE HEADACHES AND HER PARANOIA--
HOLD UP...THE COPS HAVEN'T DONE SHIT ABOUT THIS EXTORTION...
BUT YOU EXPECT THEM TO SOLVE A FUCKING MURDER?
JESUS, CAN YOU SHUT THE HELL UP, VI?!
LET THE COPS DO THEIR DAMNED JOB.
YOU'RE NOT AS SMART AS YOU THINK.
WHY DON'T YOU MAKE ME SHUT UP?
YOU STILL A BRAWLER, PUNCHY POPPY?
OR'D YOU LOSE IT AS A HOUSEWIFE?
VI...
YOU'RE LUCKY YOU'RE BLOOD OR ELSE YOU'D BE BLOODY.
"THAT NEVER STOPPED YOU BEFORE."
SHUT. UP. VIOLENT. VIOLET!
WHUD
PUNCHY POPPY'S GOT A CRUSH!
VI, POPPY'S RIGHT. WE CAN'T INTERFERE WITH THE COPS.
OF COURSE YOU'D TAKE HER SIDE.

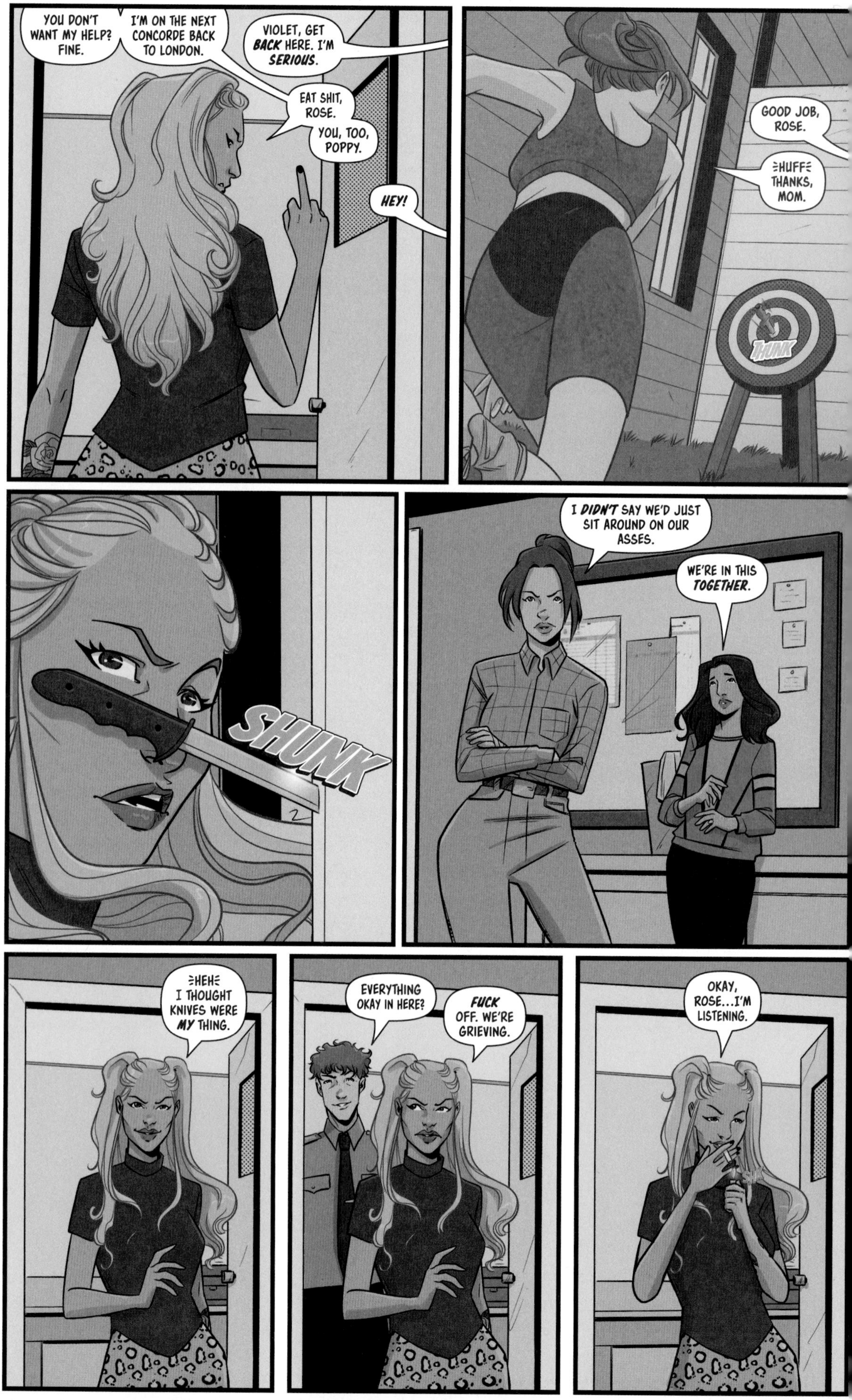
YOU DON'T WANT MY HELP? FINE.
I'M ON THE NEXT CONCORDE BACK TO LONDON.
VIOLET, GET BACK HERE. I'M SERIOUS.
EAT SHIT, ROSE.
YOU, TOO, POPPY.
HEY!
GOOD JOB, ROSE.
HUFF THANKS, MOM.
THUNK
SHUNK
I DIDN'T SAY WE'D JUST SIT AROUND ON OUR ASSES.
WE'RE IN THIS TOGETHER.
HEH I THOUGHT KNIVES WERE MY THING.
EVERYTHING OKAY IN HERE?
FUCK OFF. WE'RE GRIEVING.
OKAY, ROSE...I'M LISTENING.

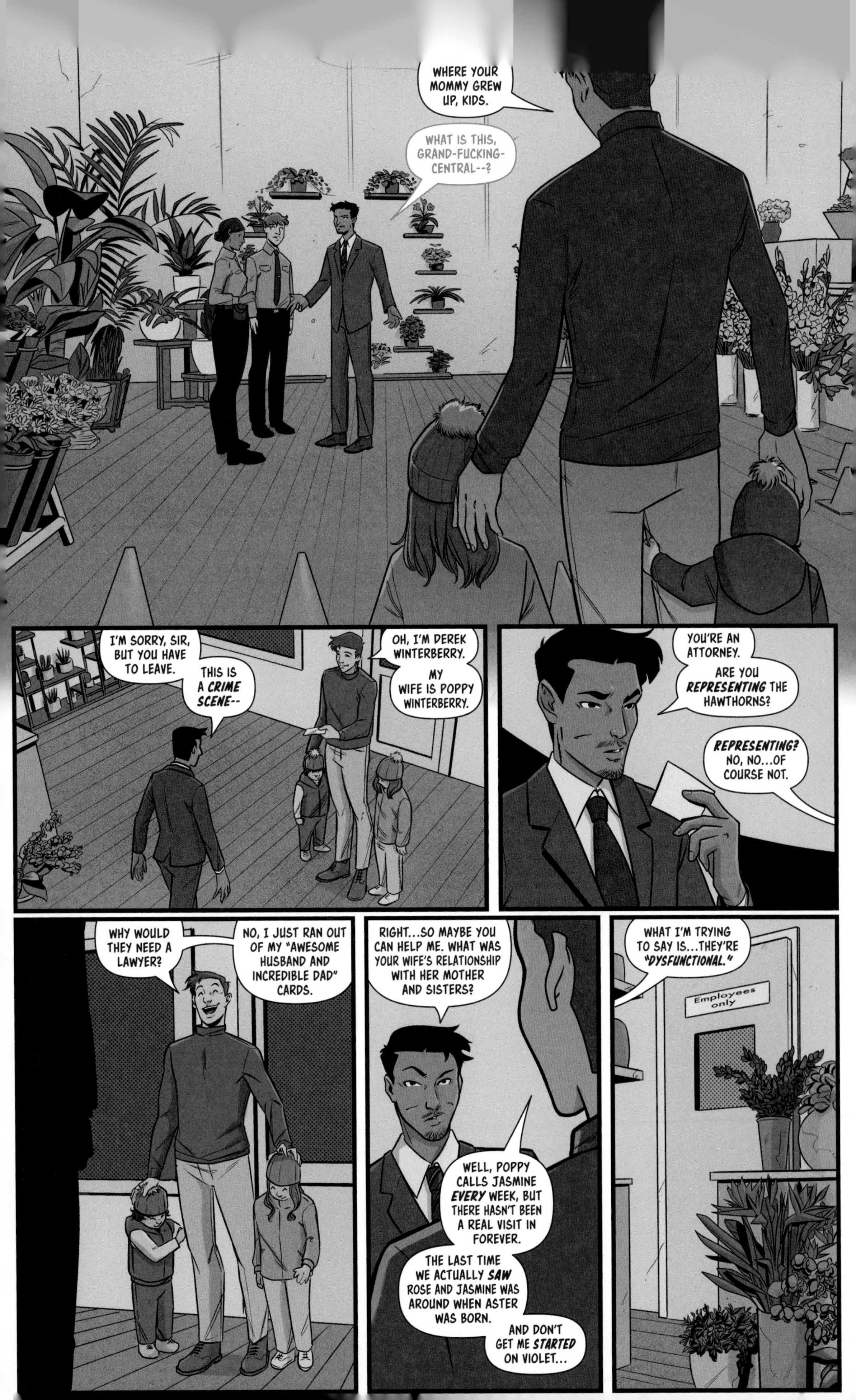
WHERE YOUR MOMMY GREW UP, KIDS.
WHAT IS THIS, GRAND-FUCKING-CENTRAL--?
I'M SORRY, SIR, BUT YOU HAVE TO LEAVE.
THIS IS A CRIME SCENE--
OH, I'M DEREK WINTERBERRY.
MY WIFE IS POPPY WINTERBERRY.
YOU'RE AN ATTORNEY.
ARE YOU REPRESENTING THE HAWTHORNS?
REPRESENTING? NO, NO...OF COURSE NOT.
WHY WOULD THEY NEED A LAWYER?
NO, I JUST RAN OUT OF MY "AWESOME HUSBAND AND INCREDIBLE DAD" CARDS.
RIGHT...SO MAYBE YOU CAN HELP ME. WHAT WAS YOUR WIFE'S RELATIONSHIP WITH HER MOTHER AND SISTERS?
WELL, POPPY CALLS JASMINE EVERY WEEK, BUT THERE HASN'T BEEN A REAL VISIT IN FOREVER.
THE LAST TIME WE ACTUALLY SAW ROSE AND JASMINE WAS AROUND WHEN ASTER WAS BORN.
AND DON'T GET ME STARTED ON VIOLET...
WHAT I'M TRYING TO SAY IS...THEY'RE "DYSFUNCTIONAL."
Employees only

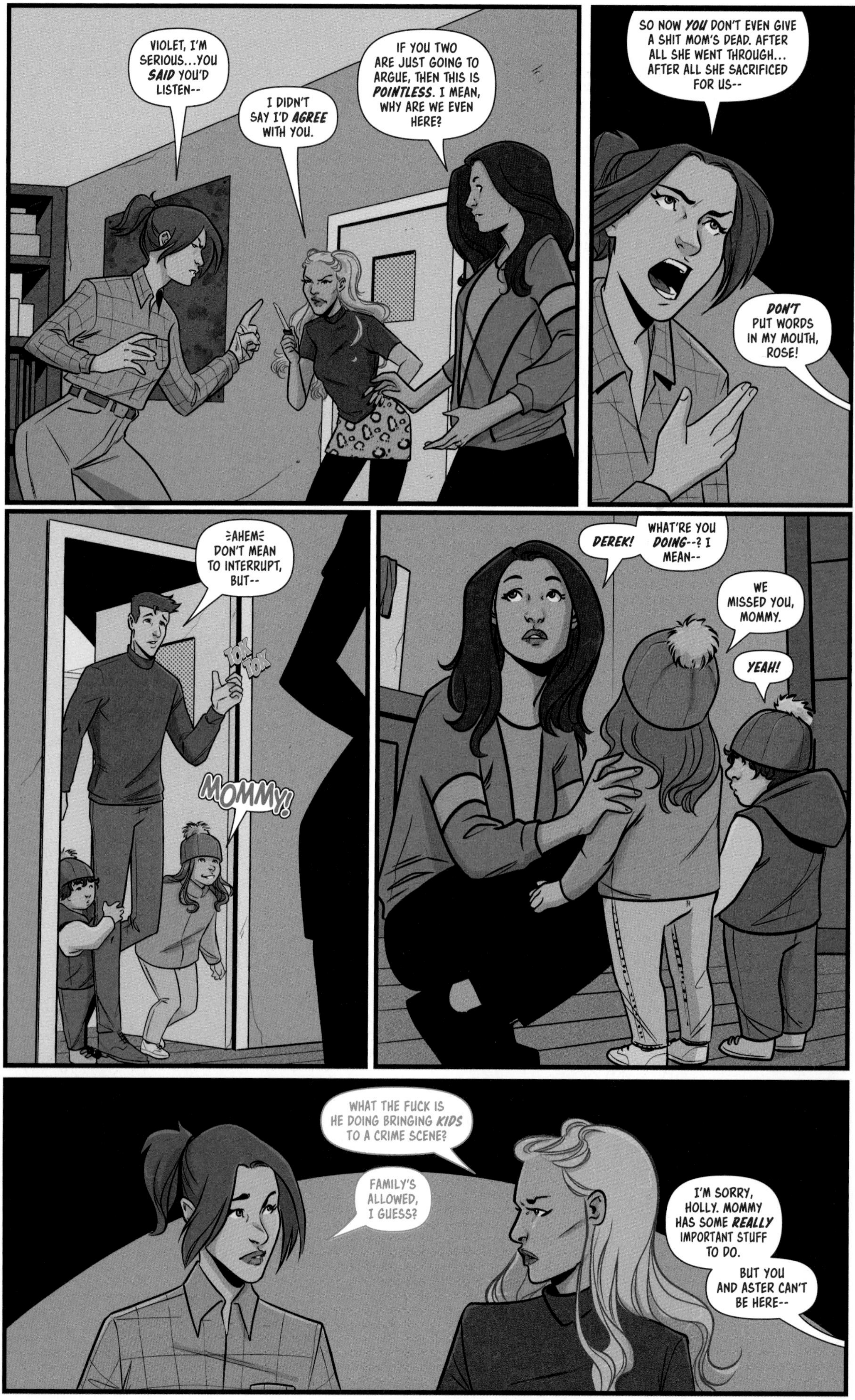
VIOLET, I'M SERIOUS...YOU SAID YOU'D LISTEN--
I DIDN'T SAY I'D AGREE WITH YOU.
IF YOU TWO ARE JUST GOING TO ARGUE, THEN THIS IS POINTLESS. I MEAN, WHY ARE WE EVEN HERE?
SO NOW YOU DON'T EVEN GIVE A SHIT MOM'S DEAD. AFTER ALL SHE WENT THROUGH... AFTER ALL SHE SACRIFICED FOR US--
DON'T PUT WORDS IN MY MOUTH, ROSE!
AHEM DON'T MEAN TO INTERRUPT, BUT--
TOK TOK
MOMMY!
DEREK!
WHAT'RE YOU DOING--? I MEAN--
WE MISSED YOU, MOMMY.
YEAH!
WHAT THE FUCK IS HE DOING BRINGING KIDS TO A CRIME SCENE?
FAMILY'S ALLOWED, I GUESS?
I'M SORRY, HOLLY. MOMMY HAS SOME REALLY IMPORTANT STUFF TO DO.
BUT YOU AND ASTER CAN'T BE HERE--

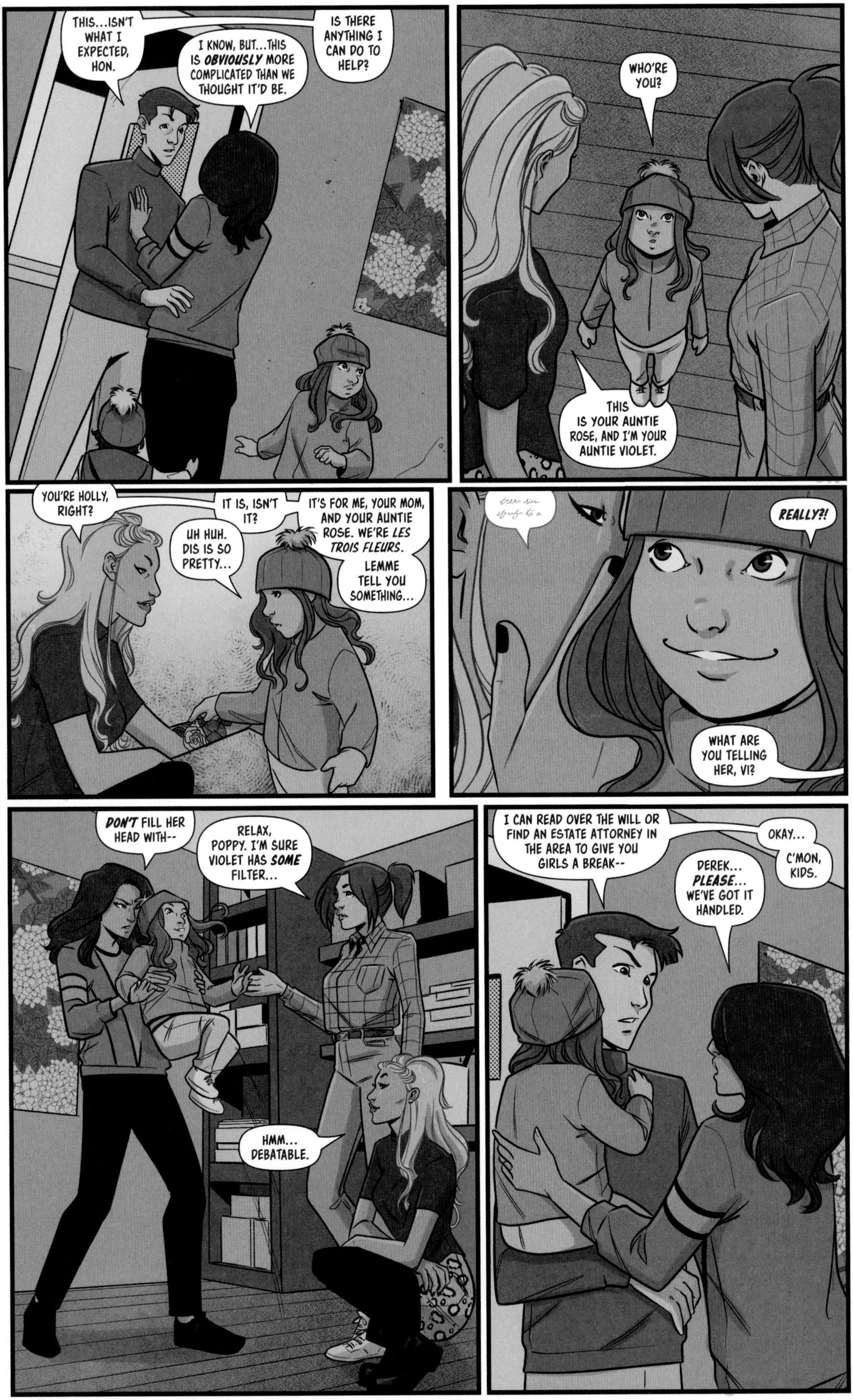
THIS...ISN'T WHAT I EXPECTED, HON.
I KNOW, BUT...THIS IS *OBVIOUSLY* MORE COMPLICATED THAN WE THOUGHT IT'D BE.
IS THERE ANYTHING I CAN DO TO HELP?
WHO'RE YOU?
THIS IS YOUR AUNTIE ROSE, AND I'M YOUR AUNTIE VIOLET.
YOU'RE HOLLY, RIGHT?
UH HUH. DIS IS SO PRETTY...
IT IS, ISN'T IT?
IT'S FOR ME, YOUR MOM, AND YOUR AUNTIE ROSE. WE'RE *LES TROIS FLEURS*.
LEMME TELL YOU SOMETHING...
REALLY?!
WHAT ARE YOU TELLING HER, VI?
DON'T FILL HER HEAD WITH--
RELAX, POPPY. I'M SURE VIOLET HAS *SOME* FILTER...
HMM... DEBATABLE.
I CAN READ OVER THE WILL OR FIND AN ESTATE ATTORNEY IN THE AREA TO GIVE YOU GIRLS A BREAK--
DEREK... *PLEASE*... WE'VE GOT IT HANDLED.
OKAY...
C'MON, KIDS.

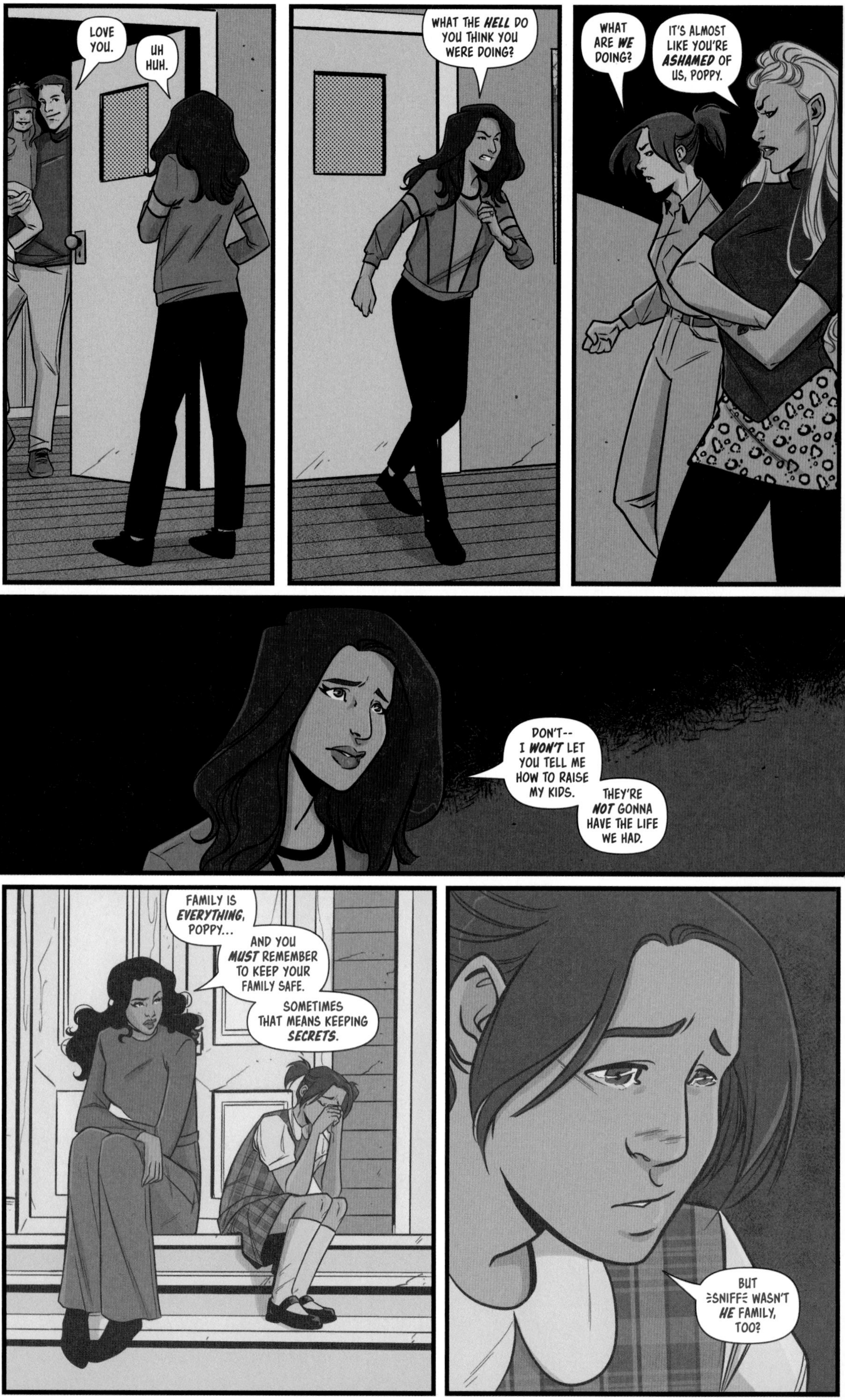
LOVE YOU.
UH HUH.
WHAT THE HELL DO YOU THINK YOU WERE DOING?
WHAT ARE WE DOING?
IT'S ALMOST LIKE YOU'RE ASHAMED OF US, POPPY.
DON'T-- I WON'T LET YOU TELL ME HOW TO RAISE MY KIDS.
THEY'RE NOT GONNA HAVE THE LIFE WE HAD.
FAMILY IS EVERYTHING, POPPY...
AND YOU MUST REMEMBER TO KEEP YOUR FAMILY SAFE.
SOMETIMES THAT MEANS KEEPING SECRETS.
BUT ≡SNIFF≡ WASN'T HE FAMILY, TOO?

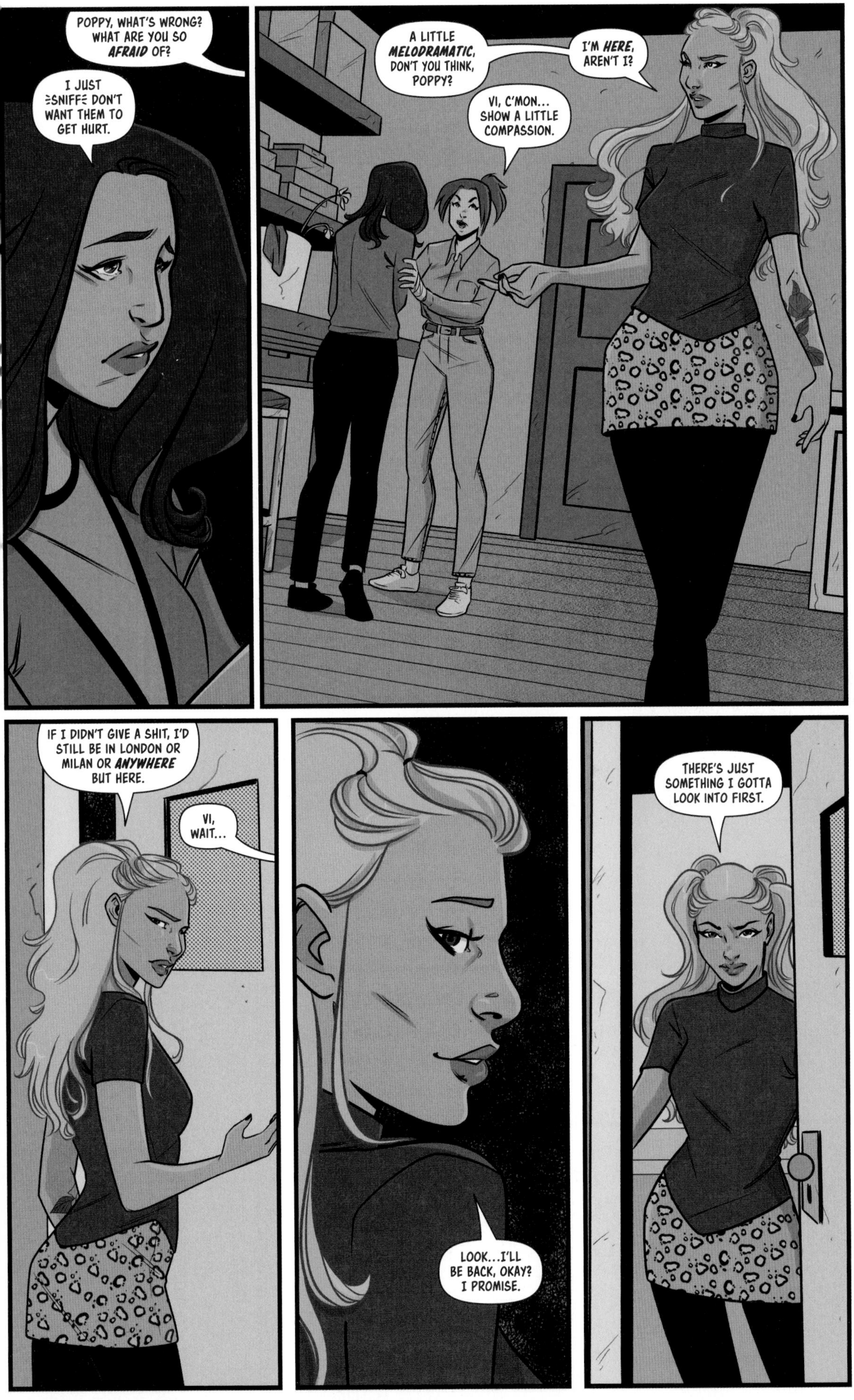
POPPY, WHAT'S WRONG? WHAT ARE YOU SO AFRAID OF?
I JUST ≡SNIFF≡ DON'T WANT THEM TO GET HURT.
A LITTLE MELODRAMATIC, DON'T YOU THINK, POPPY?
I'M HERE, AREN'T I?
VI, C'MON... SHOW A LITTLE COMPASSION.
IF I DIDN'T GIVE A SHIT, I'D STILL BE IN LONDON OR MILAN OR ANYWHERE BUT HERE.
VI, WAIT...
LOOK...I'LL BE BACK, OKAY? I PROMISE.
THERE'S JUST SOMETHING I GOTTA LOOK INTO FIRST.

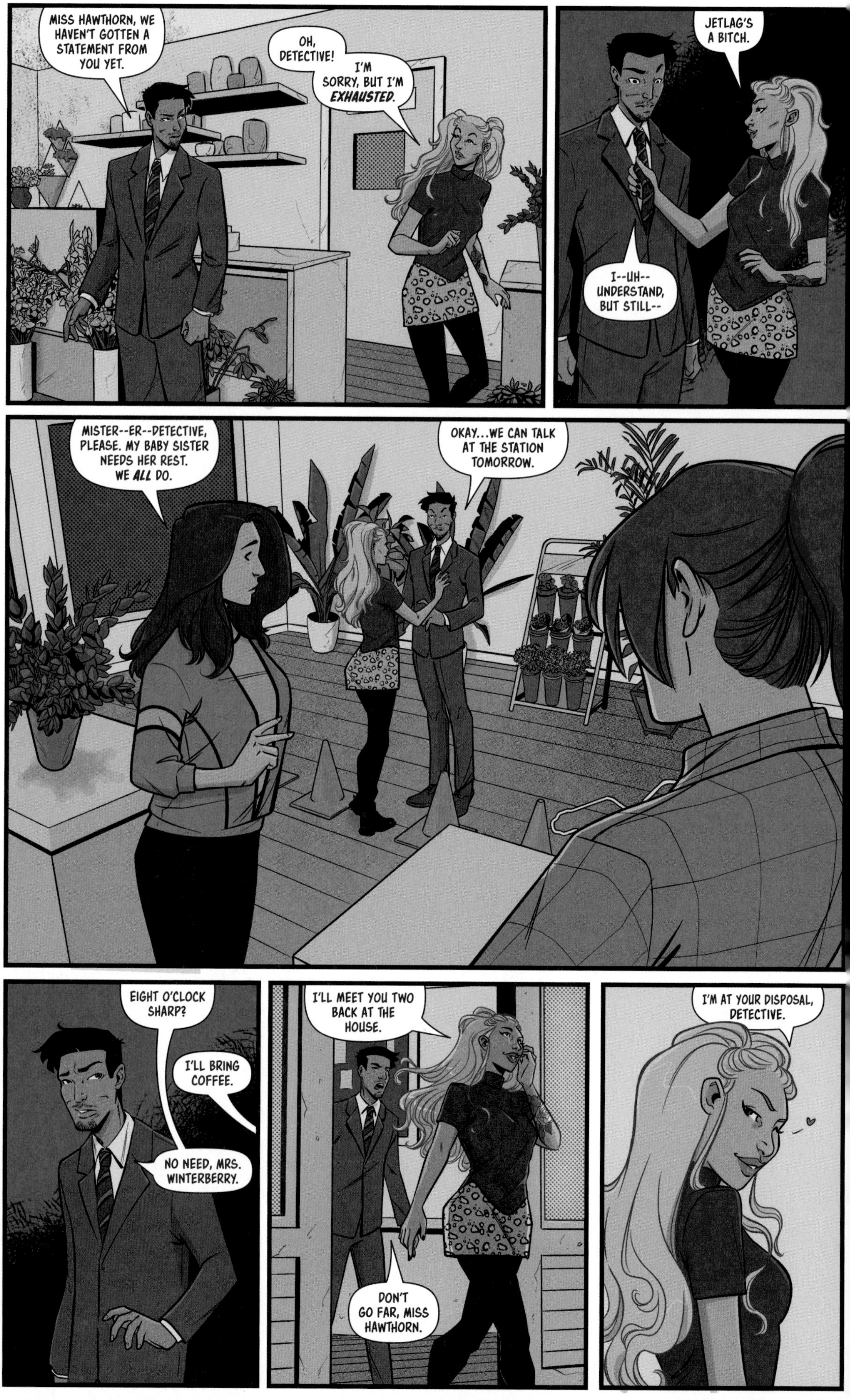
MISS HAWTHORN, WE HAVEN'T GOTTEN A STATEMENT FROM YOU YET.
OH, DETECTIVE!
I'M SORRY, BUT I'M *EXHAUSTED*.
JETLAG'S A BITCH.
I--UH--UNDERSTAND, BUT STILL--
MISTER--ER--DETECTIVE, PLEASE. MY BABY SISTER NEEDS HER REST. WE *ALL* DO.
OKAY...WE CAN TALK AT THE STATION TOMORROW.
EIGHT O'CLOCK SHARP?
I'LL BRING COFFEE.
NO NEED, MRS. WINTERBERRY.
I'LL MEET YOU TWO BACK AT THE HOUSE.
DON'T GO FAR, MISS HAWTHORN.
I'M AT YOUR DISPOSAL, DETECTIVE.

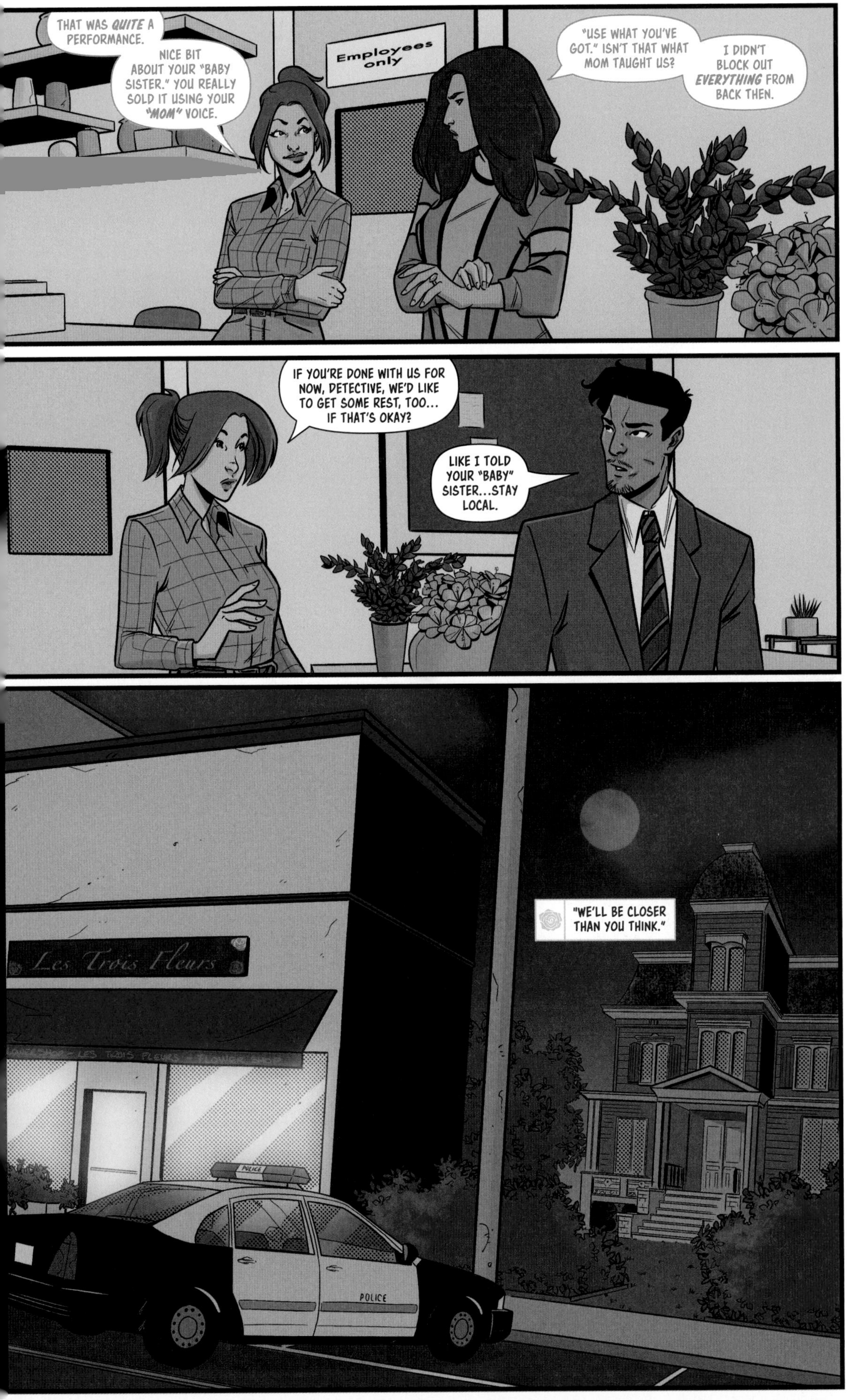

THAT WAS *QUITE* A PERFORMANCE.
NICE BIT ABOUT YOUR "BABY SISTER." YOU REALLY SOLD IT USING YOUR *"MOM"* VOICE.
Employees only
"USE WHAT YOU'VE GOT." ISN'T THAT WHAT MOM TAUGHT US?
I DIDN'T BLOCK OUT *EVERYTHING* FROM BACK THEN.
IF YOU'RE DONE WITH US FOR NOW, DETECTIVE, WE'D LIKE TO GET SOME REST, TOO... IF THAT'S OKAY?
LIKE I TOLD YOUR "BABY" SISTER...STAY LOCAL.
Les Trois Fleurs
POLICE
POLICE
"WE'LL BE CLOSER THAN YOU THINK."

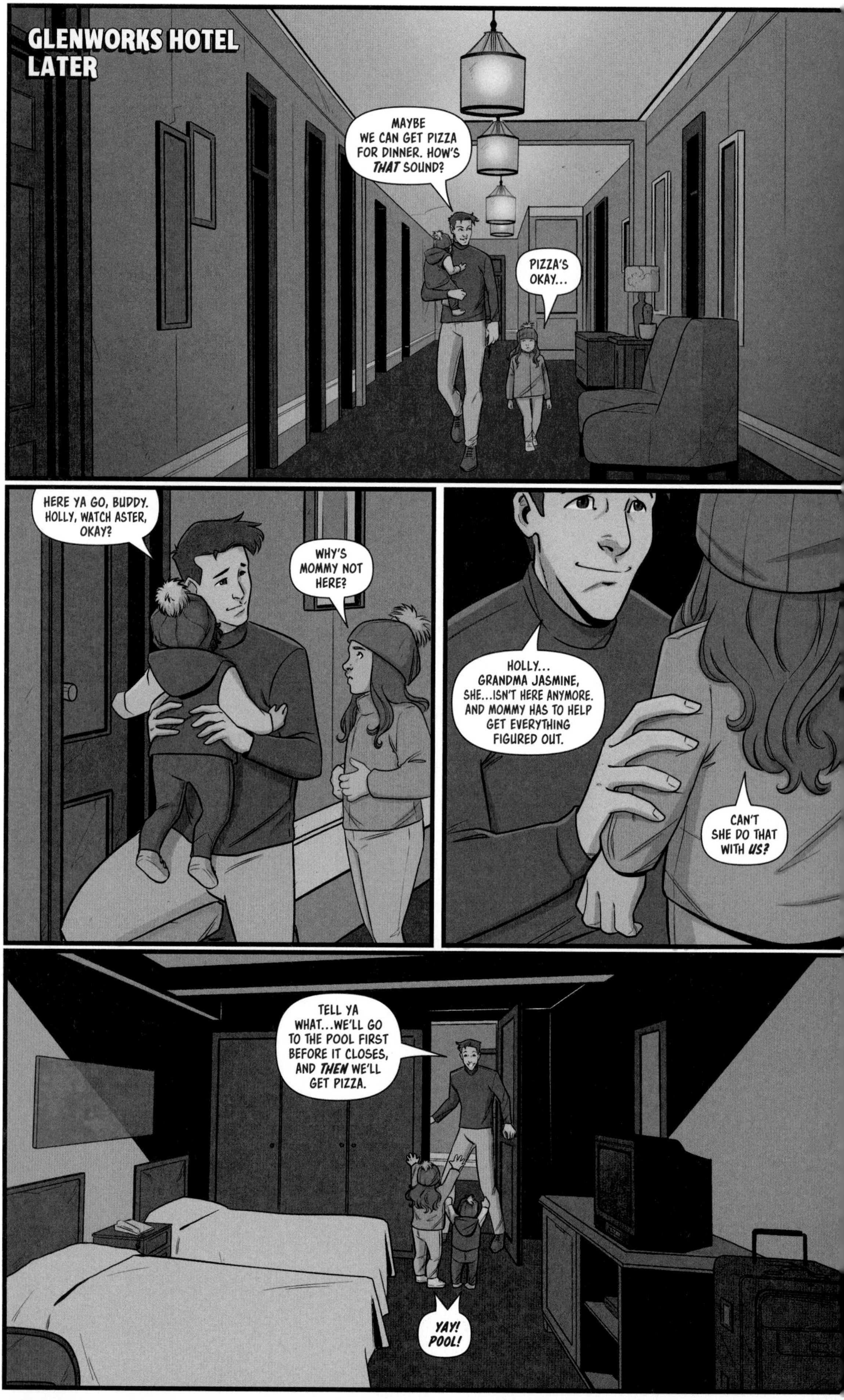
GLENWORKS HOTEL
LATER
MAYBE WE CAN GET PIZZA FOR DINNER. HOW'S *THAT* SOUND?
PIZZA'S OKAY...
HERE YA GO, BUDDY. HOLLY, WATCH ASTER, OKAY?
WHY'S MOMMY NOT HERE?
HOLLY... GRANDMA JASMINE, SHE...ISN'T HERE ANYMORE. AND MOMMY HAS TO HELP GET EVERYTHING FIGURED OUT.
CAN'T SHE DO THAT WITH *US?*
TELL YA WHAT...WE'LL GO TO THE POOL FIRST BEFORE IT CLOSES, AND *THEN* WE'LL GET PIZZA.
YAY! POOL!

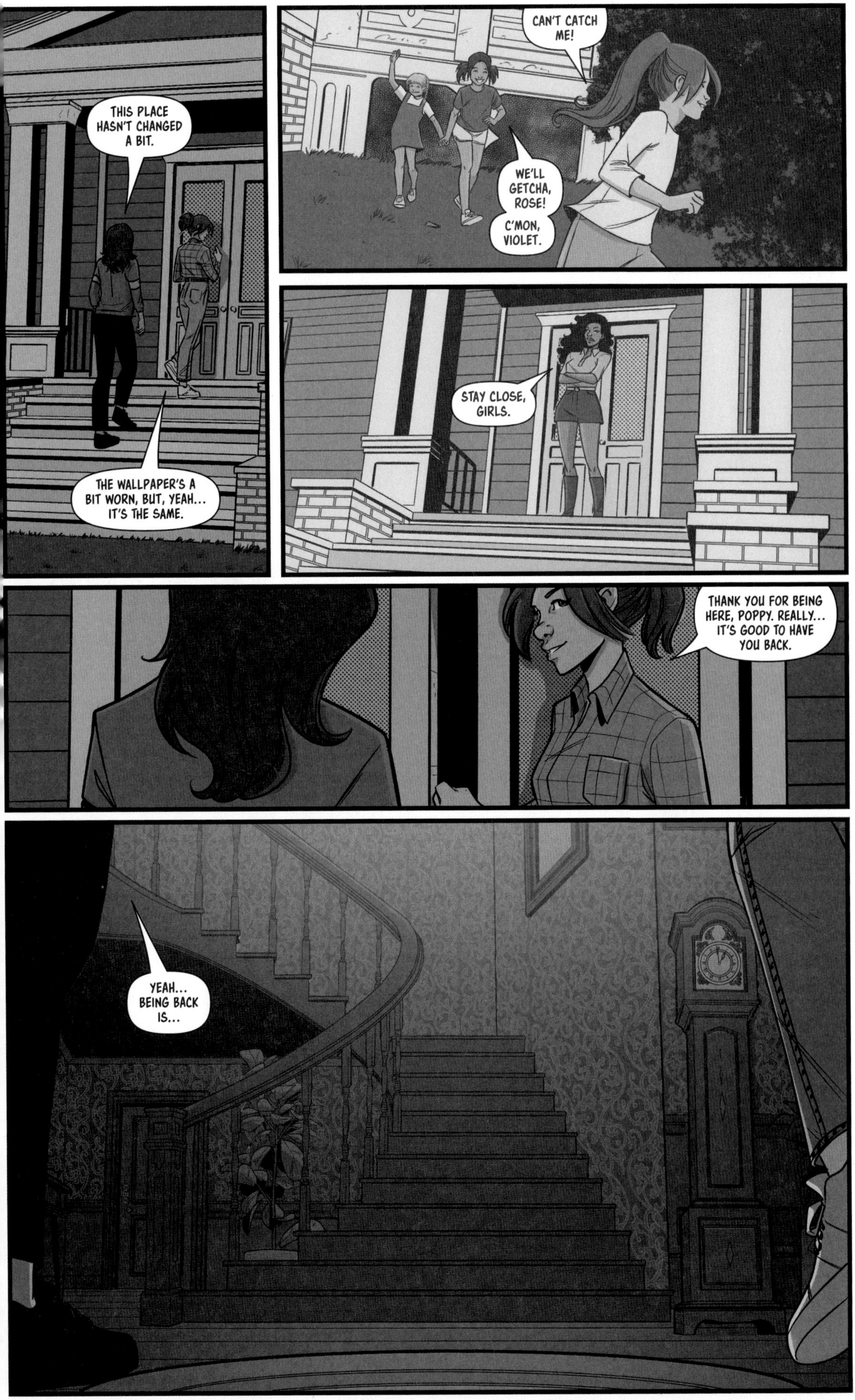
THIS PLACE HASN'T CHANGED A BIT.
THE WALLPAPER'S A BIT WORN, BUT, YEAH... IT'S THE SAME.
CAN'T CATCH ME!
WE'LL GETCHA, ROSE!
C'MON, VIOLET.
STAY CLOSE, GIRLS.
THANK YOU FOR BEING HERE, POPPY. REALLY... IT'S GOOD TO HAVE YOU BACK.
YEAH... BEING BACK IS...

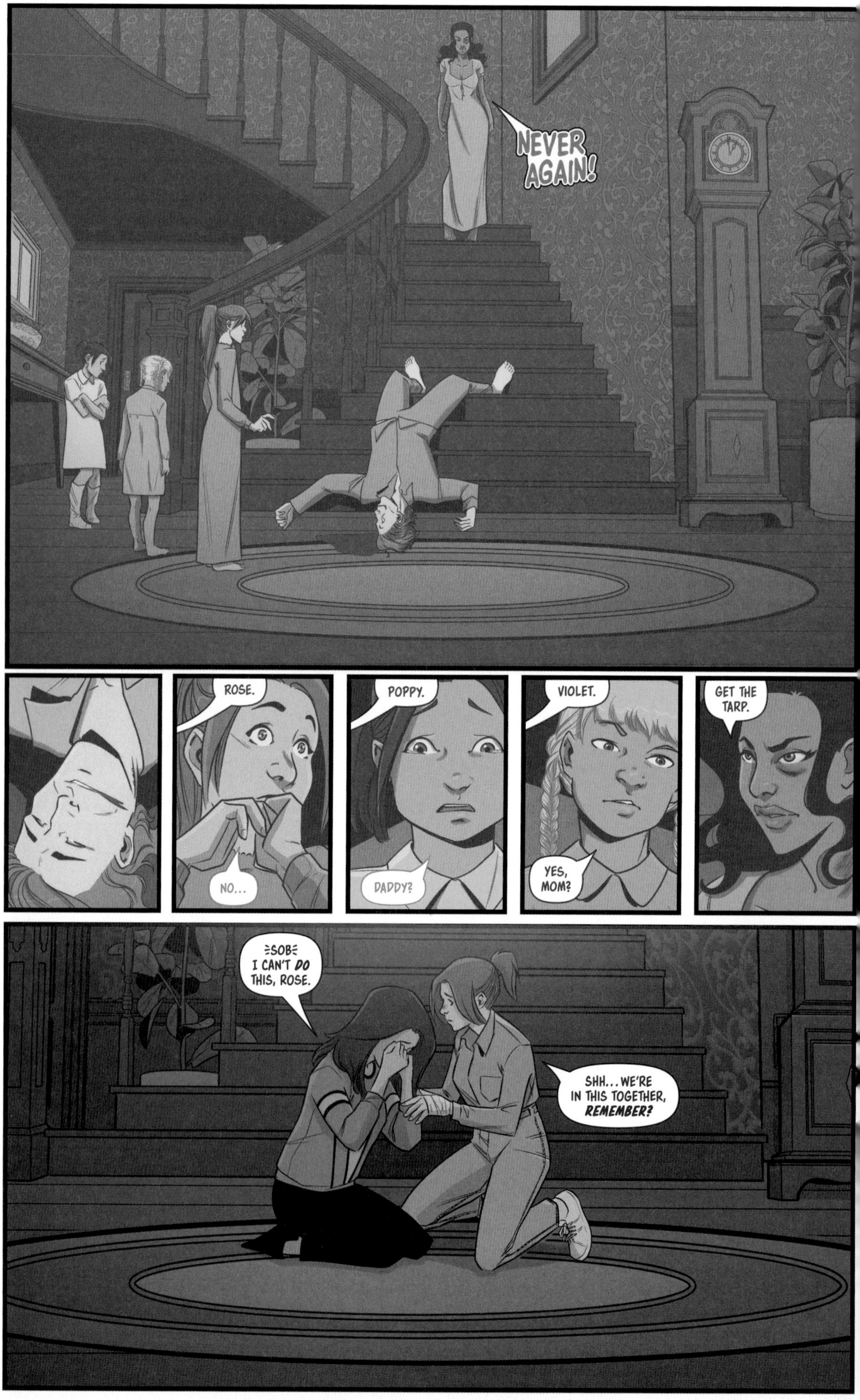
NEVER AGAIN!
ROSE.
NO...
POPPY.
DADDY?
VIOLET.
YES, MOM?
GET THE TARP.
SOB
I CAN'T DO THIS, ROSE.
SHH...WE'RE IN THIS TOGETHER, REMEMBER?

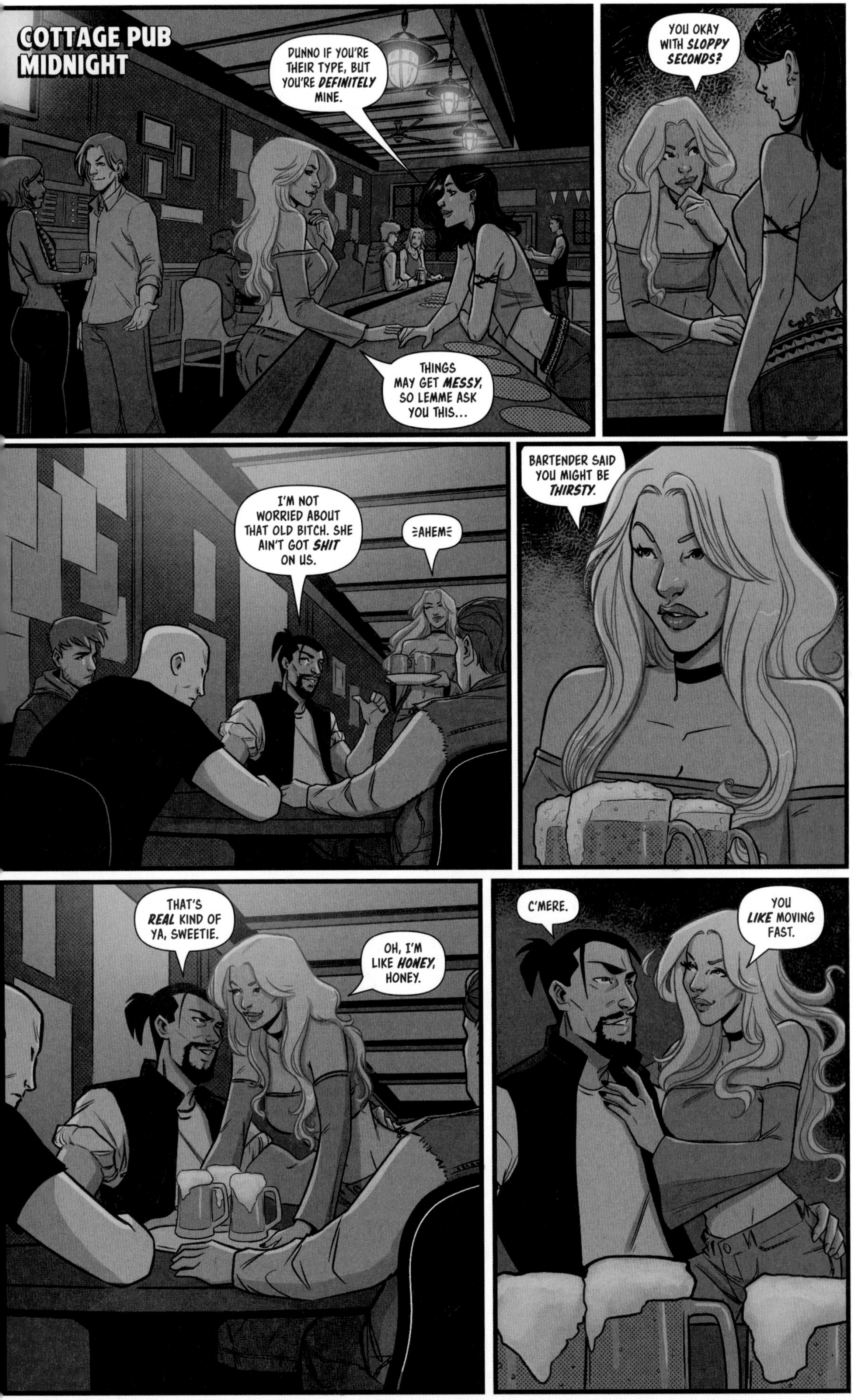
COTTAGE PUB
MIDNIGHT
DUNNO IF YOU'RE THEIR TYPE, BUT YOU'RE DEFINITELY MINE.
THINGS MAY GET MESSY, SO LEMME ASK YOU THIS...
YOU OKAY WITH SLOPPY SECONDS?
I'M NOT WORRIED ABOUT THAT OLD BITCH. SHE AIN'T GOT SHIT ON US.
AHEM
BARTENDER SAID YOU MIGHT BE THIRSTY.
THAT'S REAL KIND OF YA, SWEETIE.
OH, I'M LIKE HONEY, HONEY.
C'MERE.
YOU LIKE MOVING FAST.

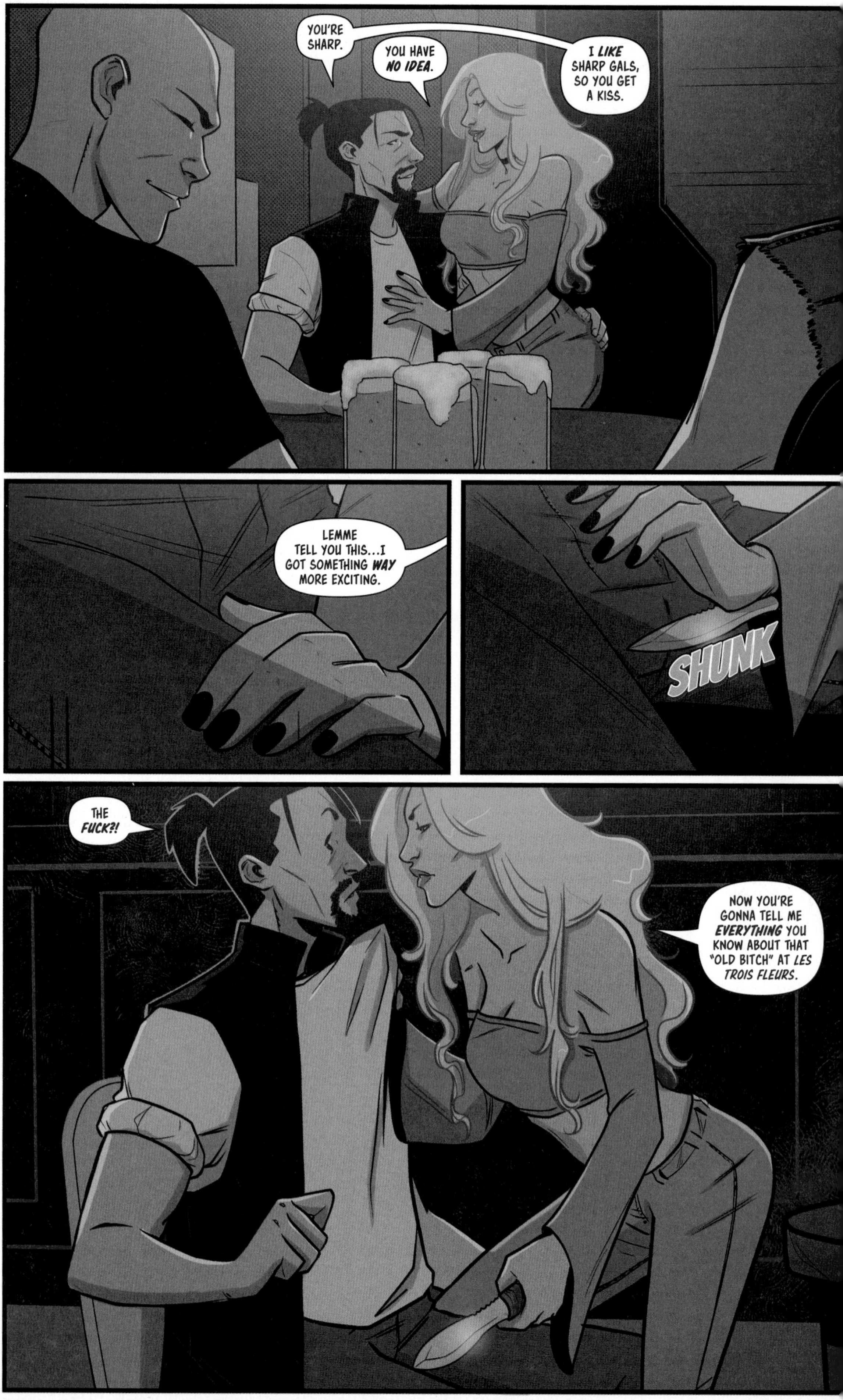
YOU'RE SHARP.
YOU HAVE NO IDEA.
I LIKE SHARP GALS, SO YOU GET A KISS.
LEMME TELL YOU THIS...I GOT SOMETHING WAY MORE EXCITING.
SHUNK
THE FUCK?!
NOW YOU'RE GONNA TELL ME EVERYTHING YOU KNOW ABOUT THAT "OLD BITCH" AT LES TROIS FLEURS.

CHAPTER *Two*

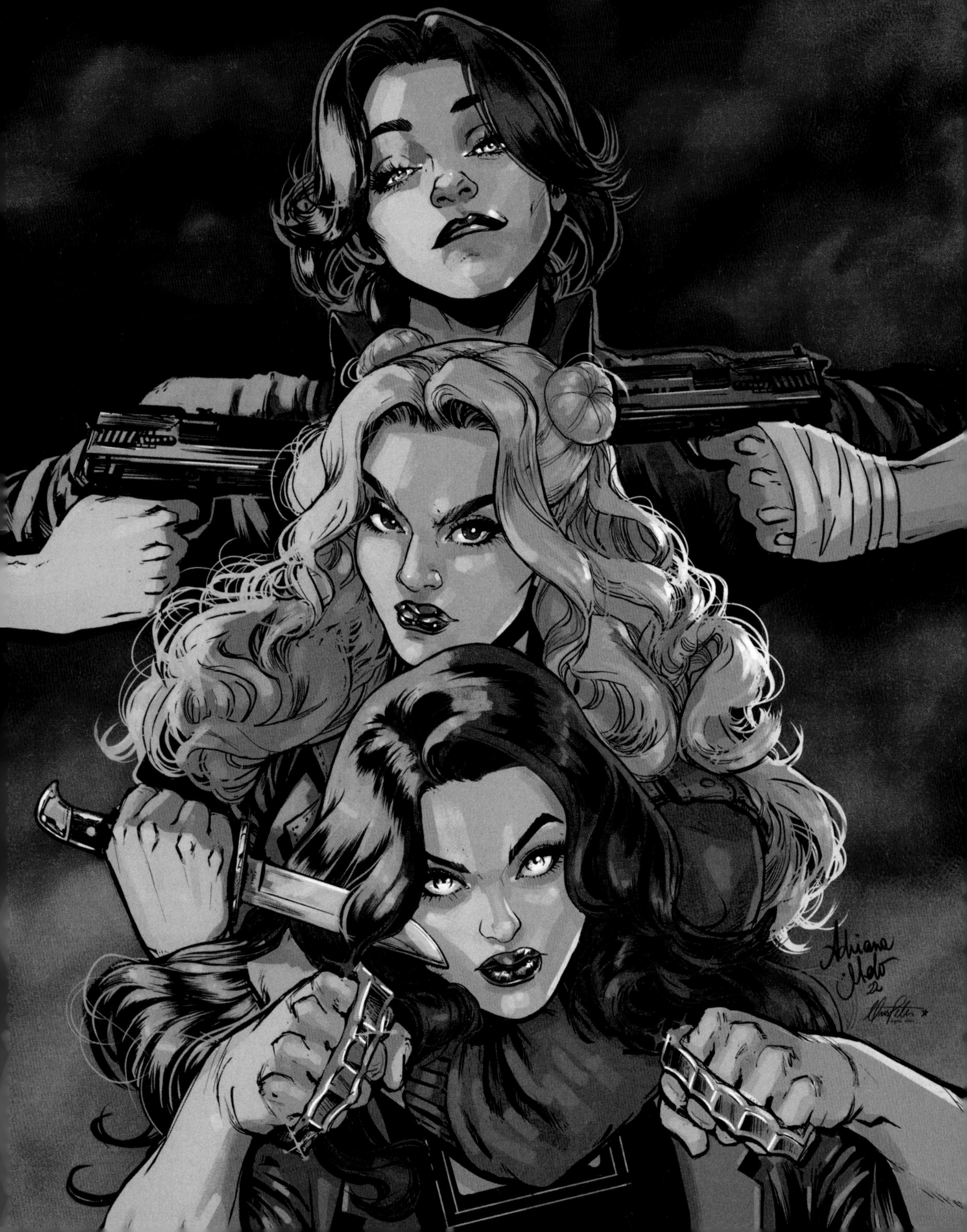

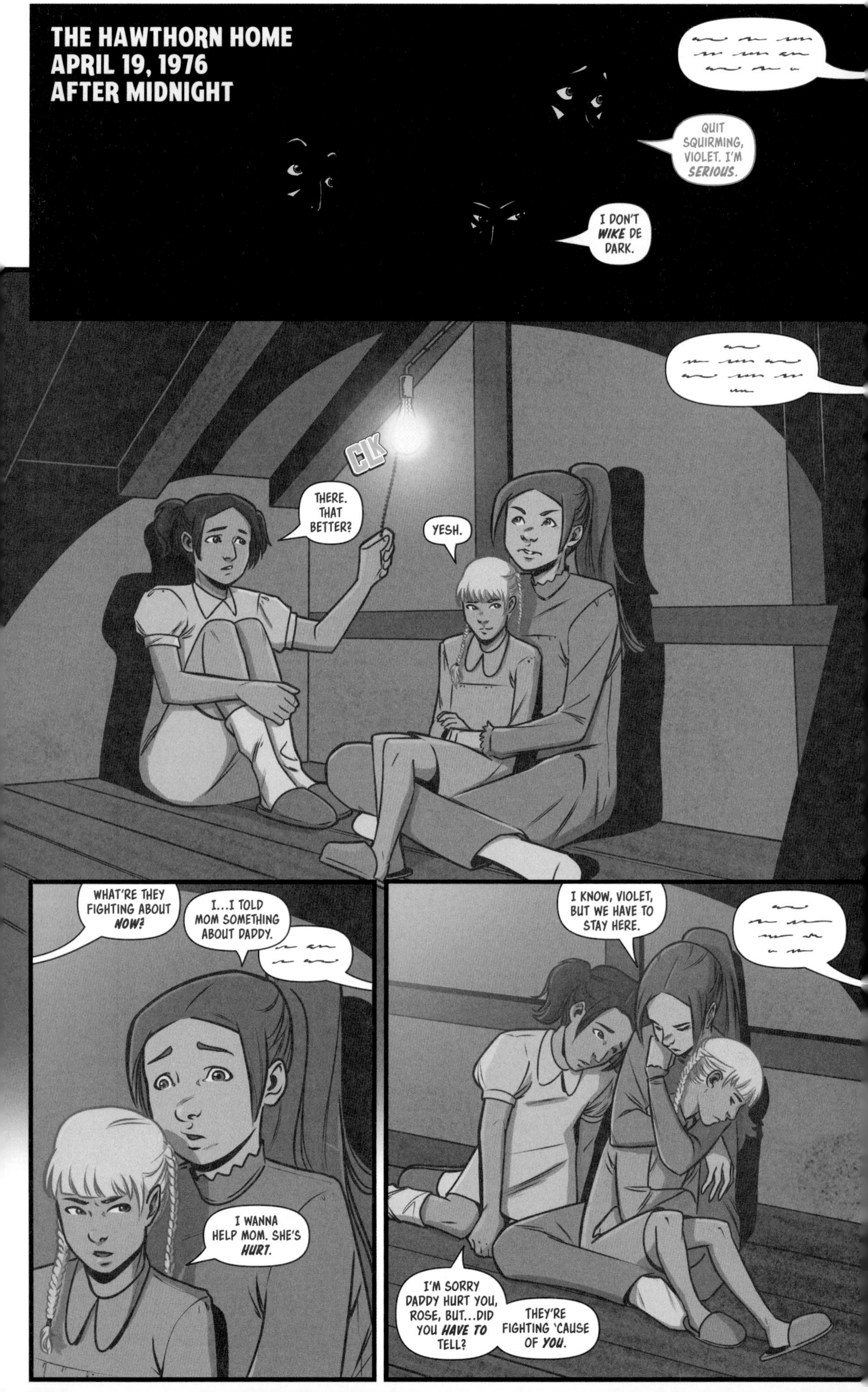
THE HAWTHORN HOME
APRIL 19, 1976
AFTER MIDNIGHT
QUIT SQUIRMING, VIOLET. I'M *SERIOUS*.
I DON'T *WIKE* DE DARK.
CLK
THERE. THAT BETTER?
YESH.
WHAT'RE THEY FIGHTING ABOUT *NOW*?
I...I TOLD MOM SOMETHING ABOUT DADDY.
I WANNA HELP MOM. SHE'S *HURT*.
I KNOW, VIOLET, BUT WE HAVE TO STAY HERE.
I'M SORRY DADDY HURT YOU, ROSE, BUT...DID YOU *HAVE TO* TELL?
THEY'RE FIGHTING 'CAUSE OF *YOU*.

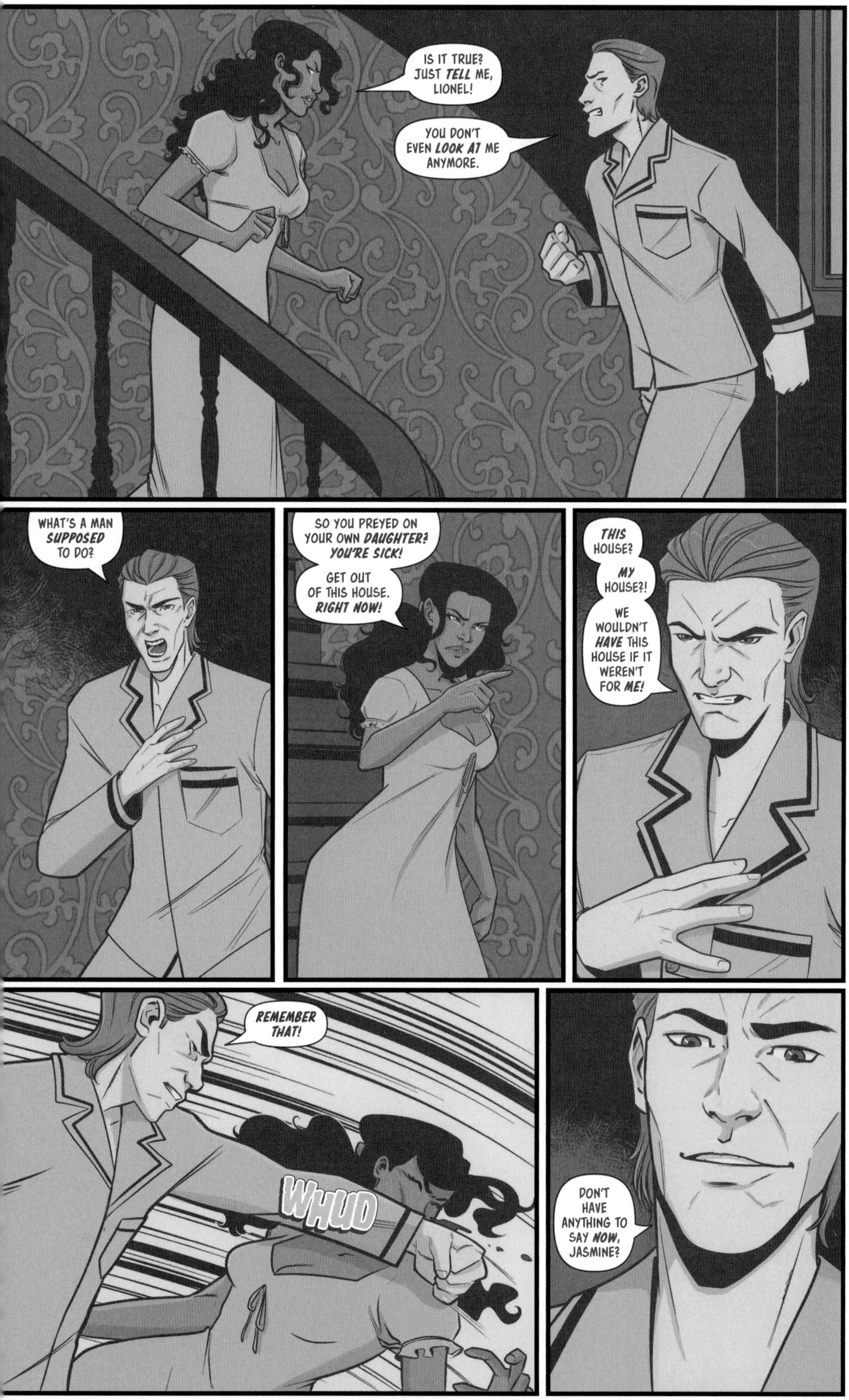
IS IT TRUE? JUST TELL ME, LIONEL!
YOU DON'T EVEN LOOK AT ME ANYMORE.
WHAT'S A MAN SUPPOSED TO DO?
SO YOU PREYED ON YOUR OWN DAUGHTER? YOU'RE SICK!
GET OUT OF THIS HOUSE. RIGHT NOW!
THIS HOUSE?
MY HOUSE?!
WE WOULDN'T HAVE THIS HOUSE IF IT WEREN'T FOR ME!
REMEMBER THAT!
WHUD
DON'T HAVE ANYTHING TO SAY NOW, JASMINE?

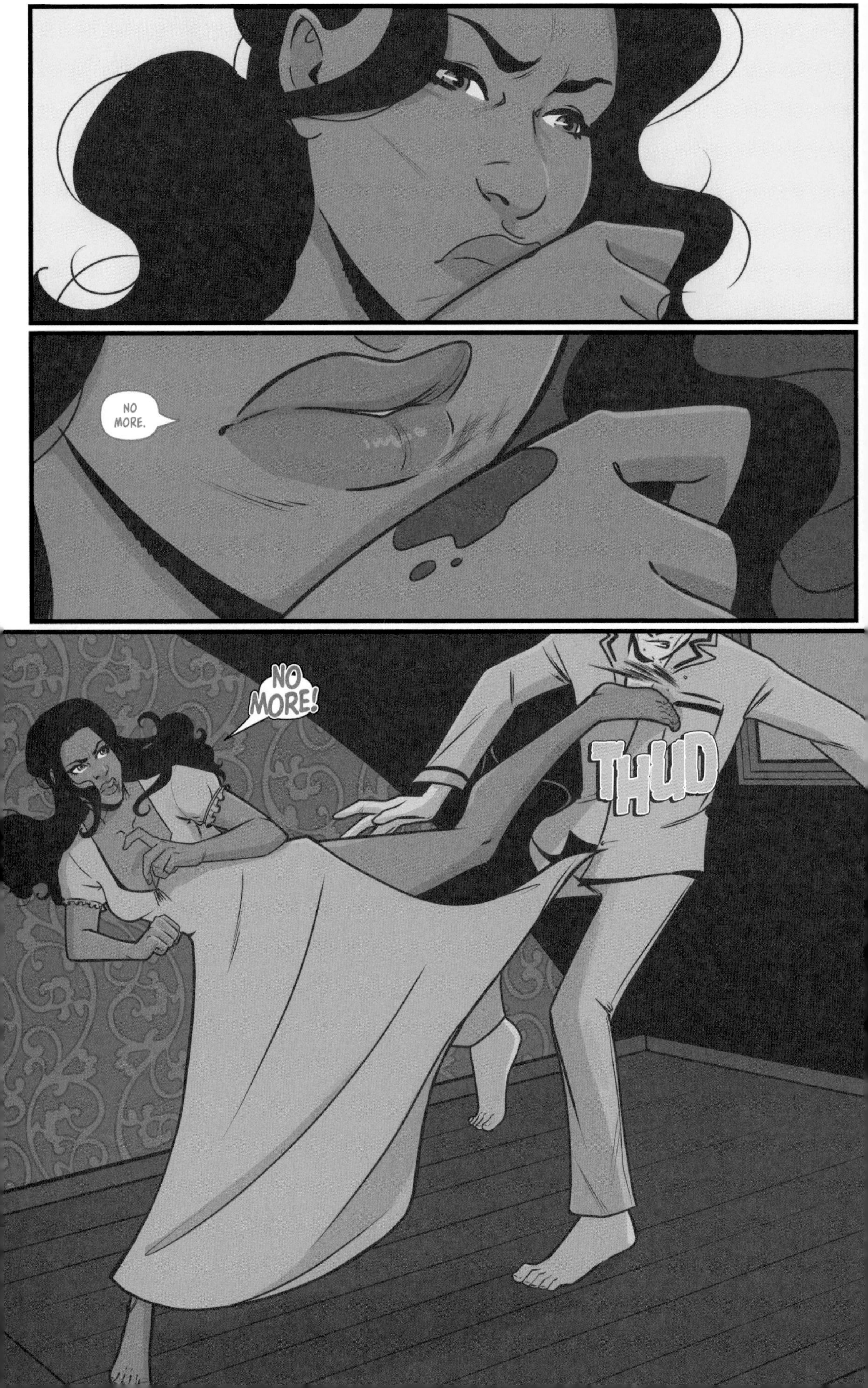
NO MORE.
NO MORE!
THUD

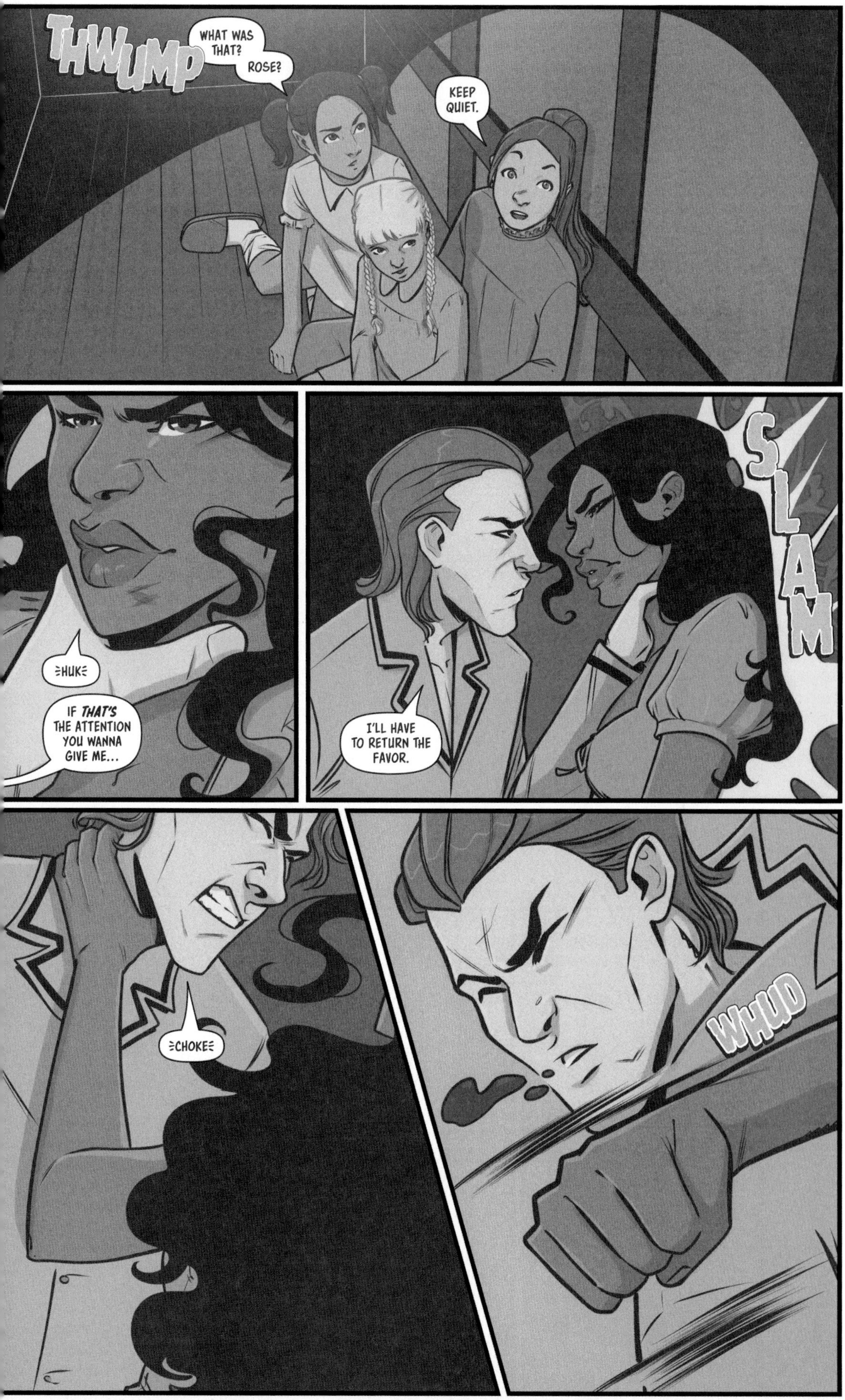
THWUMP
WHAT WAS THAT?
ROSE?
KEEP QUIET.
SLAM
HUK
IF THAT'S THE ATTENTION YOU WANNA GIVE ME...
I'LL HAVE TO RETURN THE FAVOR.
CHOKE
WHUD

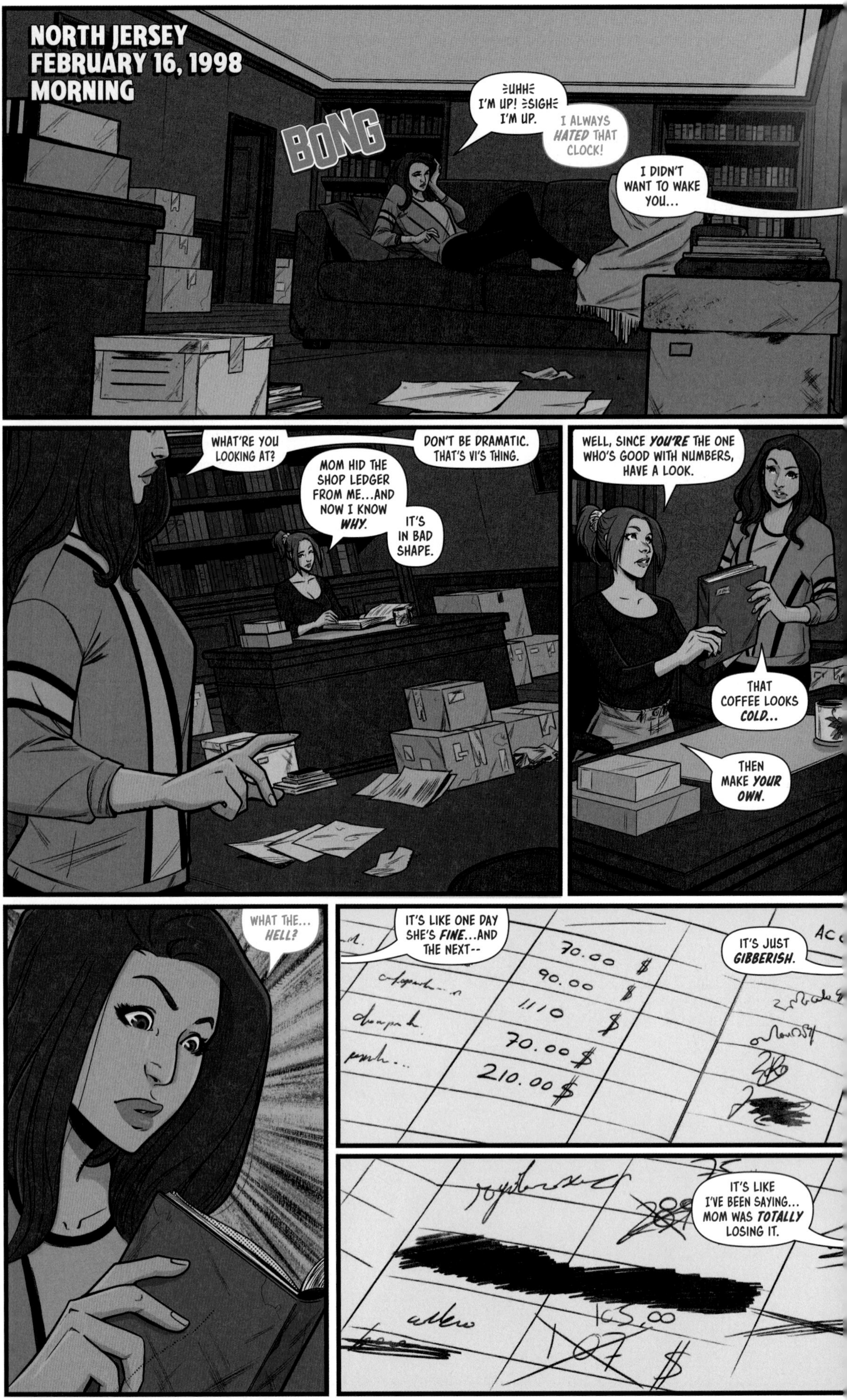
NORTH JERSEY
FEBRUARY 16, 1998
MORNING
BONG
≡UHH≡ I'M UP! ≡SIGH≡ I'M UP.
I ALWAYS HATED THAT CLOCK!
I DIDN'T WANT TO WAKE YOU...
WHAT'RE YOU LOOKING AT?
DON'T BE DRAMATIC. THAT'S VI'S THING.
MOM HID THE SHOP LEDGER FROM ME...AND NOW I KNOW WHY.
IT'S IN BAD SHAPE.
WELL, SINCE YOU'RE THE ONE WHO'S GOOD WITH NUMBERS, HAVE A LOOK.
THAT COFFEE LOOKS COLD...
THEN MAKE YOUR OWN.
WHAT THE... HELL?
IT'S LIKE ONE DAY SHE'S FINE...AND THE NEXT--
IT'S JUST GIBBERISH.
IT'S LIKE I'VE BEEN SAYING... MOM WAS TOTALLY LOSING IT.

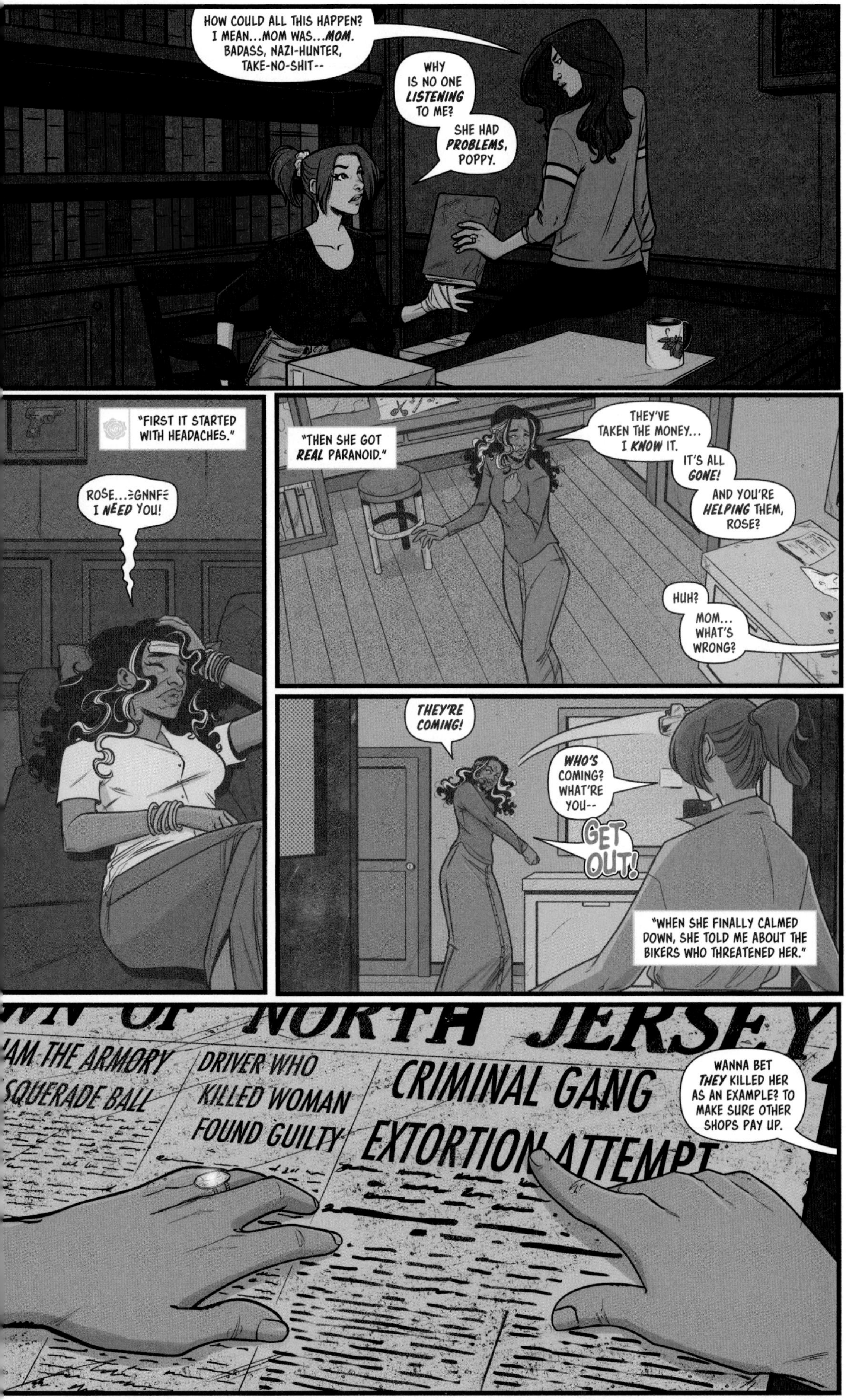
HOW COULD ALL THIS HAPPEN? I MEAN...MOM WAS...MOM. BADASS, NAZI-HUNTER, TAKE-NO-SHIT--
WHY IS NO ONE LISTENING TO ME?
SHE HAD PROBLEMS, POPPY.
"FIRST IT STARTED WITH HEADACHES."
ROSE...GNNF I NEED YOU!
"THEN SHE GOT REAL PARANOID."
THEY'VE TAKEN THE MONEY... I KNOW IT.
IT'S ALL GONE!
AND YOU'RE HELPING THEM, ROSE?
HUH?
MOM... WHAT'S WRONG?
THEY'RE COMING!
WHO'S COMING? WHAT'RE YOU--
GET OUT!
"WHEN SHE FINALLY CALMED DOWN, SHE TOLD ME ABOUT THE BIKERS WHO THREATENED HER."
NORTH JERSEY
AM THE ARMORY
SQUERADE BALL
DRIVER WHO KILLED WOMAN FOUND GUILTY
CRIMINAL GANG
EXTORTION ATTEMPT
WANNA BET THEY KILLED HER AS AN EXAMPLE? TO MAKE SURE OTHER SHOPS PAY UP.

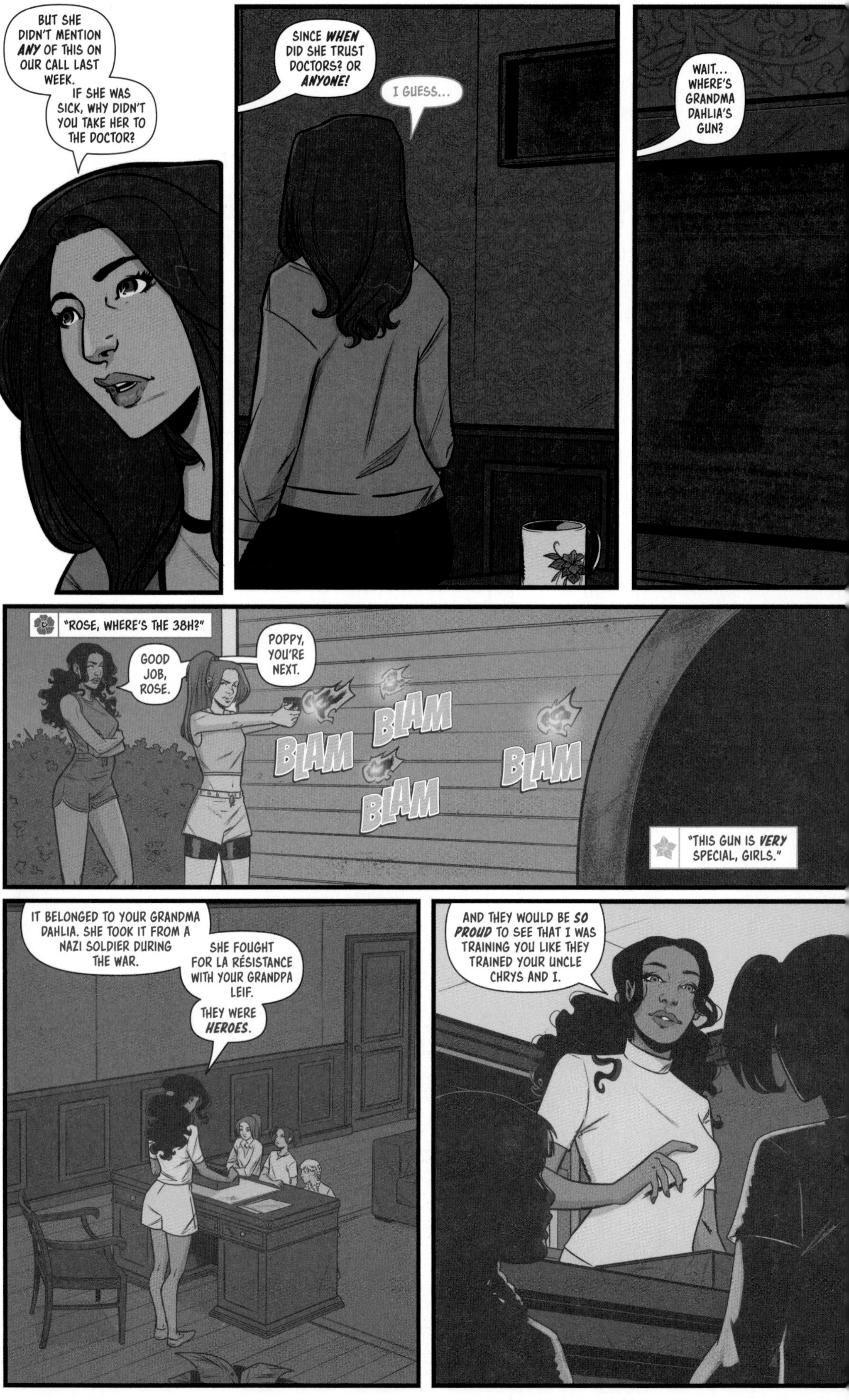
BUT SHE DIDN'T MENTION ANY OF THIS ON OUR CALL LAST WEEK.
IF SHE WAS SICK, WHY DIDN'T YOU TAKE HER TO THE DOCTOR?
SINCE WHEN DID SHE TRUST DOCTORS? OR ANYONE!
I GUESS...
WAIT... WHERE'S GRANDMA DAHLIA'S GUN?
"ROSE, WHERE'S THE 38H?"
GOOD JOB, ROSE.
POPPY, YOU'RE NEXT.
BLAM
BLAM
BLAM
BLAM
"THIS GUN IS VERY SPECIAL, GIRLS."
IT BELONGED TO YOUR GRANDMA DAHLIA. SHE TOOK IT FROM A NAZI SOLDIER DURING THE WAR.
SHE FOUGHT FOR LA RÉSISTANCE WITH YOUR GRANDPA LEIF.
THEY WERE HEROES.
AND THEY WOULD BE SO PROUD TO SEE THAT I WAS TRAINING YOU LIKE THEY TRAINED YOUR UNCLE CHRYS AND I.

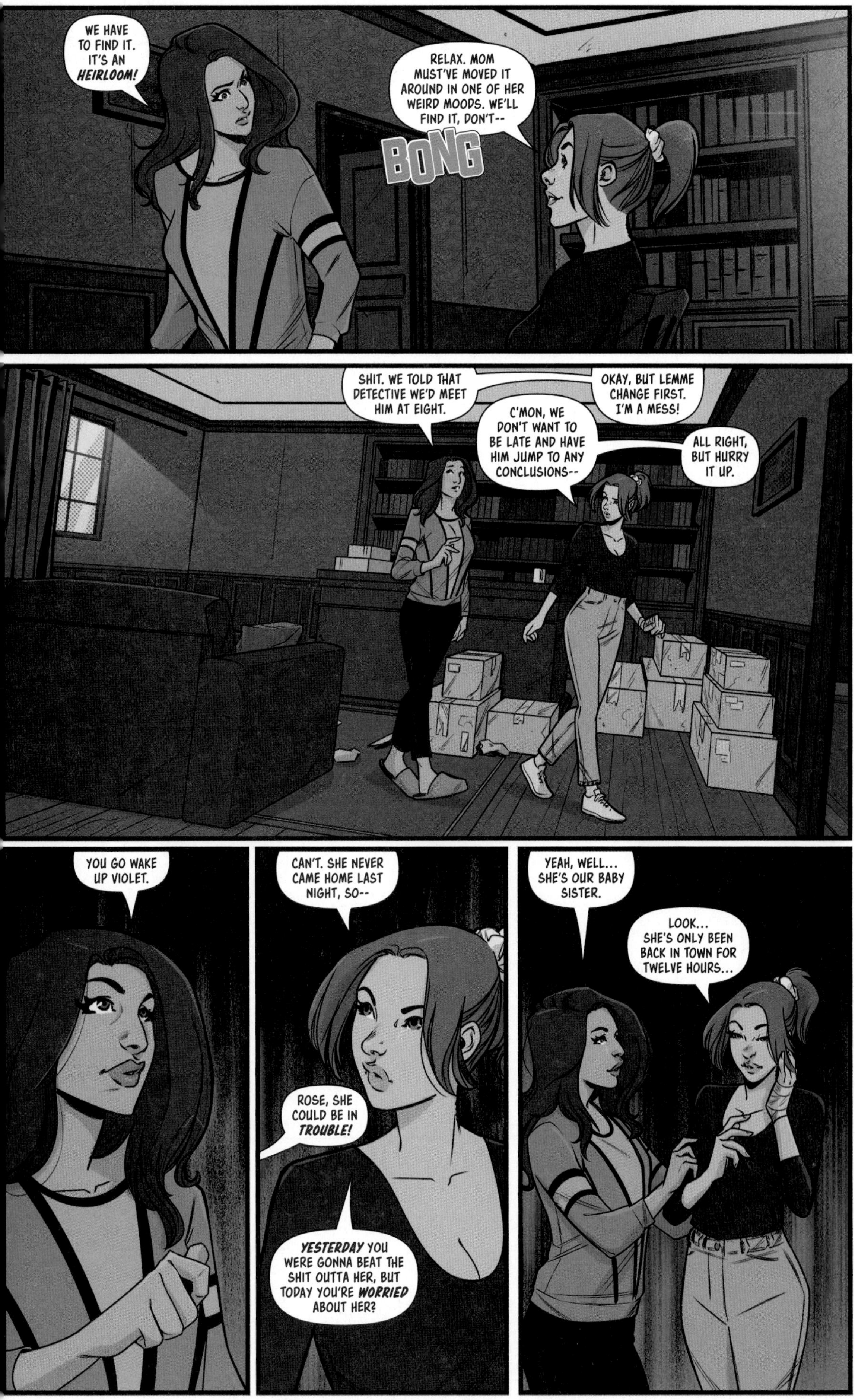
WE HAVE TO FIND IT. IT'S AN *HEIRLOOM!*
RELAX. MOM MUST'VE MOVED IT AROUND IN ONE OF HER WEIRD MOODS. WE'LL FIND IT, DON'T--
BONG
SHIT. WE TOLD THAT DETECTIVE WE'D MEET HIM AT EIGHT.
OKAY, BUT LEMME CHANGE FIRST. I'M A MESS!
C'MON, WE DON'T WANT TO BE LATE AND HAVE HIM JUMP TO ANY CONCLUSIONS--
ALL RIGHT, BUT HURRY IT UP.
YOU GO WAKE UP VIOLET.
CAN'T. SHE NEVER CAME HOME LAST NIGHT, SO--
ROSE, SHE COULD BE IN *TROUBLE!*
YESTERDAY YOU WERE GONNA BEAT THE SHIT OUTTA HER, BUT TODAY YOU'RE *WORRIED* ABOUT HER?
YEAH, WELL... SHE'S OUR BABY SISTER.
LOOK... SHE'S ONLY BEEN BACK IN TOWN FOR TWELVE HOURS...

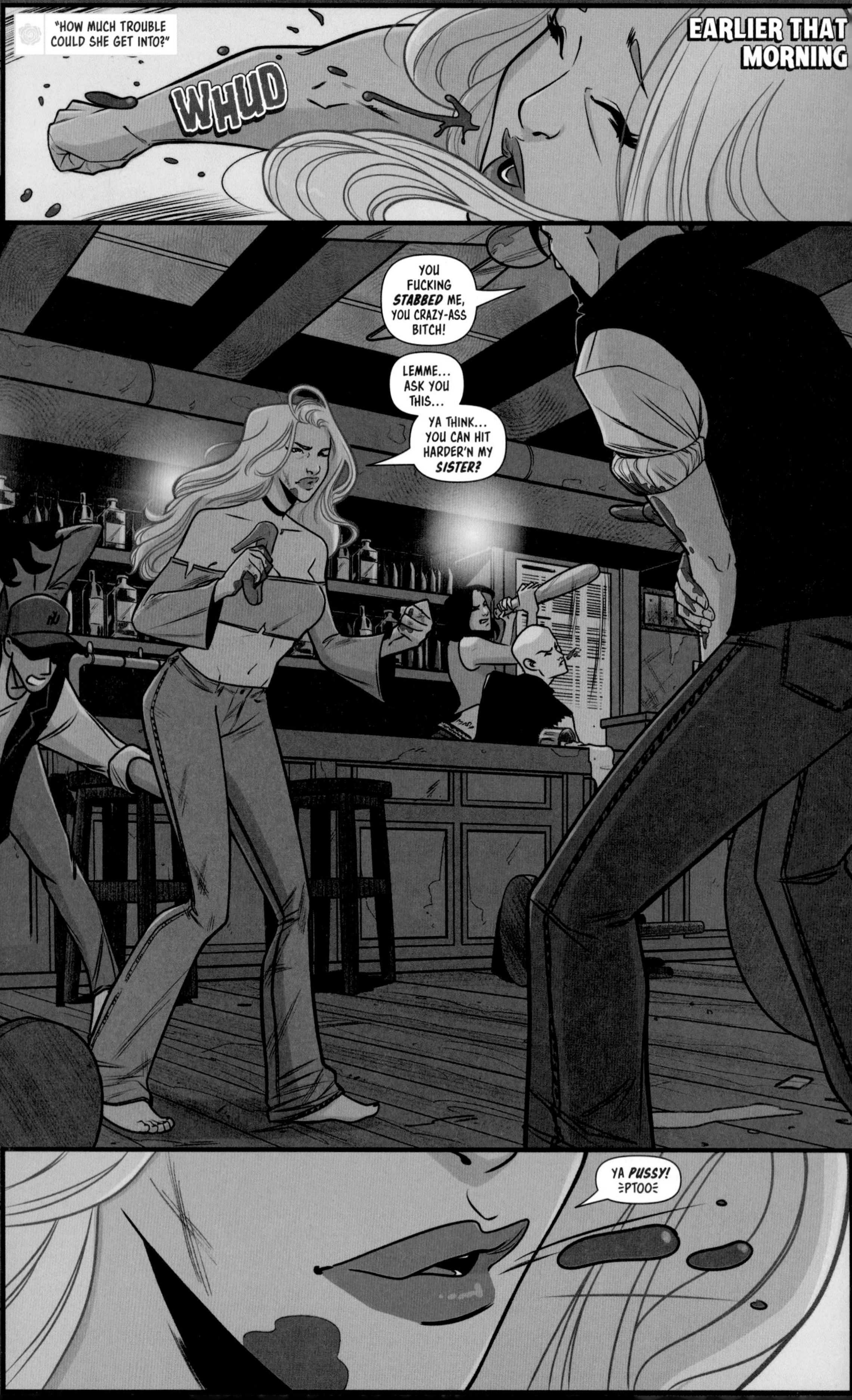
"HOW MUCH TROUBLE COULD SHE GET INTO?"
EARLIER THAT MORNING
WHUD
YOU FUCKING STABBED ME, YOU CRAZY-ASS BITCH!
LEMME... ASK YOU THIS...
YA THINK... YOU CAN HIT HARDER'N MY SISTER?
YA PUSSY!
PTOO

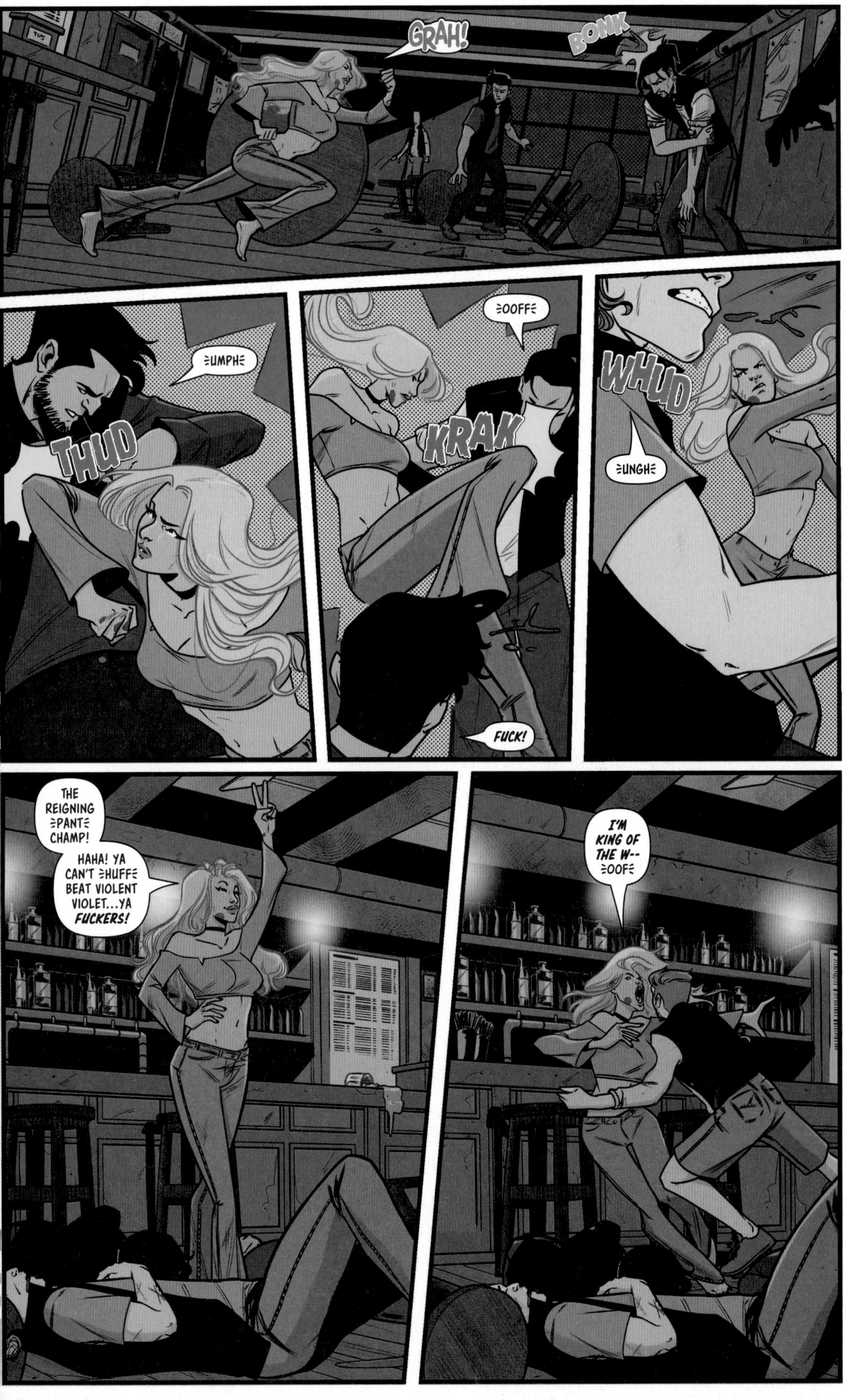
GRAH!
BONK
UMPH
THUD
OOFF
KRAK
FUCK!
WHUD
UNGH
THE REIGNING PANT CHAMP!
HAHA! YA CAN'T HUFF BEAT VIOLENT VIOLET...YA FUCKERS!
I'M KING OF THE W-- OOF

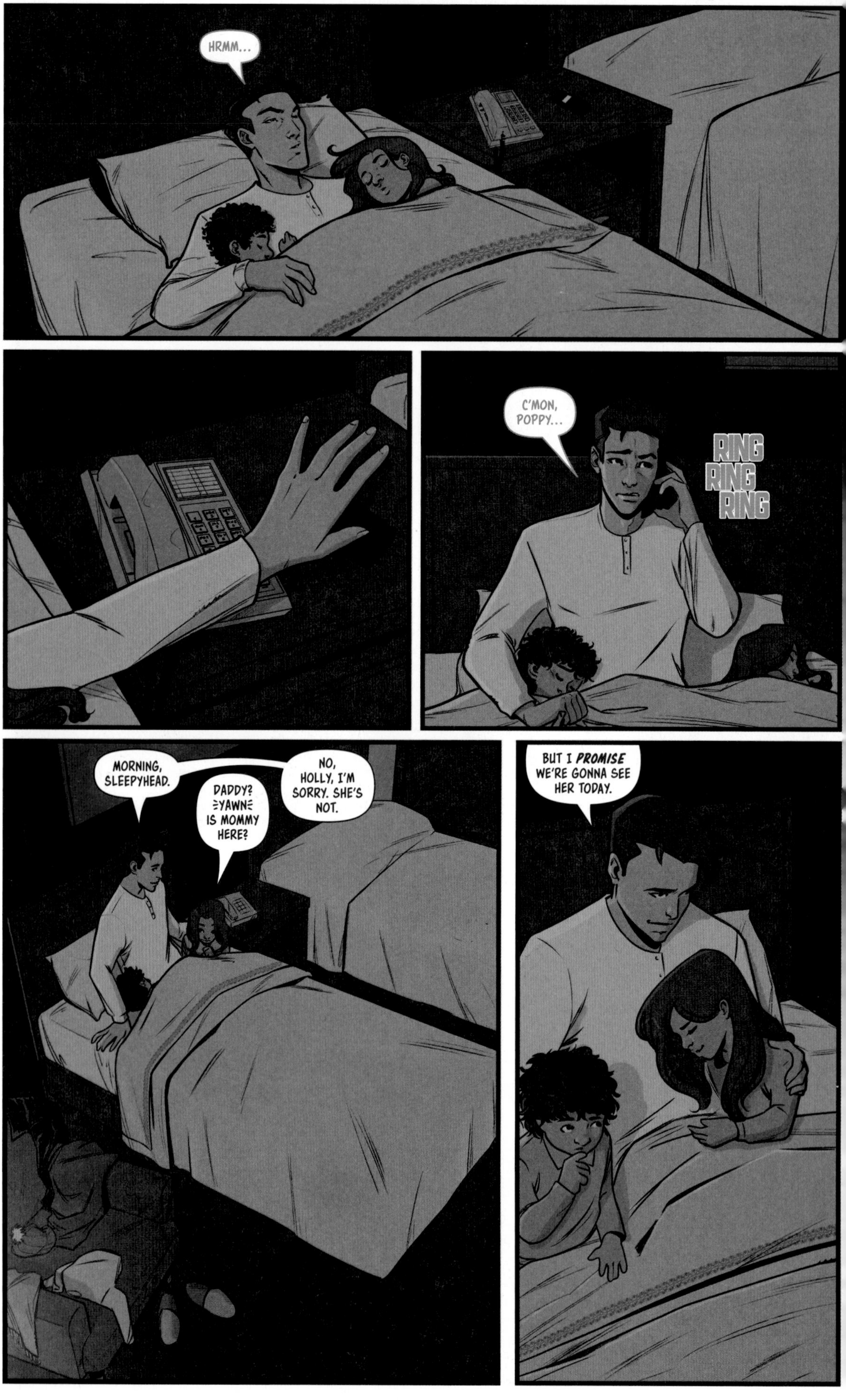
HRMM...
C'MON, POPPY...
RING RING RING
MORNING, SLEEPYHEAD.
DADDY? =YAWN= IS MOMMY HERE?
NO, HOLLY, I'M SORRY. SHE'S NOT.
BUT I *PROMISE* WE'RE GONNA SEE HER TODAY.

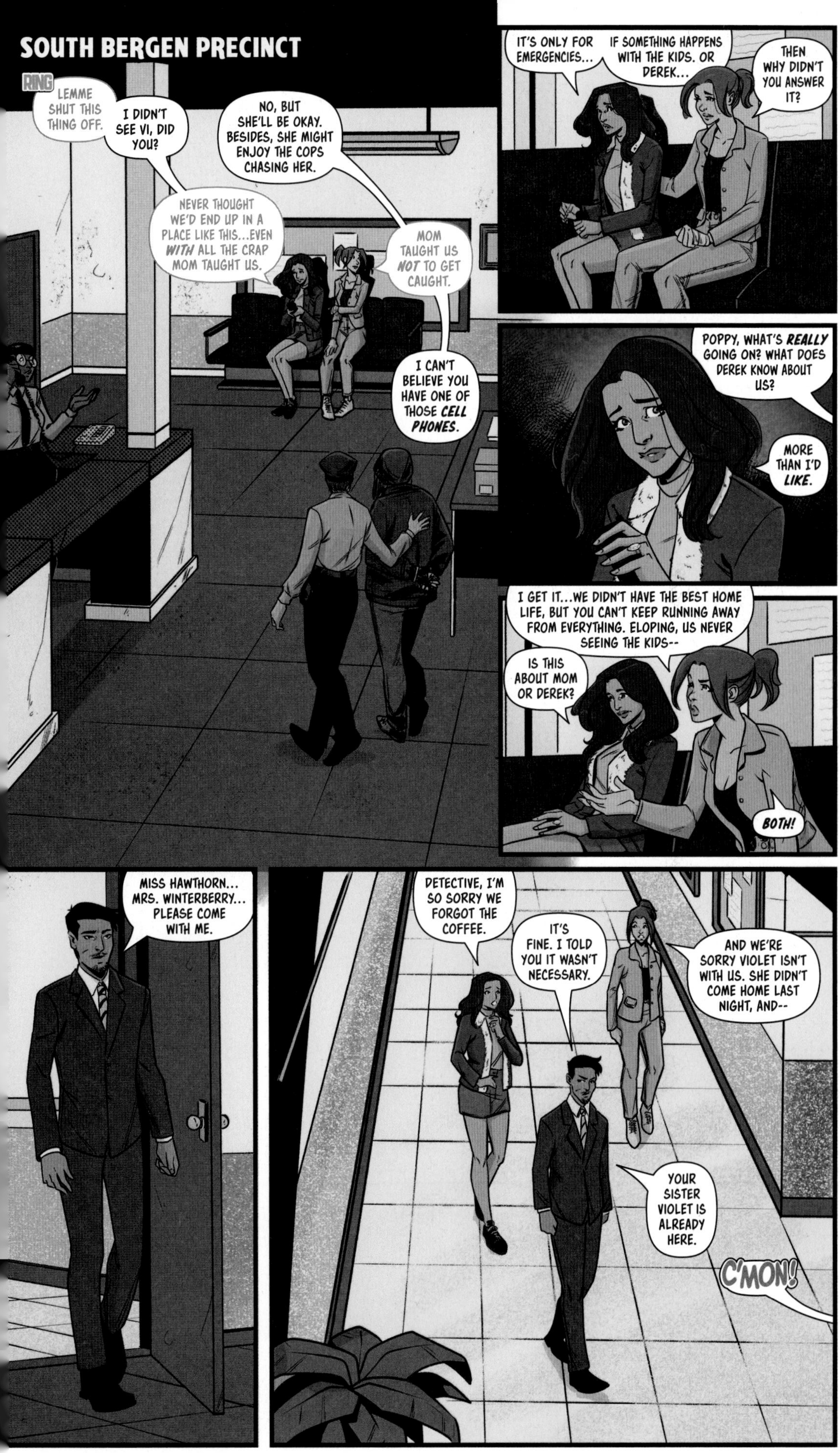
SOUTH BERGEN PRECINCT
RING
LEMME SHUT THIS THING OFF.
I DIDN'T SEE VI, DID YOU?
NO, BUT SHE'LL BE OKAY. BESIDES, SHE MIGHT ENJOY THE COPS CHASING HER.
NEVER THOUGHT WE'D END UP IN A PLACE LIKE THIS...EVEN WITH ALL THE CRAP MOM TAUGHT US.
MOM TAUGHT US NOT TO GET CAUGHT.
I CAN'T BELIEVE YOU HAVE ONE OF THOSE CELL PHONES.
IT'S ONLY FOR EMERGENCIES...
IF SOMETHING HAPPENS WITH THE KIDS. OR DEREK...
THEN WHY DIDN'T YOU ANSWER IT?
POPPY, WHAT'S REALLY GOING ON? WHAT DOES DEREK KNOW ABOUT US?
MORE THAN I'D LIKE.
I GET IT...WE DIDN'T HAVE THE BEST HOME LIFE, BUT YOU CAN'T KEEP RUNNING AWAY FROM EVERYTHING. ELOPING, US NEVER SEEING THE KIDS--
IS THIS ABOUT MOM OR DEREK?
BOTH!
MISS HAWTHORN... MRS. WINTERBERRY... PLEASE COME WITH ME.
DETECTIVE, I'M SO SORRY WE FORGOT THE COFFEE.
IT'S FINE. I TOLD YOU IT WASN'T NECESSARY.
AND WE'RE SORRY VIOLET ISN'T WITH US. SHE DIDN'T COME HOME LAST NIGHT, AND--
YOUR SISTER VIOLET IS ALREADY HERE.
C'MON!

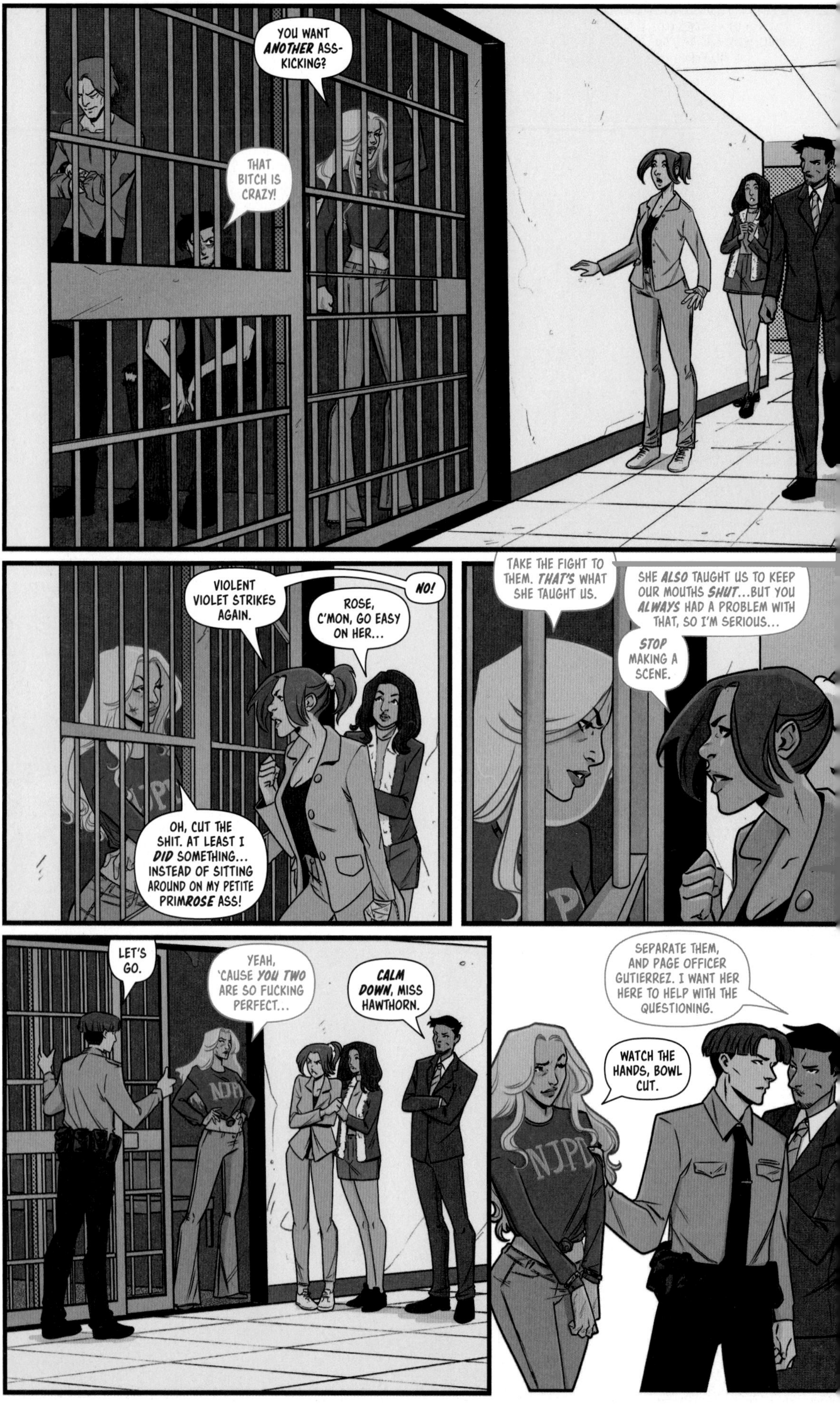
YOU WANT ANOTHER ASS-KICKING?
THAT BITCH IS CRAZY!
VIOLENT VIOLET STRIKES AGAIN.
NO!
ROSE, C'MON, GO EASY ON HER...
OH, CUT THE SHIT. AT LEAST I DID SOMETHING... INSTEAD OF SITTING AROUND ON MY PETITE PRIMROSE ASS!
TAKE THE FIGHT TO THEM. THAT'S WHAT SHE TAUGHT US.
SHE ALSO TAUGHT US TO KEEP OUR MOUTHS SHUT...BUT YOU ALWAYS HAD A PROBLEM WITH THAT, SO I'M SERIOUS...
STOP MAKING A SCENE.
LET'S GO.
YEAH, 'CAUSE YOU TWO ARE SO FUCKING PERFECT...
CALM DOWN, MISS HAWTHORN.
SEPARATE THEM, AND PAGE OFFICER GUTIERREZ. I WANT HER HERE TO HELP WITH THE QUESTIONING.
WATCH THE HANDS, BOWL CUT.

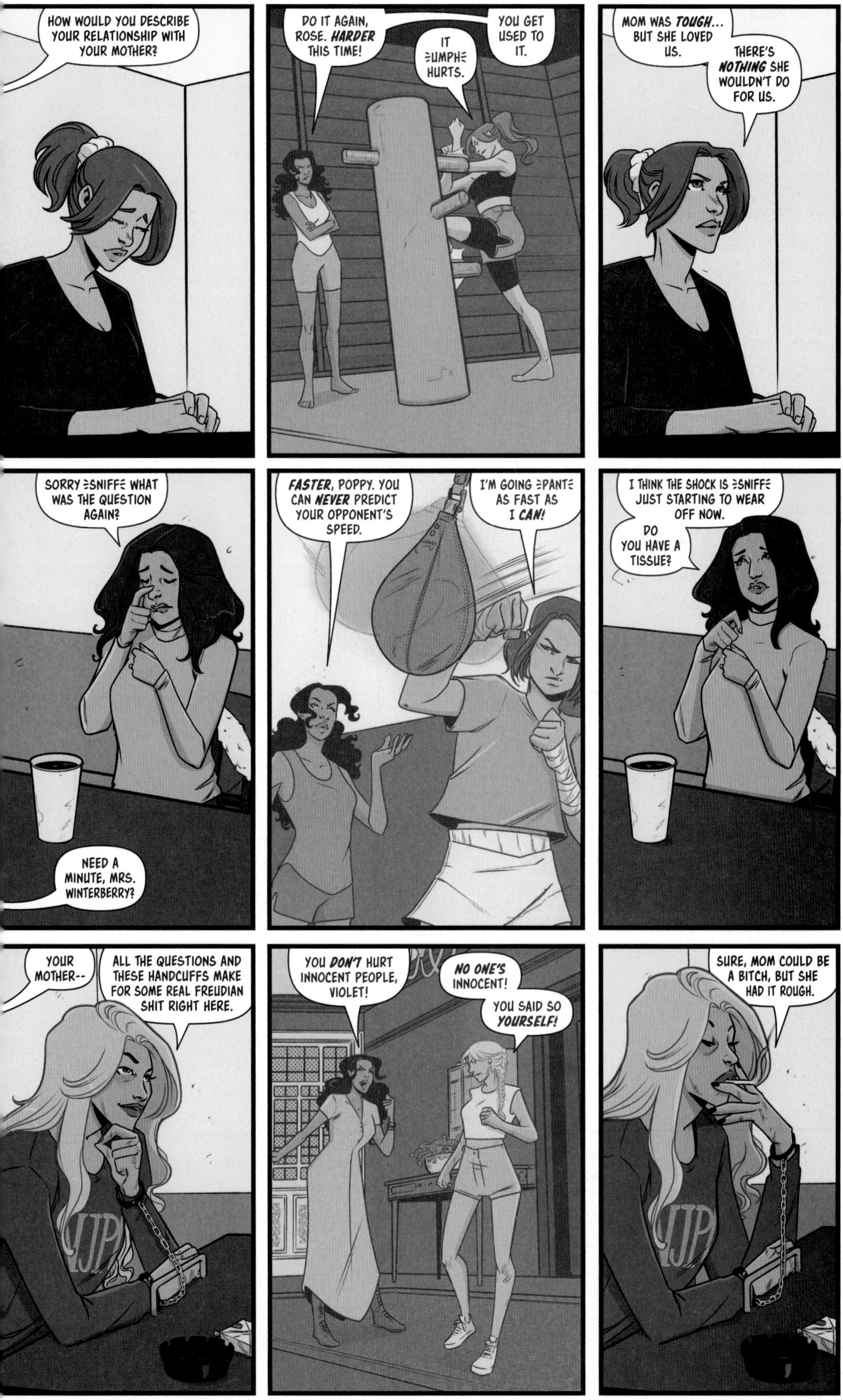
HOW WOULD YOU DESCRIBE YOUR RELATIONSHIP WITH YOUR MOTHER?
DO IT AGAIN, ROSE. HARDER THIS TIME!
IT ≡UMPH≡ HURTS.
YOU GET USED TO IT.
MOM WAS TOUGH... BUT SHE LOVED US.
THERE'S NOTHING SHE WOULDN'T DO FOR US.
SORRY ≡SNIFF≡ WHAT WAS THE QUESTION AGAIN?
NEED A MINUTE, MRS. WINTERBERRY?
FASTER, POPPY. YOU CAN NEVER PREDICT YOUR OPPONENT'S SPEED.
I'M GOING ≡PANT≡ AS FAST AS I CAN!
I THINK THE SHOCK IS ≡SNIFF≡ JUST STARTING TO WEAR OFF NOW.
DO YOU HAVE A TISSUE?
YOUR MOTHER--
ALL THE QUESTIONS AND THESE HANDCUFFS MAKE FOR SOME REAL FREUDIAN SHIT RIGHT HERE.
YOU DON'T HURT INNOCENT PEOPLE, VIOLET!
NO ONE'S INNOCENT!
YOU SAID SO YOURSELF!
SURE, MOM COULD BE A BITCH, BUT SHE HAD IT ROUGH.

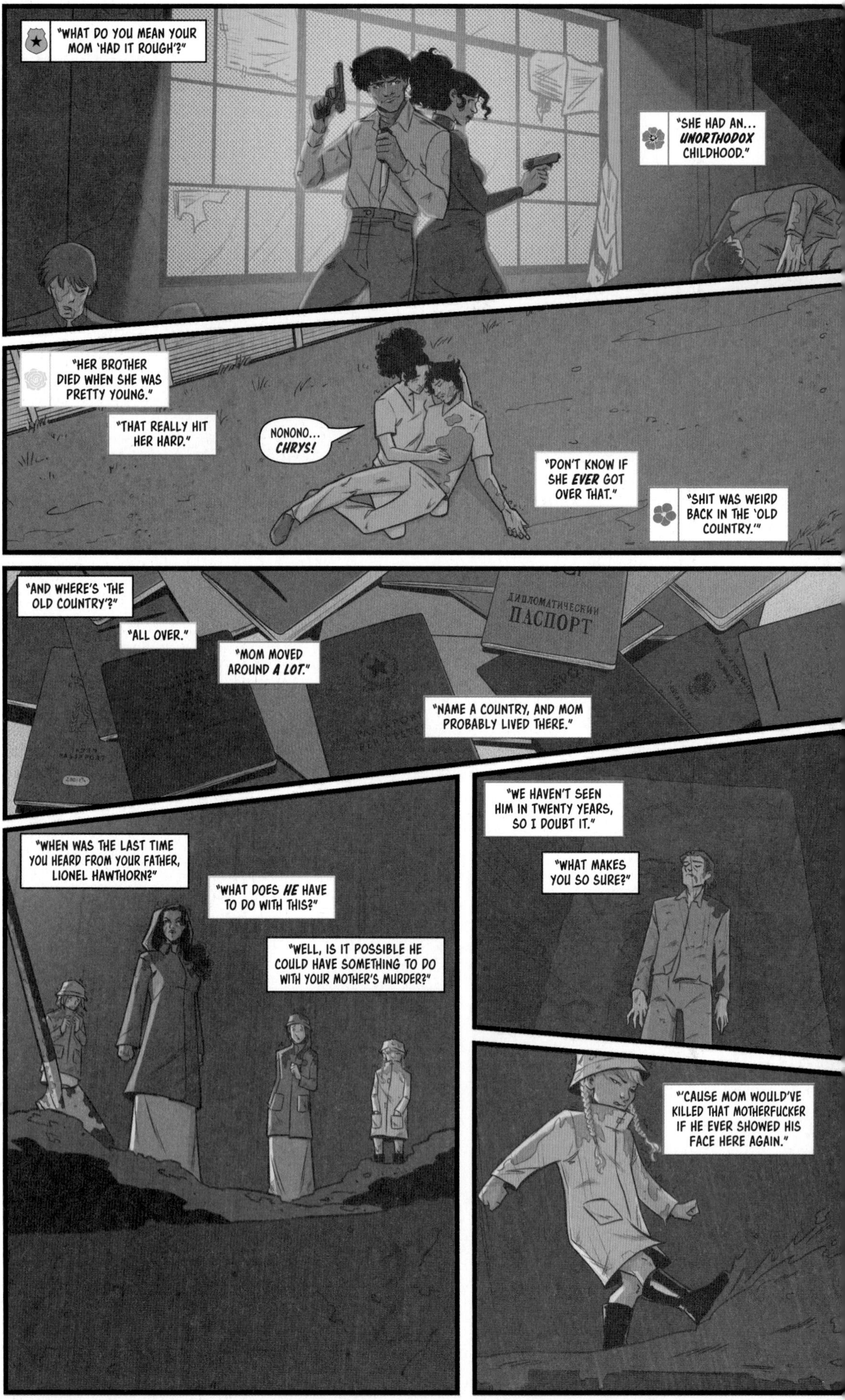
"WHAT DO YOU MEAN YOUR MOM 'HAD IT ROUGH'?"
"SHE HAD AN... UNORTHODOX CHILDHOOD."
"HER BROTHER DIED WHEN SHE WAS PRETTY YOUNG."
"THAT REALLY HIT HER HARD."
NONONO... CHRYS!
"DON'T KNOW IF SHE EVER GOT OVER THAT."
"SHIT WAS WEIRD BACK IN THE 'OLD COUNTRY.'"
"AND WHERE'S 'THE OLD COUNTRY'?"
"ALL OVER."
"MOM MOVED AROUND A LOT."
ДИПЛОМАТИЧЕСКИЙ
ПАСПОРТ
"NAME A COUNTRY, AND MOM PROBABLY LIVED THERE."
"WHEN WAS THE LAST TIME YOU HEARD FROM YOUR FATHER, LIONEL HAWTHORN?"
"WHAT DOES HE HAVE TO DO WITH THIS?"
"WELL, IS IT POSSIBLE HE COULD HAVE SOMETHING TO DO WITH YOUR MOTHER'S MURDER?"
"WE HAVEN'T SEEN HIM IN TWENTY YEARS, SO I DOUBT IT."
"WHAT MAKES YOU SO SURE?"
"CAUSE MOM WOULD'VE KILLED THAT MOTHERFUCKER IF HE EVER SHOWED HIS FACE HERE AGAIN."

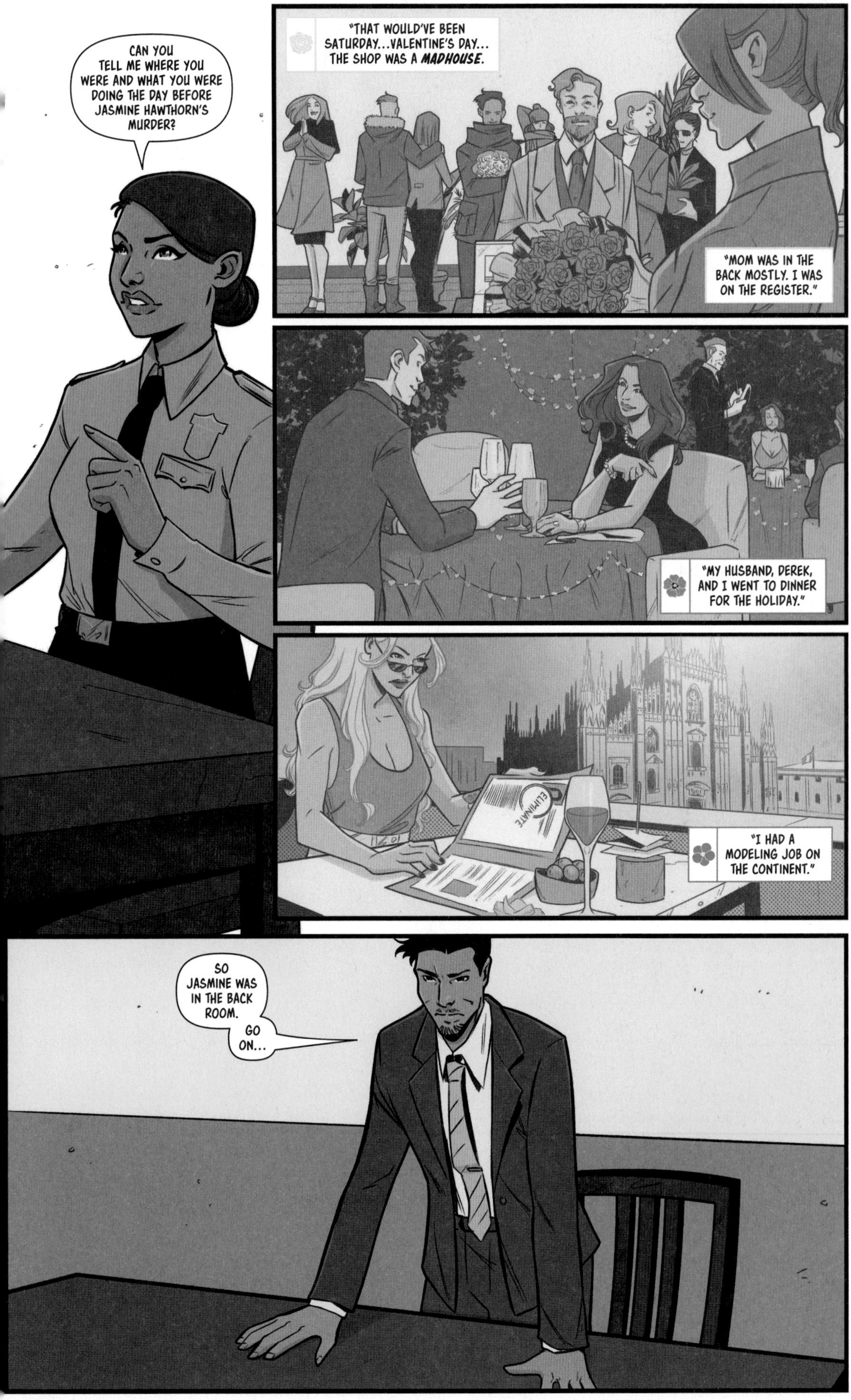
CAN YOU TELL ME WHERE YOU WERE AND WHAT YOU WERE DOING THE DAY BEFORE JASMINE HAWTHORN'S MURDER?
"THAT WOULD'VE BEEN SATURDAY...VALENTINE'S DAY... THE SHOP WAS A MADHOUSE.
"MOM WAS IN THE BACK MOSTLY. I WAS ON THE REGISTER."
"MY HUSBAND, DEREK, AND I WENT TO DINNER FOR THE HOLIDAY."
ELIMINATE
"I HAD A MODELING JOB ON THE CONTINENT."
SO JASMINE WAS IN THE BACK ROOM.
GO ON...

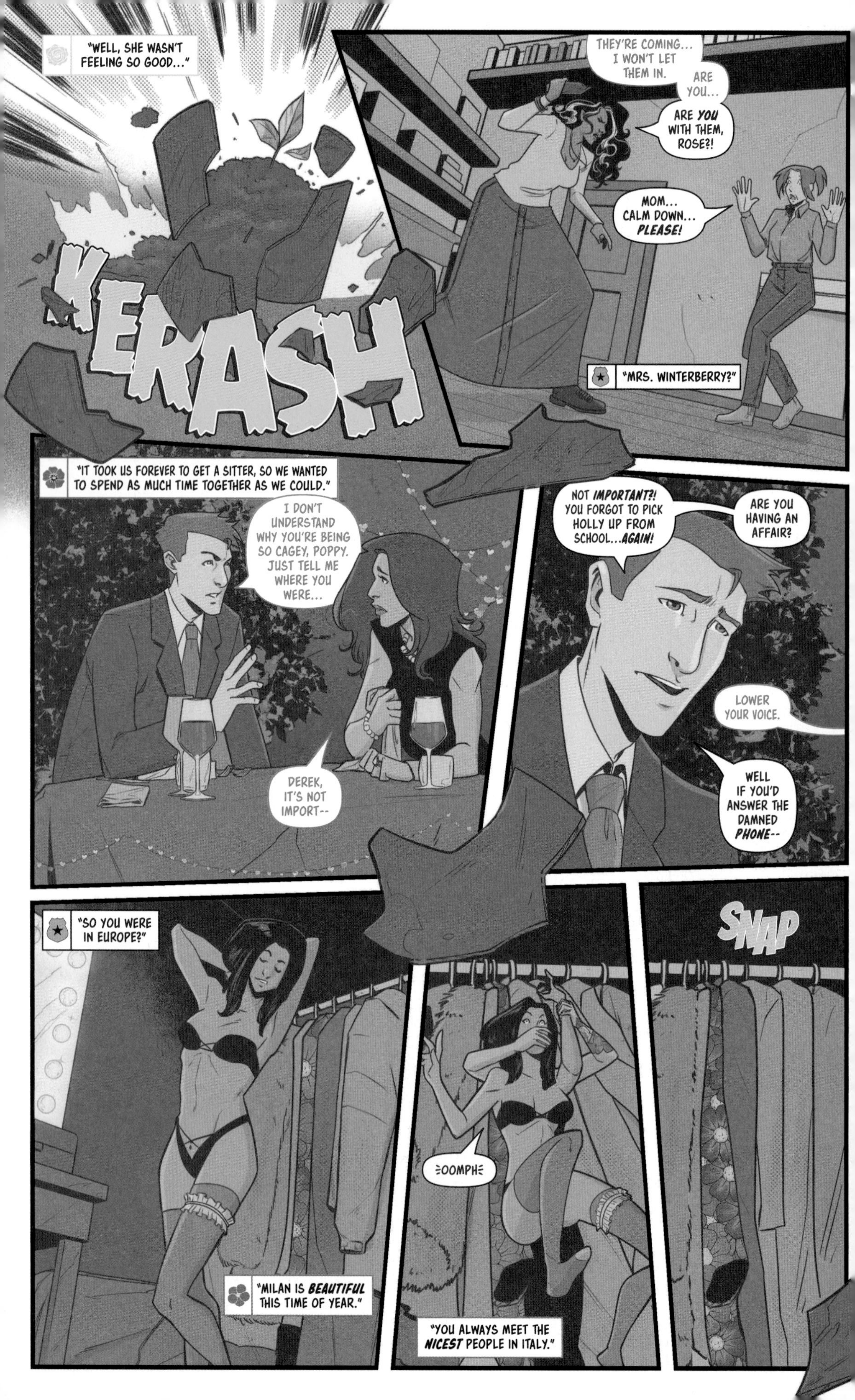
"WELL, SHE WASN'T FEELING SO GOOD..."
KERASH
THEY'RE COMING... I WON'T LET THEM IN.
ARE YOU...
ARE YOU WITH THEM, ROSE?!
MOM... CALM DOWN... PLEASE!
"MRS. WINTERBERRY?"
"IT TOOK US FOREVER TO GET A SITTER, SO WE WANTED TO SPEND AS MUCH TIME TOGETHER AS WE COULD."
I DON'T UNDERSTAND WHY YOU'RE BEING SO CAGEY, POPPY. JUST TELL ME WHERE YOU WERE...
DEREK, IT'S NOT IMPORT--
NOT IMPORTANT?! YOU FORGOT TO PICK HOLLY UP FROM SCHOOL...AGAIN!
ARE YOU HAVING AN AFFAIR?
LOWER YOUR VOICE.
WELL IF YOU'D ANSWER THE DAMNED PHONE--
"SO YOU WERE IN EUROPE?"
"MILAN IS BEAUTIFUL THIS TIME OF YEAR."
OOMPH
"YOU ALWAYS MEET THE NICEST PEOPLE IN ITALY."
SNAP

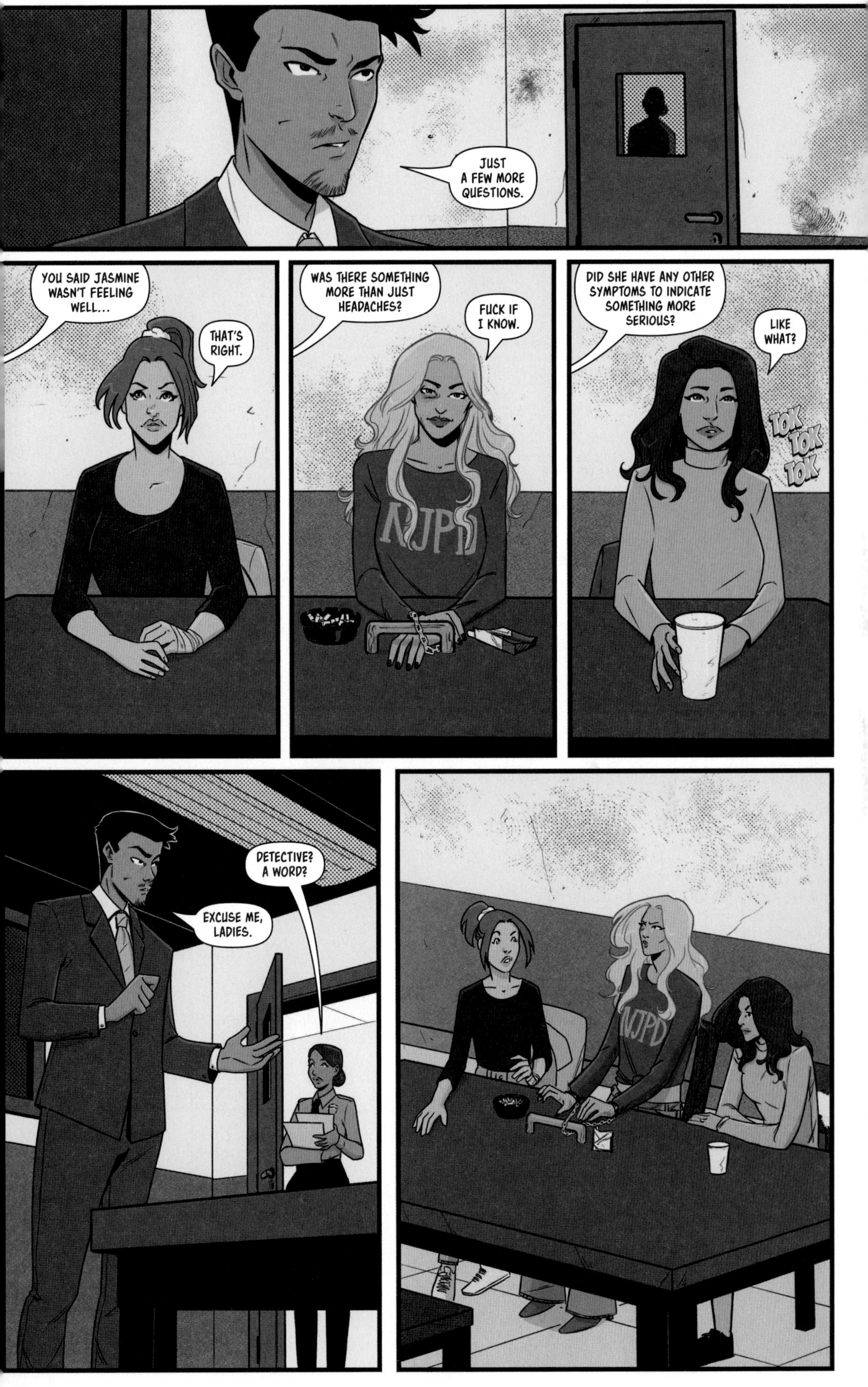
JUST A FEW MORE QUESTIONS.
YOU SAID JASMINE WASN'T FEELING WELL...
THAT'S RIGHT.
WAS THERE SOMETHING MORE THAN JUST HEADACHES?
FUCK IF I KNOW.
NJPD
DID SHE HAVE ANY OTHER SYMPTOMS TO INDICATE SOMETHING MORE SERIOUS?
LIKE WHAT?
TOK TOK TOK
DETECTIVE? A WORD?
EXCUSE ME, LADIES.
NJPD

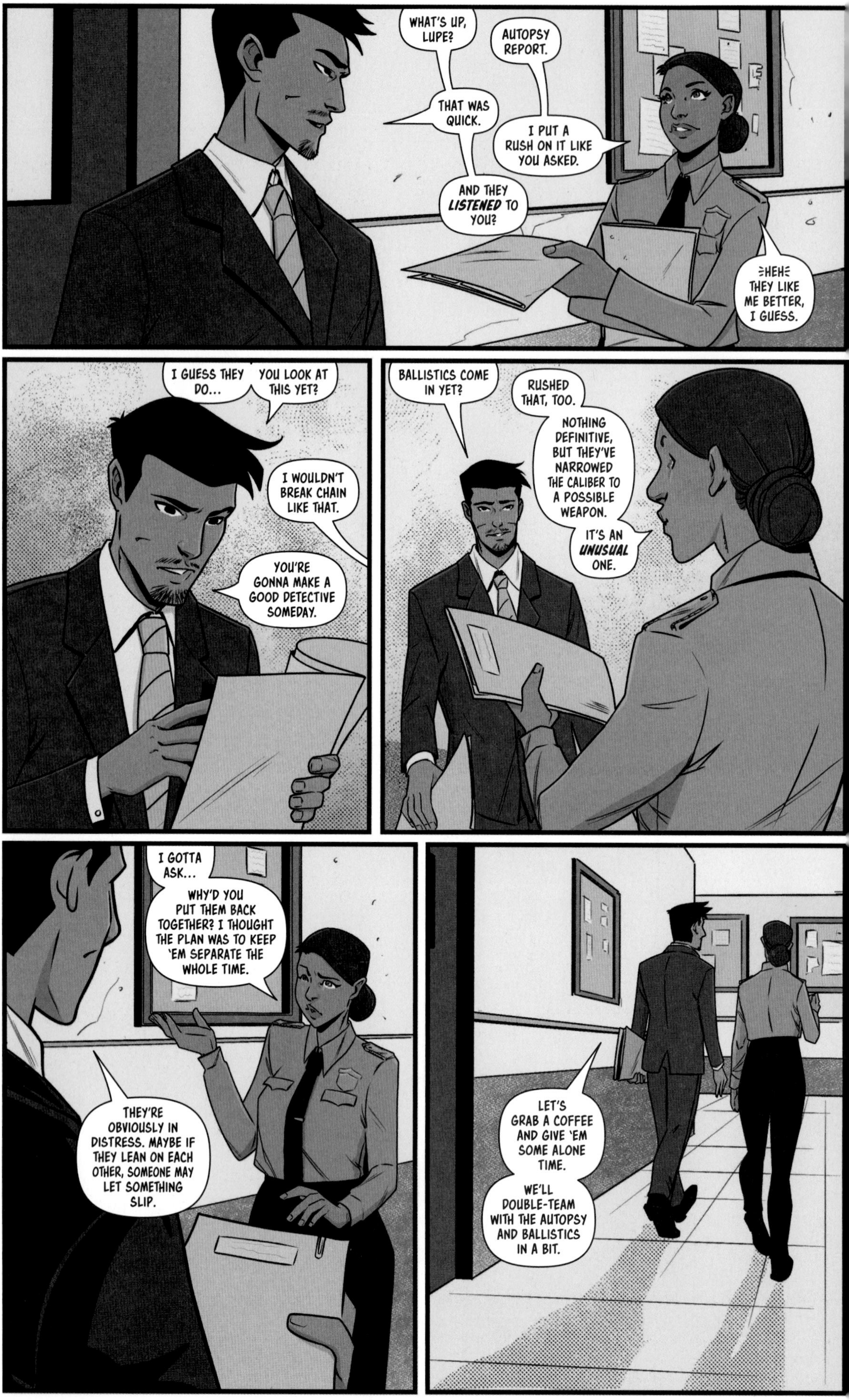

WHAT'S UP, LUPE?
AUTOPSY REPORT.
THAT WAS QUICK.
I PUT A RUSH ON IT LIKE YOU ASKED.
AND THEY *LISTENED* TO YOU?
HEH
THEY LIKE ME BETTER, I GUESS.
I GUESS THEY DO...
YOU LOOK AT THIS YET?
I WOULDN'T BREAK CHAIN LIKE THAT.
YOU'RE GONNA MAKE A GOOD DETECTIVE SOMEDAY.
BALLISTICS COME IN YET?
RUSHED THAT, TOO.
NOTHING DEFINITIVE, BUT THEY'VE NARROWED THE CALIBER TO A POSSIBLE WEAPON.
IT'S AN *UNUSUAL* ONE.
I GOTTA ASK...
WHY'D YOU PUT THEM BACK TOGETHER? I THOUGHT THE PLAN WAS TO KEEP 'EM SEPARATE THE WHOLE TIME.
THEY'RE OBVIOUSLY IN DISTRESS. MAYBE IF THEY LEAN ON EACH OTHER, SOMEONE MAY LET SOMETHING SLIP.
LET'S GRAB A COFFEE AND GIVE 'EM SOME ALONE TIME.
WE'LL DOUBLE-TEAM WITH THE AUTOPSY AND BALLISTICS IN A BIT.

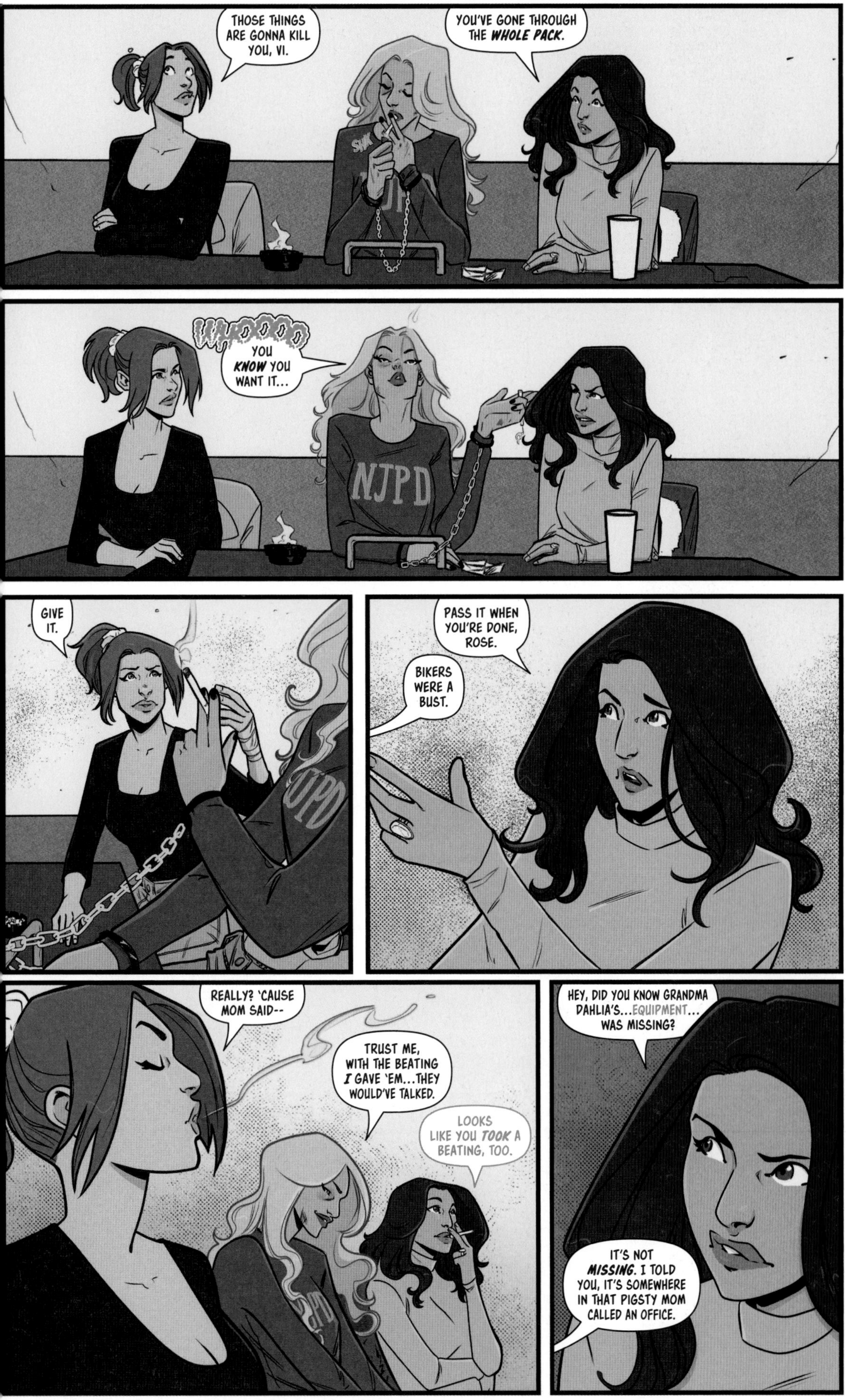
THOSE THINGS ARE GONNA KILL YOU, VI.
YOU'VE GONE THROUGH THE *WHOLE PACK*.
YOU *KNOW* YOU WANT IT...
NJPD
GIVE IT.
PASS IT WHEN YOU'RE DONE, ROSE.
BIKERS WERE A BUST.
REALLY? 'CAUSE MOM SAID--
TRUST ME, WITH THE BEATING *I* GAVE 'EM...THEY WOULD'VE TALKED.
LOOKS LIKE YOU *TOOK* A BEATING, TOO.
HEY, DID YOU KNOW GRANDMA DAHLIA'S...EQUIPMENT...WAS MISSING?
IT'S NOT *MISSING*. I TOLD YOU, IT'S SOMEWHERE IN THAT PIGSTY MOM CALLED AN OFFICE.

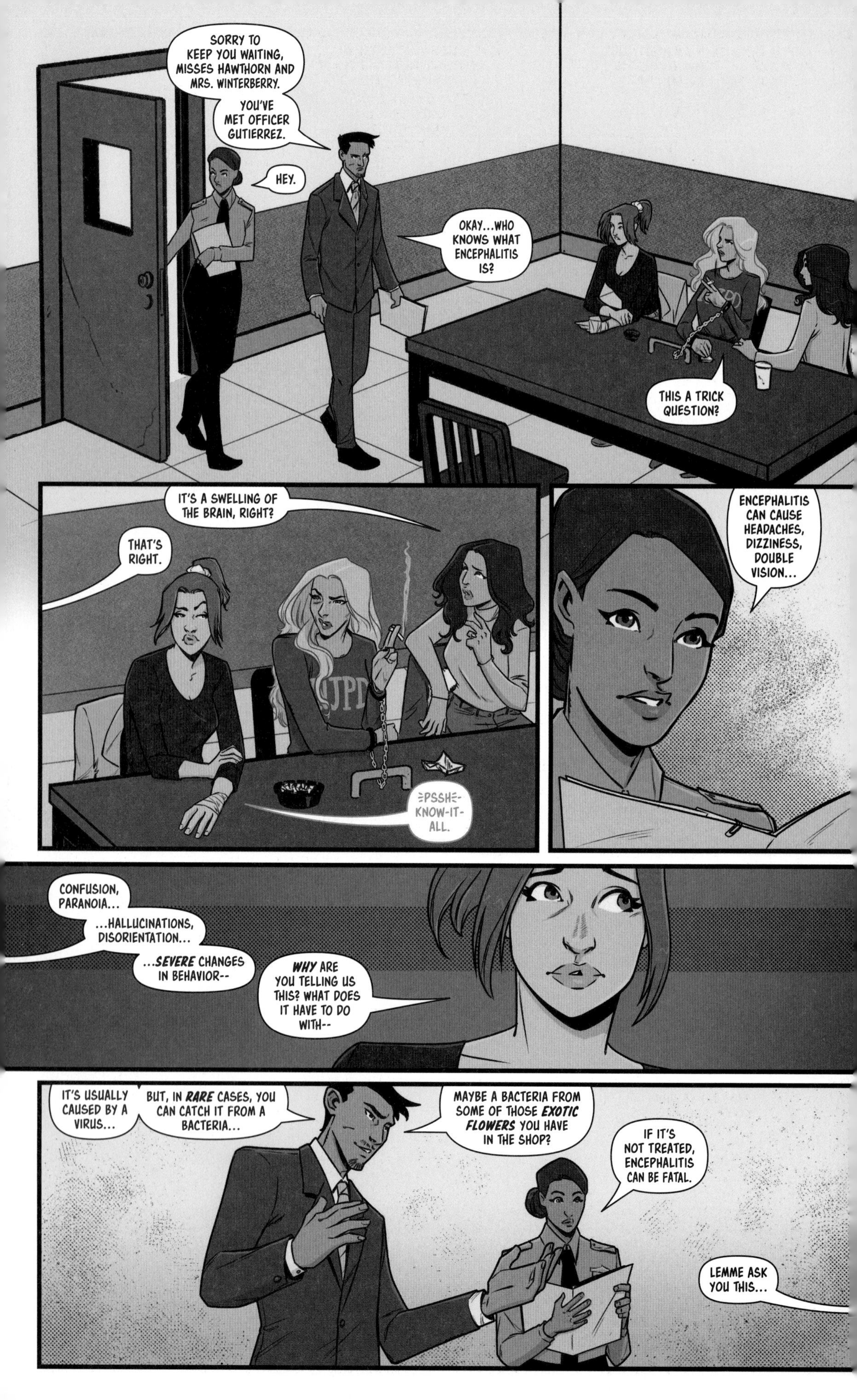
SORRY TO KEEP YOU WAITING, MISSES HAWTHORN AND MRS. WINTERBERRY.
YOU'VE MET OFFICER GUTIERREZ.
HEY.
OKAY...WHO KNOWS WHAT ENCEPHALITIS IS?
THIS A TRICK QUESTION?
IT'S A SWELLING OF THE BRAIN, RIGHT?
THAT'S RIGHT.
PSSH- KNOW-IT-ALL.
ENCEPHALITIS CAN CAUSE HEADACHES, DIZZINESS, DOUBLE VISION...
CONFUSION, PARANOIA...
...HALLUCINATIONS, DISORIENTATION...
...SEVERE CHANGES IN BEHAVIOR--
WHY ARE YOU TELLING US THIS? WHAT DOES IT HAVE TO DO WITH--
IT'S USUALLY CAUSED BY A VIRUS...
BUT, IN RARE CASES, YOU CAN CATCH IT FROM A BACTERIA...
MAYBE A BACTERIA FROM SOME OF THOSE EXOTIC FLOWERS YOU HAVE IN THE SHOP?
IF IT'S NOT TREATED, ENCEPHALITIS CAN BE FATAL.
LEMME ASK YOU THIS...

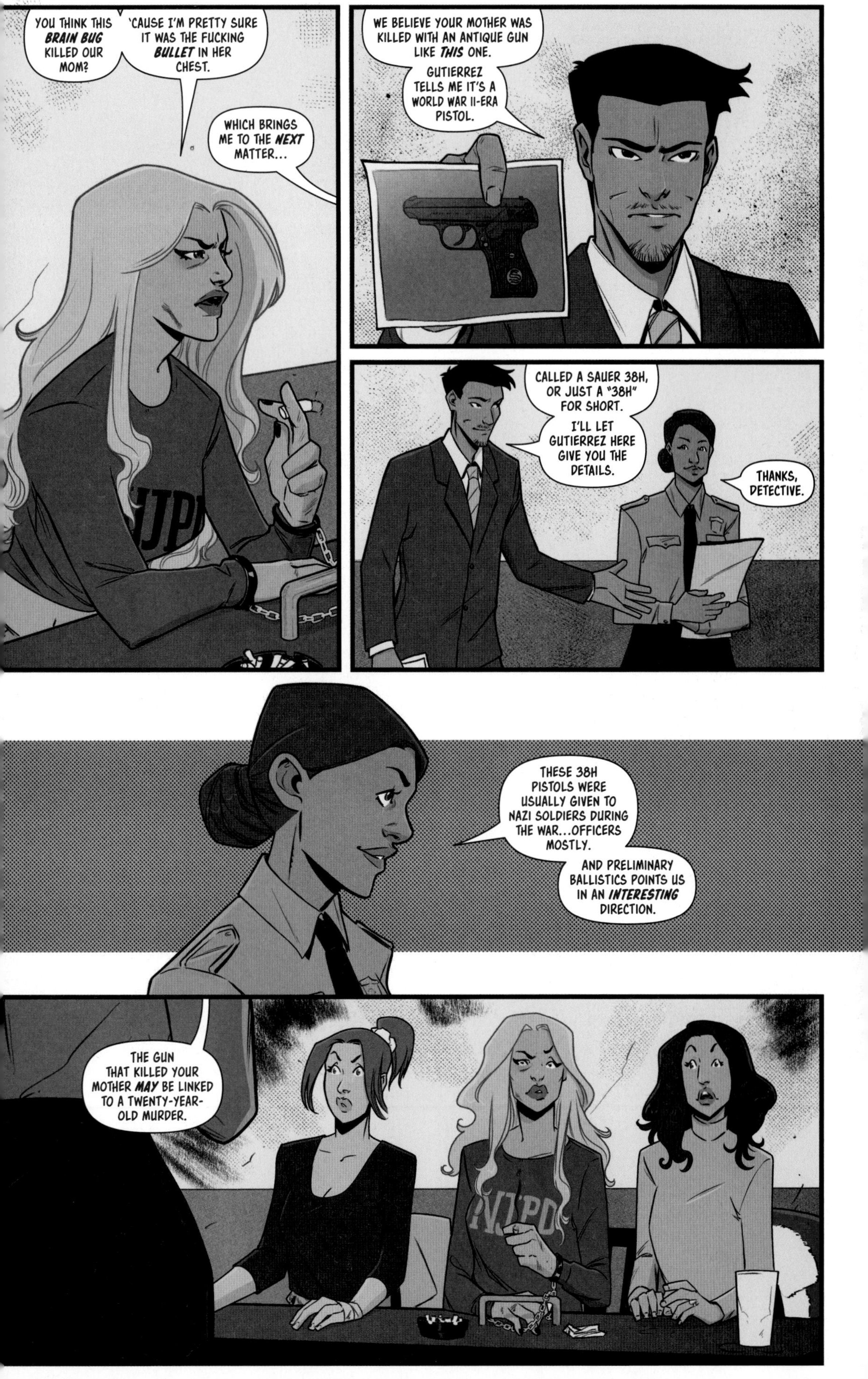

YOU THINK THIS BRAIN BUG KILLED OUR MOM?
'CAUSE I'M PRETTY SURE IT WAS THE FUCKING BULLET IN HER CHEST.
WHICH BRINGS ME TO THE NEXT MATTER...
WE BELIEVE YOUR MOTHER WAS KILLED WITH AN ANTIQUE GUN LIKE THIS ONE.
GUTIERREZ TELLS ME IT'S A WORLD WAR II-ERA PISTOL.
CALLED A SAUER 38H, OR JUST A "38H" FOR SHORT.
I'LL LET GUTIERREZ HERE GIVE YOU THE DETAILS.
THANKS, DETECTIVE.
THESE 38H PISTOLS WERE USUALLY GIVEN TO NAZI SOLDIERS DURING THE WAR...OFFICERS MOSTLY.
AND PRELIMINARY BALLISTICS POINTS US IN AN INTERESTING DIRECTION.
THE GUN THAT KILLED YOUR MOTHER MAY BE LINKED TO A TWENTY-YEAR-OLD MURDER.

CHAPTER *Three*

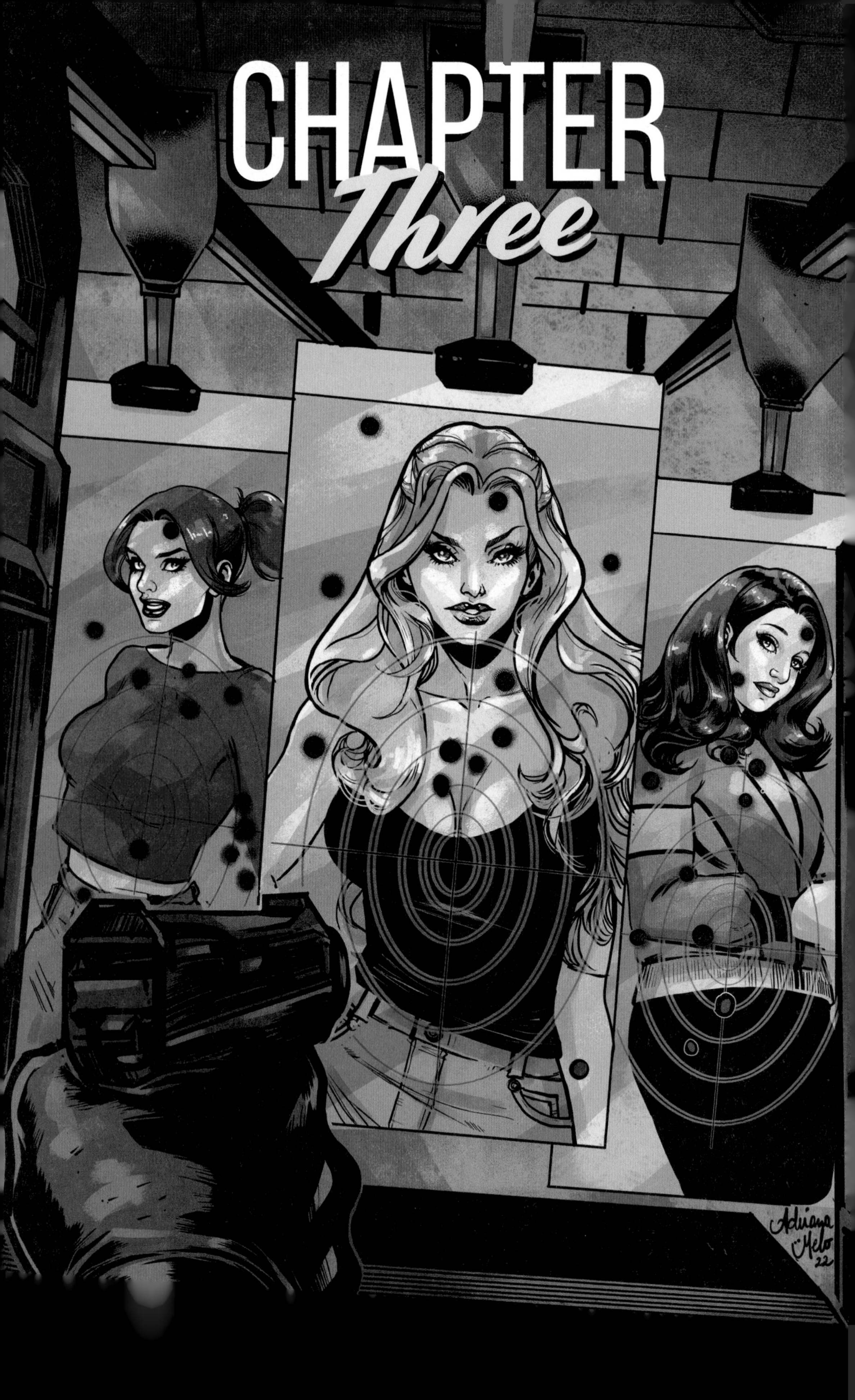
Adriana Melo 22

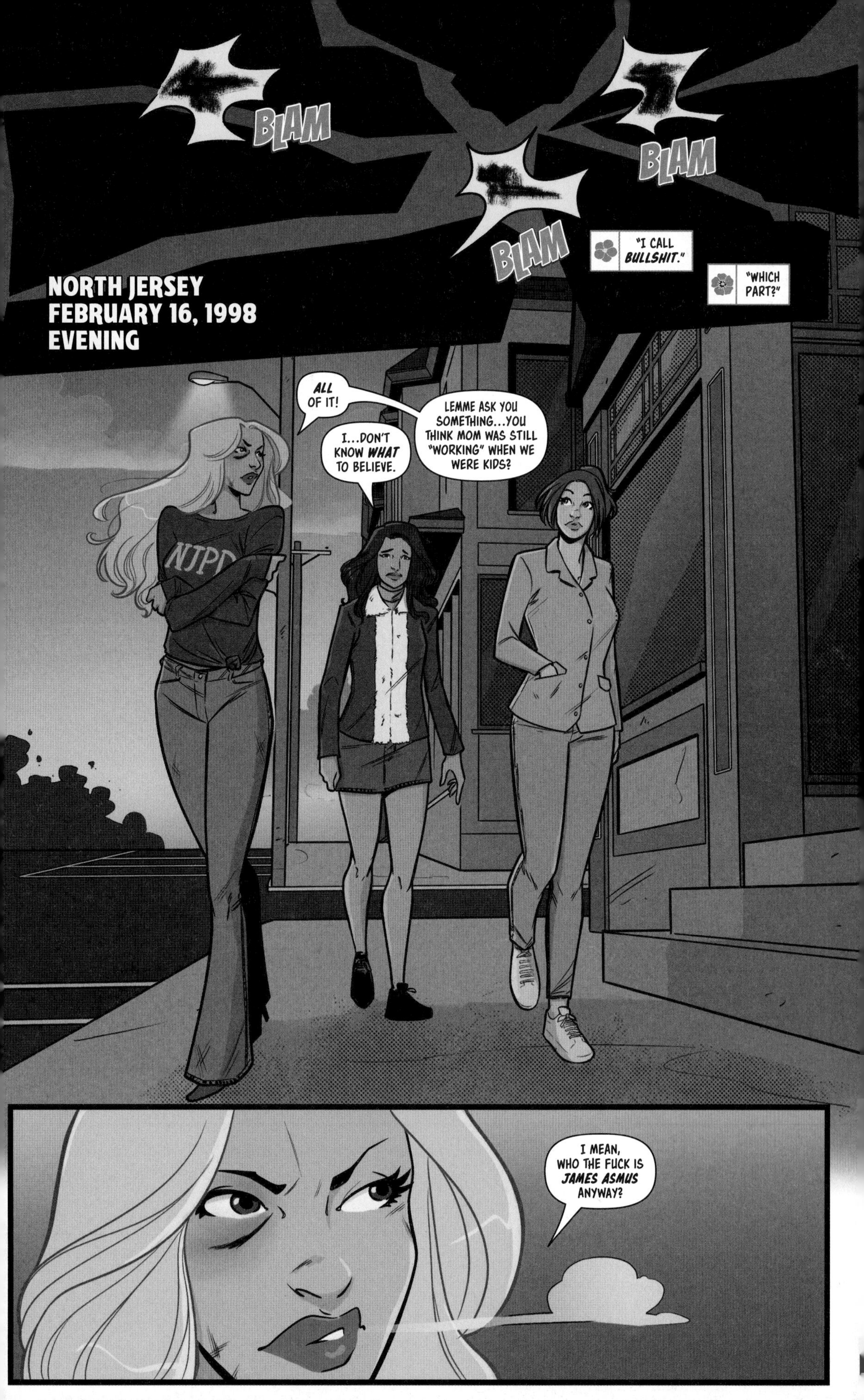
BLAM
BLAM
BLAM
"I CALL BULLSHIT."
"WHICH PART?"
NORTH JERSEY
FEBRUARY 16, 1998
EVENING
ALL OF IT!
I...DON'T KNOW WHAT TO BELIEVE.
LEMME ASK YOU SOMETHING...YOU THINK MOM WAS STILL "WORKING" WHEN WE WERE KIDS?
NJPD
I MEAN, WHO THE FUCK IS JAMES ASMUS ANYWAY?

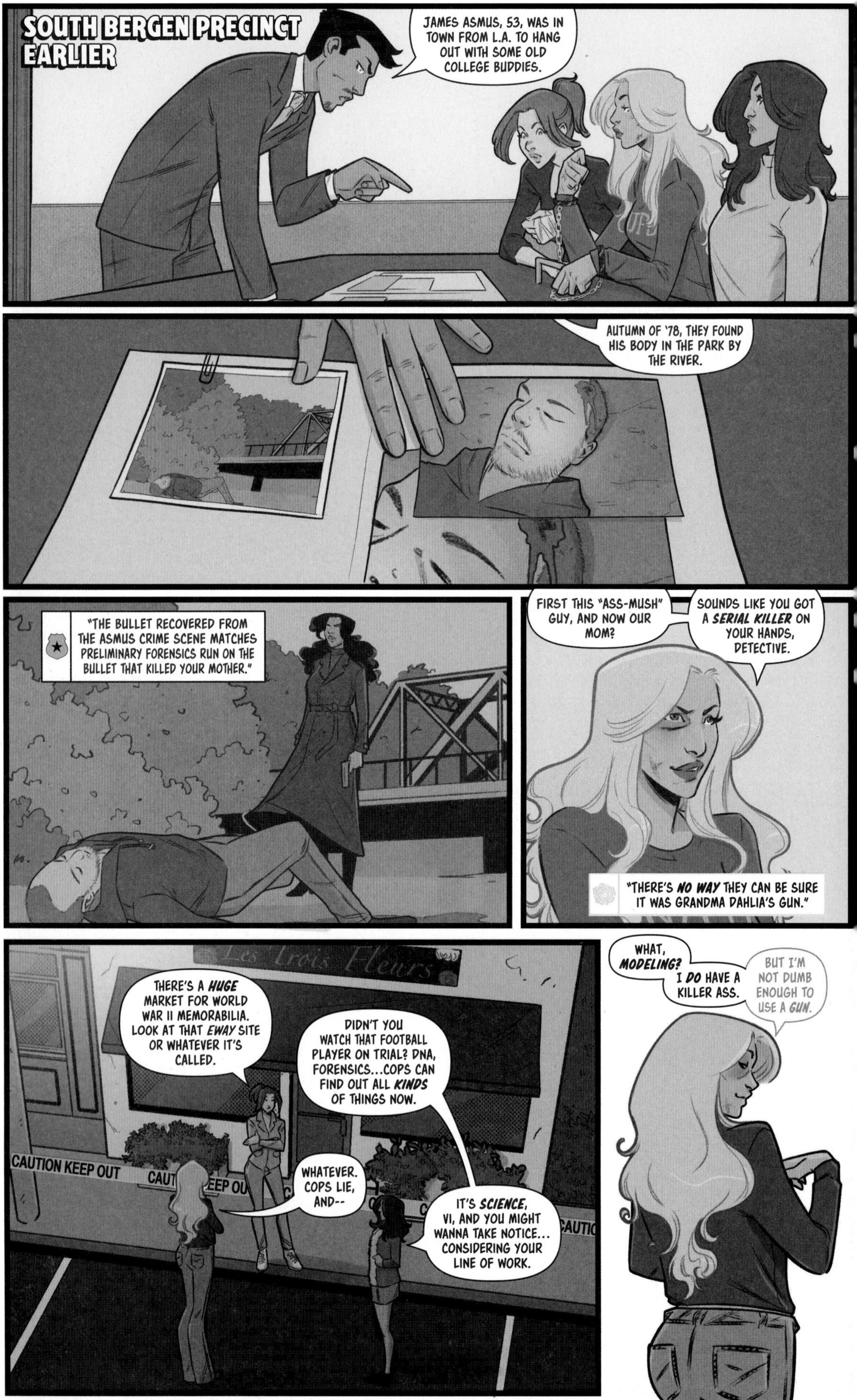

SOUTH BERGEN PRECINCT
EARLIER
JAMES ASMUS, 53, WAS IN TOWN FROM L.A. TO HANG OUT WITH SOME OLD COLLEGE BUDDIES.
AUTUMN OF '78, THEY FOUND HIS BODY IN THE PARK BY THE RIVER.
"THE BULLET RECOVERED FROM THE ASMUS CRIME SCENE MATCHES PRELIMINARY FORENSICS RUN ON THE BULLET THAT KILLED YOUR MOTHER."
FIRST THIS "ASS-MUSH" GUY, AND NOW OUR MOM?
SOUNDS LIKE YOU GOT A SERIAL KILLER ON YOUR HANDS, DETECTIVE.
"THERE'S NO WAY THEY CAN BE SURE IT WAS GRANDMA DAHLIA'S GUN."
Les Trois Fleurs
THERE'S A HUGE MARKET FOR WORLD WAR II MEMORABILIA. LOOK AT THAT EWAY SITE OR WHATEVER IT'S CALLED.
DIDN'T YOU WATCH THAT FOOTBALL PLAYER ON TRIAL? DNA, FORENSICS...COPS CAN FIND OUT ALL KINDS OF THINGS NOW.
CAUTION KEEP OUT
WHATEVER. COPS LIE, AND--
IT'S SCIENCE, VI, AND YOU MIGHT WANNA TAKE NOTICE... CONSIDERING YOUR LINE OF WORK.
WHAT, MODELING? I DO HAVE A KILLER ASS.
BUT I'M NOT DUMB ENOUGH TO USE A GUN.

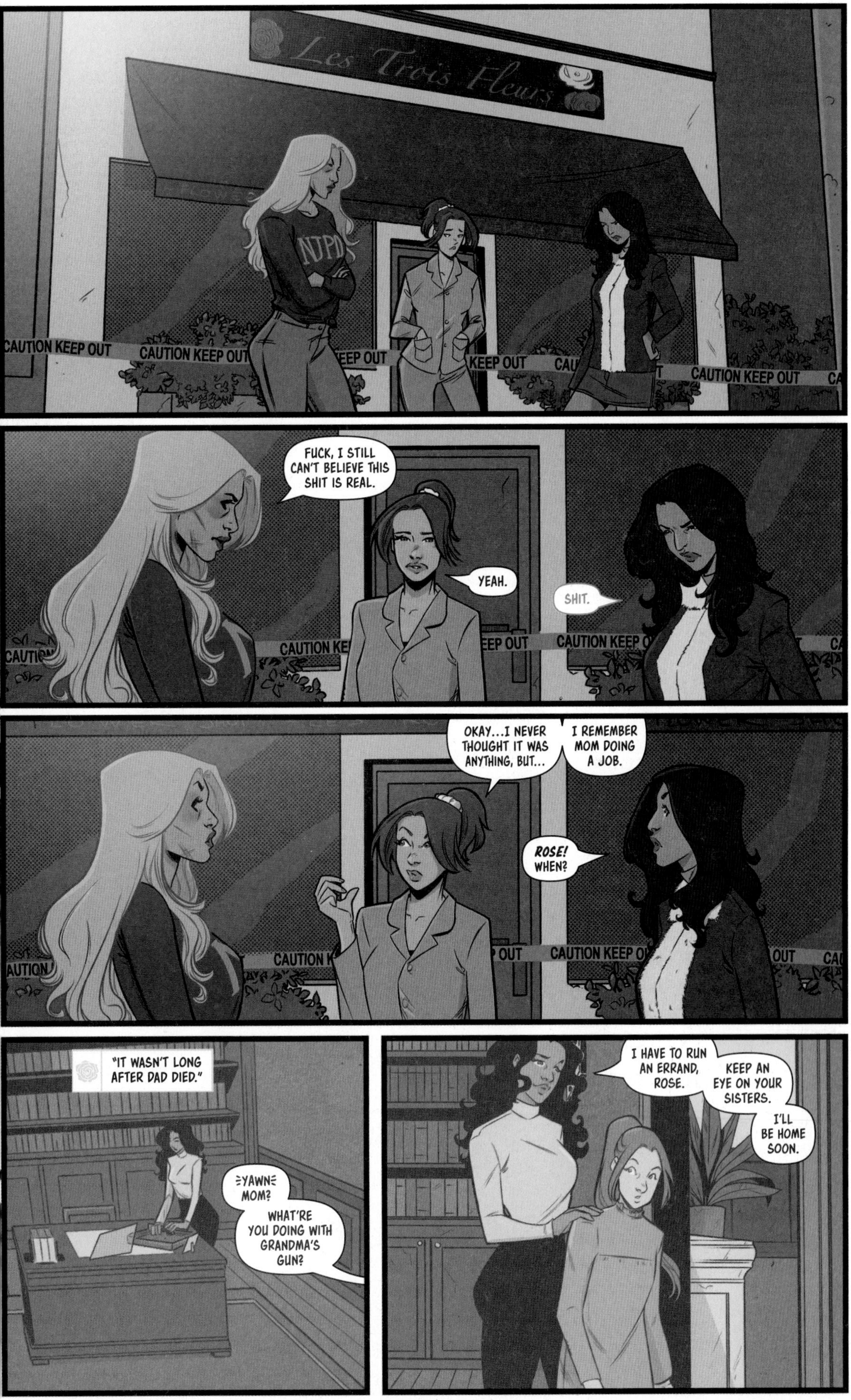

Les Trois Fleurs
CAUTION KEEP OUT
FUCK, I STILL CAN'T BELIEVE THIS SHIT IS REAL.
YEAH.
SHIT.
OKAY...I NEVER THOUGHT IT WAS ANYTHING, BUT...
I REMEMBER MOM DOING A JOB.
ROSE! WHEN?
"IT WASN'T LONG AFTER DAD DIED."
≡YAWN≡ MOM?
WHAT'RE YOU DOING WITH GRANDMA'S GUN?
I HAVE TO RUN AN ERRAND, ROSE.
KEEP AN EYE ON YOUR SISTERS.
I'LL BE HOME SOON.

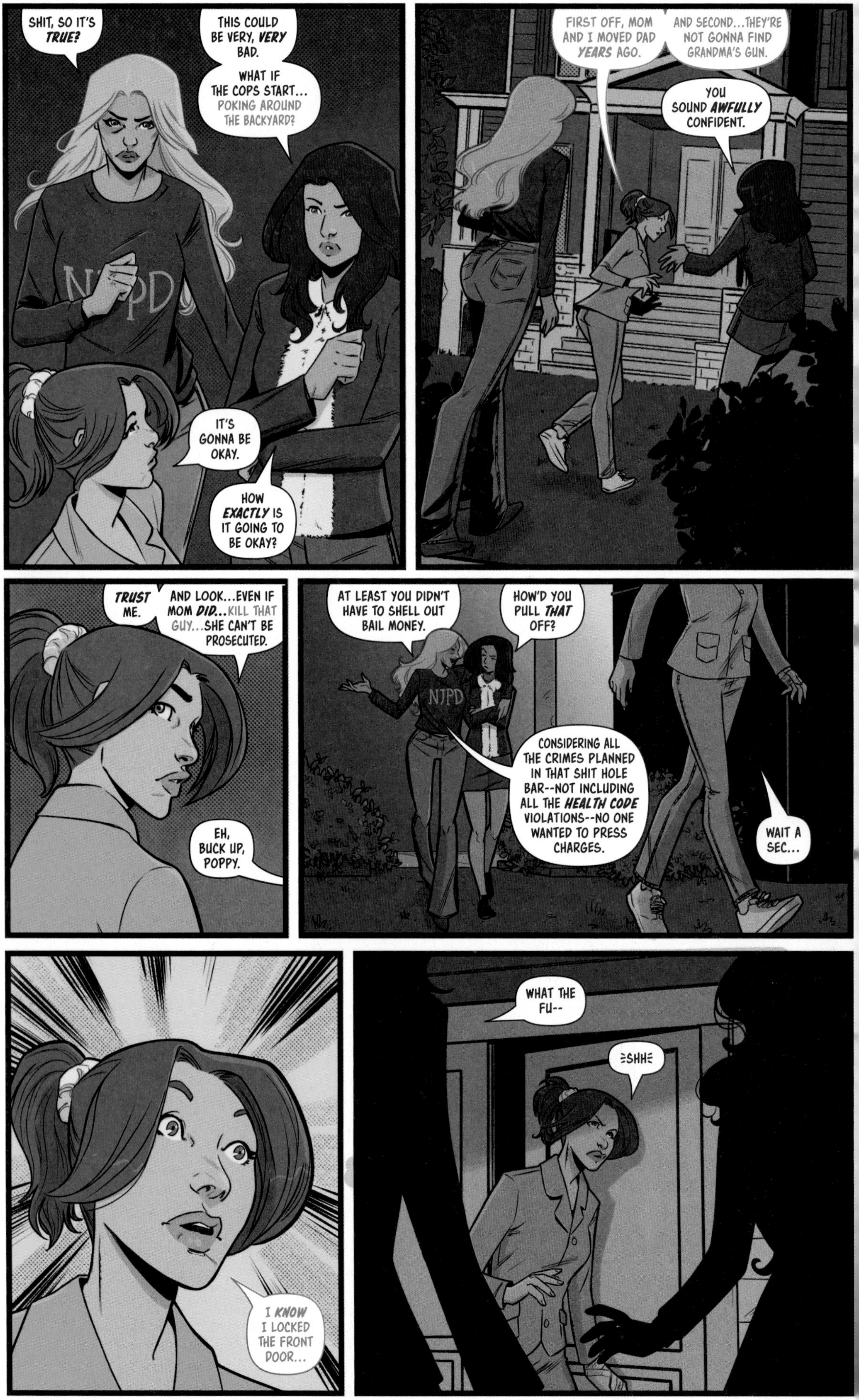
SHIT, SO IT'S TRUE?
THIS COULD BE VERY, VERY BAD.
WHAT IF THE COPS START... POKING AROUND THE BACKYARD?
NJPD
IT'S GONNA BE OKAY.
HOW EXACTLY IS IT GOING TO BE OKAY?
FIRST OFF, MOM AND I MOVED DAD YEARS AGO.
AND SECOND...THEY'RE NOT GONNA FIND GRANDMA'S GUN.
YOU SOUND AWFULLY CONFIDENT.
TRUST ME.
AND LOOK...EVEN IF MOM DID...KILL THAT GUY...SHE CAN'T BE PROSECUTED.
EH, BUCK UP, POPPY.
AT LEAST YOU DIDN'T HAVE TO SHELL OUT BAIL MONEY.
HOW'D YOU PULL THAT OFF?
NJPD
CONSIDERING ALL THE CRIMES PLANNED IN THAT SHIT HOLE BAR--NOT INCLUDING ALL THE HEALTH CODE VIOLATIONS--NO ONE WANTED TO PRESS CHARGES.
WAIT A SEC...
I KNOW I LOCKED THE FRONT DOOR...
WHAT THE FU--
SHH

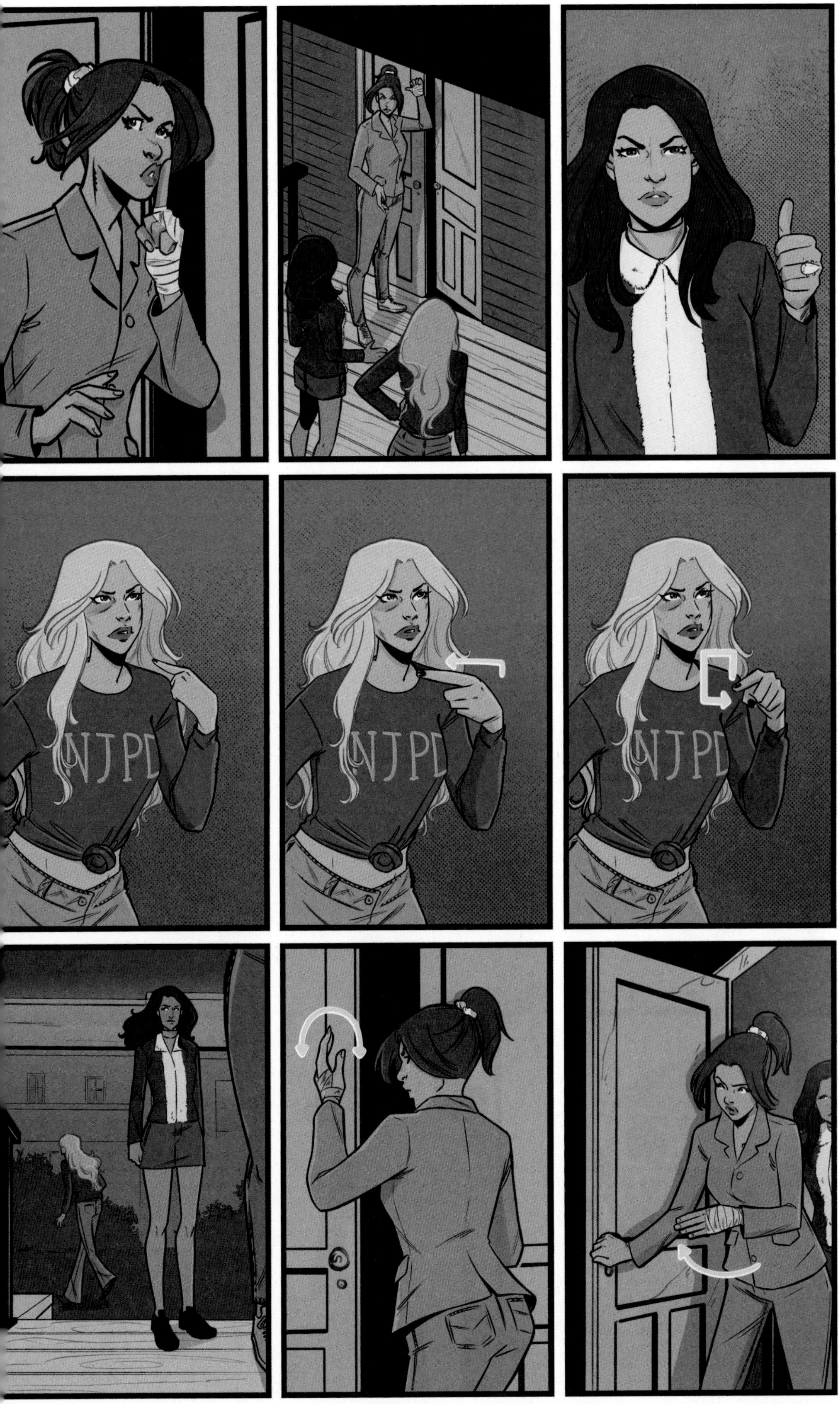
NJPD
NJPD
NJPD

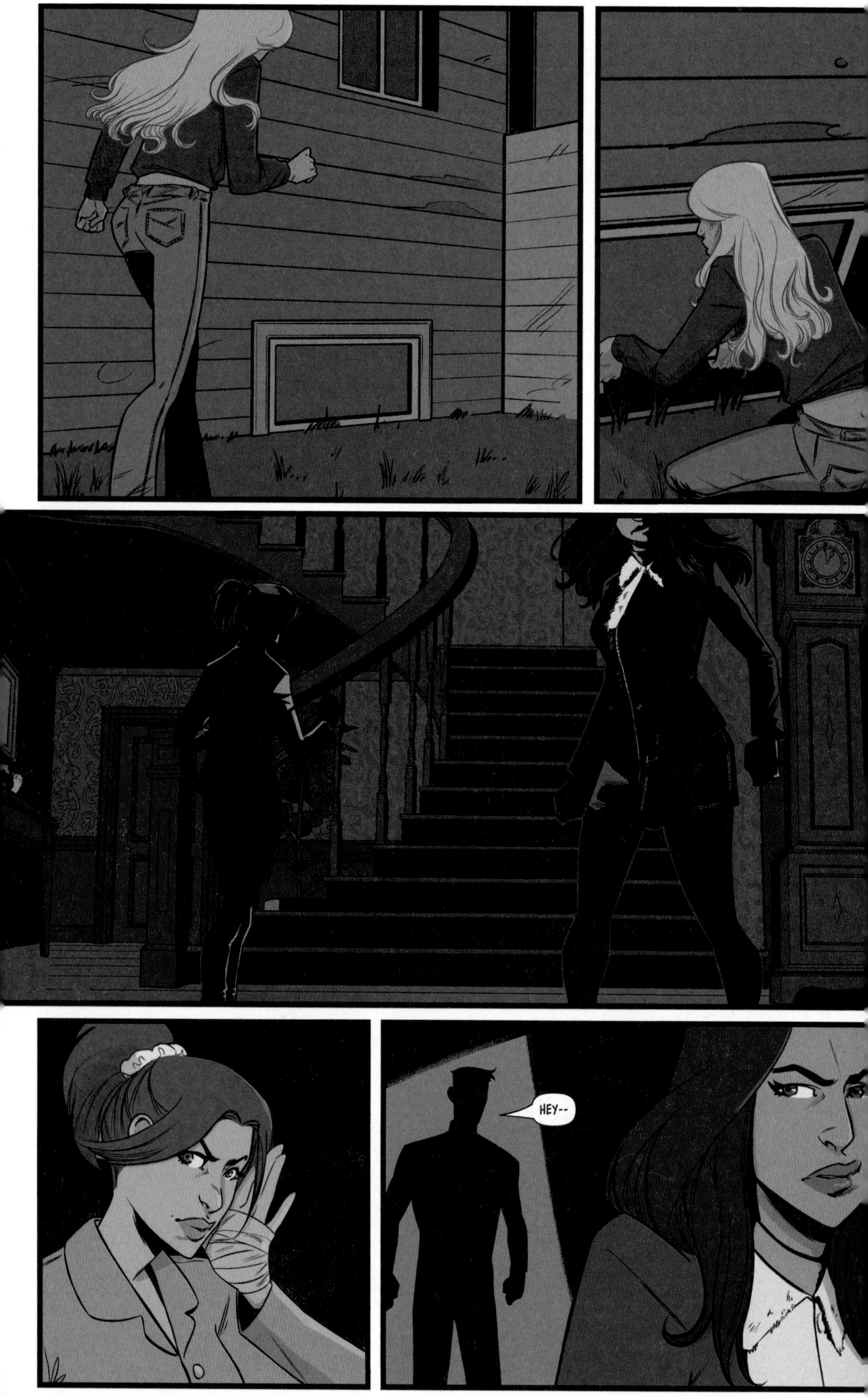
HEY--

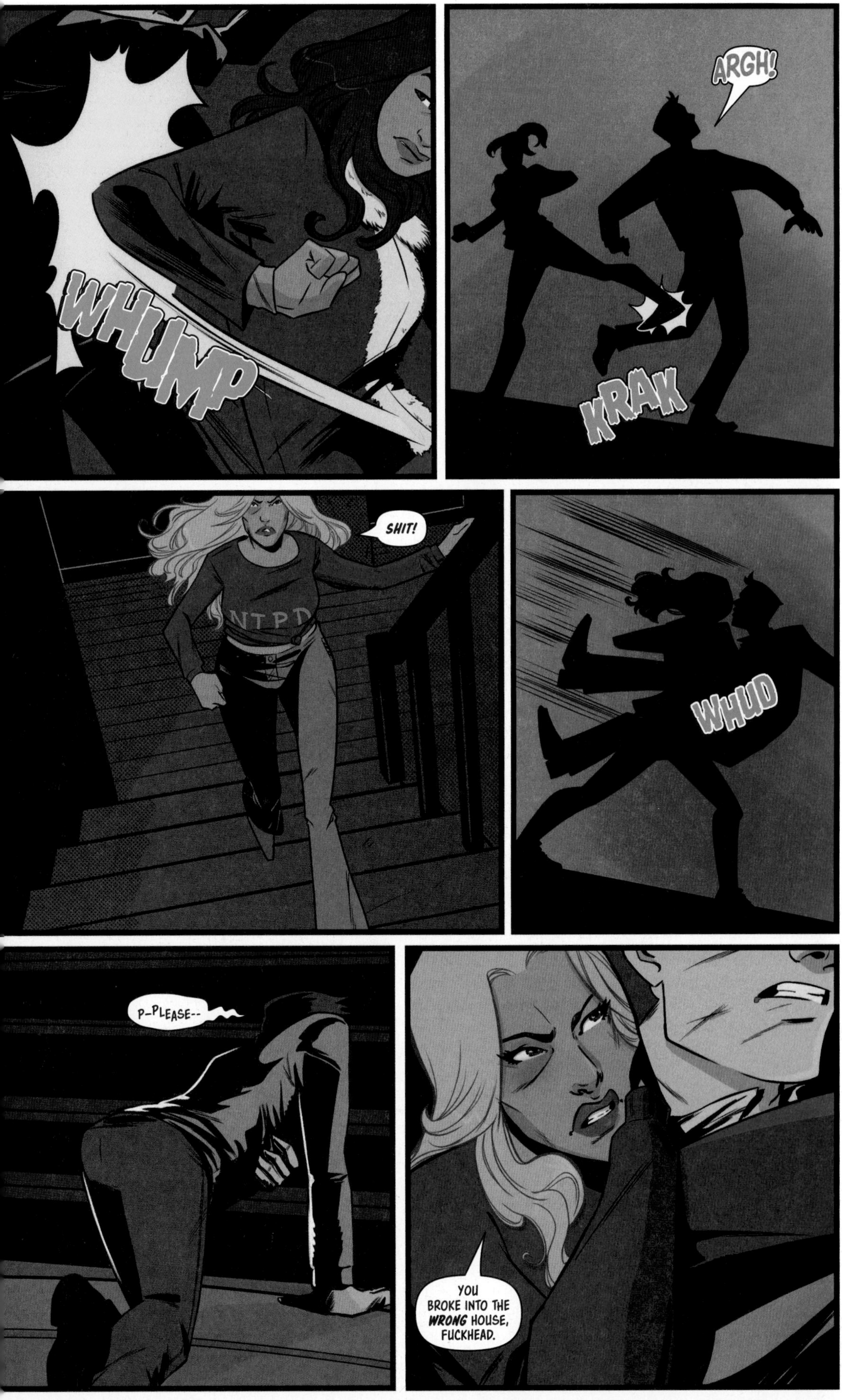
WHUMP
ARGH!
KRAK
SHIT!
NTPD
WHUD
P-PLEASE--
YOU BROKE INTO THE ***WRONG*** HOUSE, FUCKHEAD.

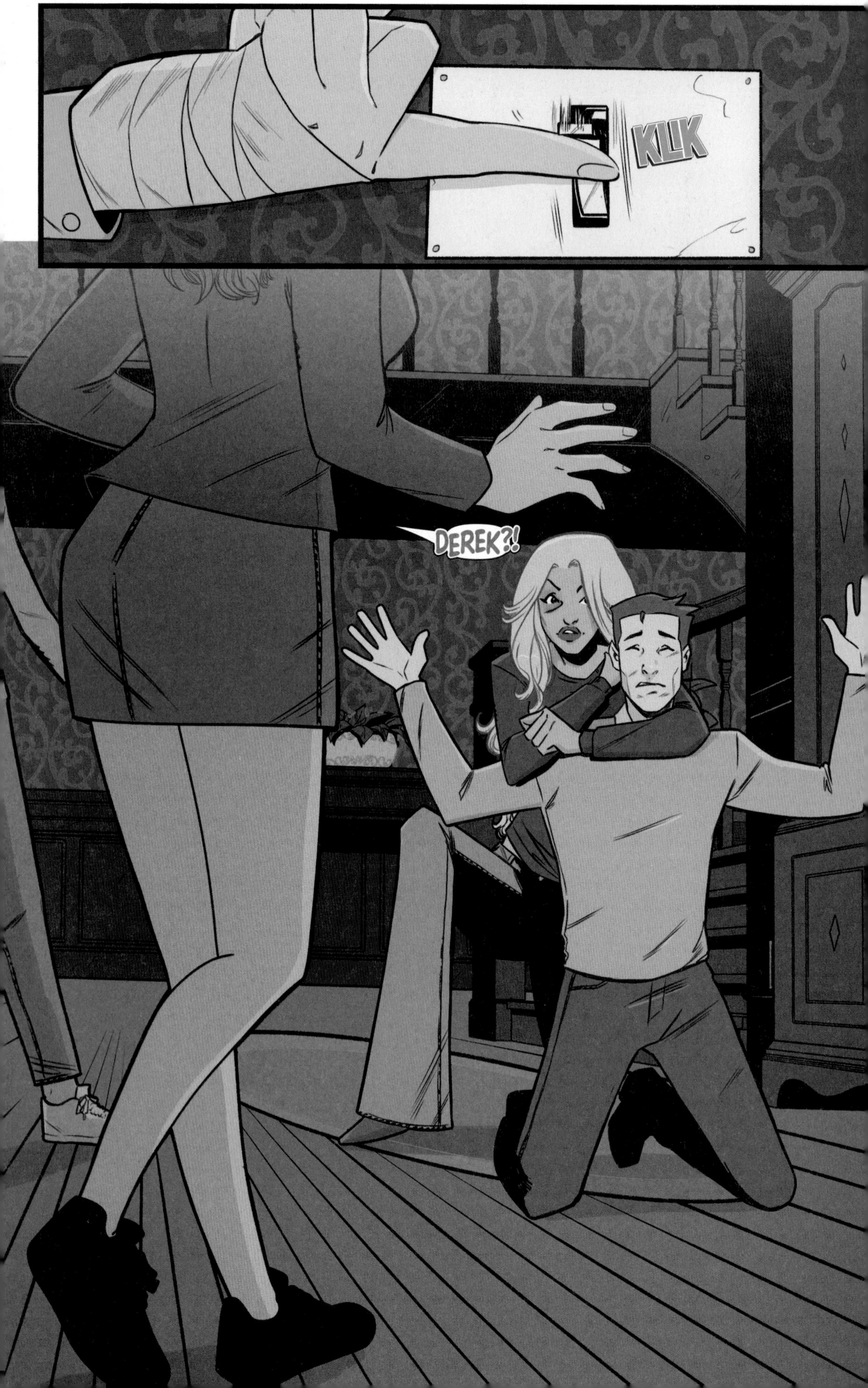
KLIK
DEREK?!

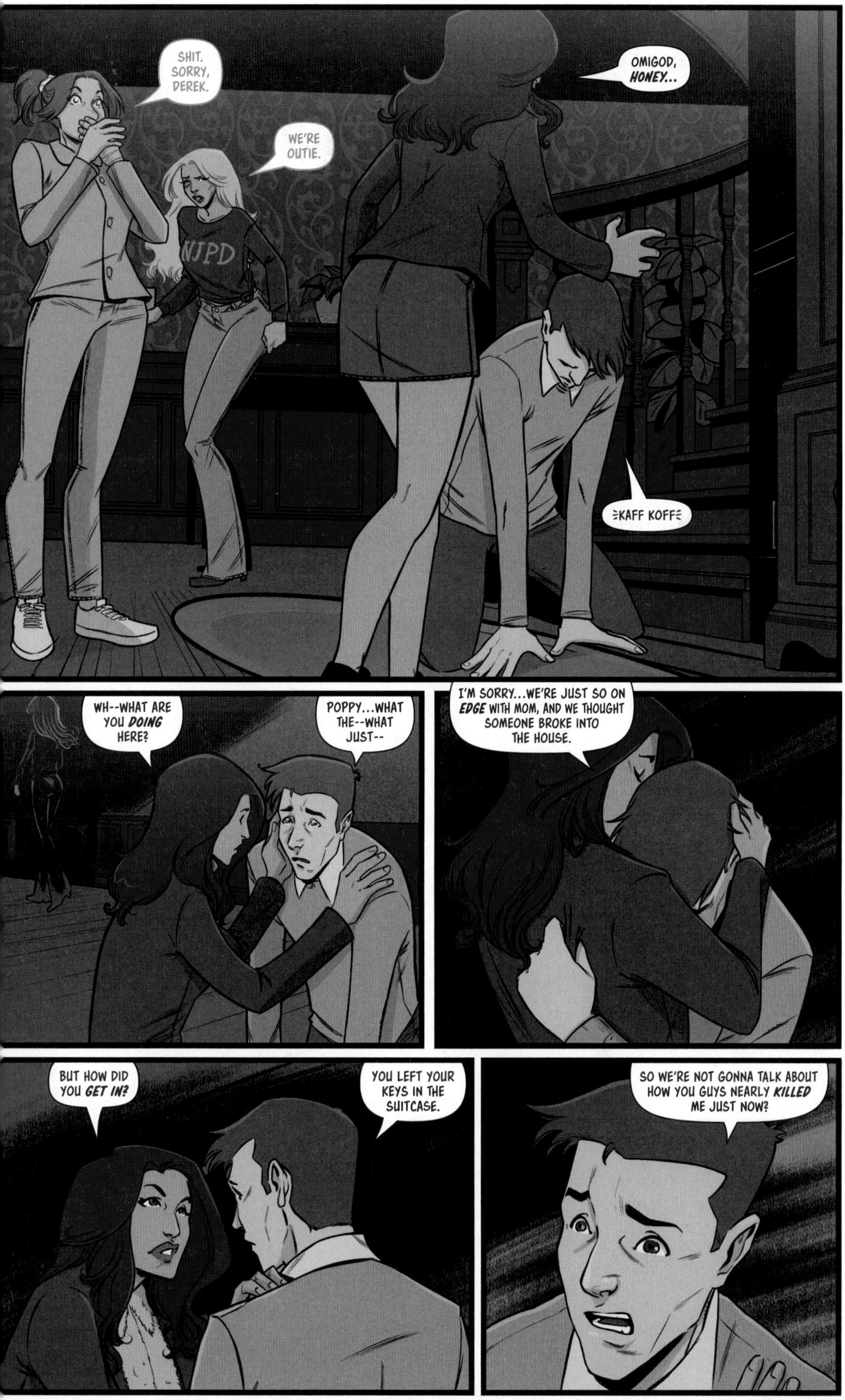
SHIT. SORRY, DEREK.
WE'RE OUTIE.
OMIGOD, ***HONEY...***
KAFF KOFF
WH--WHAT ARE YOU ***DOING*** HERE?
POPPY...WHAT THE--WHAT JUST--
I'M SORRY...WE'RE JUST SO ON ***EDGE*** WITH MOM, AND WE THOUGHT SOMEONE BROKE INTO THE HOUSE.
BUT HOW DID YOU ***GET IN?***
YOU LEFT YOUR KEYS IN THE SUITCASE.
SO WE'RE NOT GONNA TALK ABOUT HOW YOU GUYS NEARLY ***KILLED*** ME JUST NOW?

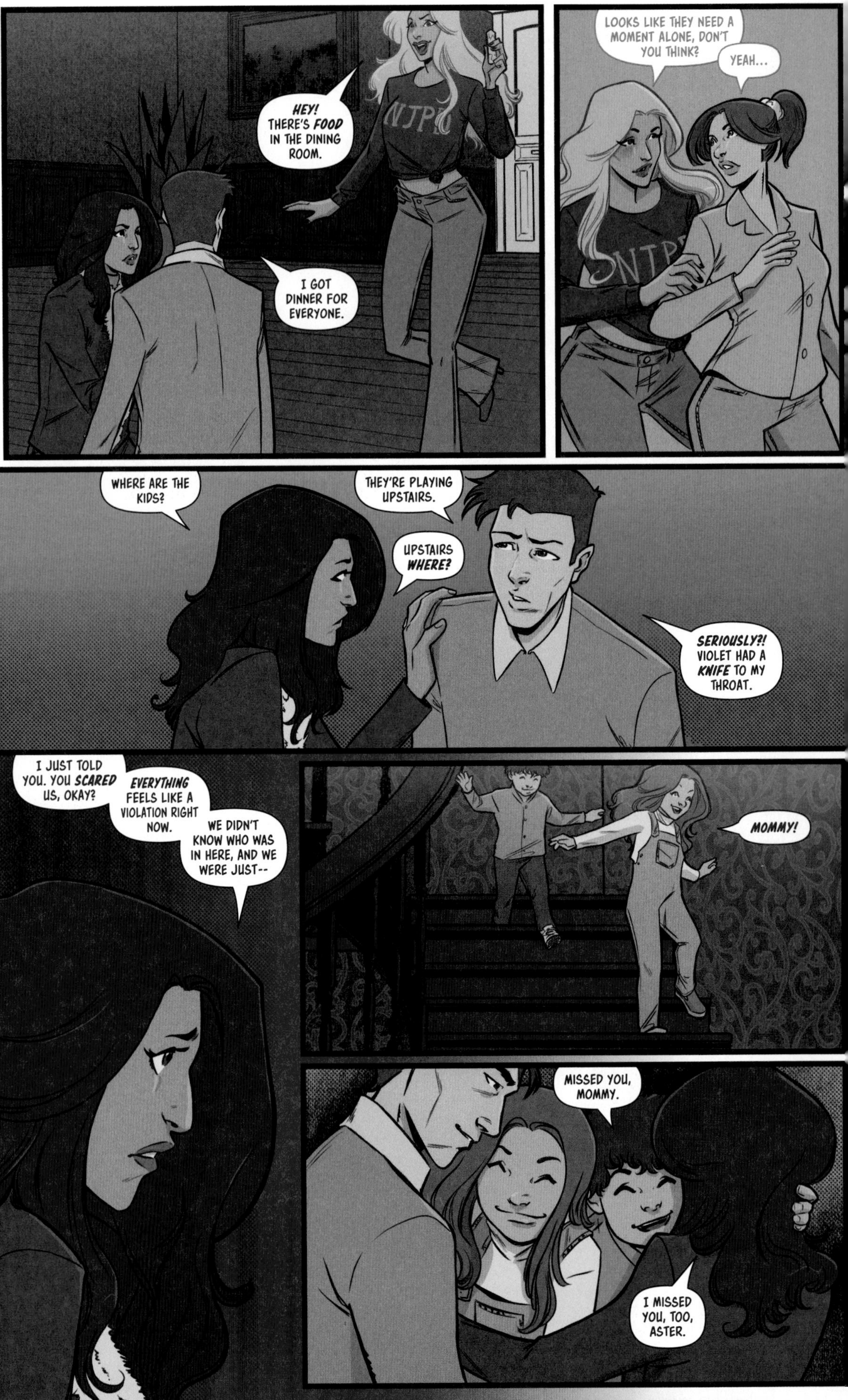
HEY! THERE'S FOOD IN THE DINING ROOM.
I GOT DINNER FOR EVERYONE.
LOOKS LIKE THEY NEED A MOMENT ALONE, DON'T YOU THINK?
YEAH...
WHERE ARE THE KIDS?
THEY'RE PLAYING UPSTAIRS.
UPSTAIRS WHERE?
SERIOUSLY?! VIOLET HAD A KNIFE TO MY THROAT.
I JUST TOLD YOU. YOU SCARED US, OKAY?
EVERYTHING FEELS LIKE A VIOLATION RIGHT NOW.
WE DIDN'T KNOW WHO WAS IN HERE, AND WE WERE JUST--
MOMMY!
MISSED YOU, MOMMY.
I MISSED YOU, TOO, ASTER.

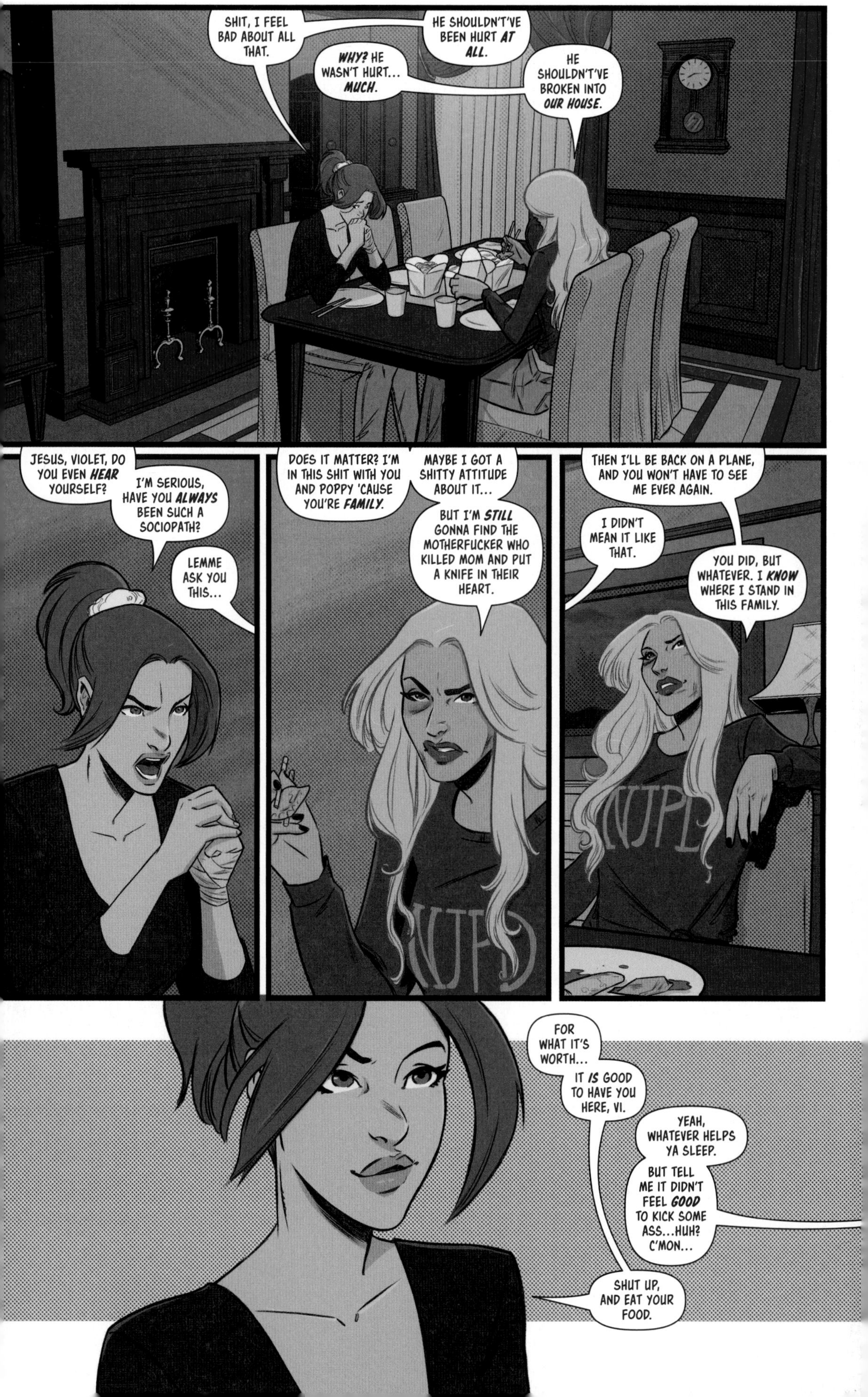
SHIT, I FEEL BAD ABOUT ALL THAT.
HE SHOULDN'T'VE BEEN HURT AT ALL.
WHY? HE WASN'T HURT... MUCH.
HE SHOULDN'T'VE BROKEN INTO OUR HOUSE.
JESUS, VIOLET, DO YOU EVEN HEAR YOURSELF?
I'M SERIOUS, HAVE YOU ALWAYS BEEN SUCH A SOCIOPATH?
LEMME ASK YOU THIS...
DOES IT MATTER? I'M IN THIS SHIT WITH YOU AND POPPY 'CAUSE YOU'RE FAMILY.
MAYBE I GOT A SHITTY ATTITUDE ABOUT IT...
BUT I'M STILL GONNA FIND THE MOTHERFUCKER WHO KILLED MOM AND PUT A KNIFE IN THEIR HEART.
THEN I'LL BE BACK ON A PLANE, AND YOU WON'T HAVE TO SEE ME EVER AGAIN.
I DIDN'T MEAN IT LIKE THAT.
YOU DID, BUT WHATEVER. I KNOW WHERE I STAND IN THIS FAMILY.
FOR WHAT IT'S WORTH...
IT IS GOOD TO HAVE YOU HERE, VI.
YEAH, WHATEVER HELPS YA SLEEP.
BUT TELL ME IT DIDN'T FEEL GOOD TO KICK SOME ASS...HUH? C'MON...
SHUT UP, AND EAT YOUR FOOD.

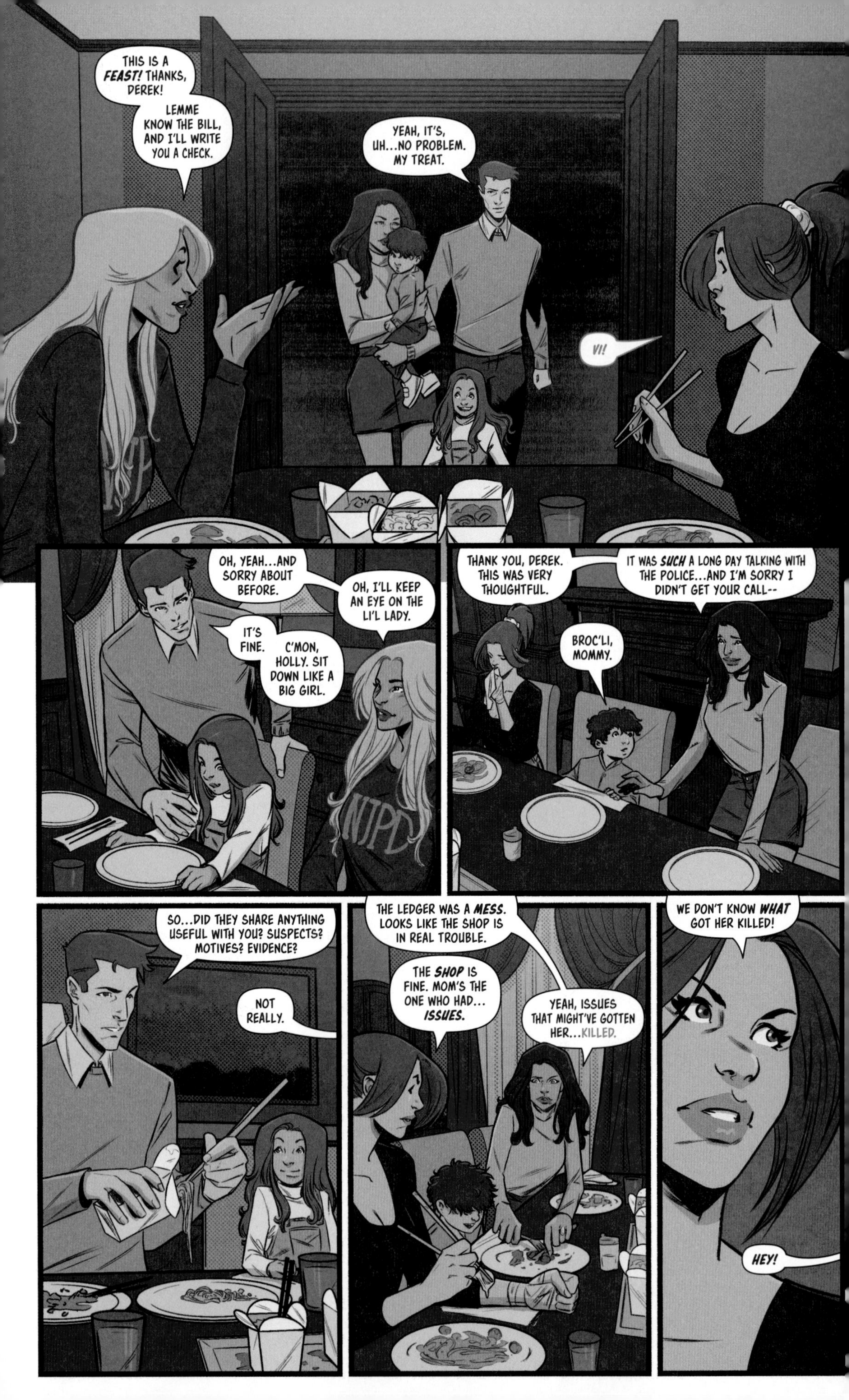
THIS IS A FEAST! THANKS, DEREK!
LEMME KNOW THE BILL, AND I'LL WRITE YOU A CHECK.
YEAH, IT'S, UH...NO PROBLEM. MY TREAT.
VI!
OH, YEAH...AND SORRY ABOUT BEFORE.
OH, I'LL KEEP AN EYE ON THE LI'L LADY.
IT'S FINE.
C'MON, HOLLY. SIT DOWN LIKE A BIG GIRL.
THANK YOU, DEREK. THIS WAS VERY THOUGHTFUL.
IT WAS SUCH A LONG DAY TALKING WITH THE POLICE...AND I'M SORRY I DIDN'T GET YOUR CALL--
BROC'LI, MOMMY.
SO...DID THEY SHARE ANYTHING USEFUL WITH YOU? SUSPECTS? MOTIVES? EVIDENCE?
NOT REALLY.
THE LEDGER WAS A MESS. LOOKS LIKE THE SHOP IS IN REAL TROUBLE.
THE SHOP IS FINE. MOM'S THE ONE WHO HAD... ISSUES.
YEAH, ISSUES THAT MIGHT'VE GOTTEN HER...KILLED.
WE DON'T KNOW WHAT GOT HER KILLED!
HEY!

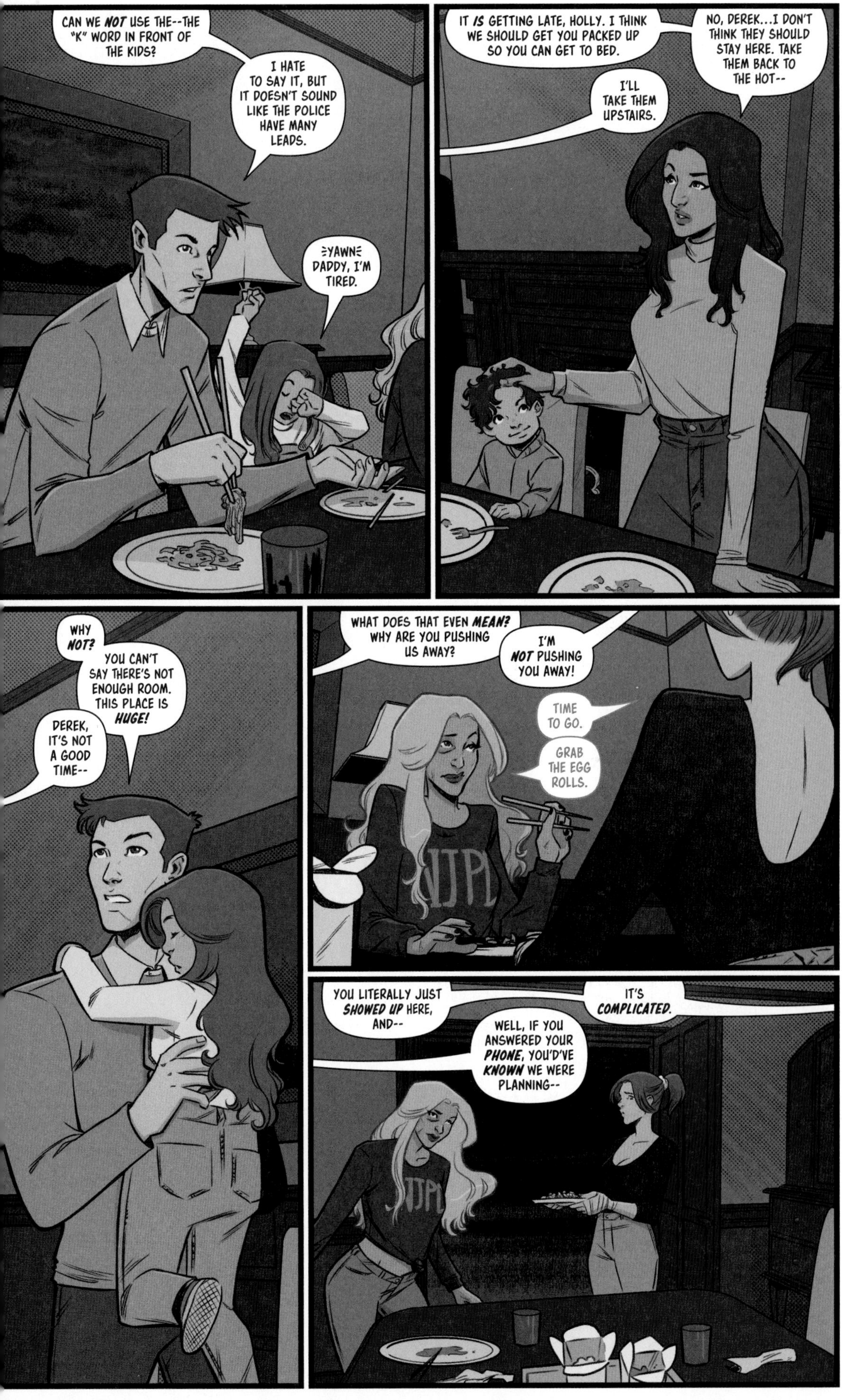

CAN WE NOT USE THE--THE "K" WORD IN FRONT OF THE KIDS?
I HATE TO SAY IT, BUT IT DOESN'T SOUND LIKE THE POLICE HAVE MANY LEADS.
=YAWN= DADDY, I'M TIRED.
IT IS GETTING LATE, HOLLY. I THINK WE SHOULD GET YOU PACKED UP SO YOU CAN GET TO BED.
I'LL TAKE THEM UPSTAIRS.
NO, DEREK...I DON'T THINK THEY SHOULD STAY HERE. TAKE THEM BACK TO THE HOT--
WHY NOT?
YOU CAN'T SAY THERE'S NOT ENOUGH ROOM. THIS PLACE IS HUGE!
DEREK, IT'S NOT A GOOD TIME--
WHAT DOES THAT EVEN MEAN? WHY ARE YOU PUSHING US AWAY?
I'M NOT PUSHING YOU AWAY!
TIME TO GO.
GRAB THE EGG ROLLS.
YOU LITERALLY JUST SHOWED UP HERE, AND--
IT'S COMPLICATED.
WELL, IF YOU ANSWERED YOUR PHONE, YOU'D'VE KNOWN WE WERE PLANNING--

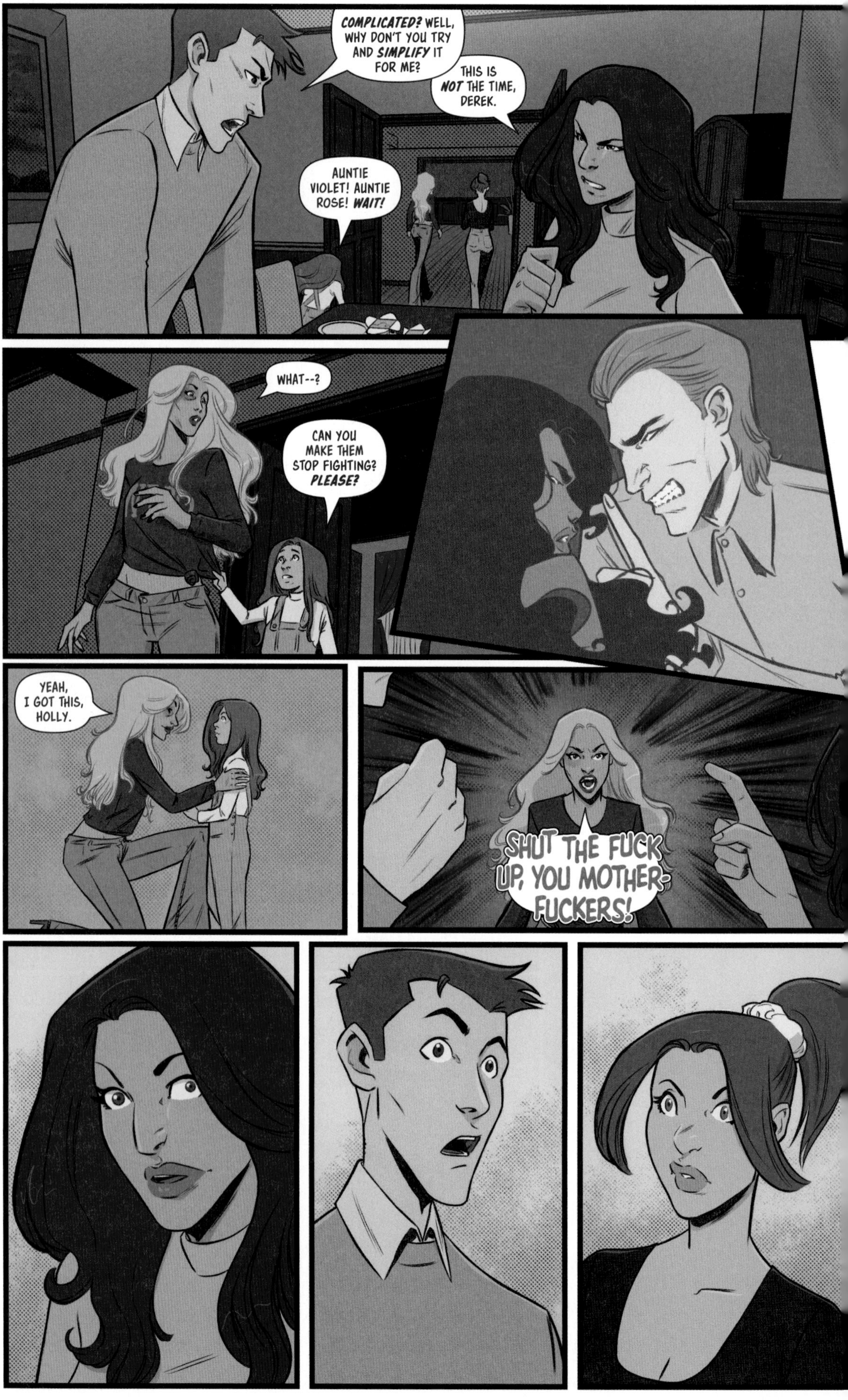

COMPLICATED? WELL, WHY DON'T YOU TRY AND SIMPLIFY IT FOR ME?
THIS IS NOT THE TIME, DEREK.
AUNTIE VIOLET! AUNTIE ROSE! WAIT!
WHAT--?
CAN YOU MAKE THEM STOP FIGHTING? PLEASE?
YEAH, I GOT THIS, HOLLY.
SHUT THE FUCK UP, YOU MOTHER-FUCKERS!

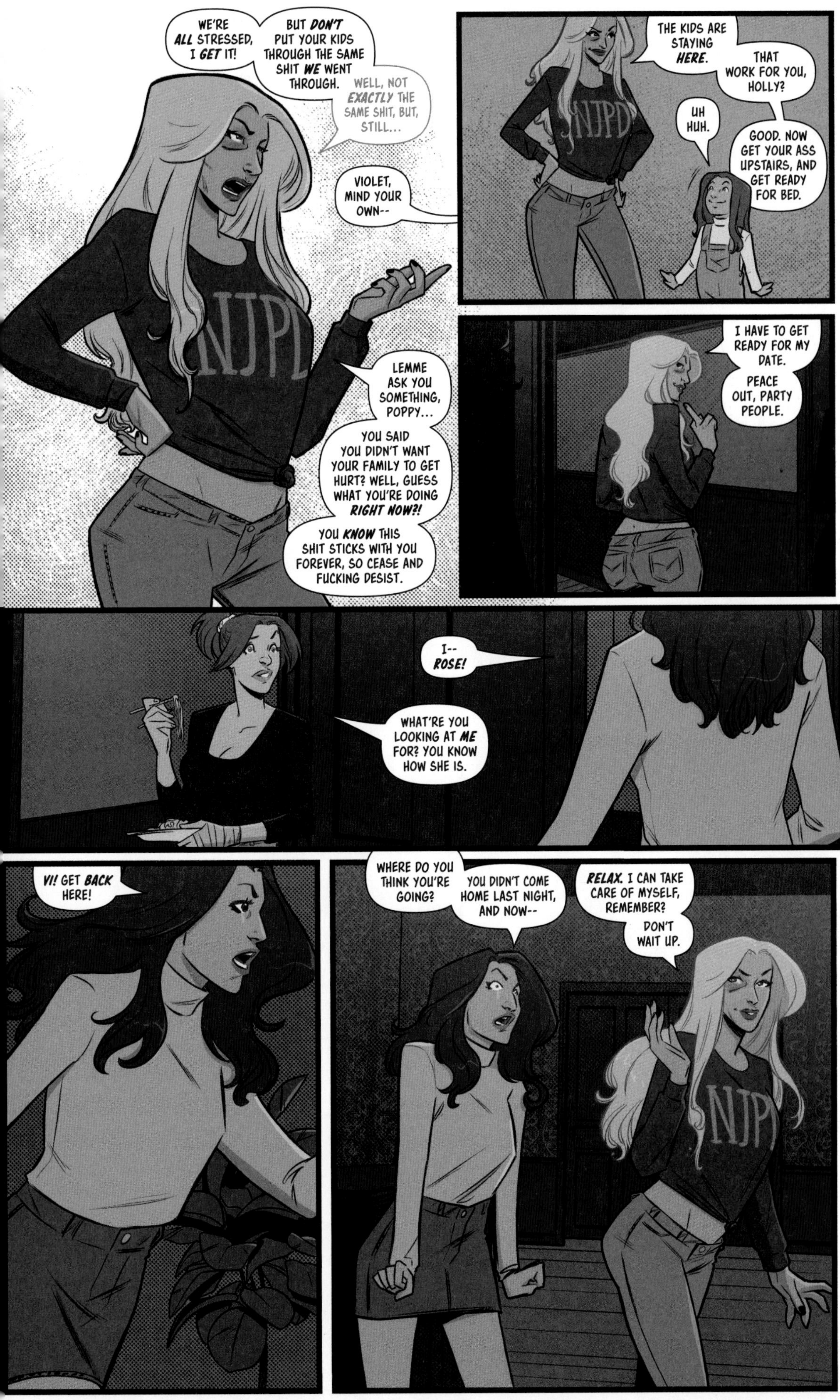
WE'RE ALL STRESSED, I GET IT!
BUT DON'T PUT YOUR KIDS THROUGH THE SAME SHIT WE WENT THROUGH.
WELL, NOT EXACTLY THE SAME SHIT, BUT, STILL...
VIOLET, MIND YOUR OWN--
LEMME ASK YOU SOMETHING, POPPY...
YOU SAID YOU DIDN'T WANT YOUR FAMILY TO GET HURT? WELL, GUESS WHAT YOU'RE DOING RIGHT NOW?!
YOU KNOW THIS SHIT STICKS WITH YOU FOREVER, SO CEASE AND FUCKING DESIST.
THE KIDS ARE STAYING HERE.
THAT WORK FOR YOU, HOLLY?
UH HUH.
GOOD. NOW GET YOUR ASS UPSTAIRS, AND GET READY FOR BED.
I HAVE TO GET READY FOR MY DATE.
PEACE OUT, PARTY PEOPLE.
I-- ROSE!
WHAT'RE YOU LOOKING AT ME FOR? YOU KNOW HOW SHE IS.
VI! GET BACK HERE!
WHERE DO YOU THINK YOU'RE GOING?
YOU DIDN'T COME HOME LAST NIGHT, AND NOW--
RELAX. I CAN TAKE CARE OF MYSELF, REMEMBER?
DON'T WAIT UP.

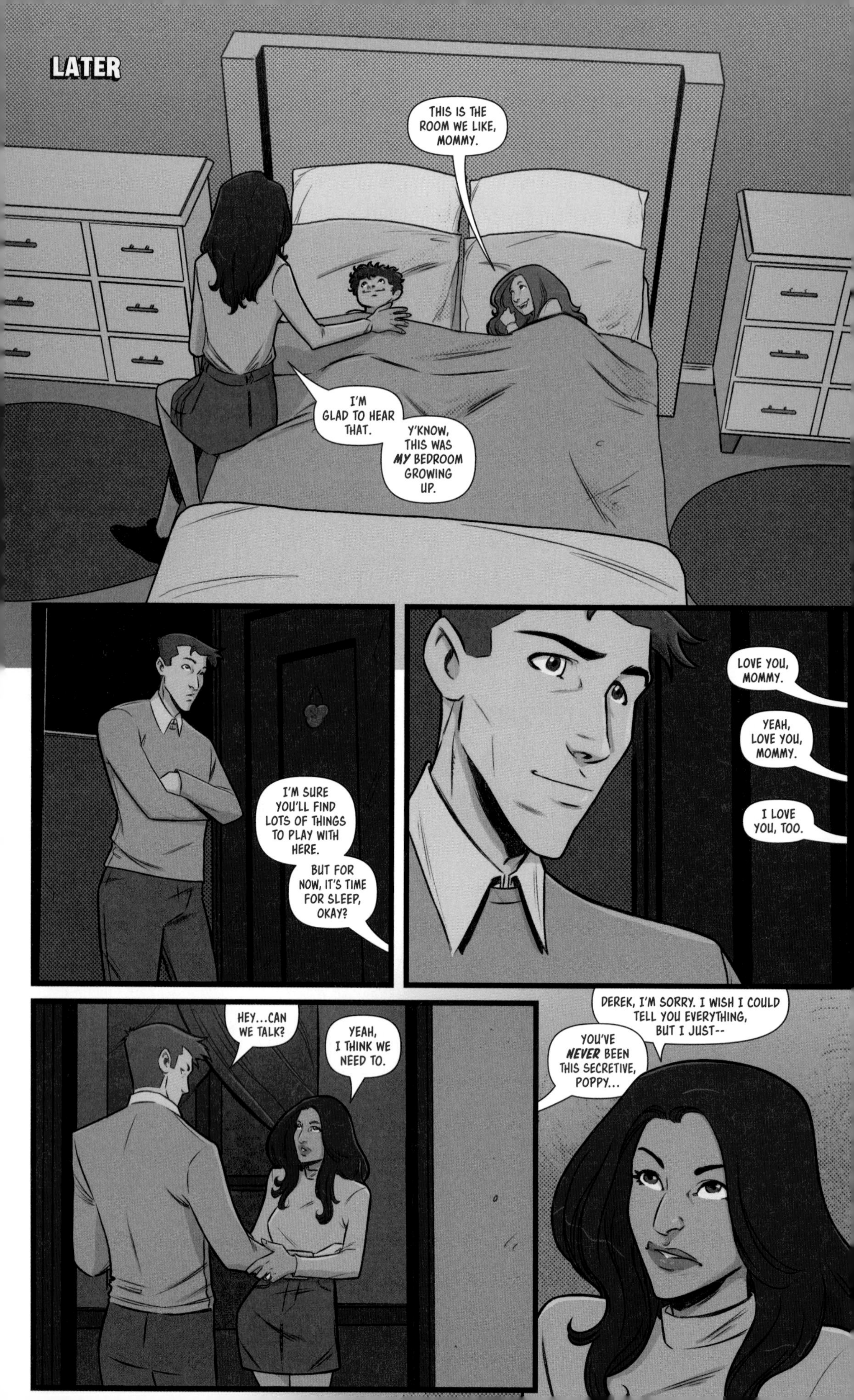
LATER
THIS IS THE ROOM WE LIKE, MOMMY.
I'M GLAD TO HEAR THAT.
Y'KNOW, THIS WAS *MY* BEDROOM GROWING UP.
I'M SURE YOU'LL FIND LOTS OF THINGS TO PLAY WITH HERE.
BUT FOR NOW, IT'S TIME FOR SLEEP, OKAY?
LOVE YOU, MOMMY.
YEAH, LOVE YOU, MOMMY.
I LOVE YOU, TOO.
HEY...CAN WE TALK?
YEAH, I THINK WE NEED TO.
DEREK, I'M SORRY. I WISH I COULD TELL YOU EVERYTHING, BUT I JUST--
YOU'VE *NEVER* BEEN THIS SECRETIVE, POPPY...

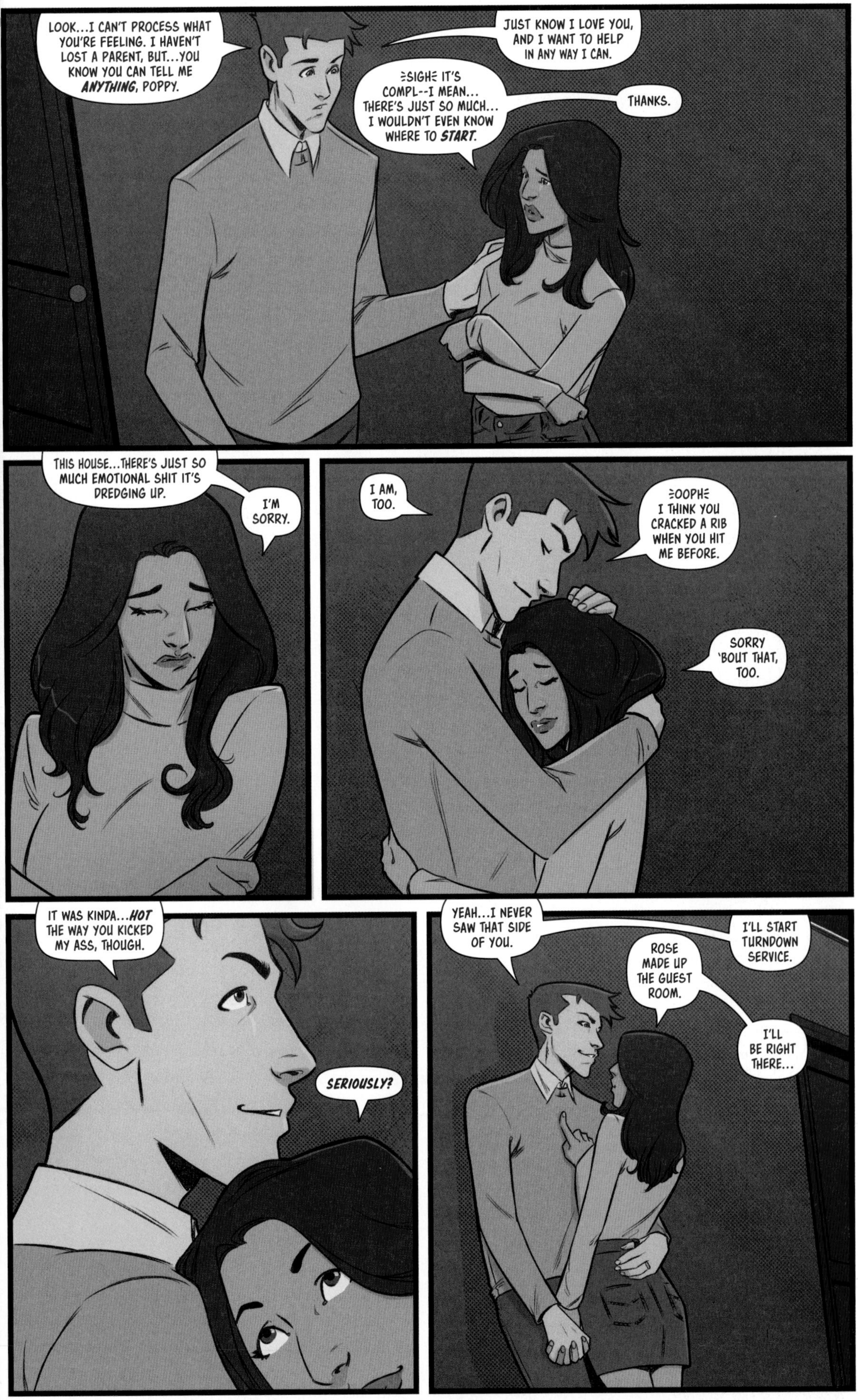
LOOK...I CAN'T PROCESS WHAT YOU'RE FEELING. I HAVEN'T LOST A PARENT, BUT...YOU KNOW YOU CAN TELL ME *ANYTHING*, POPPY.
JUST KNOW I LOVE YOU, AND I WANT TO HELP IN ANY WAY I CAN.
=SIGH= IT'S COMPL--I MEAN... THERE'S JUST SO MUCH... I WOULDN'T EVEN KNOW WHERE TO *START*.
THANKS.
THIS HOUSE...THERE'S JUST SO MUCH EMOTIONAL SHIT IT'S DREDGING UP.
I'M SORRY.
I AM, TOO.
=OOPH= I THINK YOU CRACKED A RIB WHEN YOU HIT ME BEFORE.
SORRY 'BOUT THAT, TOO.
IT WAS KINDA...*HOT* THE WAY YOU KICKED MY ASS, THOUGH.
SERIOUSLY?
YEAH...I NEVER SAW THAT SIDE OF YOU.
I'LL START TURNDOWN SERVICE.
ROSE MADE UP THE GUEST ROOM.
I'LL BE RIGHT THERE...

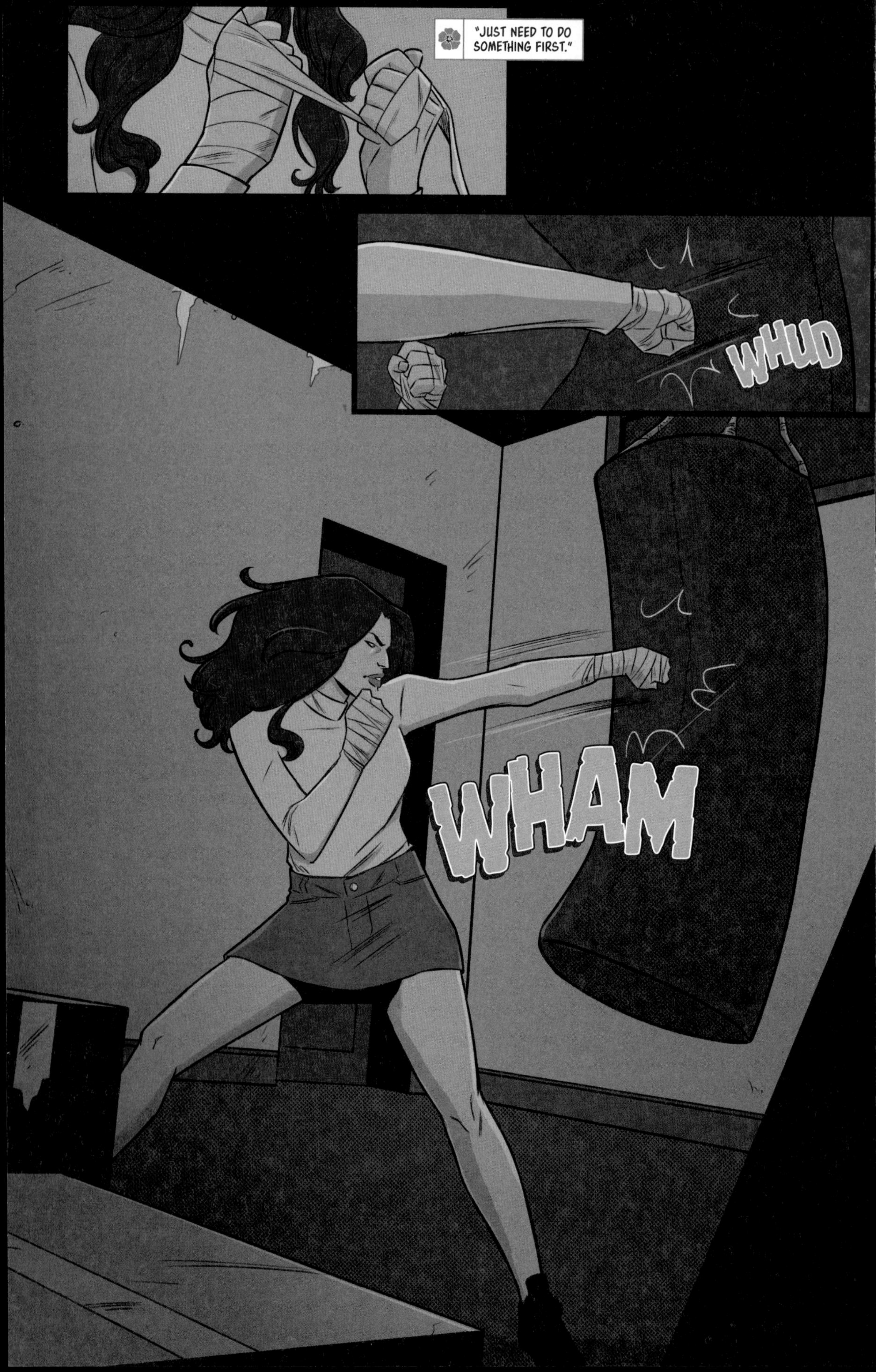
"JUST NEED TO DO SOMETHING FIRST."
WHUD
WHAM

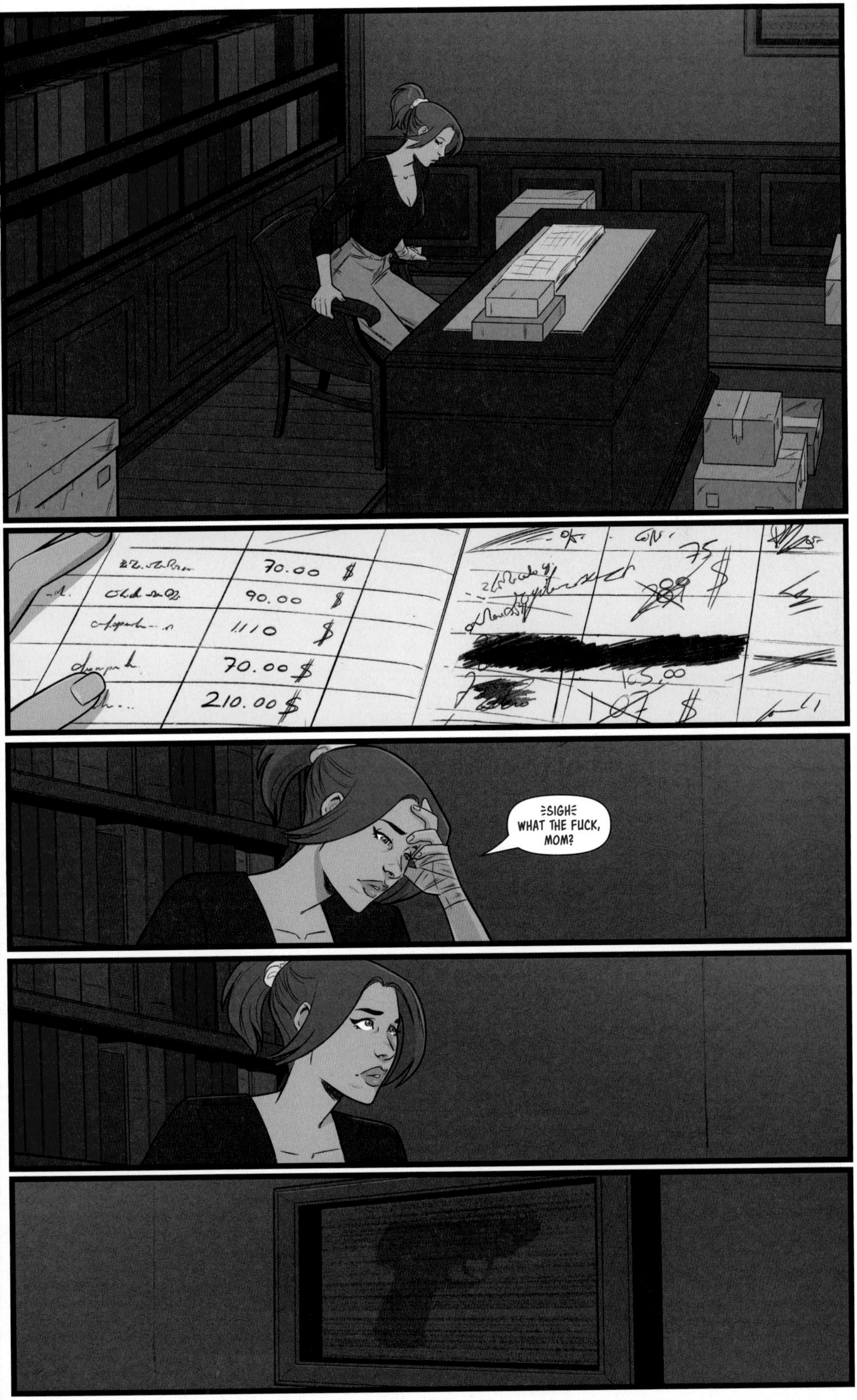
70.00 $
90.00 $
1110 $
70.00 $
210.00 $
≡SIGH≡ WHAT THE FUCK, MOM?

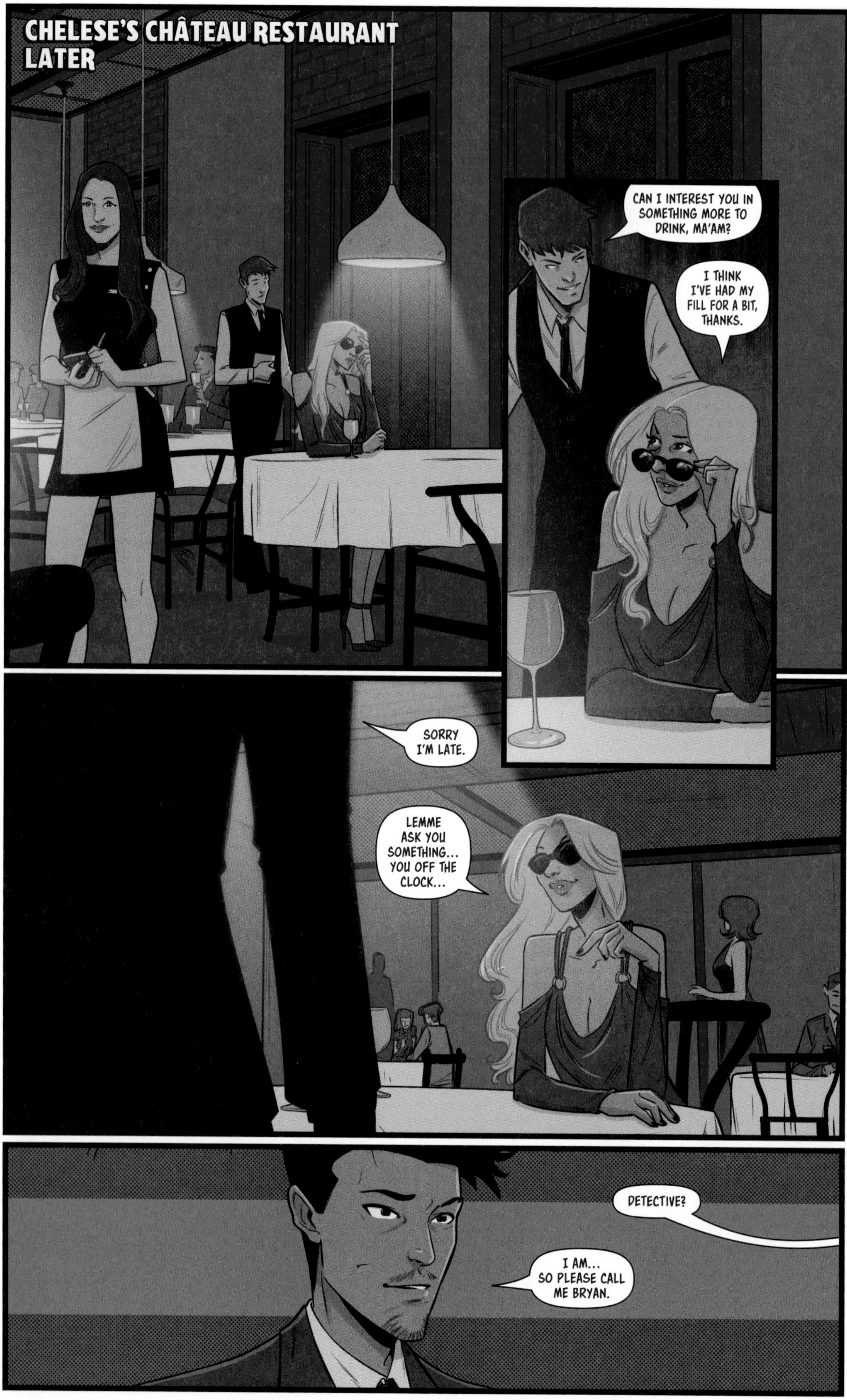
CHELESE'S CHÂTEAU RESTAURANT
LATER
CAN I INTEREST YOU IN SOMETHING MORE TO DRINK, MA'AM?
I THINK I'VE HAD MY FILL FOR A BIT, THANKS.
SORRY I'M LATE.
LEMME ASK YOU SOMETHING... YOU OFF THE CLOCK...
DETECTIVE?
I AM... SO PLEASE CALL ME BRYAN.

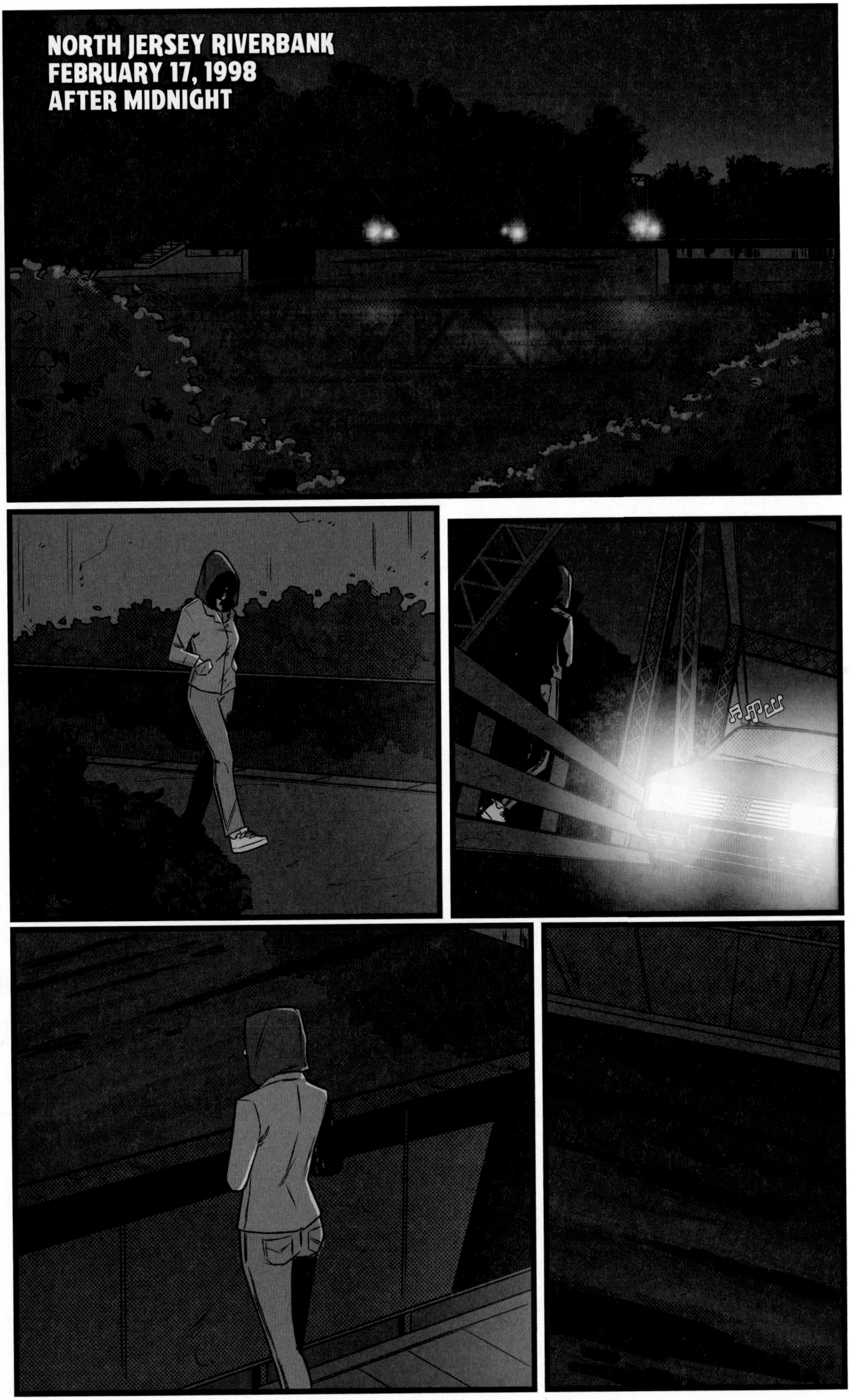
NORTH JERSEY RIVERBANK
FEBRUARY 17, 1998
AFTER MIDNIGHT

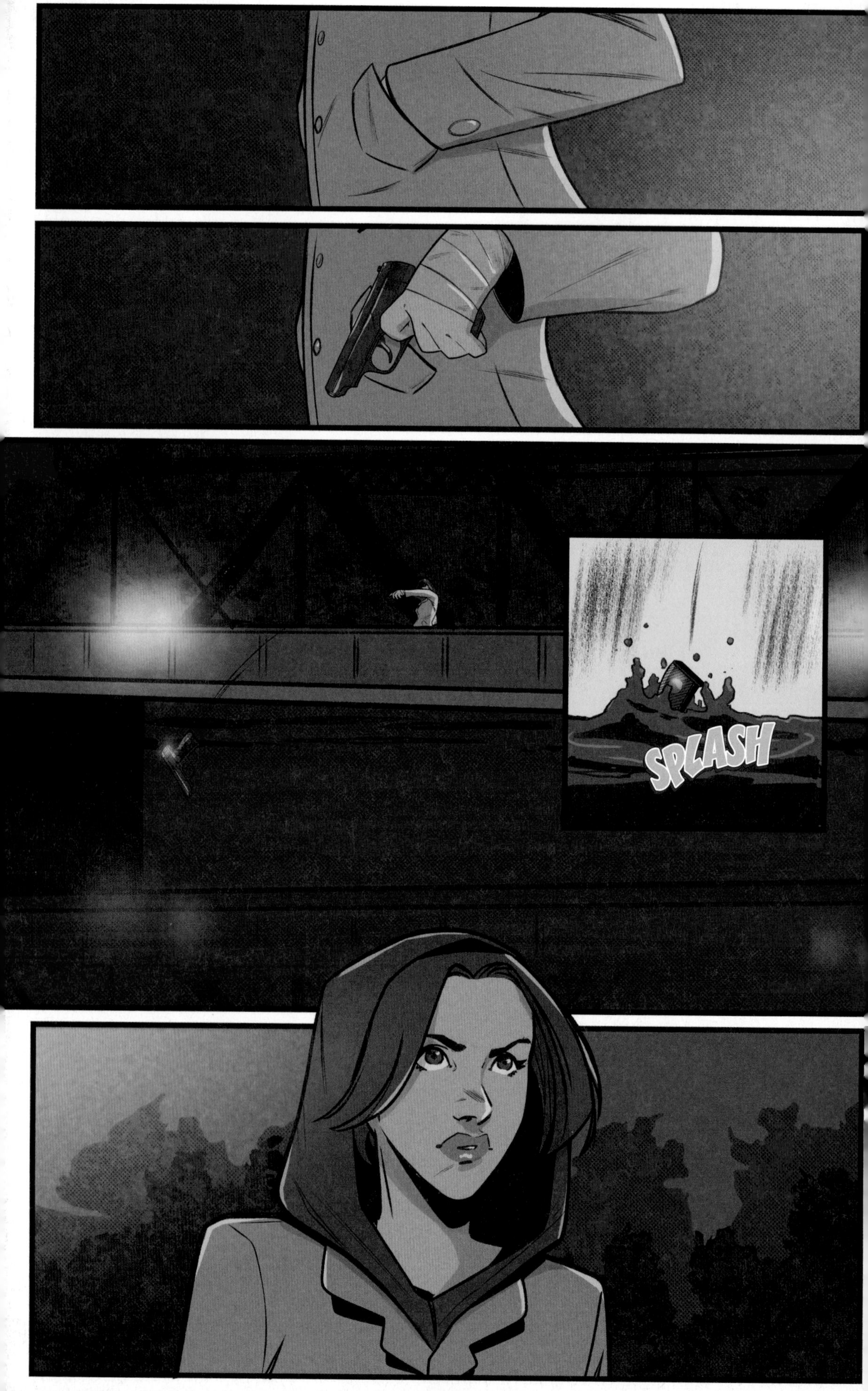
SPLASH

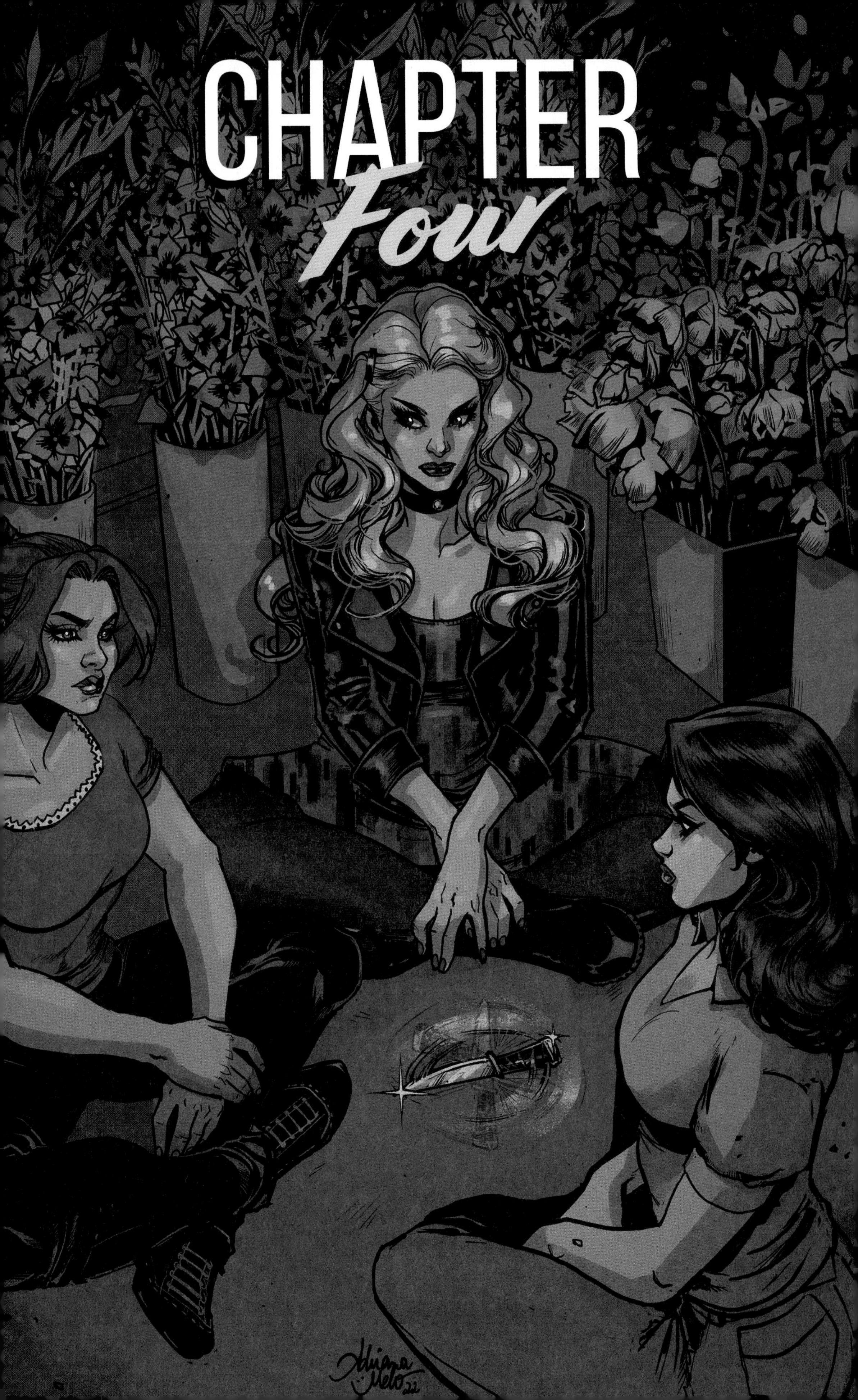
CHAPTER
Four

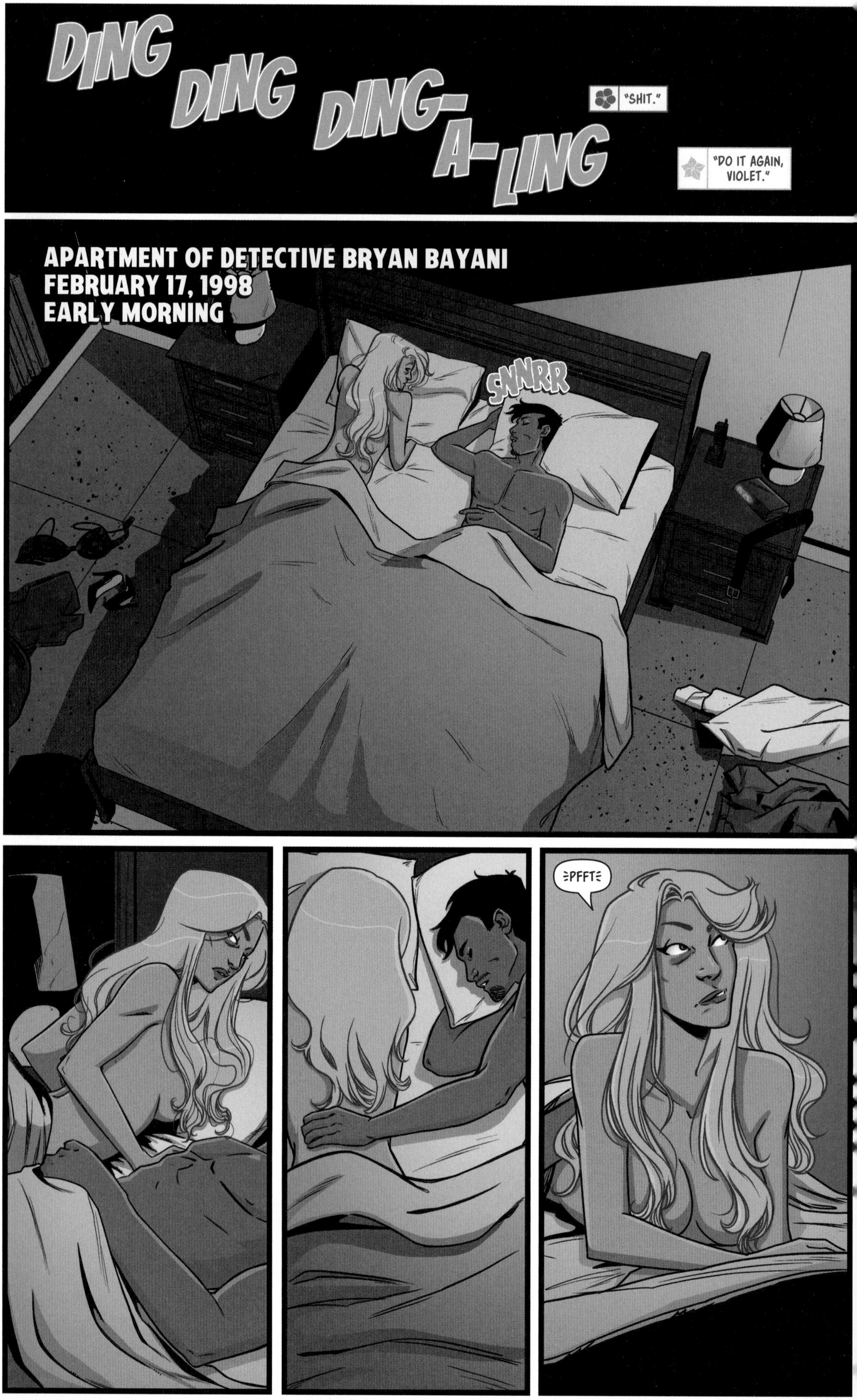
DING DING DING-A-LING
"SHIT."
"DO IT AGAIN, VIOLET."
APARTMENT OF DETECTIVE BRYAN BAYANI
FEBRUARY 17, 1998
EARLY MORNING
SNNRR
PFFT

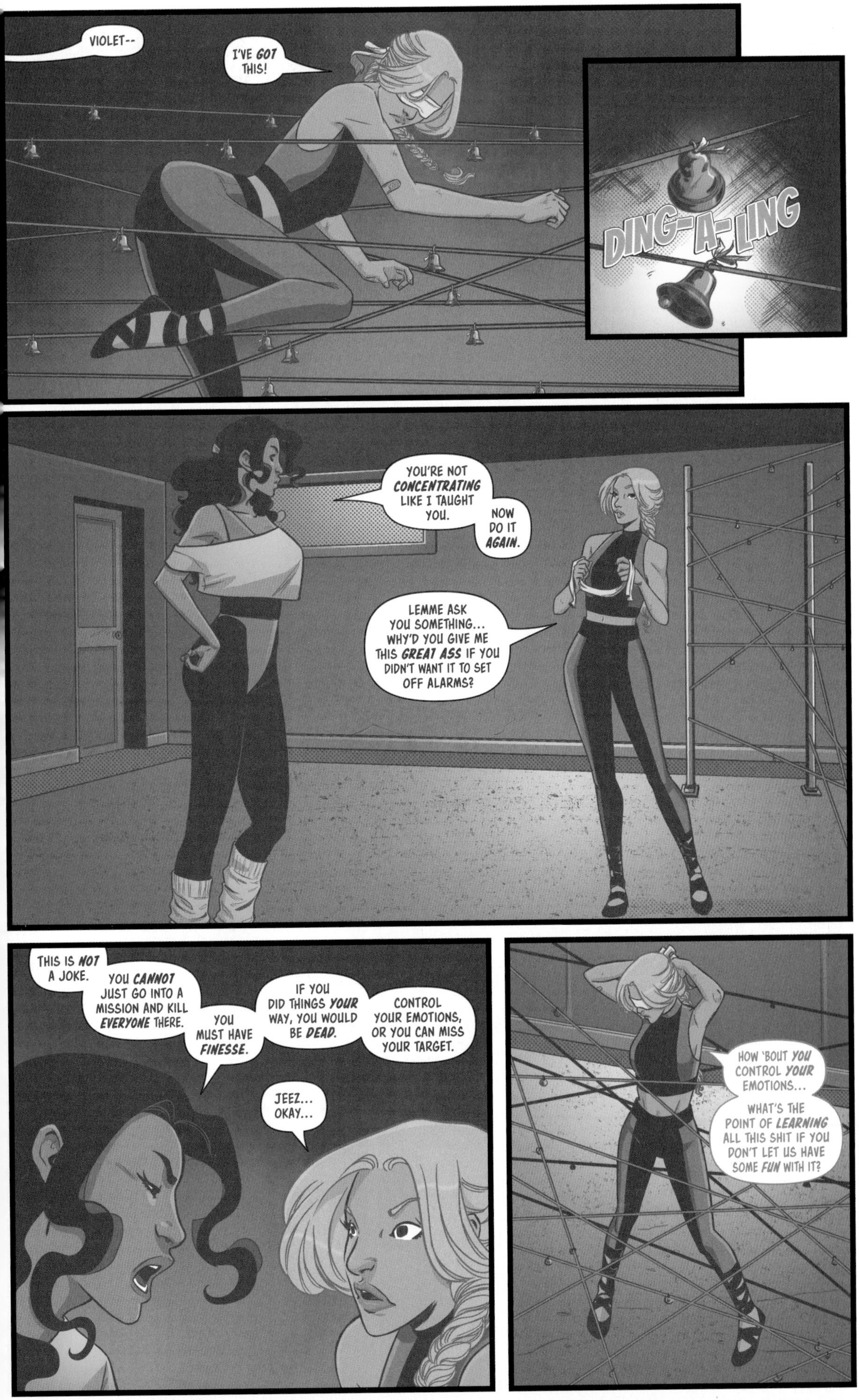
VIOLET--
I'VE GOT THIS!
DING-A-LING
YOU'RE NOT CONCENTRATING LIKE I TAUGHT YOU.
NOW DO IT AGAIN.
LEMME ASK YOU SOMETHING... WHY'D YOU GIVE ME THIS GREAT ASS IF YOU DIDN'T WANT IT TO SET OFF ALARMS?
THIS IS NOT A JOKE.
YOU CANNOT JUST GO INTO A MISSION AND KILL EVERYONE THERE.
YOU MUST HAVE FINESSE.
IF YOU DID THINGS YOUR WAY, YOU WOULD BE DEAD.
CONTROL YOUR EMOTIONS, OR YOU CAN MISS YOUR TARGET.
JEEZ... OKAY...
HOW 'BOUT YOU CONTROL YOUR EMOTIONS...
WHAT'S THE POINT OF LEARNING ALL THIS SHIT IF YOU DON'T LET US HAVE SOME FUN WITH IT?

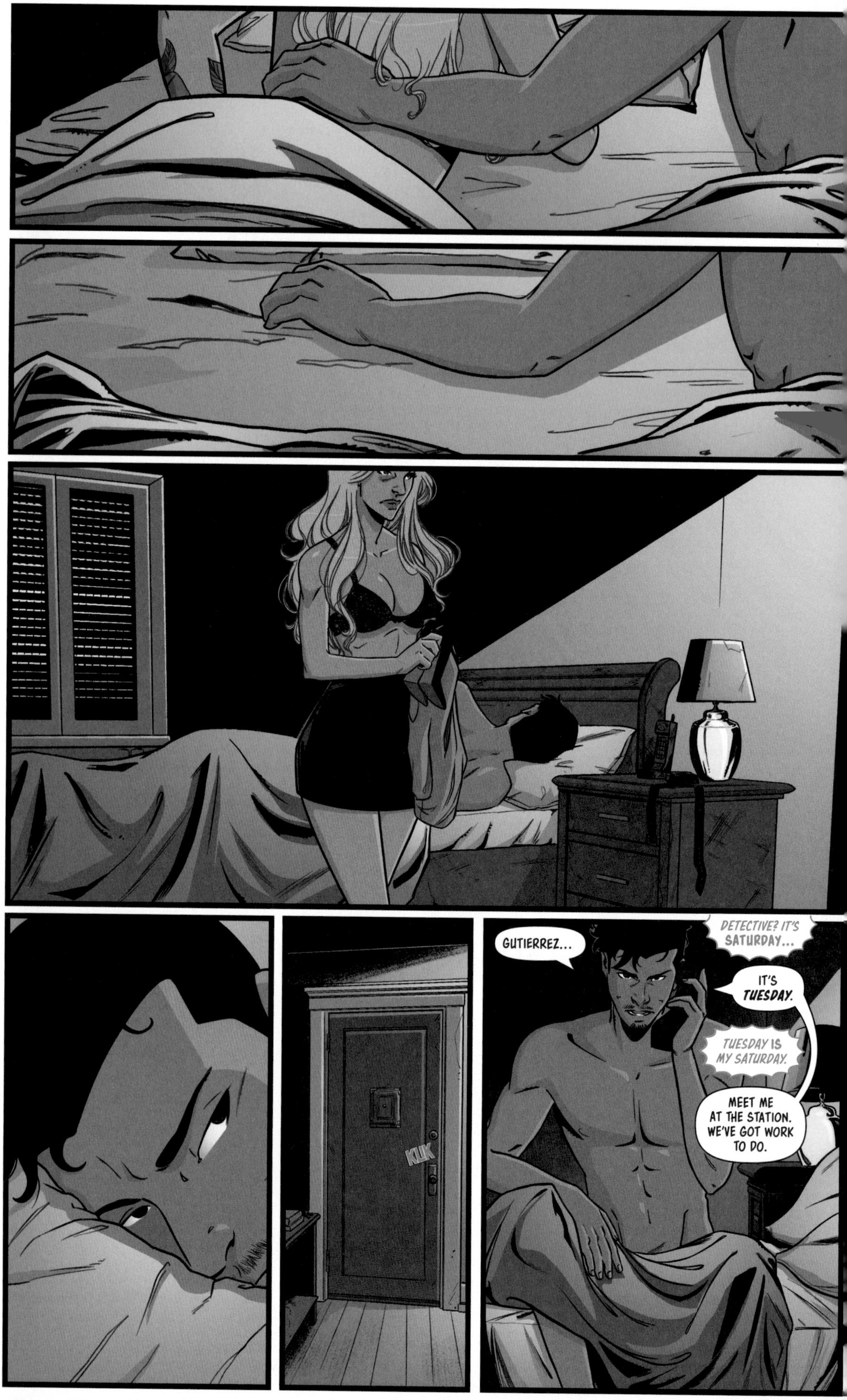
KLIK
GUTIERREZ...
DETECTIVE? IT'S SATURDAY...
IT'S TUESDAY.
TUESDAY IS MY SATURDAY.
MEET ME AT THE STATION. WE'VE GOT WORK TO DO.

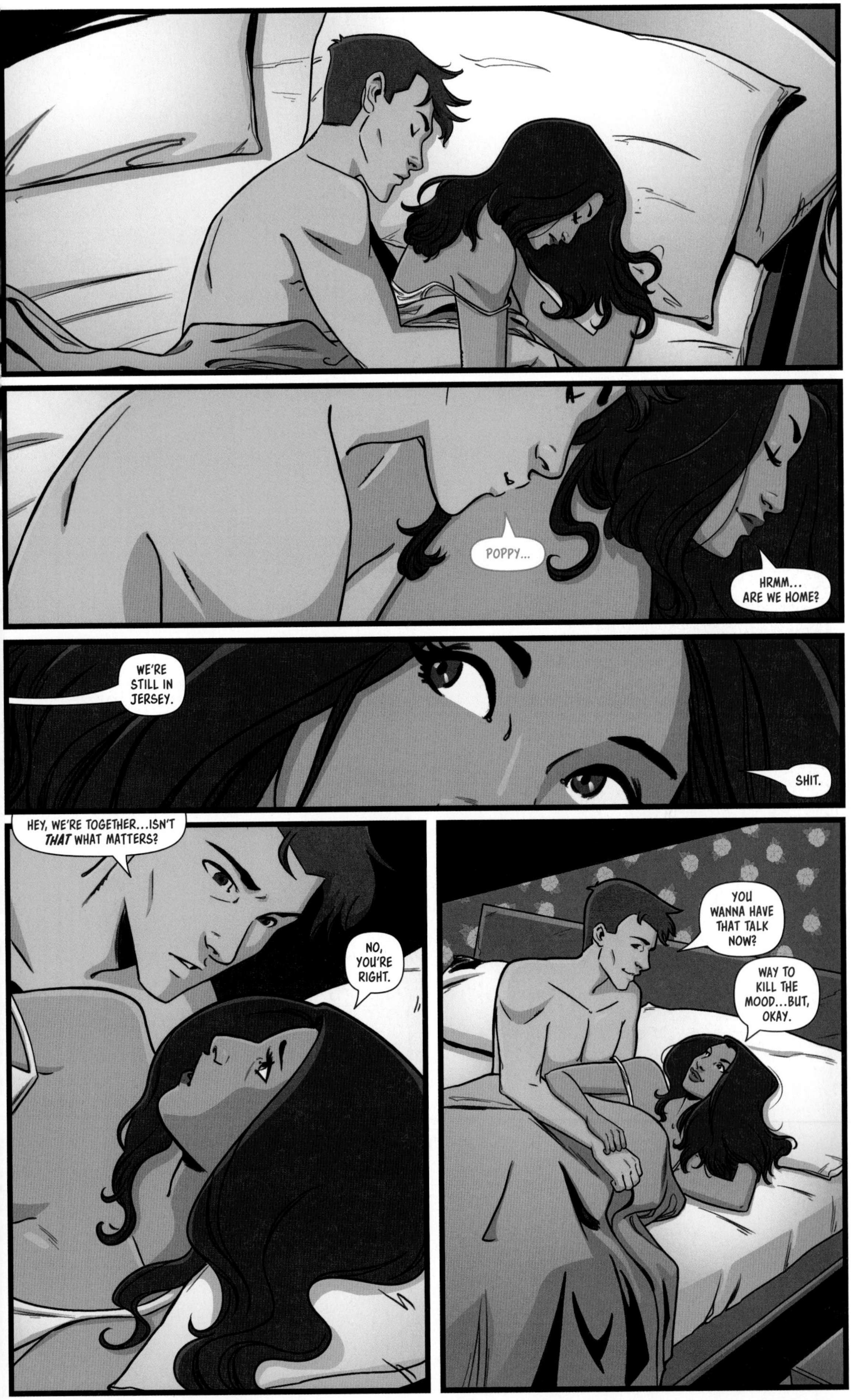
POPPY...
HRMM... ARE WE HOME?
WE'RE STILL IN JERSEY.
SHIT.
HEY, WE'RE TOGETHER...ISN'T *THAT* WHAT MATTERS?
NO, YOU'RE RIGHT.
YOU WANNA HAVE THAT TALK NOW?
WAY TO KILL THE MOOD...BUT, OKAY.

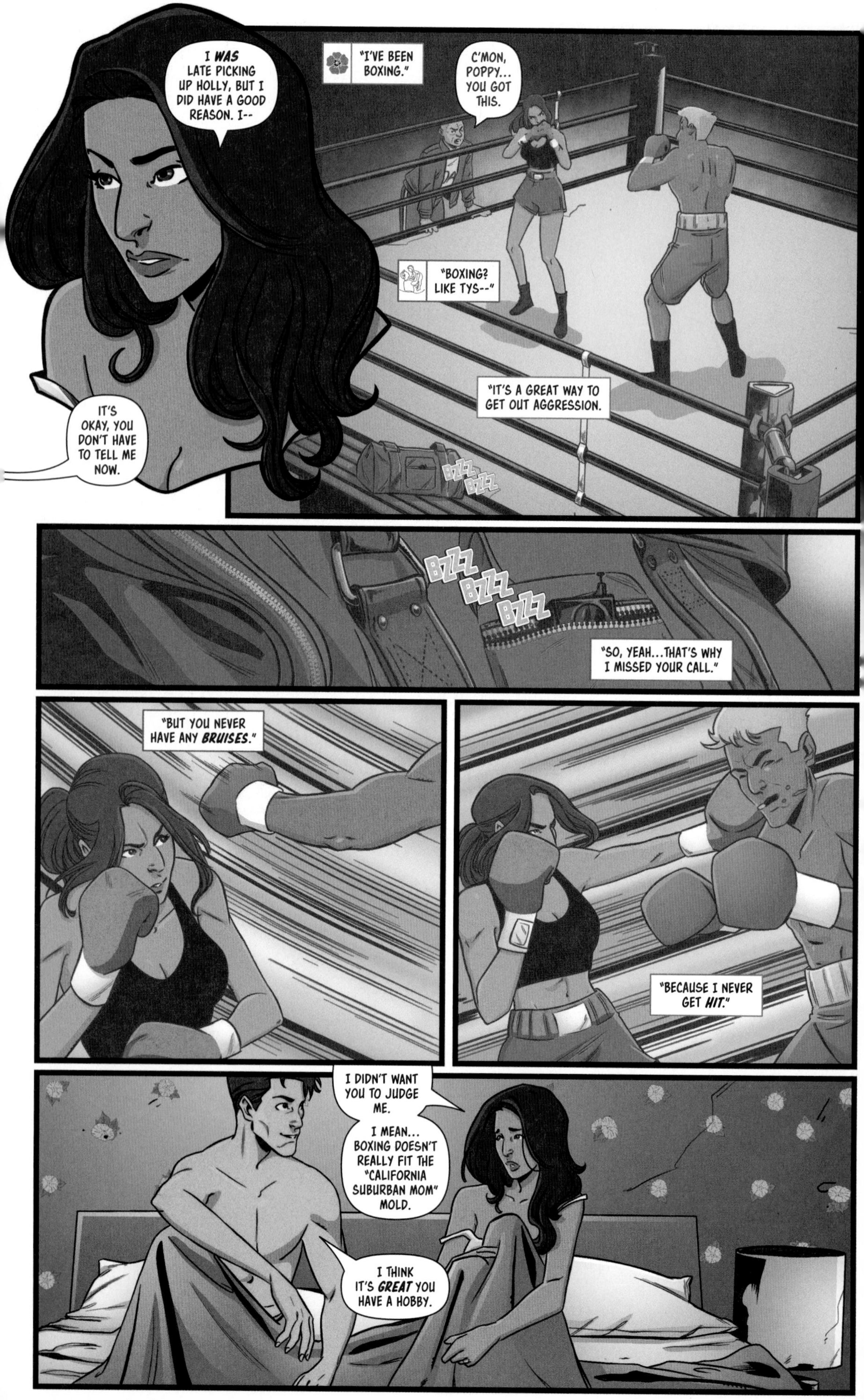
I *WAS* LATE PICKING UP HOLLY, BUT I DID HAVE A GOOD REASON. I--
"I'VE BEEN BOXING."
C'MON, POPPY... YOU GOT THIS.
"BOXING? LIKE TYS--"
"IT'S A GREAT WAY TO GET OUT AGGRESSION.
IT'S OKAY, YOU DON'T HAVE TO TELL ME NOW.
BZZZ BZZZ
BZZZ BZZZ BZZZ
"SO, YEAH...THAT'S WHY I MISSED YOUR CALL."
"BUT YOU NEVER HAVE ANY *BRUISES*."
"BECAUSE I NEVER GET *HIT*."
I DIDN'T WANT YOU TO JUDGE ME.
I MEAN... BOXING DOESN'T REALLY FIT THE "CALIFORNIA SUBURBAN MOM" MOLD.
I THINK IT'S *GREAT* YOU HAVE A HOBBY.

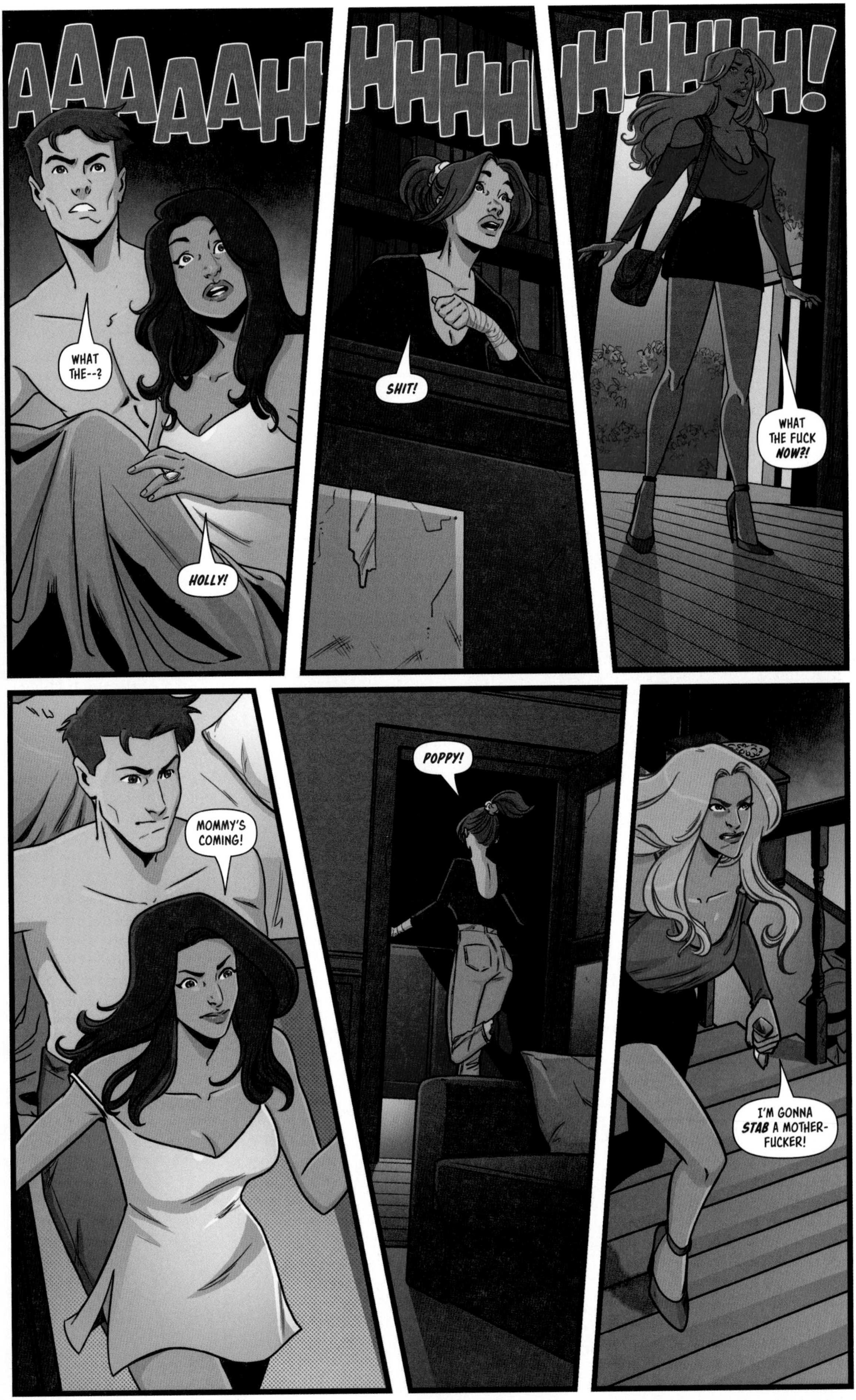
AAAAAAHHHHHHHHHHHHHHH!
WHAT THE--?
HOLLY!
SHIT!
WHAT THE FUCK NOW?!
MOMMY'S COMING!
POPPY!
I'M GONNA STAB A MOTHER-FUCKER!

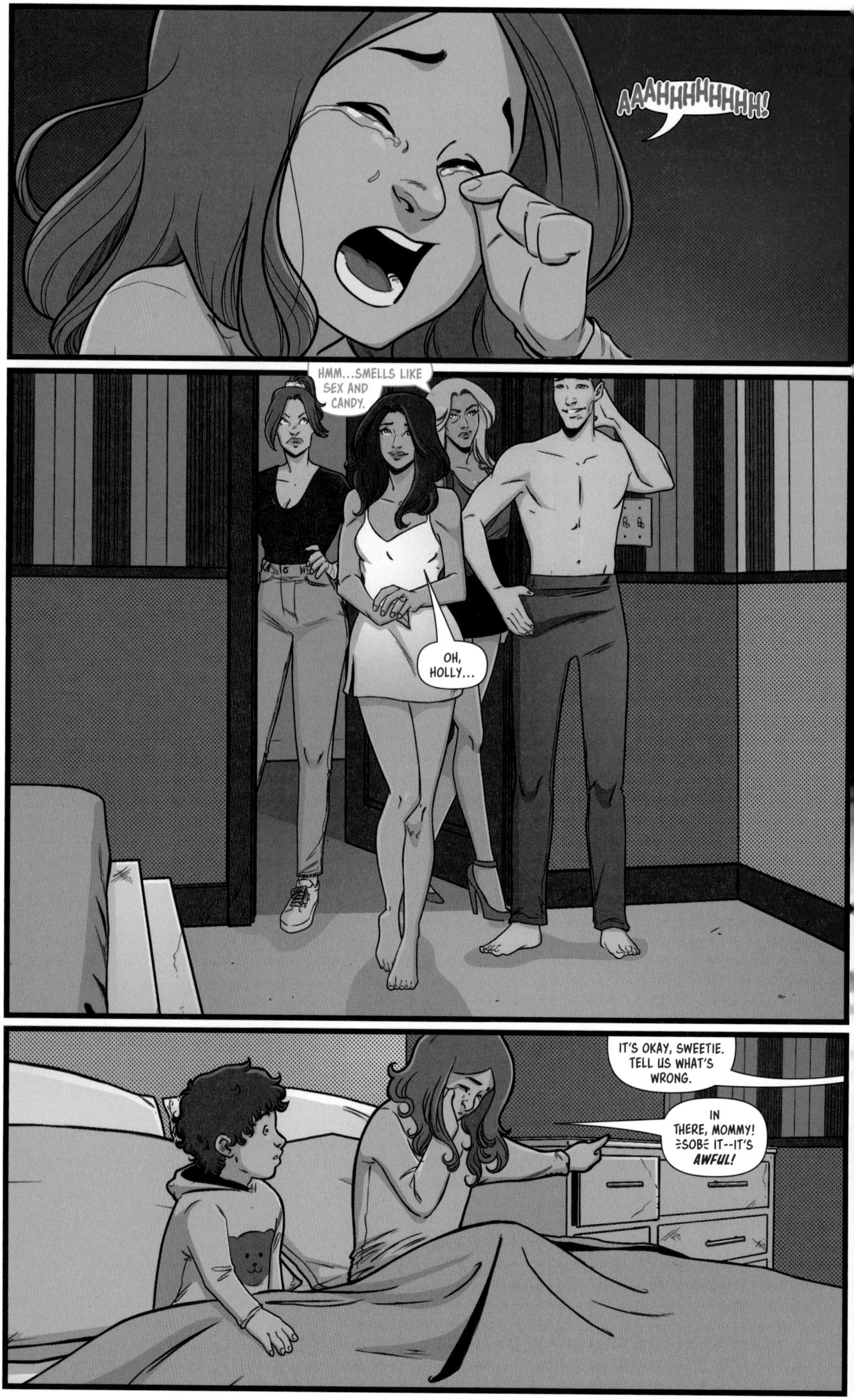
AAAHHHHHHHH!
HMM...SMELLS LIKE SEX AND CANDY.
OH, HOLLY...
IT'S OKAY, SWEETIE. TELL US WHAT'S WRONG.
IN THERE, MOMMY! ≋SOB≋ IT--IT'S *AWFUL!*

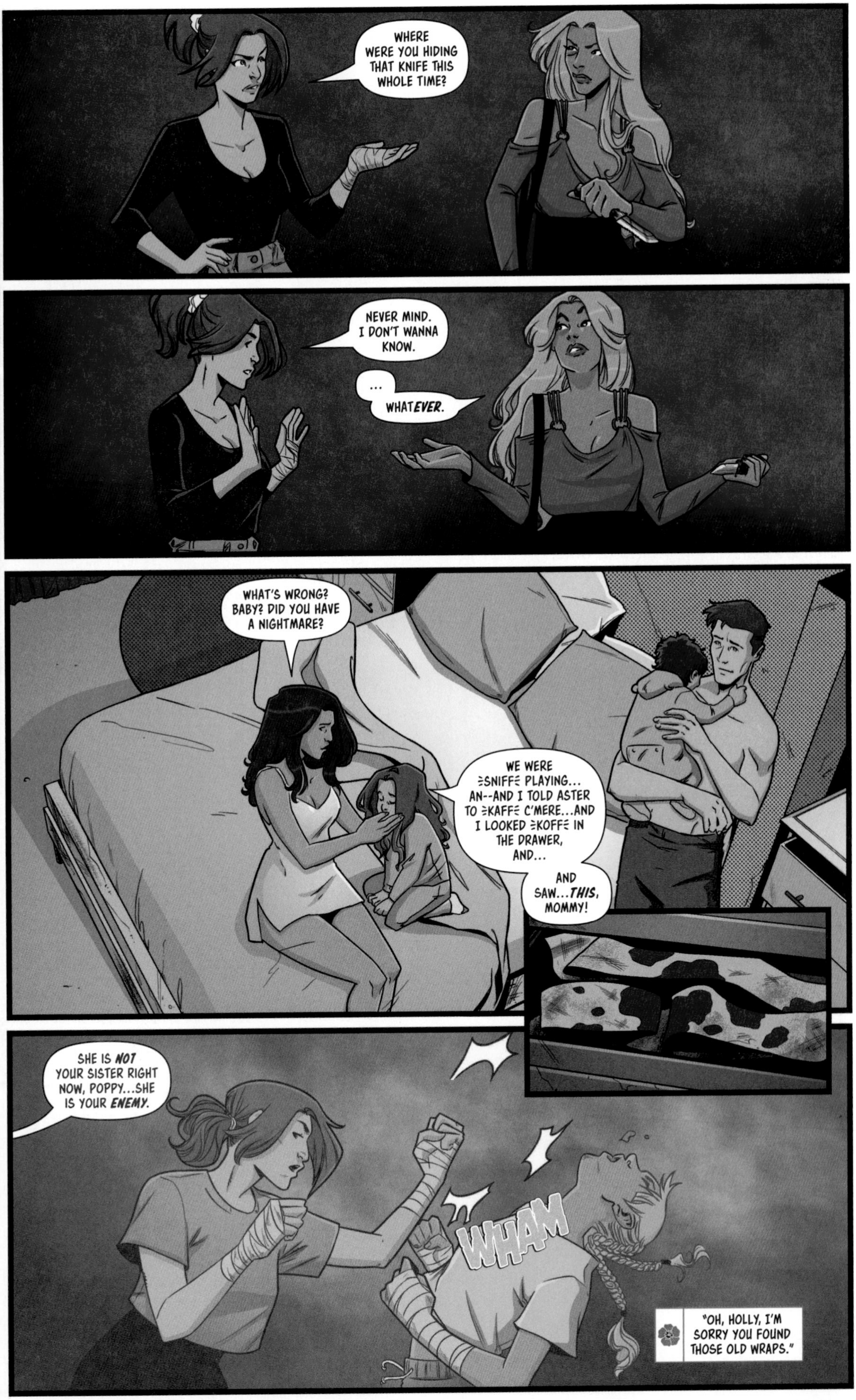
WHERE WERE YOU HIDING THAT KNIFE THIS WHOLE TIME?
NEVER MIND. I DON'T WANNA KNOW.
...
WHAT*EVER*.
WHAT'S WRONG? BABY? DID YOU HAVE A NIGHTMARE?
WE WERE ≡SNIFF≡ PLAYING... AN--AND I TOLD ASTER TO ≡KAFF≡ C'MERE...AND I LOOKED ≡KOFF≡ IN THE DRAWER, AND...
AND SAW...*THIS*, MOMMY!
SHE IS *NOT* YOUR SISTER RIGHT NOW, POPPY...SHE IS YOUR *ENEMY*.
WHAM
"OH, HOLLY, I'M SORRY YOU FOUND THOSE OLD WRAPS."

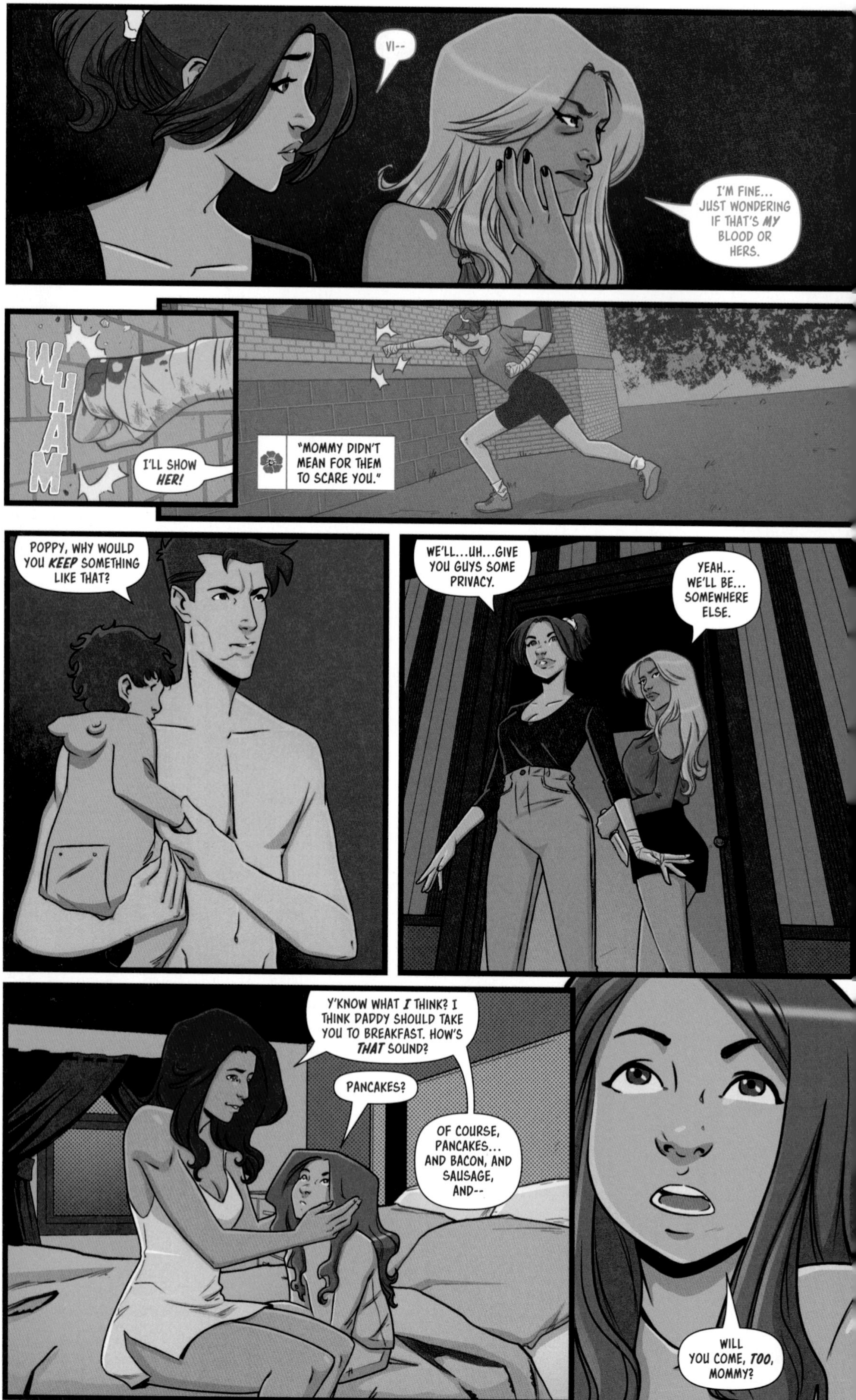
VI--
I'M FINE... JUST WONDERING IF THAT'S MY BLOOD OR HERS.
WHAM
I'LL SHOW HER!
"MOMMY DIDN'T MEAN FOR THEM TO SCARE YOU."
POPPY, WHY WOULD YOU KEEP SOMETHING LIKE THAT?
WE'LL...UH...GIVE YOU GUYS SOME PRIVACY.
YEAH... WE'LL BE... SOMEWHERE ELSE.
Y'KNOW WHAT I THINK? I THINK DADDY SHOULD TAKE YOU TO BREAKFAST. HOW'S THAT SOUND?
PANCAKES?
OF COURSE, PANCAKES... AND BACON, AND SAUSAGE, AND--
WILL YOU COME, TOO, MOMMY?

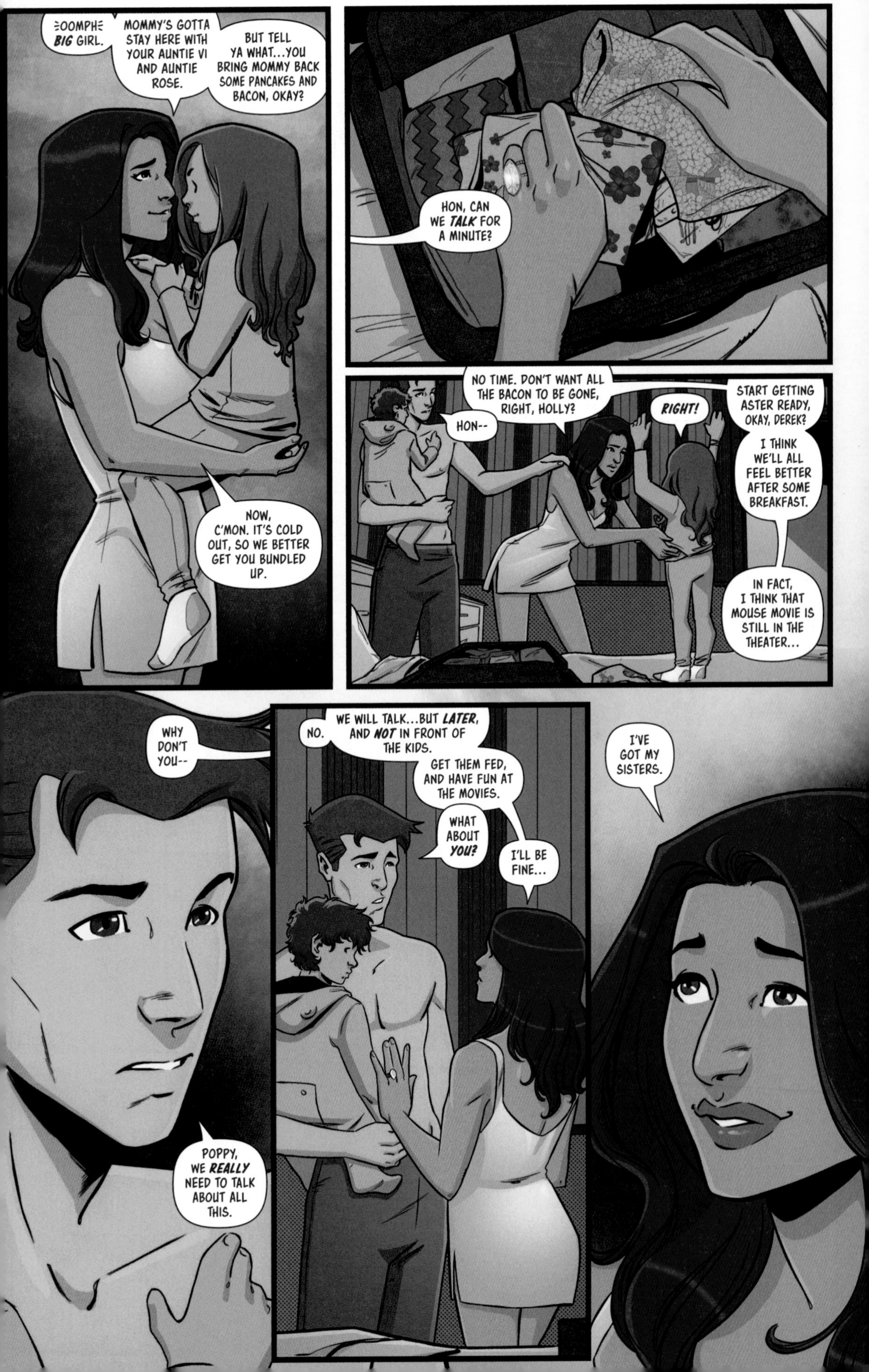
OOMPH
BIG GIRL.
MOMMY'S GOTTA STAY HERE WITH YOUR AUNTIE VI AND AUNTIE ROSE.
BUT TELL YA WHAT...YOU BRING MOMMY BACK SOME PANCAKES AND BACON, OKAY?
NOW, C'MON. IT'S COLD OUT, SO WE BETTER GET YOU BUNDLED UP.
HON, CAN WE TALK FOR A MINUTE?
HON--
NO TIME. DON'T WANT ALL THE BACON TO BE GONE, RIGHT, HOLLY?
RIGHT!
START GETTING ASTER READY, OKAY, DEREK?
I THINK WE'LL ALL FEEL BETTER AFTER SOME BREAKFAST.
IN FACT, I THINK THAT MOUSE MOVIE IS STILL IN THE THEATER...
WHY DON'T YOU--
POPPY, WE REALLY NEED TO TALK ABOUT ALL THIS.
NO.
WE WILL TALK...BUT LATER, AND NOT IN FRONT OF THE KIDS.
GET THEM FED, AND HAVE FUN AT THE MOVIES.
WHAT ABOUT YOU?
I'LL BE FINE...
I'VE GOT MY SISTERS.

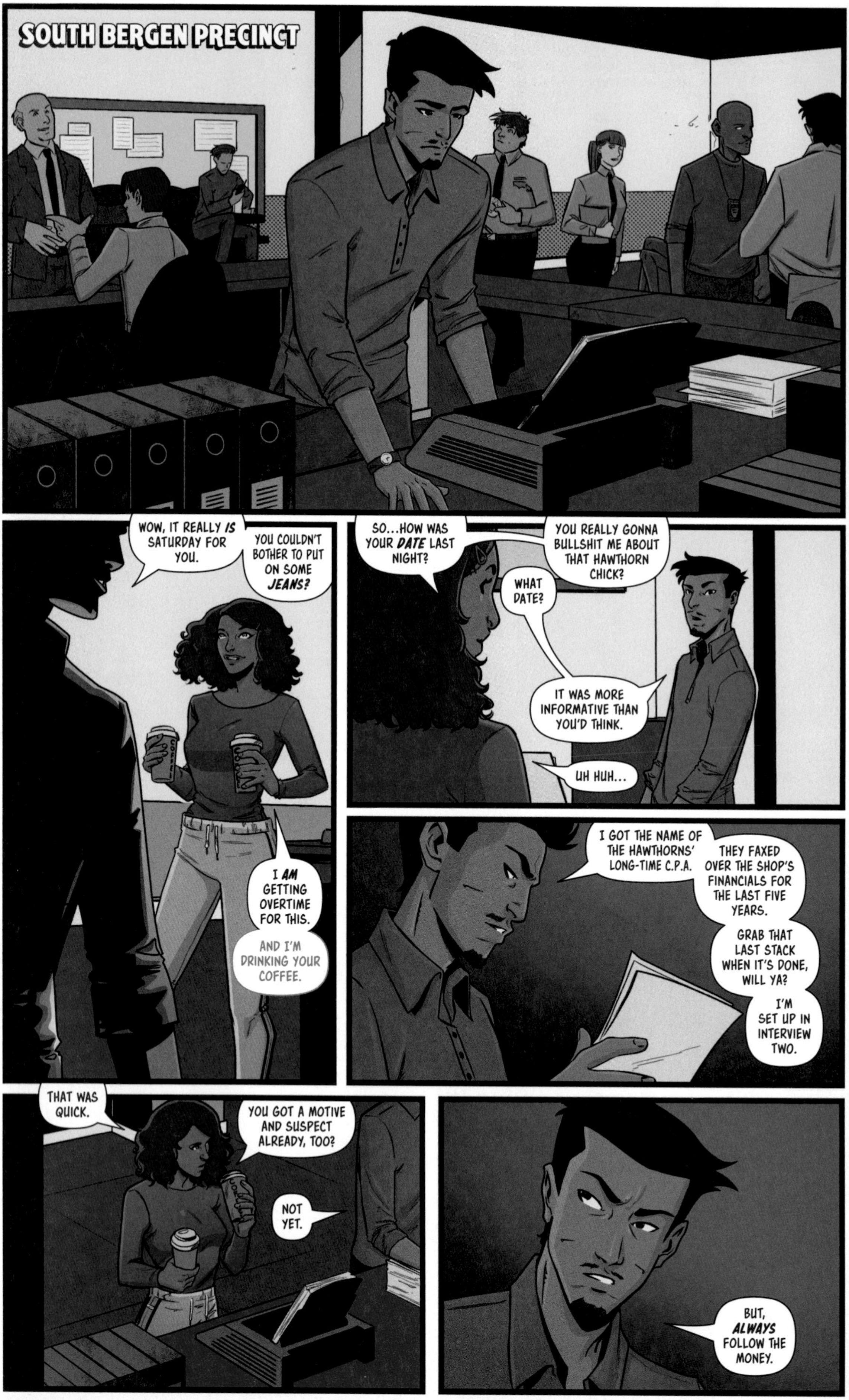
SOUTH BERGEN PRECINCT
WOW, IT REALLY *IS* SATURDAY FOR YOU.
YOU COULDN'T BOTHER TO PUT ON SOME *JEANS?*
I *AM* GETTING OVERTIME FOR THIS.
AND I'M DRINKING YOUR COFFEE.
SO...HOW WAS YOUR *DATE* LAST NIGHT?
YOU REALLY GONNA BULLSHIT ME ABOUT THAT HAWTHORN CHICK?
WHAT DATE?
IT WAS MORE INFORMATIVE THAN YOU'D THINK.
UH HUH...
I GOT THE NAME OF THE HAWTHORNS' LONG-TIME C.P.A.
THEY FAXED OVER THE SHOP'S FINANCIALS FOR THE LAST FIVE YEARS.
GRAB THAT LAST STACK WHEN IT'S DONE, WILL YA?
I'M SET UP IN INTERVIEW TWO.
THAT WAS QUICK.
YOU GOT A MOTIVE AND SUSPECT ALREADY, TOO?
NOT YET.
BUT, *ALWAYS* FOLLOW THE MONEY.

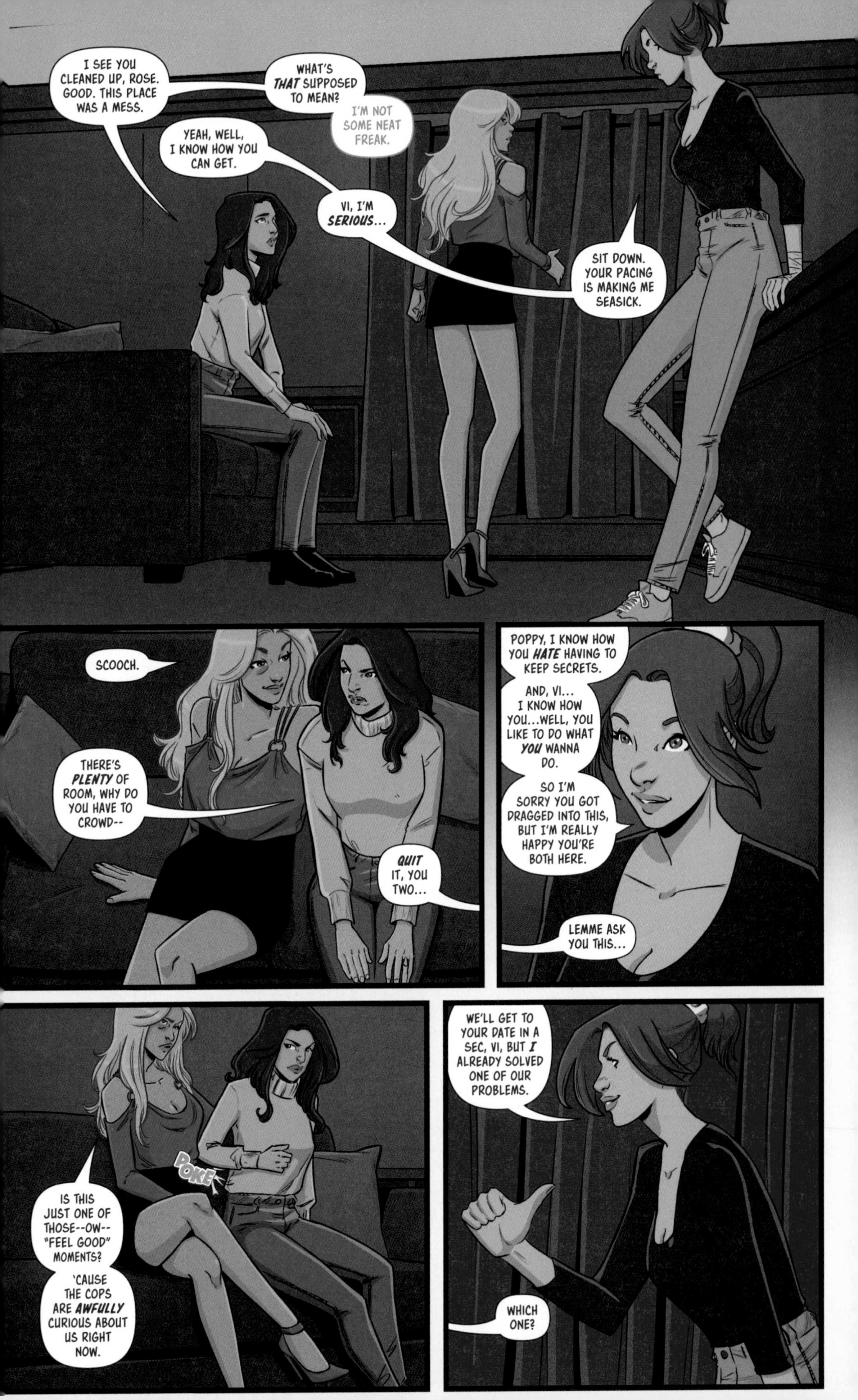
I SEE YOU CLEANED UP, ROSE. GOOD. THIS PLACE WAS A MESS.
WHAT'S *THAT* SUPPOSED TO MEAN?
I'M NOT SOME NEAT FREAK.
YEAH, WELL, I KNOW HOW YOU CAN GET.
VI, I'M *SERIOUS*...
SIT DOWN. YOUR PACING IS MAKING ME SEASICK.
SCOOCH.
THERE'S *PLENTY* OF ROOM, WHY DO YOU HAVE TO CROWD--
QUIT IT, YOU TWO...
POPPY, I KNOW HOW YOU *HATE* HAVING TO KEEP SECRETS.
AND, VI... I KNOW HOW YOU...WELL, YOU LIKE TO DO WHAT *YOU* WANNA DO.
SO I'M SORRY YOU GOT DRAGGED INTO THIS, BUT I'M REALLY HAPPY YOU'RE BOTH HERE.
LEMME ASK YOU THIS...
POKE
IS THIS JUST ONE OF THOSE--OW-- "FEEL GOOD" MOMENTS?
'CAUSE THE COPS ARE *AWFULLY* CURIOUS ABOUT US RIGHT NOW.
WE'LL GET TO YOUR DATE IN A SEC, VI, BUT *I* ALREADY SOLVED ONE OF OUR PROBLEMS.
WHICH ONE?

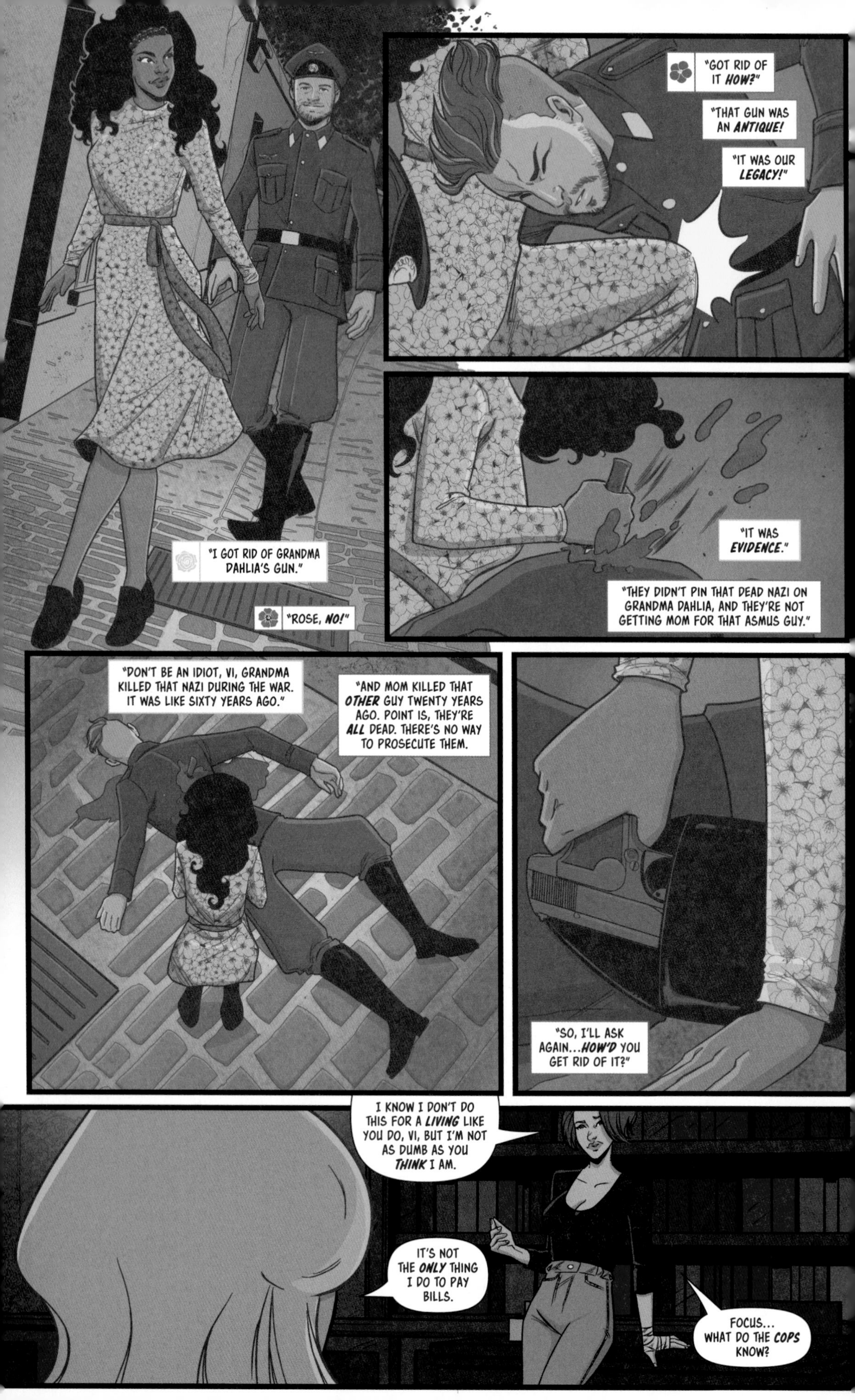
"I GOT RID OF GRANDMA DAHLIA'S GUN."
"ROSE, NO!"
"GOT RID OF IT HOW?"
"THAT GUN WAS AN ANTIQUE!
"IT WAS OUR LEGACY!"
"IT WAS EVIDENCE."
"THEY DIDN'T PIN THAT DEAD NAZI ON GRANDMA DAHLIA, AND THEY'RE NOT GETTING MOM FOR THAT ASMUS GUY."
"DON'T BE AN IDIOT, VI, GRANDMA KILLED THAT NAZI DURING THE WAR. IT WAS LIKE SIXTY YEARS AGO."
"AND MOM KILLED THAT OTHER GUY TWENTY YEARS AGO. POINT IS, THEY'RE ALL DEAD. THERE'S NO WAY TO PROSECUTE THEM.
"SO, I'LL ASK AGAIN...HOW'D YOU GET RID OF IT?"
I KNOW I DON'T DO THIS FOR A LIVING LIKE YOU DO, VI, BUT I'M NOT AS DUMB AS YOU THINK I AM.
IT'S NOT THE ONLY THING I DO TO PAY BILLS.
FOCUS... WHAT DO THE COPS KNOW?

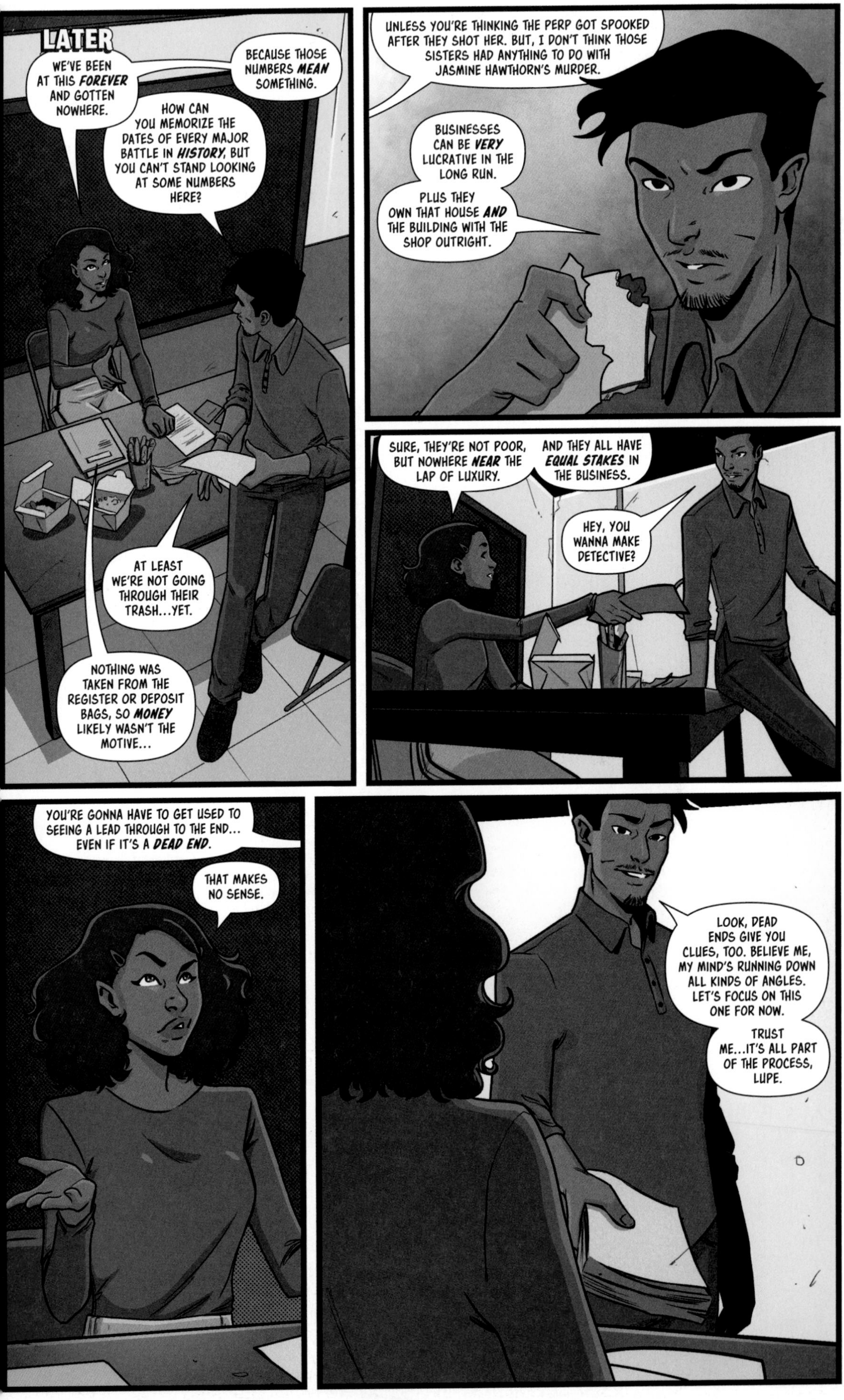
LATER
WE'VE BEEN AT THIS FOREVER AND GOTTEN NOWHERE.
BECAUSE THOSE NUMBERS MEAN SOMETHING.
HOW CAN YOU MEMORIZE THE DATES OF EVERY MAJOR BATTLE IN HISTORY, BUT YOU CAN'T STAND LOOKING AT SOME NUMBERS HERE?
AT LEAST WE'RE NOT GOING THROUGH THEIR TRASH...YET.
NOTHING WAS TAKEN FROM THE REGISTER OR DEPOSIT BAGS, SO MONEY LIKELY WASN'T THE MOTIVE...
UNLESS YOU'RE THINKING THE PERP GOT SPOOKED AFTER THEY SHOT HER. BUT, I DON'T THINK THOSE SISTERS HAD ANYTHING TO DO WITH JASMINE HAWTHORN'S MURDER.
BUSINESSES CAN BE VERY LUCRATIVE IN THE LONG RUN.
PLUS THEY OWN THAT HOUSE AND THE BUILDING WITH THE SHOP OUTRIGHT.
SURE, THEY'RE NOT POOR, BUT NOWHERE NEAR THE LAP OF LUXURY.
AND THEY ALL HAVE EQUAL STAKES IN THE BUSINESS.
HEY, YOU WANNA MAKE DETECTIVE?
YOU'RE GONNA HAVE TO GET USED TO SEEING A LEAD THROUGH TO THE END... EVEN IF IT'S A DEAD END.
THAT MAKES NO SENSE.
LOOK, DEAD ENDS GIVE YOU CLUES, TOO. BELIEVE ME, MY MIND'S RUNNING DOWN ALL KINDS OF ANGLES. LET'S FOCUS ON THIS ONE FOR NOW.
TRUST ME...IT'S ALL PART OF THE PROCESS, LUPE.

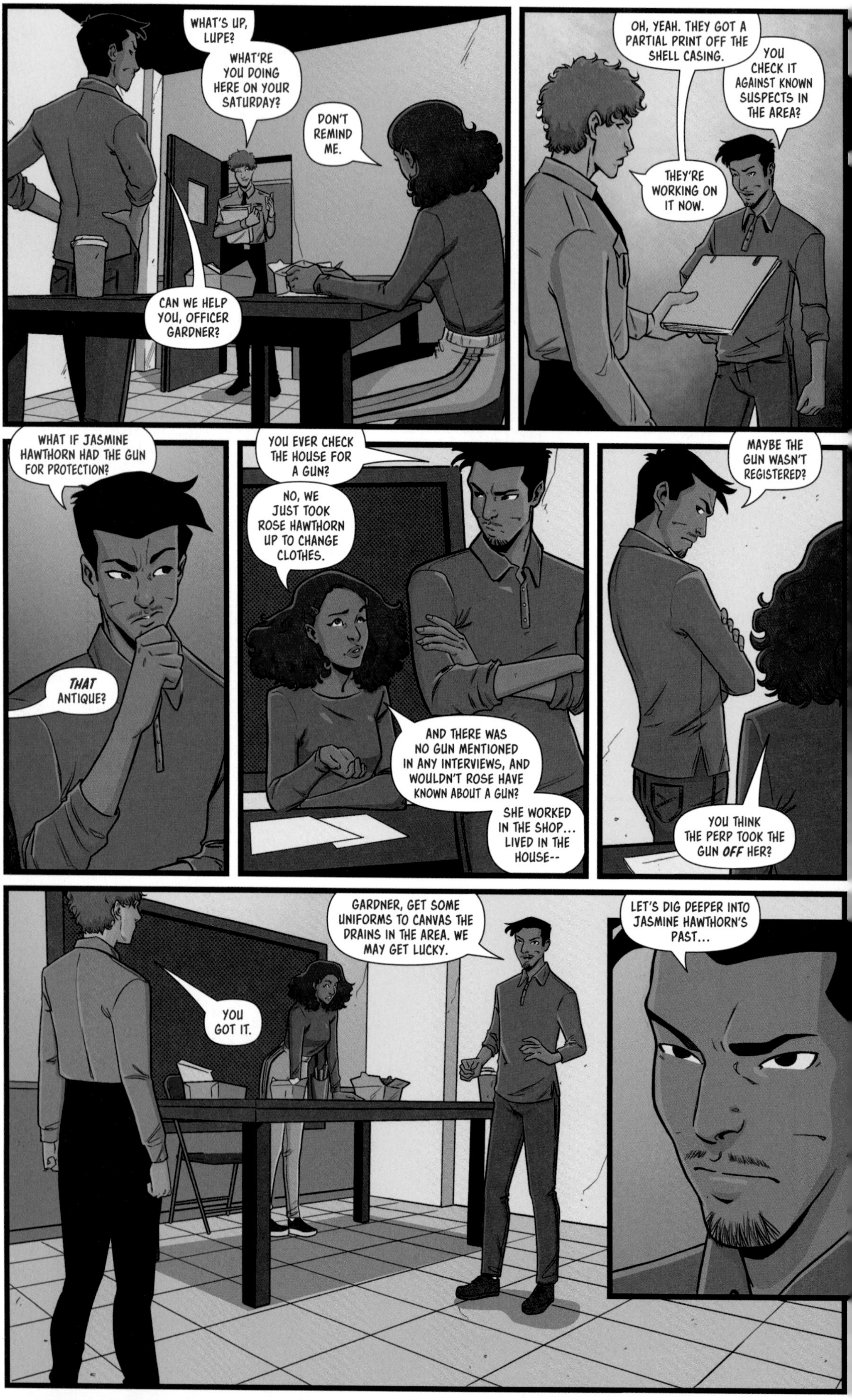
WHAT'S UP, LUPE?
WHAT'RE YOU DOING HERE ON YOUR SATURDAY?
DON'T REMIND ME.
CAN WE HELP YOU, OFFICER GARDNER?
OH, YEAH. THEY GOT A PARTIAL PRINT OFF THE SHELL CASING.
YOU CHECK IT AGAINST KNOWN SUSPECTS IN THE AREA?
THEY'RE WORKING ON IT NOW.
WHAT IF JASMINE HAWTHORN HAD THE GUN FOR PROTECTION?
THAT ANTIQUE?
YOU EVER CHECK THE HOUSE FOR A GUN?
NO, WE JUST TOOK ROSE HAWTHORN UP TO CHANGE CLOTHES.
AND THERE WAS NO GUN MENTIONED IN ANY INTERVIEWS, AND WOULDN'T ROSE HAVE KNOWN ABOUT A GUN?
SHE WORKED IN THE SHOP... LIVED IN THE HOUSE--
MAYBE THE GUN WASN'T REGISTERED?
YOU THINK THE PERP TOOK THE GUN OFF HER?
GARDNER, GET SOME UNIFORMS TO CANVAS THE DRAINS IN THE AREA. WE MAY GET LUCKY.
YOU GOT IT.
LET'S DIG DEEPER INTO JASMINE HAWTHORN'S PAST...

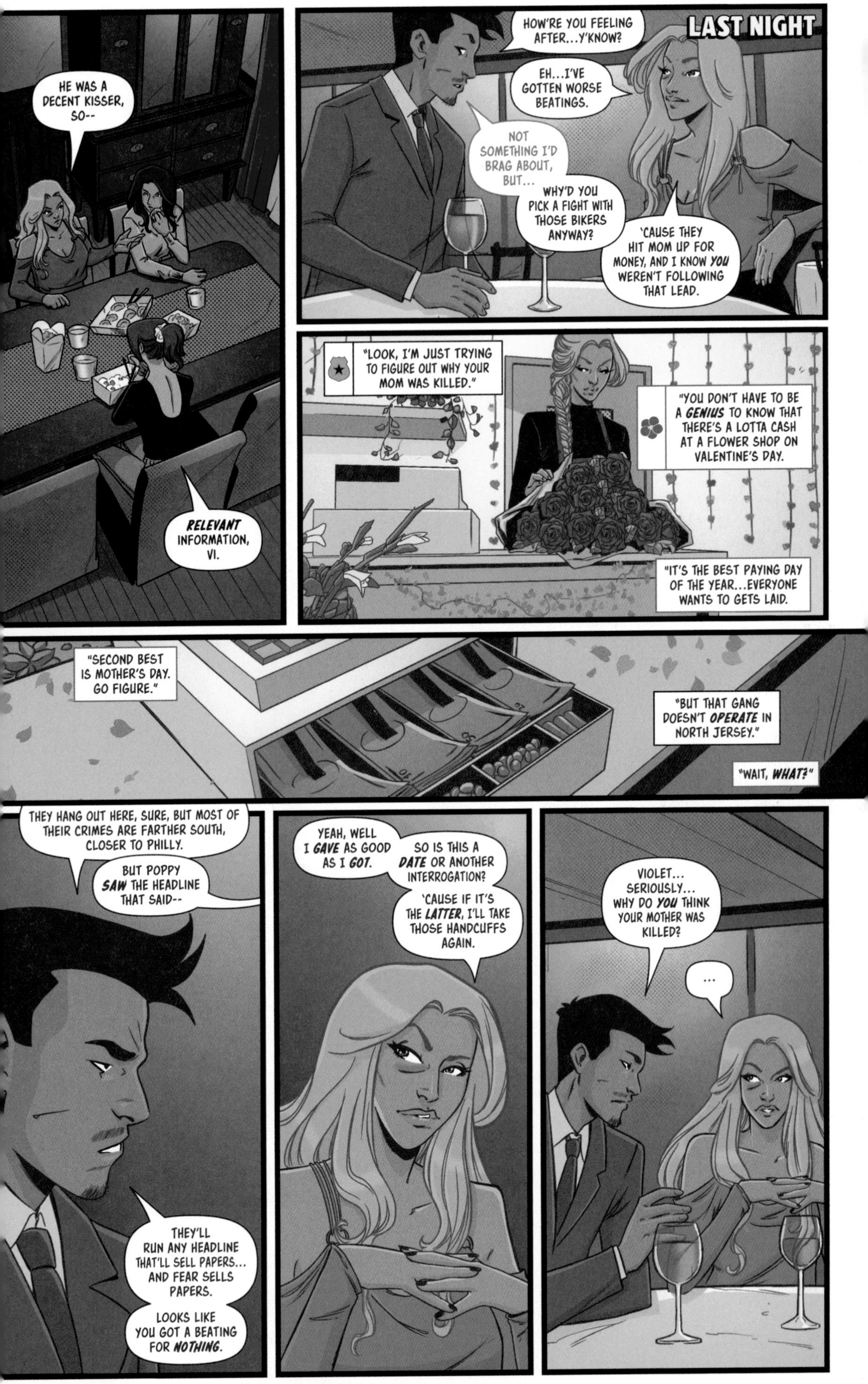
HE WAS A DECENT KISSER, SO--
RELEVANT INFORMATION, VI.
LAST NIGHT
HOW'RE YOU FEELING AFTER...Y'KNOW?
EH...I'VE GOTTEN WORSE BEATINGS.
NOT SOMETHING I'D BRAG ABOUT, BUT...
WHY'D YOU PICK A FIGHT WITH THOSE BIKERS ANYWAY?
'CAUSE THEY HIT MOM UP FOR MONEY, AND I KNOW YOU WEREN'T FOLLOWING THAT LEAD.
"LOOK, I'M JUST TRYING TO FIGURE OUT WHY YOUR MOM WAS KILLED."
"YOU DON'T HAVE TO BE A GENIUS TO KNOW THAT THERE'S A LOTTA CASH AT A FLOWER SHOP ON VALENTINE'S DAY.
"IT'S THE BEST PAYING DAY OF THE YEAR...EVERYONE WANTS TO GETS LAID.
"SECOND BEST IS MOTHER'S DAY. GO FIGURE."
"BUT THAT GANG DOESN'T OPERATE IN NORTH JERSEY."
"WAIT, WHAT?"
THEY HANG OUT HERE, SURE, BUT MOST OF THEIR CRIMES ARE FARTHER SOUTH, CLOSER TO PHILLY.
BUT POPPY SAW THE HEADLINE THAT SAID--
THEY'LL RUN ANY HEADLINE THAT'LL SELL PAPERS... AND FEAR SELLS PAPERS.
LOOKS LIKE YOU GOT A BEATING FOR NOTHING.
YEAH, WELL I GAVE AS GOOD AS I GOT.
SO IS THIS A DATE OR ANOTHER INTERROGATION?
'CAUSE IF IT'S THE LATTER, I'LL TAKE THOSE HANDCUFFS AGAIN.
VIOLET... SERIOUSLY... WHY DO YOU THINK YOUR MOTHER WAS KILLED?
...

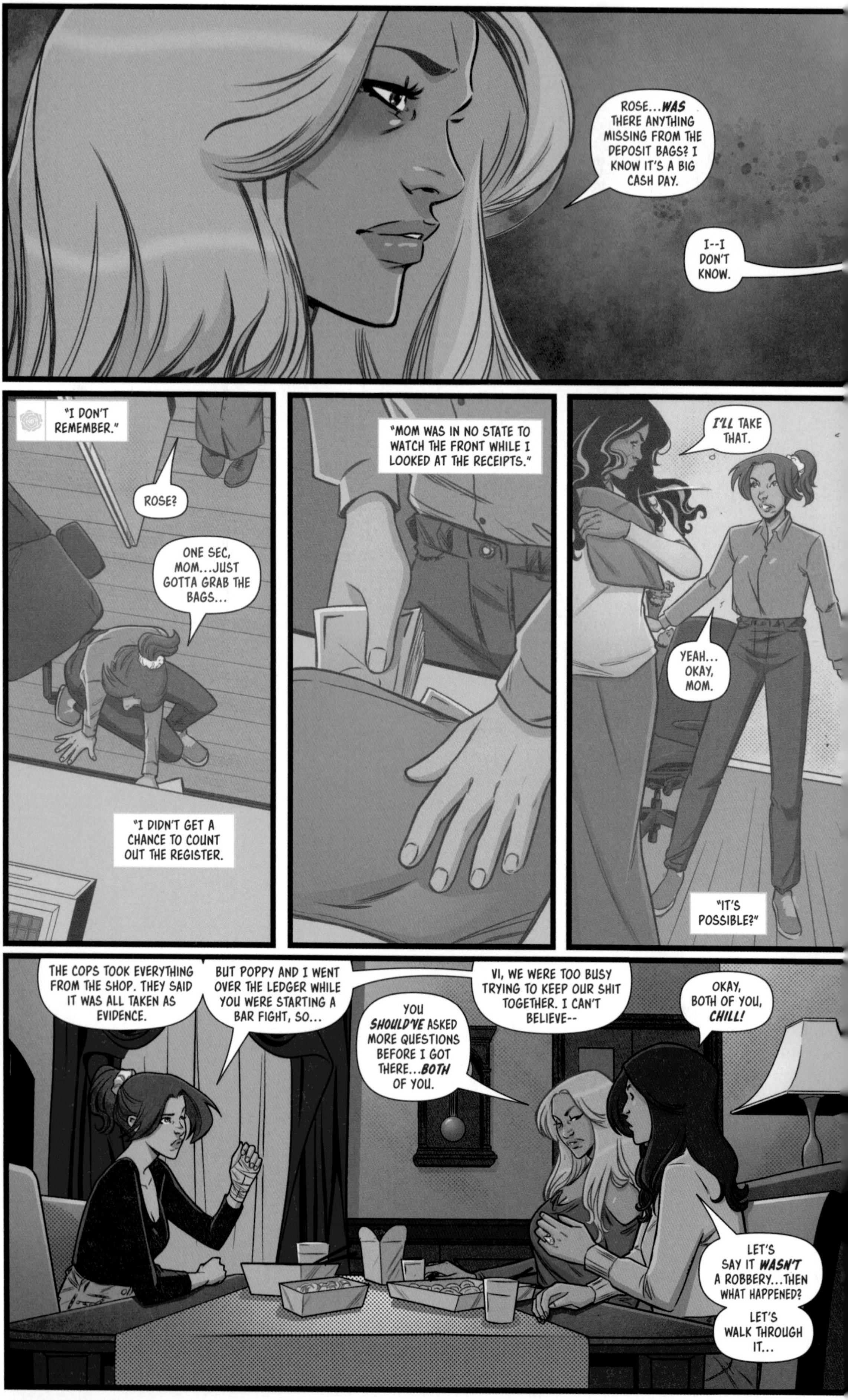

ROSE...WAS THERE ANYTHING MISSING FROM THE DEPOSIT BAGS? I KNOW IT'S A BIG CASH DAY.
I--I DON'T KNOW.
"I DON'T REMEMBER."
ROSE?
ONE SEC, MOM...JUST GOTTA GRAB THE BAGS...
"I DIDN'T GET A CHANCE TO COUNT OUT THE REGISTER.
"MOM WAS IN NO STATE TO WATCH THE FRONT WHILE I LOOKED AT THE RECEIPTS."
I'LL TAKE THAT.
YEAH... OKAY, MOM.
"IT'S POSSIBLE?"
THE COPS TOOK EVERYTHING FROM THE SHOP. THEY SAID IT WAS ALL TAKEN AS EVIDENCE.
BUT POPPY AND I WENT OVER THE LEDGER WHILE YOU WERE STARTING A BAR FIGHT, SO...
YOU SHOULD'VE ASKED MORE QUESTIONS BEFORE I GOT THERE...BOTH OF YOU.
VI, WE WERE TOO BUSY TRYING TO KEEP OUR SHIT TOGETHER. I CAN'T BELIEVE--
OKAY, BOTH OF YOU, CHILL!
LET'S SAY IT WASN'T A ROBBERY...THEN WHAT HAPPENED?
LET'S WALK THROUGH IT...

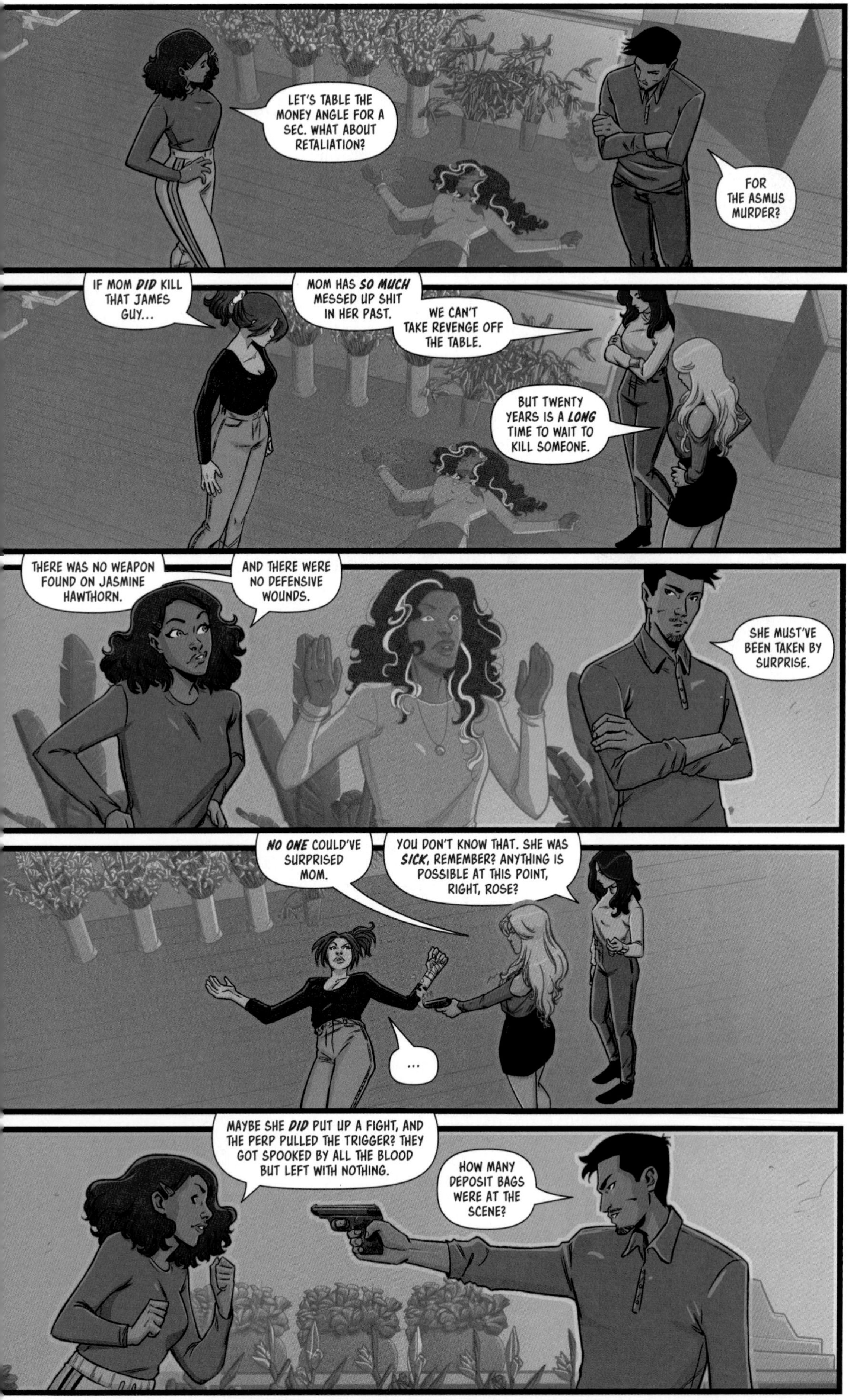
LET'S TABLE THE MONEY ANGLE FOR A SEC. WHAT ABOUT RETALIATION?
FOR THE ASMUS MURDER?
IF MOM DID KILL THAT JAMES GUY...
MOM HAS SO MUCH MESSED UP SHIT IN HER PAST.
WE CAN'T TAKE REVENGE OFF THE TABLE.
BUT TWENTY YEARS IS A LONG TIME TO WAIT TO KILL SOMEONE.
THERE WAS NO WEAPON FOUND ON JASMINE HAWTHORN.
AND THERE WERE NO DEFENSIVE WOUNDS.
SHE MUST'VE BEEN TAKEN BY SURPRISE.
NO ONE COULD'VE SURPRISED MOM.
YOU DON'T KNOW THAT. SHE WAS SICK, REMEMBER? ANYTHING IS POSSIBLE AT THIS POINT, RIGHT, ROSE?
...
MAYBE SHE DID PUT UP A FIGHT, AND THE PERP PULLED THE TRIGGER? THEY GOT SPOOKED BY ALL THE BLOOD BUT LEFT WITH NOTHING.
HOW MANY DEPOSIT BAGS WERE AT THE SCENE?

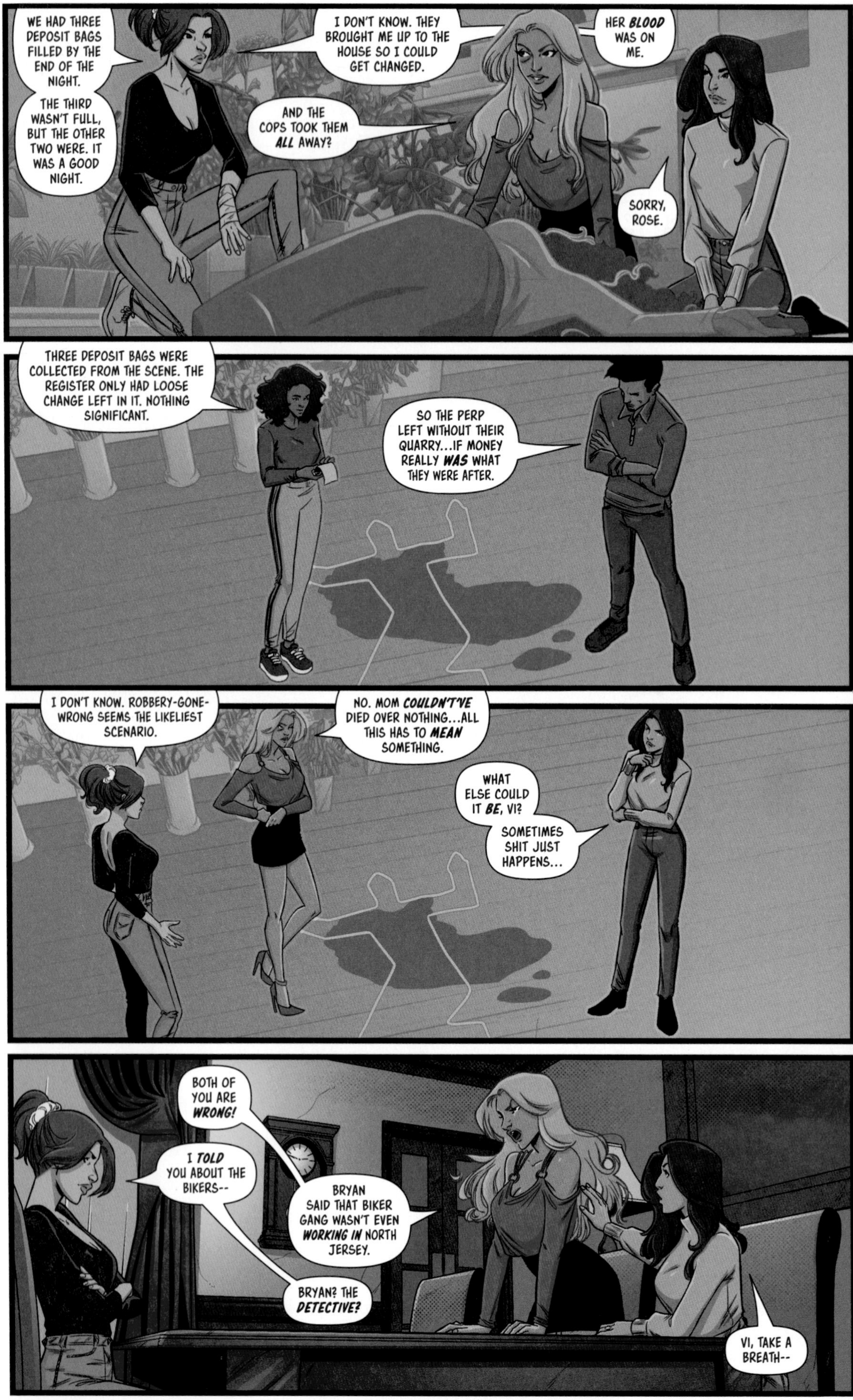
WE HAD THREE DEPOSIT BAGS FILLED BY THE END OF THE NIGHT.
THE THIRD WASN'T FULL, BUT THE OTHER TWO WERE. IT WAS A GOOD NIGHT.
AND THE COPS TOOK THEM ALL AWAY?
I DON'T KNOW. THEY BROUGHT ME UP TO THE HOUSE SO I COULD GET CHANGED.
HER BLOOD WAS ON ME.
SORRY, ROSE.
THREE DEPOSIT BAGS WERE COLLECTED FROM THE SCENE. THE REGISTER ONLY HAD LOOSE CHANGE LEFT IN IT. NOTHING SIGNIFICANT.
SO THE PERP LEFT WITHOUT THEIR QUARRY...IF MONEY REALLY WAS WHAT THEY WERE AFTER.
I DON'T KNOW. ROBBERY-GONE-WRONG SEEMS THE LIKELIEST SCENARIO.
NO. MOM COULDN'T'VE DIED OVER NOTHING...ALL THIS HAS TO MEAN SOMETHING.
WHAT ELSE COULD IT BE, VI?
SOMETIMES SHIT JUST HAPPENS...
BOTH OF YOU ARE WRONG!
I TOLD YOU ABOUT THE BIKERS--
BRYAN SAID THAT BIKER GANG WASN'T EVEN WORKING IN NORTH JERSEY.
BRYAN? THE DETECTIVE?
VI, TAKE A BREATH--

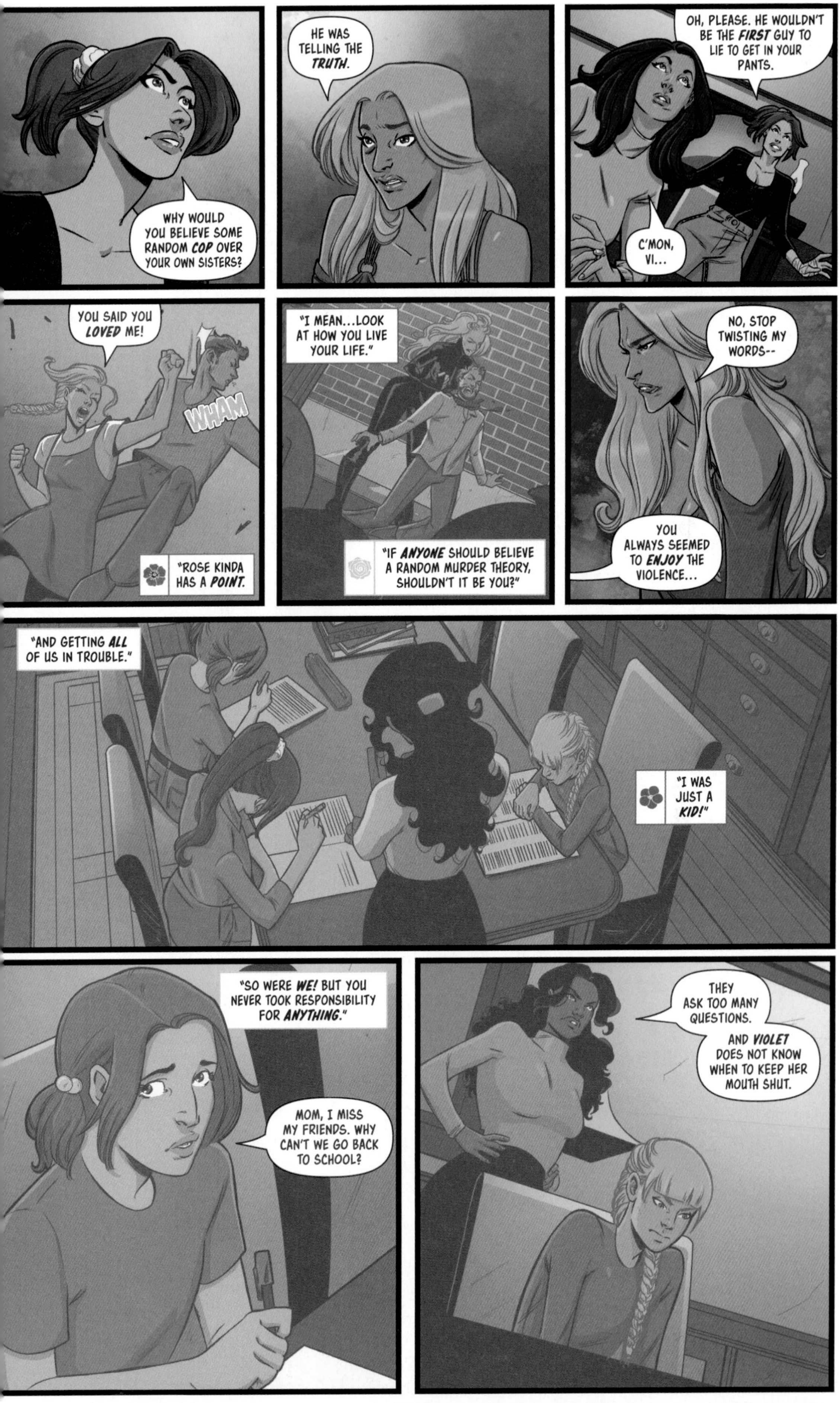
WHY WOULD YOU BELIEVE SOME RANDOM COP OVER YOUR OWN SISTERS?
HE WAS TELLING THE TRUTH.
OH, PLEASE. HE WOULDN'T BE THE FIRST GUY TO LIE TO GET IN YOUR PANTS.
C'MON, VI...
YOU SAID YOU LOVED ME!
WHAM
"ROSE KINDA HAS A POINT.
"I MEAN...LOOK AT HOW YOU LIVE YOUR LIFE."
"IF ANYONE SHOULD BELIEVE A RANDOM MURDER THEORY, SHOULDN'T IT BE YOU?"
NO, STOP TWISTING MY WORDS--
YOU ALWAYS SEEMED TO ENJOY THE VIOLENCE...
"AND GETTING ALL OF US IN TROUBLE."
"I WAS JUST A KID!"
"SO WERE WE! BUT YOU NEVER TOOK RESPONSIBILITY FOR ANYTHING."
MOM, I MISS MY FRIENDS. WHY CAN'T WE GO BACK TO SCHOOL?
THEY ASK TOO MANY QUESTIONS.
AND VIOLET DOES NOT KNOW WHEN TO KEEP HER MOUTH SHUT.

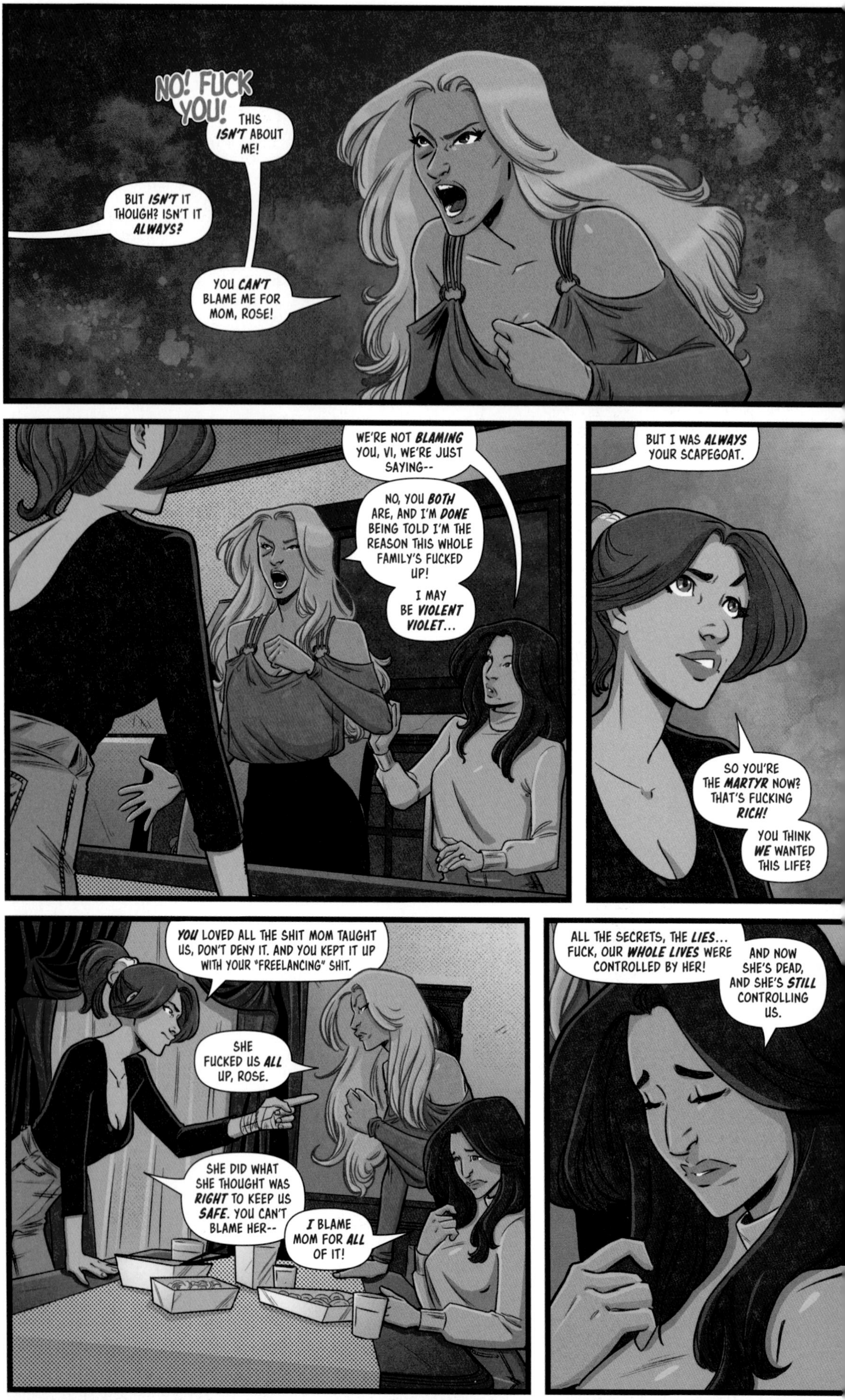
NO! FUCK YOU!
THIS ISN'T ABOUT ME!
BUT ISN'T IT THOUGH? ISN'T IT ALWAYS?
YOU CAN'T BLAME ME FOR MOM, ROSE!
WE'RE NOT BLAMING YOU, VI, WE'RE JUST SAYING--
NO, YOU BOTH ARE, AND I'M DONE BEING TOLD I'M THE REASON THIS WHOLE FAMILY'S FUCKED UP!
I MAY BE VIOLENT VIOLET...
BUT I WAS ALWAYS YOUR SCAPEGOAT.
SO YOU'RE THE MARTYR NOW? THAT'S FUCKING RICH!
YOU THINK WE WANTED THIS LIFE?
YOU LOVED ALL THE SHIT MOM TAUGHT US, DON'T DENY IT. AND YOU KEPT IT UP WITH YOUR "FREELANCING" SHIT.
SHE FUCKED US ALL UP, ROSE.
SHE DID WHAT SHE THOUGHT WAS RIGHT TO KEEP US SAFE. YOU CAN'T BLAME HER--
I BLAME MOM FOR ALL OF IT!
ALL THE SECRETS, THE LIES... FUCK, OUR WHOLE LIVES WERE CONTROLLED BY HER!
AND NOW SHE'S DEAD, AND SHE'S STILL CONTROLLING US.

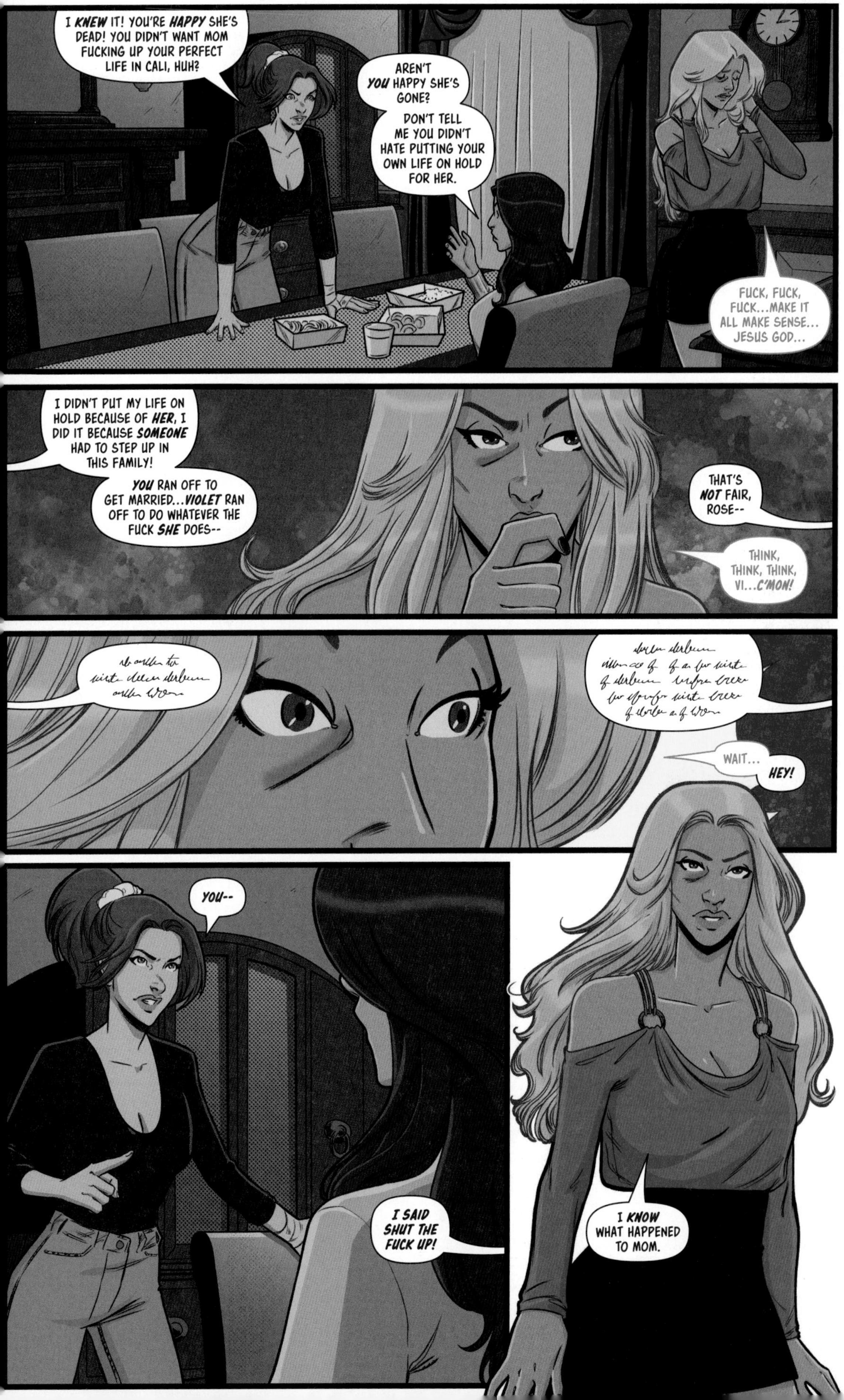
I KNEW IT! YOU'RE HAPPY SHE'S DEAD! YOU DIDN'T WANT MOM FUCKING UP YOUR PERFECT LIFE IN CALI, HUH?
AREN'T YOU HAPPY SHE'S GONE?
DON'T TELL ME YOU DIDN'T HATE PUTTING YOUR OWN LIFE ON HOLD FOR HER.
FUCK, FUCK, FUCK...MAKE IT ALL MAKE SENSE... JESUS GOD...
I DIDN'T PUT MY LIFE ON HOLD BECAUSE OF HER, I DID IT BECAUSE SOMEONE HAD TO STEP UP IN THIS FAMILY!
YOU RAN OFF TO GET MARRIED...VIOLET RAN OFF TO DO WHATEVER THE FUCK SHE DOES--
THAT'S NOT FAIR, ROSE--
THINK, THINK, THINK, VI...C'MON!
WAIT... HEY!
YOU--
I SAID SHUT THE FUCK UP!
I KNOW WHAT HAPPENED TO MOM.

CHAPTER *Five*

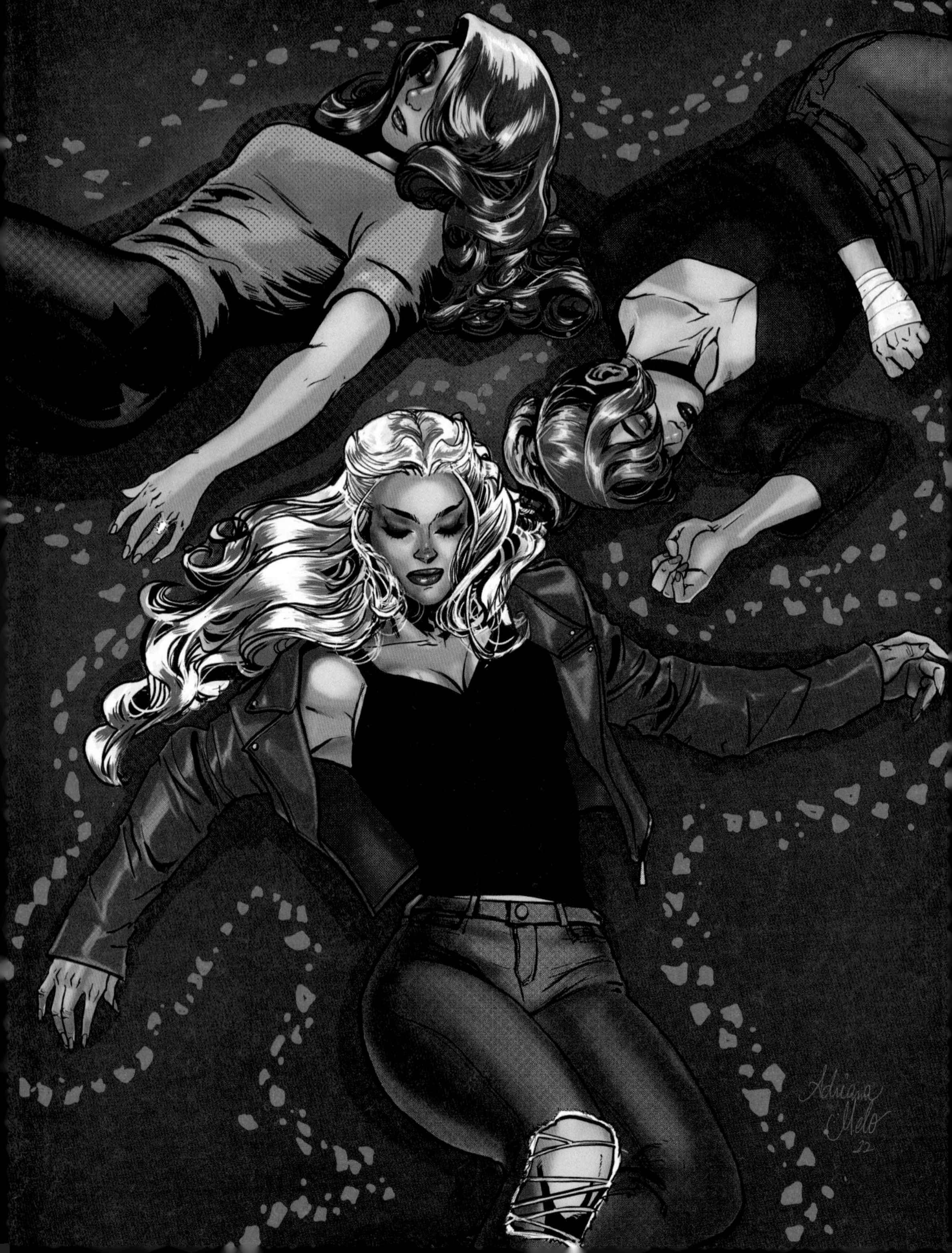
Adriana Melo 22

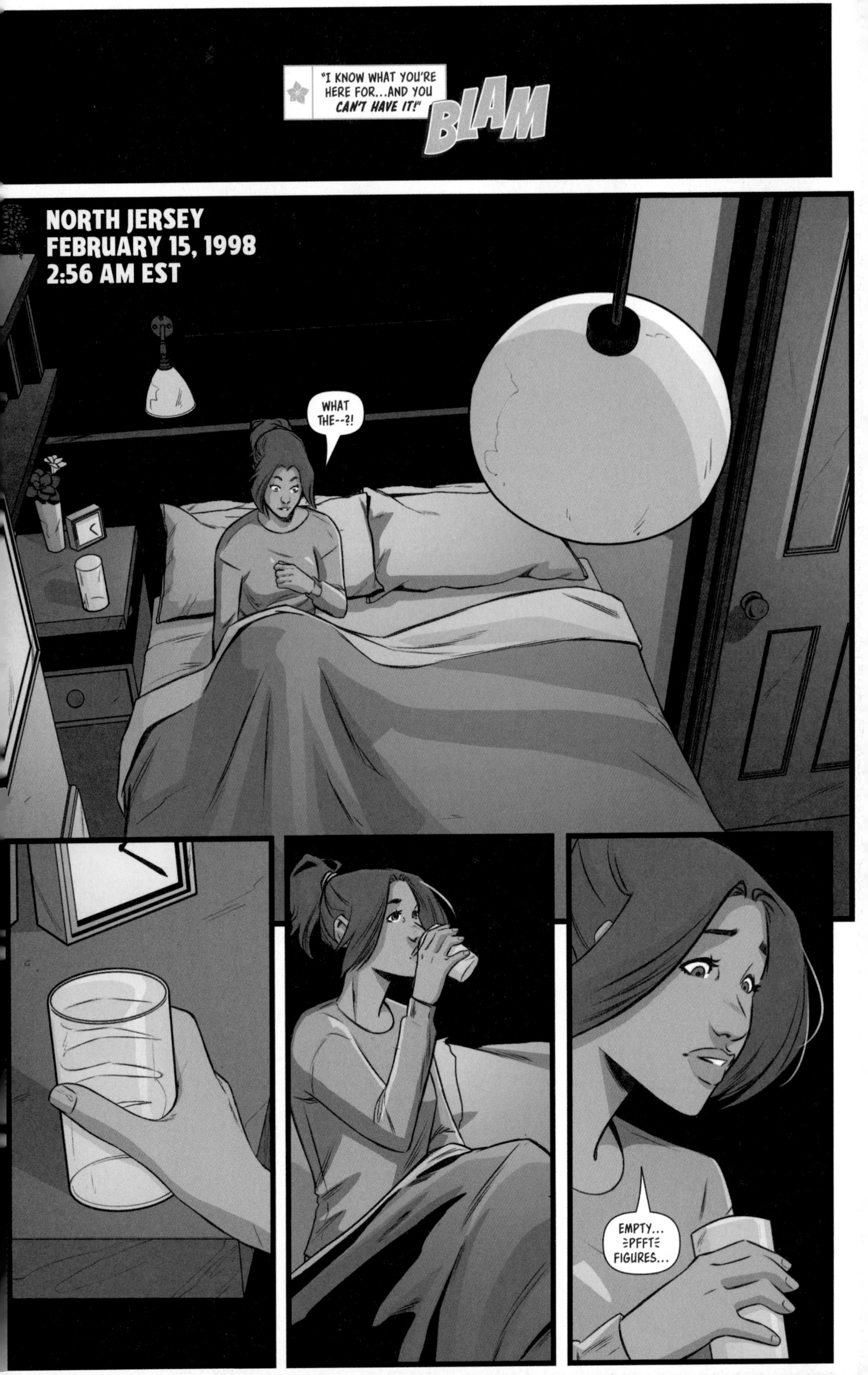
"I KNOW WHAT YOU'RE HERE FOR...AND YOU *CAN'T HAVE IT!*"
BLAM
NORTH JERSEY
FEBRUARY 15, 1998
2:56 AM EST
WHAT THE--?!
EMPTY...
≡PFFT≡
FIGURES...

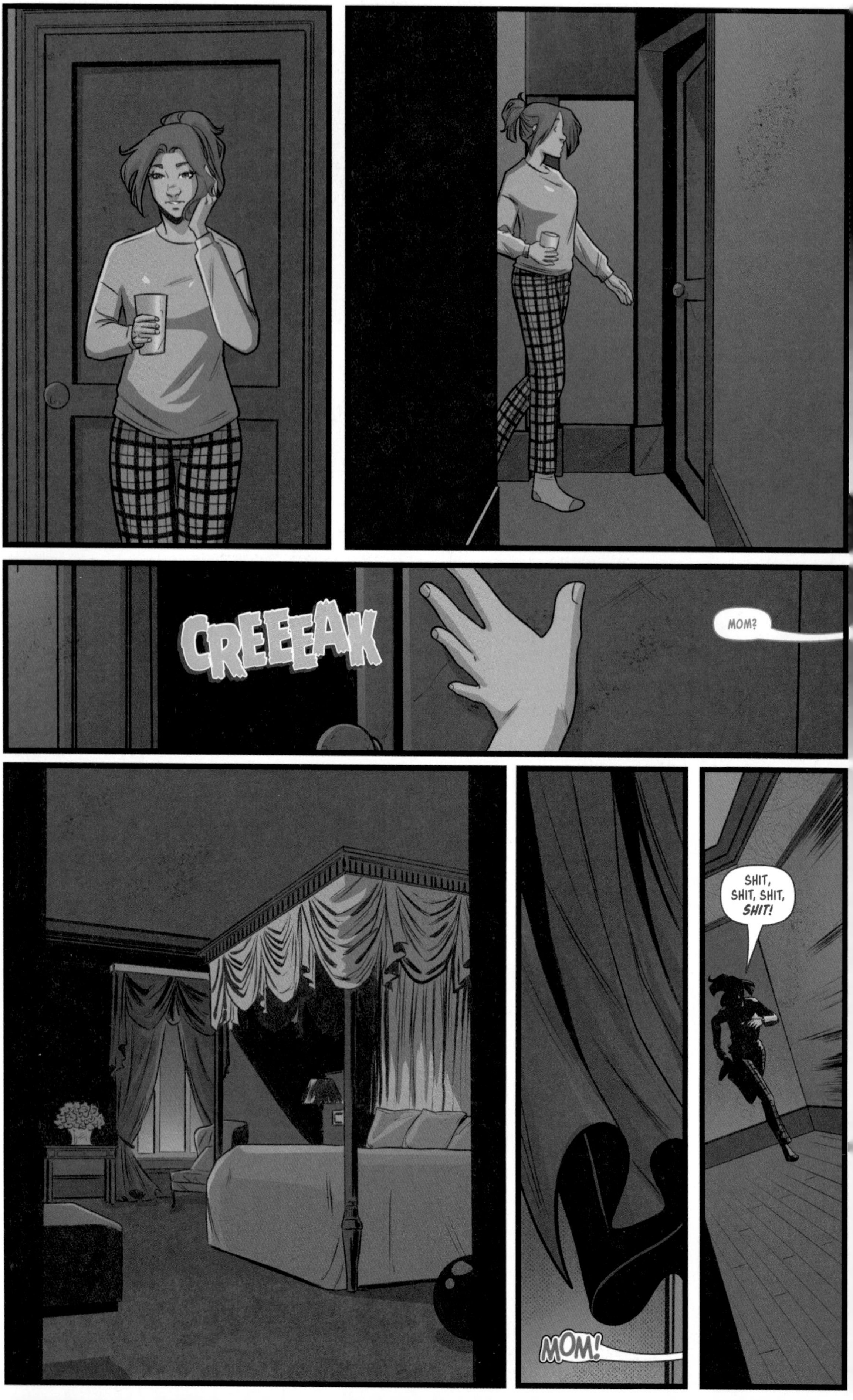
CREEEAK
MOM?
MOM!
SHIT, SHIT, SHIT, SHIT!

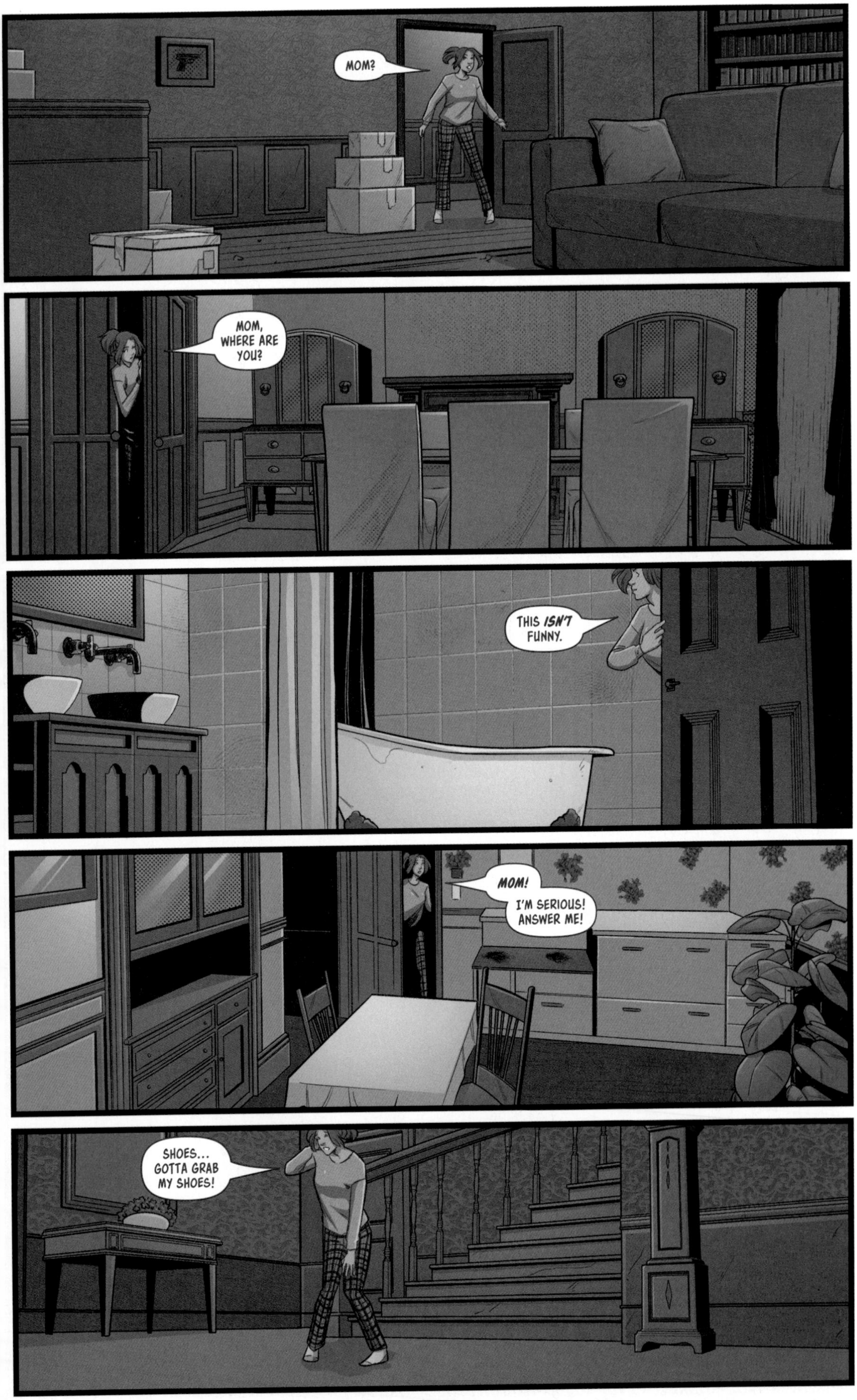
MOM?
MOM, WHERE ARE YOU?
THIS *ISN'T* FUNNY.
MOM!
I'M SERIOUS! ANSWER ME!
SHOES... GOTTA GRAB MY SHOES!

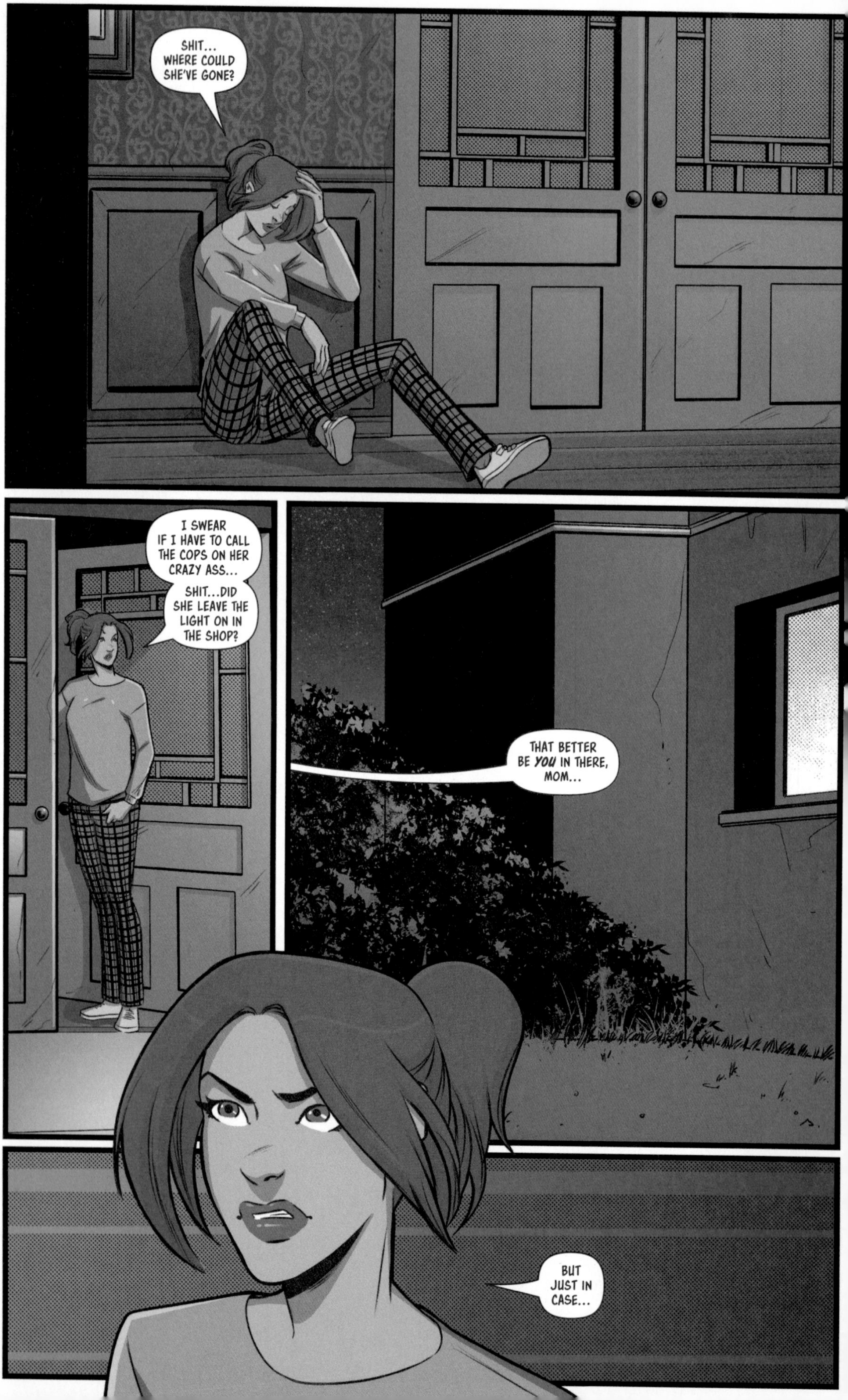
SHIT... WHERE COULD SHE'VE GONE?
I SWEAR IF I HAVE TO CALL THE COPS ON HER CRAZY ASS...
SHIT...DID SHE LEAVE THE LIGHT ON IN THE SHOP?
THAT BETTER BE YOU IN THERE, MOM...
BUT JUST IN CASE...

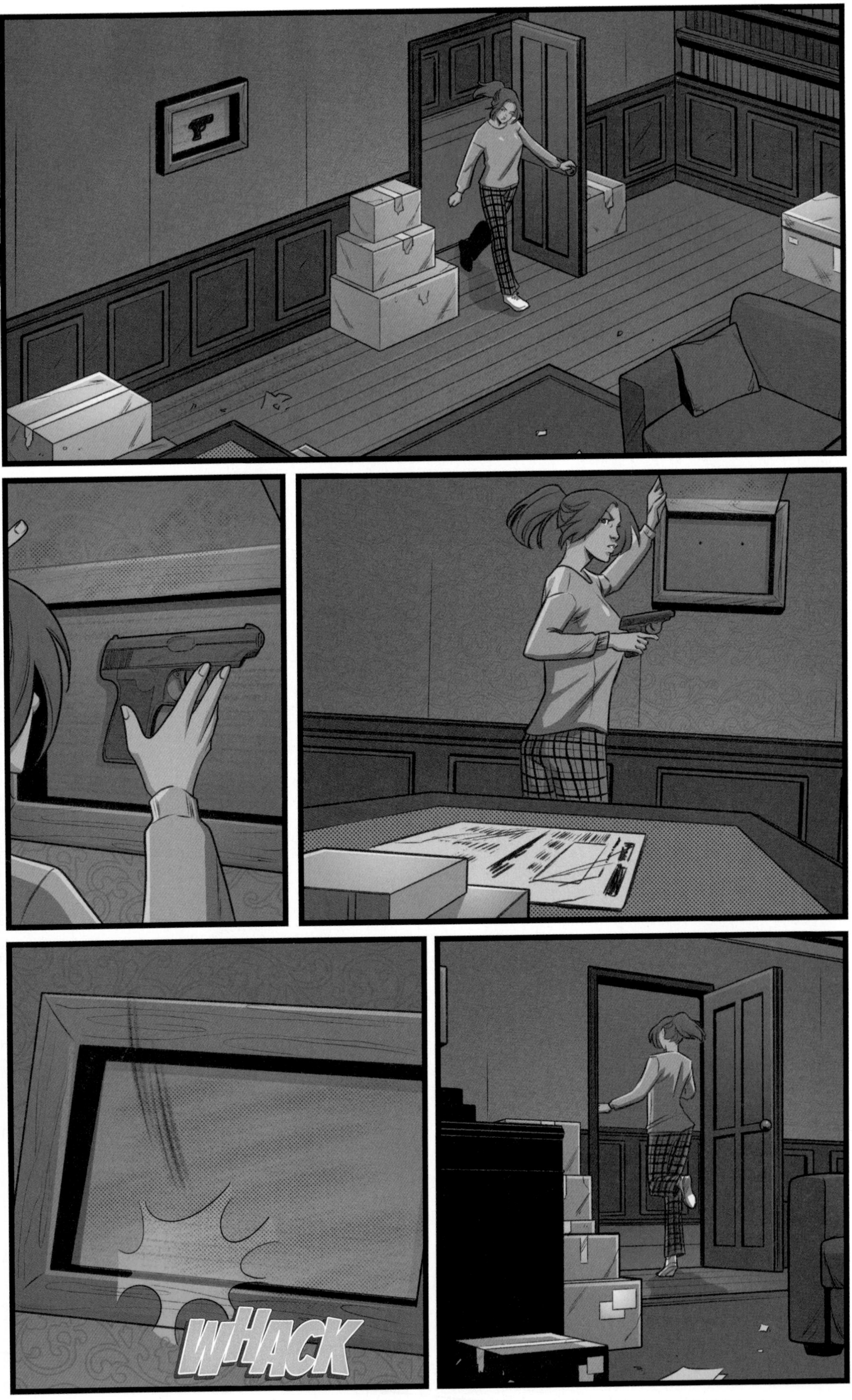
WHACK

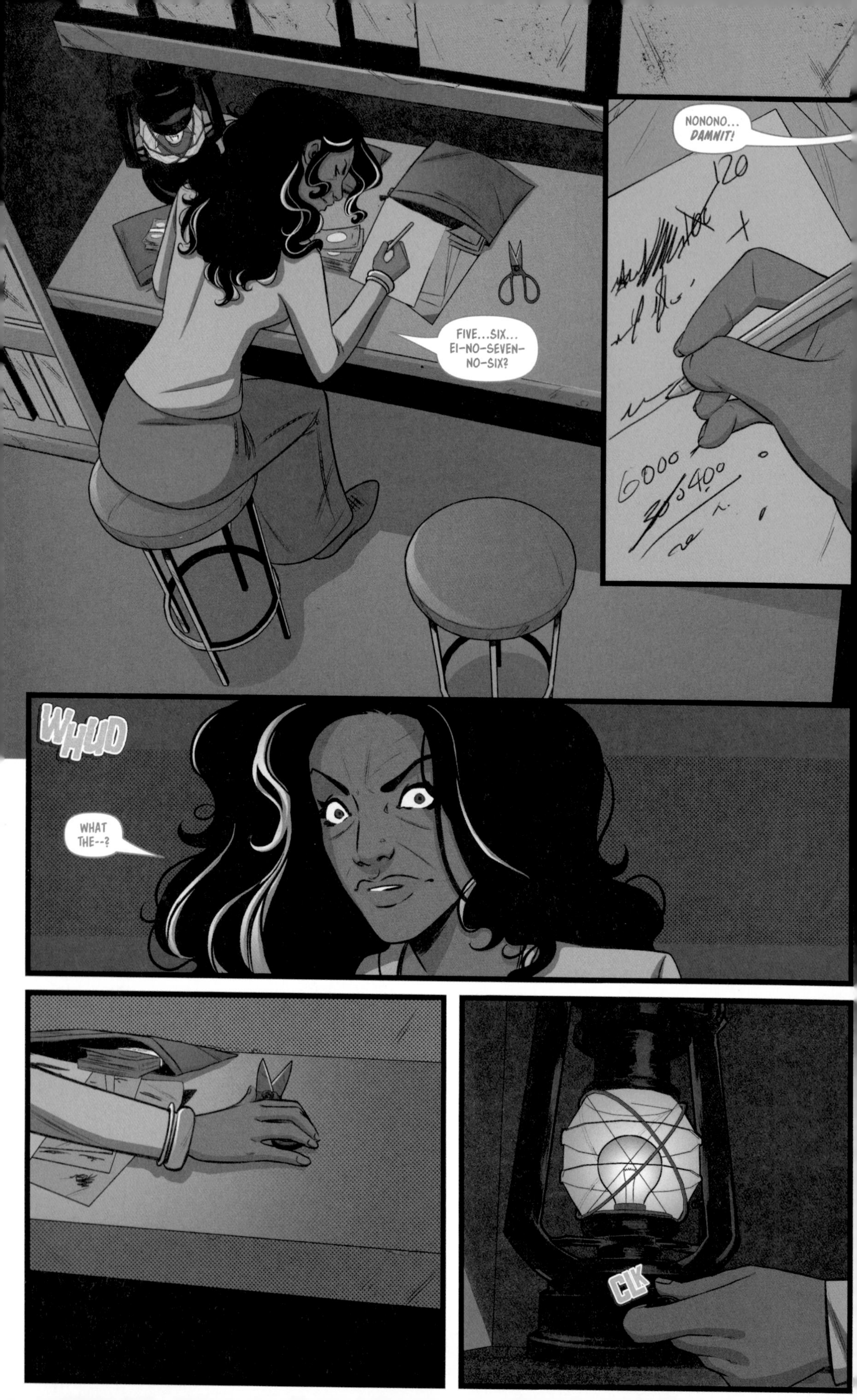
FIVE...SIX... EI-NO-SEVEN-NO-SIX?
NONONO... DAMNIT!
WHUD
WHAT THE--?
CLK

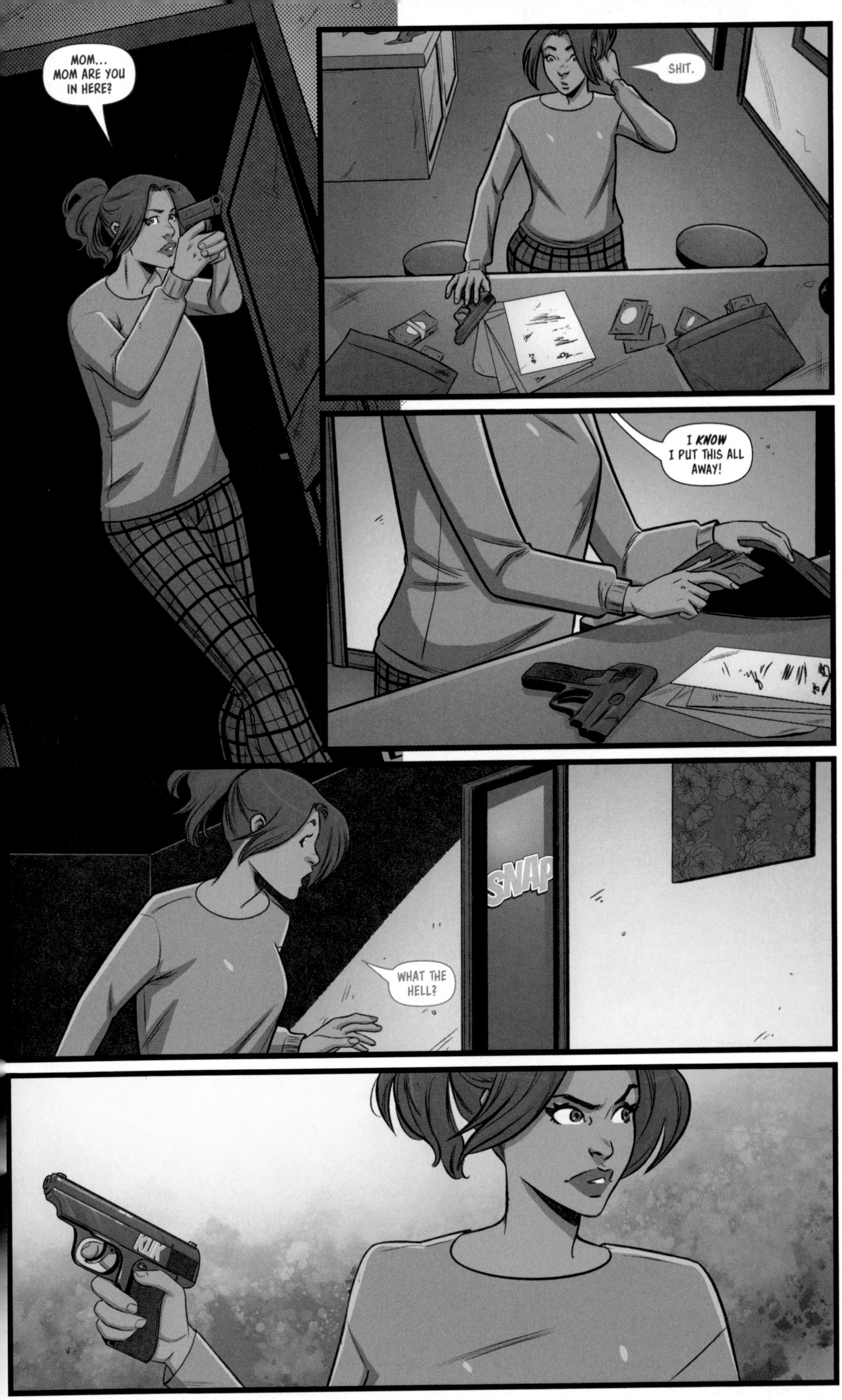
MOM...
MOM ARE YOU
IN HERE?
SHIT.
I KNOW
I PUT THIS ALL
AWAY!
SNAP
WHAT THE
HELL?
KLIK

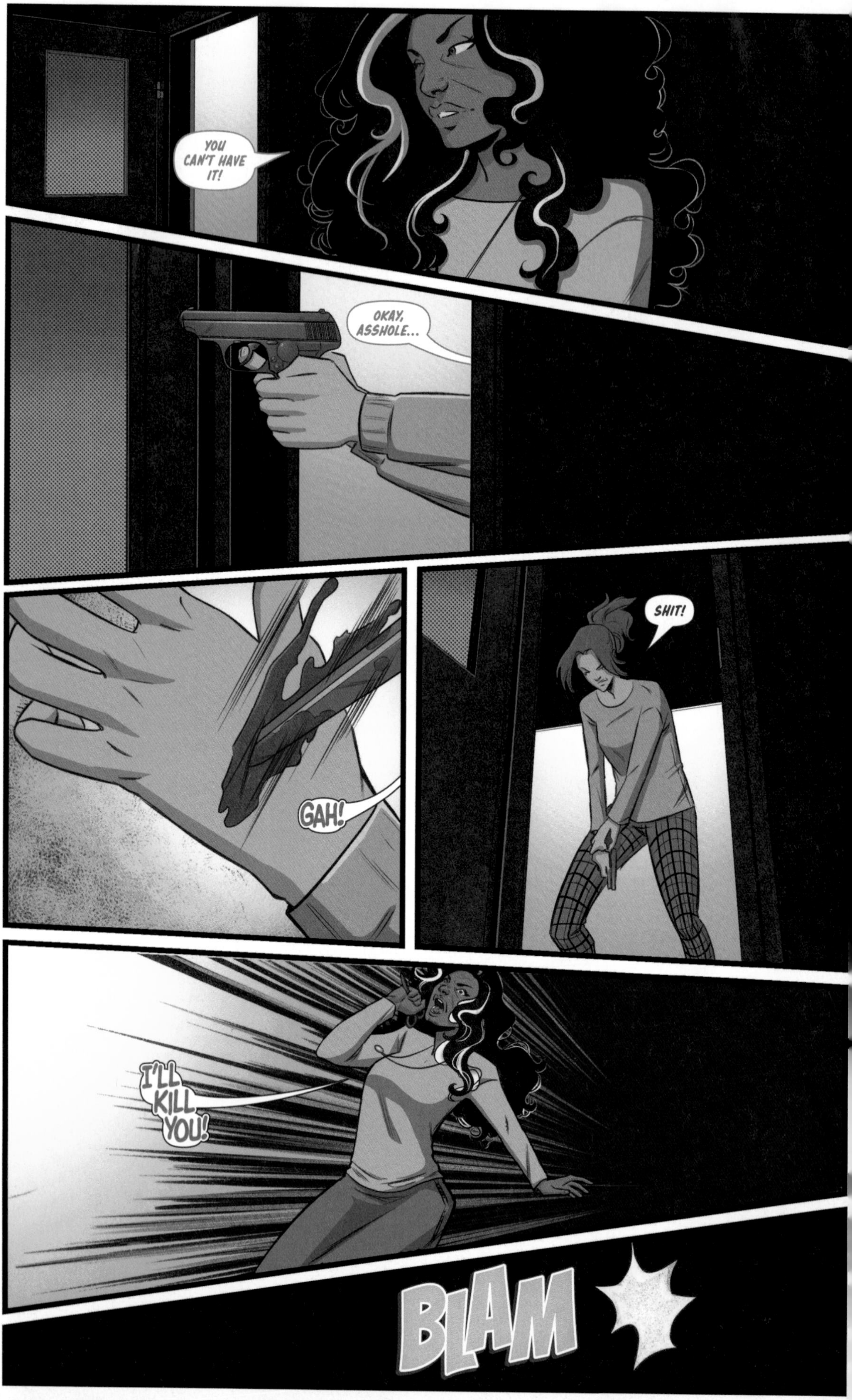
YOU CAN'T HAVE IT!
OKAY, ASSHOLE...
GAH!
SHIT!
I'LL KILL YOU!
BLAM

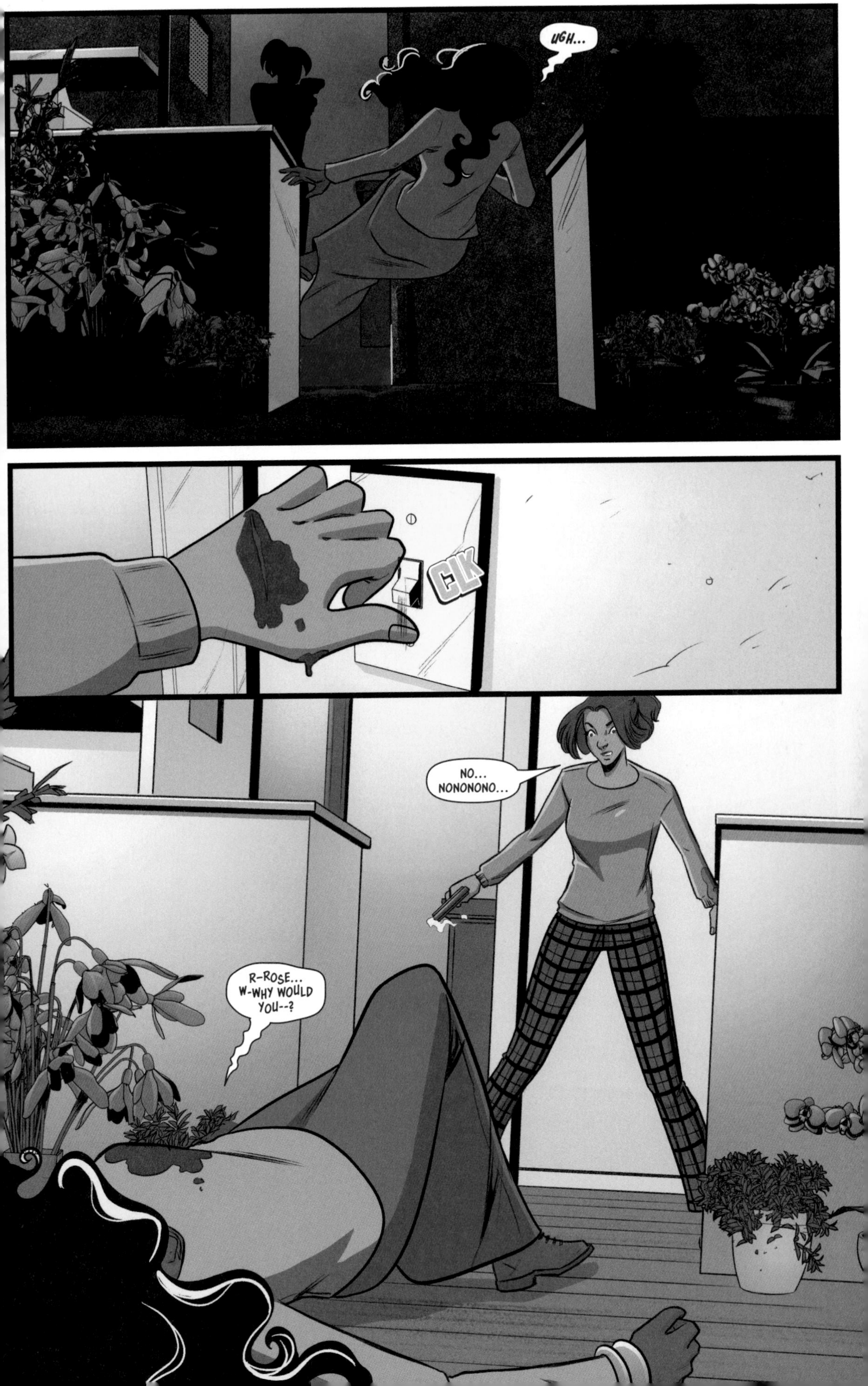
UGH...
CLK
NO...
NONONONO...
R-ROSE...
W-WHY WOULD
YOU--?

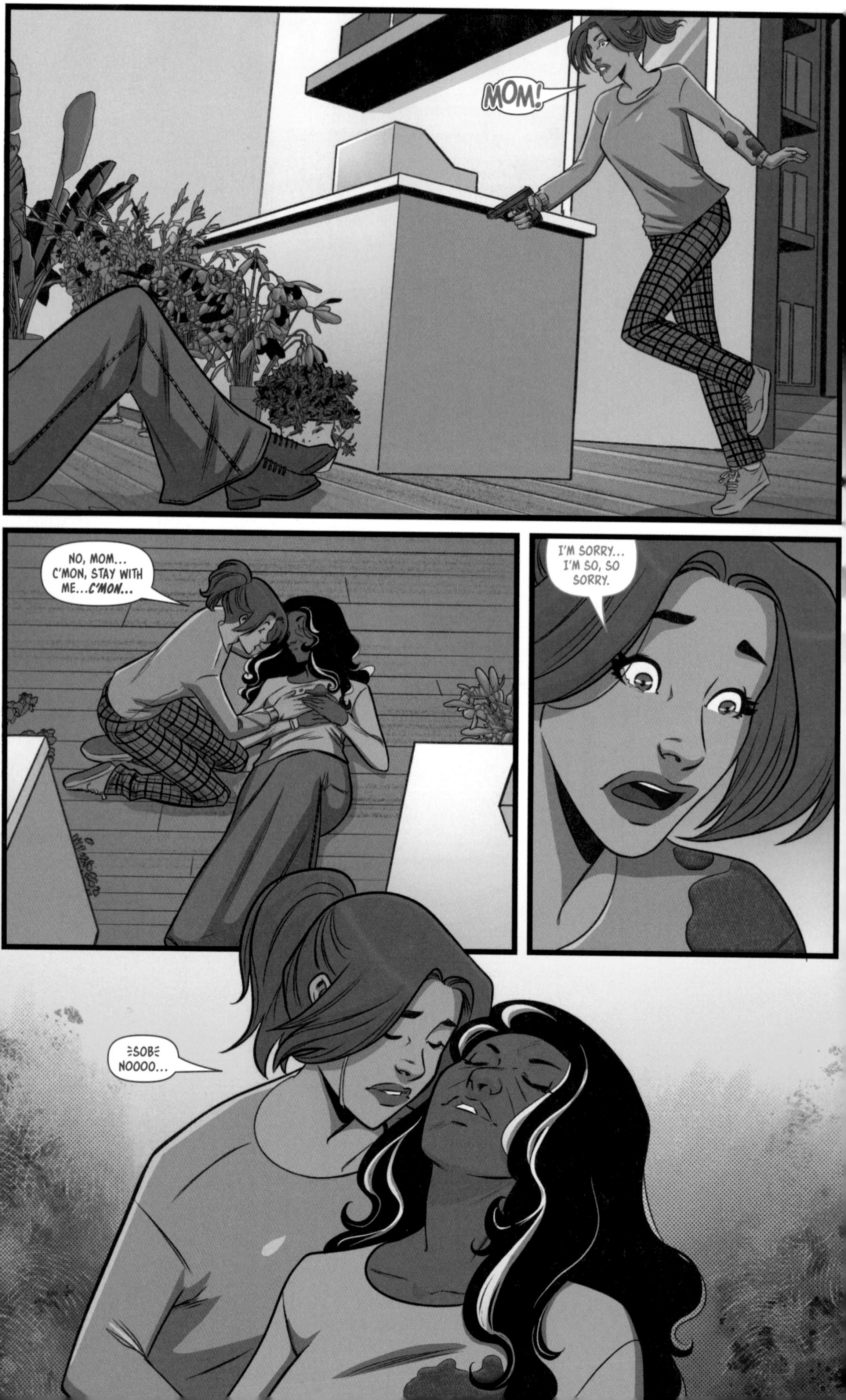
MOM!
NO, MOM... C'MON, STAY WITH ME...C'MON...
I'M SORRY... I'M SO, SO SORRY.
SOB NOOOO...

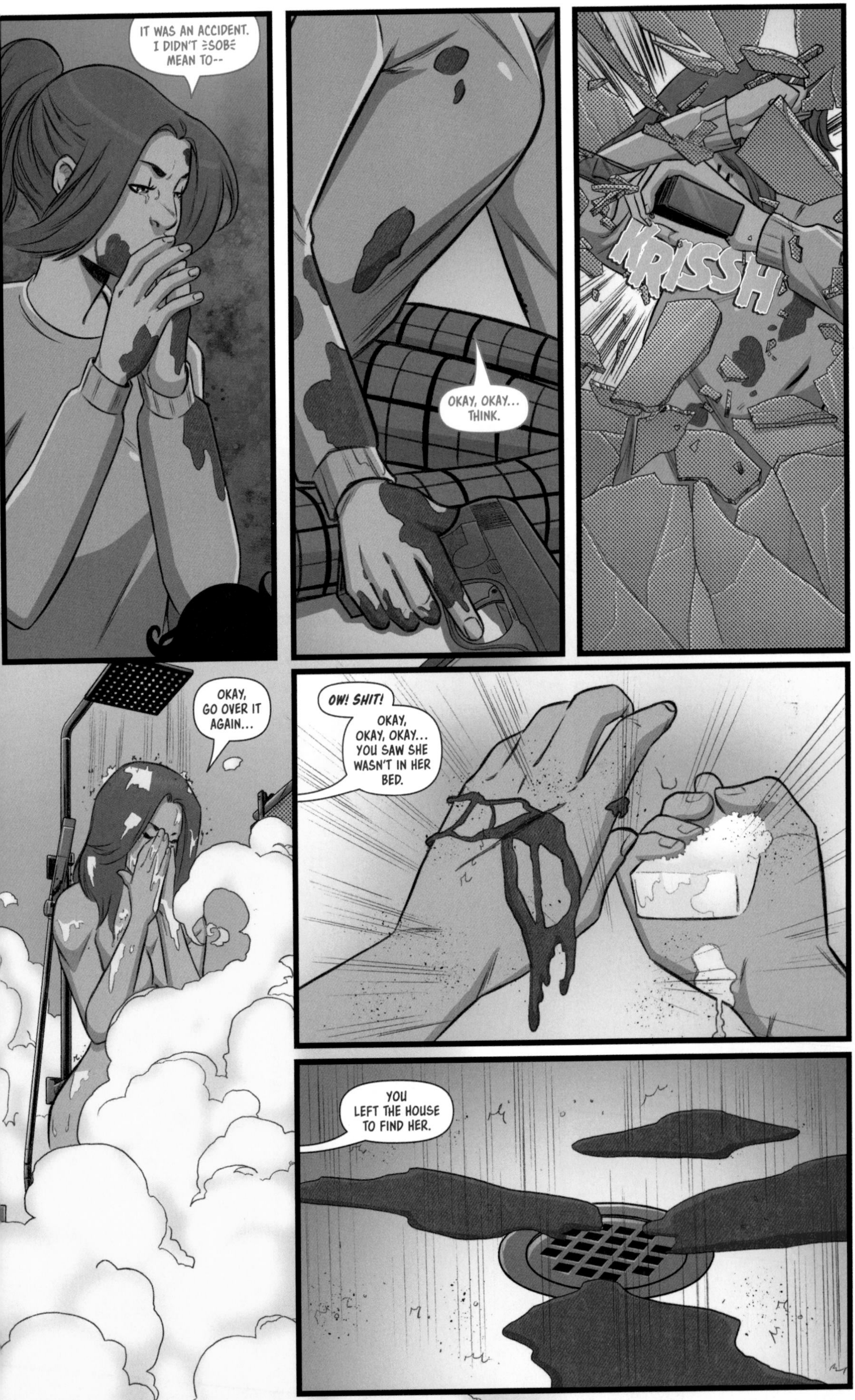
IT WAS AN ACCIDENT. I DIDN'T =SOB= MEAN TO--
OKAY, OKAY... THINK.
KRISSH
OKAY, GO OVER IT AGAIN...
OW! SHIT!
OKAY, OKAY, OKAY... YOU SAW SHE WASN'T IN HER BED.
YOU LEFT THE HOUSE TO FIND HER.

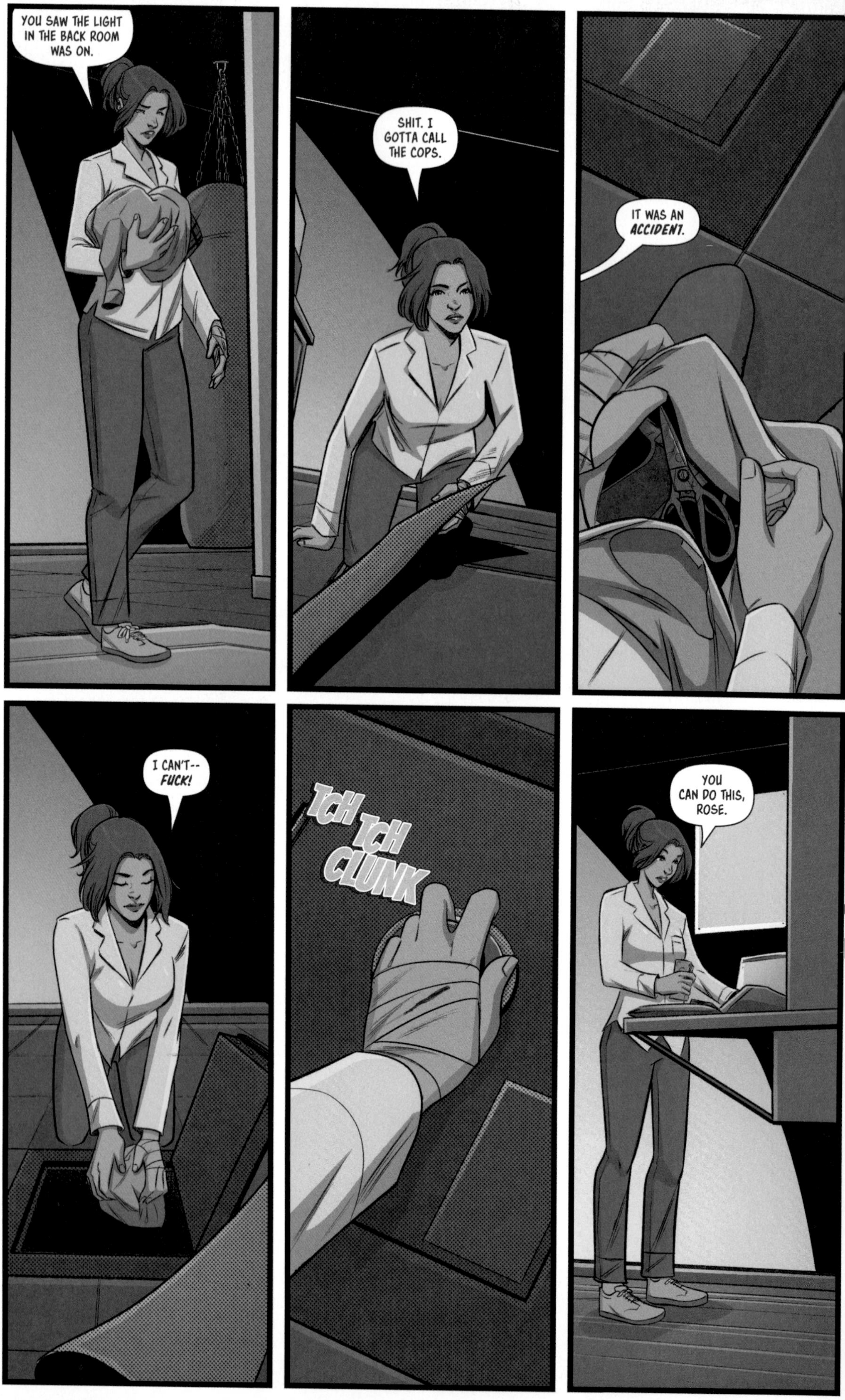
YOU SAW THE LIGHT IN THE BACK ROOM WAS ON.
SHIT. I GOTTA CALL THE COPS.
IT WAS AN ACCIDENT.
I CAN'T-- FUCK!
TCH TCH CLUNK
YOU CAN DO THIS, ROSE.

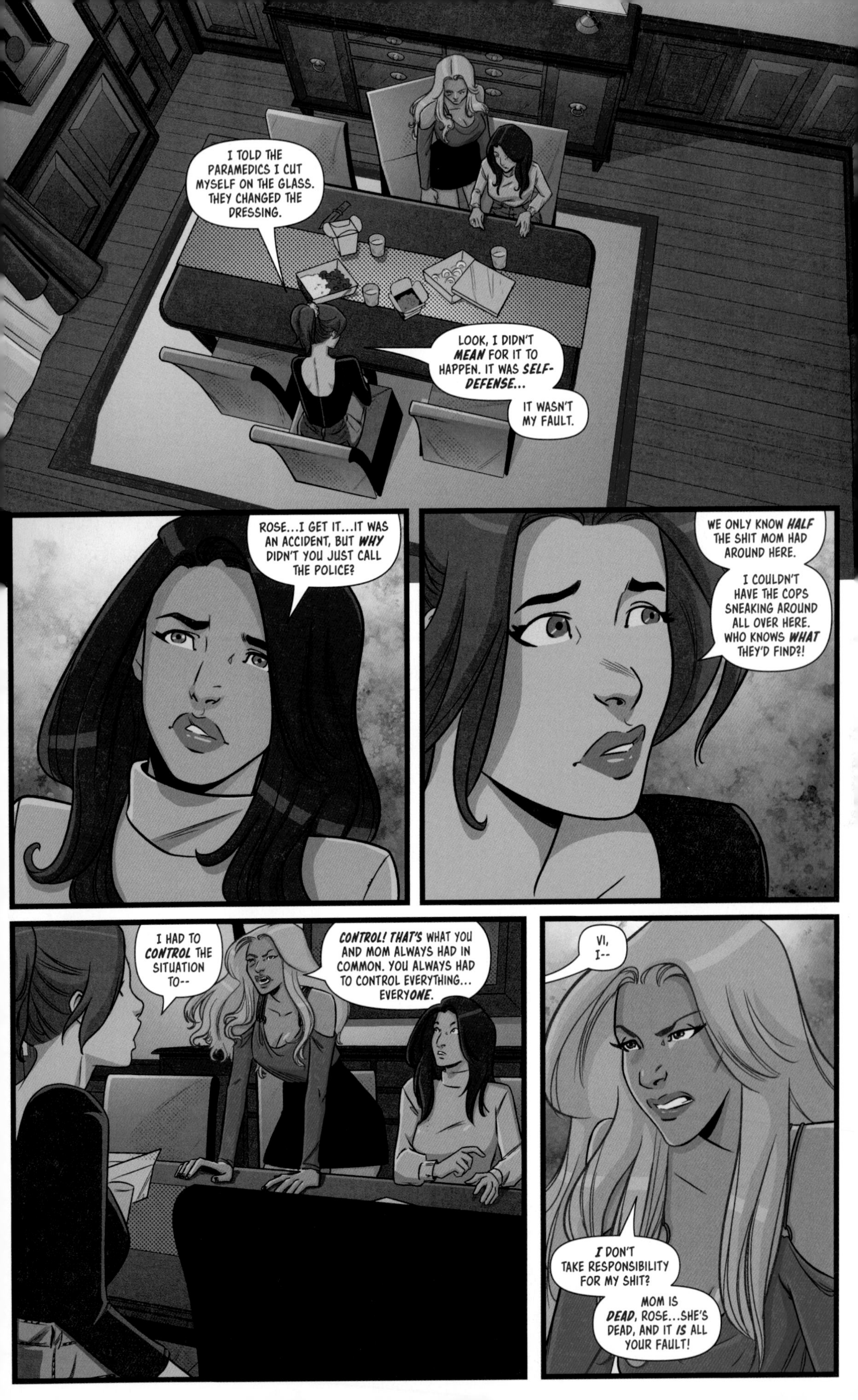
I TOLD THE PARAMEDICS I CUT MYSELF ON THE GLASS. THEY CHANGED THE DRESSING.
LOOK, I DIDN'T MEAN FOR IT TO HAPPEN. IT WAS SELF-DEFENSE...
IT WASN'T MY FAULT.
ROSE...I GET IT...IT WAS AN ACCIDENT, BUT WHY DIDN'T YOU JUST CALL THE POLICE?
WE ONLY KNOW HALF THE SHIT MOM HAD AROUND HERE.
I COULDN'T HAVE THE COPS SNEAKING AROUND ALL OVER HERE. WHO KNOWS WHAT THEY'D FIND?!
I HAD TO CONTROL THE SITUATION TO--
CONTROL! THAT'S WHAT YOU AND MOM ALWAYS HAD IN COMMON. YOU ALWAYS HAD TO CONTROL EVERYTHING... EVERYONE.
VI, I--
I DON'T TAKE RESPONSIBILITY FOR MY SHIT?
MOM IS DEAD, ROSE...SHE'S DEAD, AND IT IS ALL YOUR FAULT!

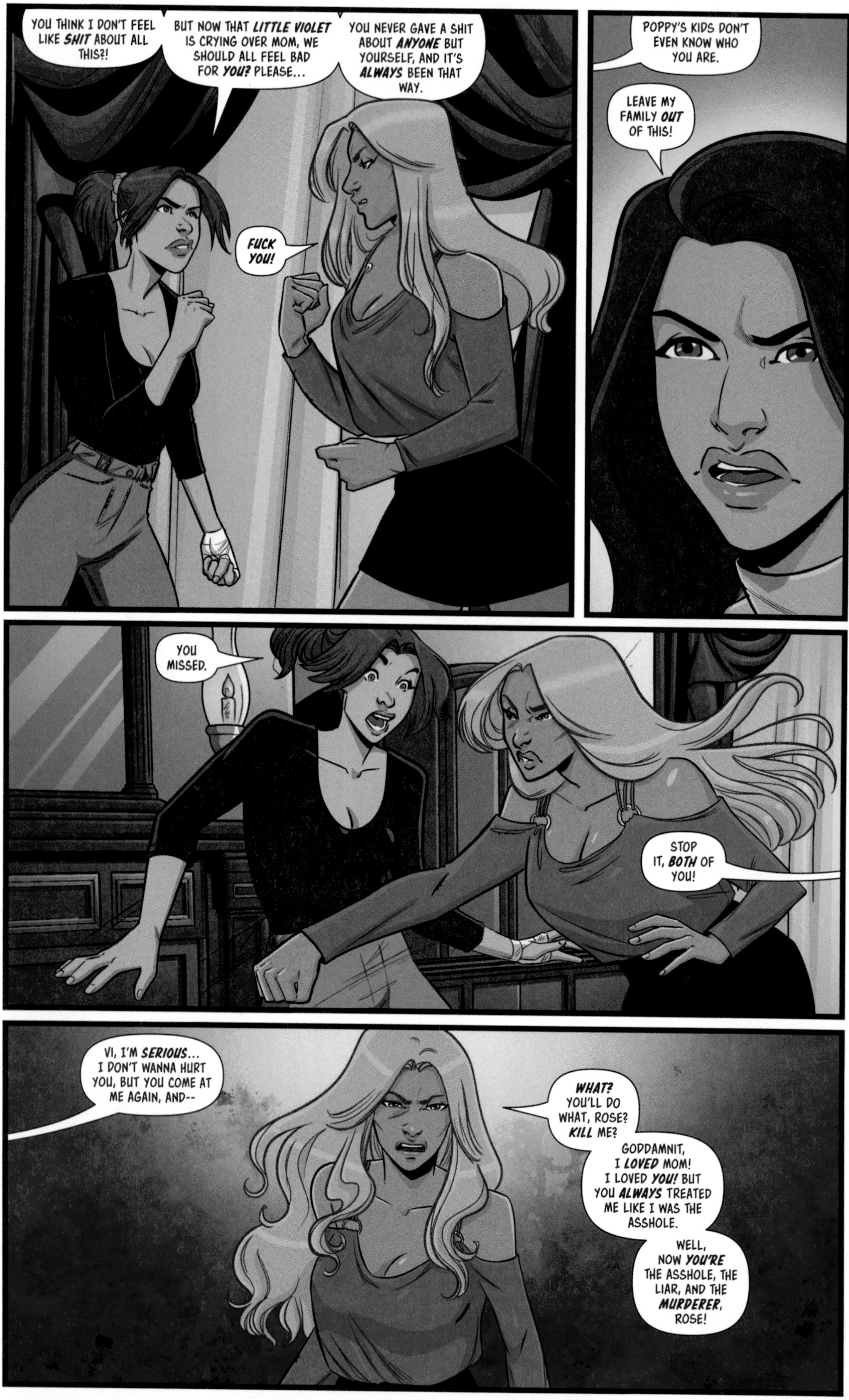
YOU THINK I DON'T FEEL LIKE SHIT ABOUT ALL THIS?!
BUT NOW THAT LITTLE VIOLET IS CRYING OVER MOM, WE SHOULD ALL FEEL BAD FOR YOU? PLEASE...
YOU NEVER GAVE A SHIT ABOUT ANYONE BUT YOURSELF, AND IT'S ALWAYS BEEN THAT WAY.
FUCK YOU!
POPPY'S KIDS DON'T EVEN KNOW WHO YOU ARE.
LEAVE MY FAMILY OUT OF THIS!
YOU MISSED.
STOP IT, BOTH OF YOU!
VI, I'M SERIOUS... I DON'T WANNA HURT YOU, BUT YOU COME AT ME AGAIN, AND--
WHAT? YOU'LL DO WHAT, ROSE? KILL ME?
GODDAMNIT, I LOVED MOM! I LOVED YOU! BUT YOU ALWAYS TREATED ME LIKE I WAS THE ASSHOLE.
WELL, NOW YOU'RE THE ASSHOLE, THE LIAR, AND THE MURDERER, ROSE!

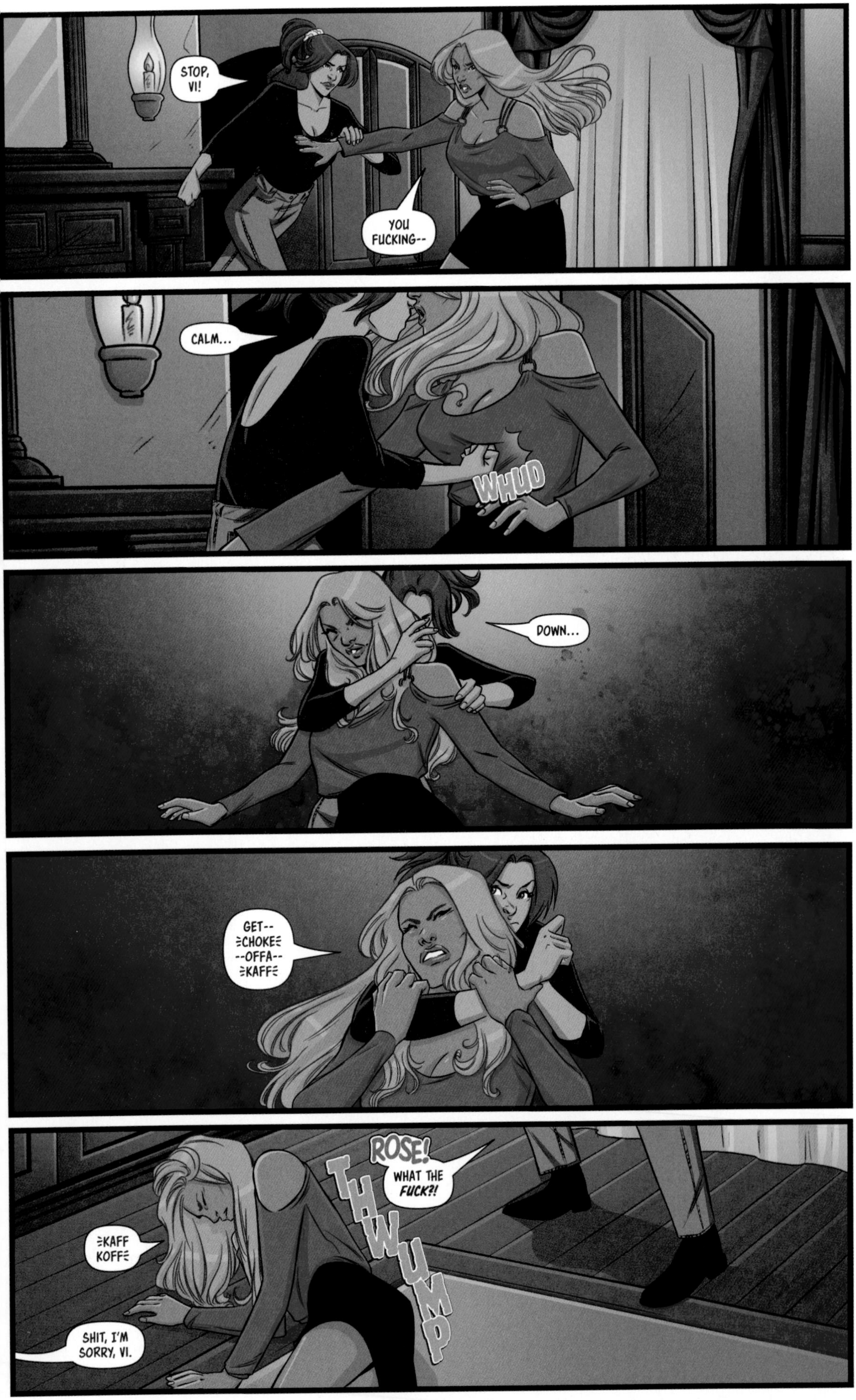
STOP, VI!
YOU FUCKING--
CALM...
WHUD
DOWN...
GET-- ≡CHOKE≡ --OFFA-- ≡KAFF≡
ROSE! WHAT THE *FUCK?!*
THWUMP
≡KAFF KOFF≡
SHIT, I'M SORRY, VI.

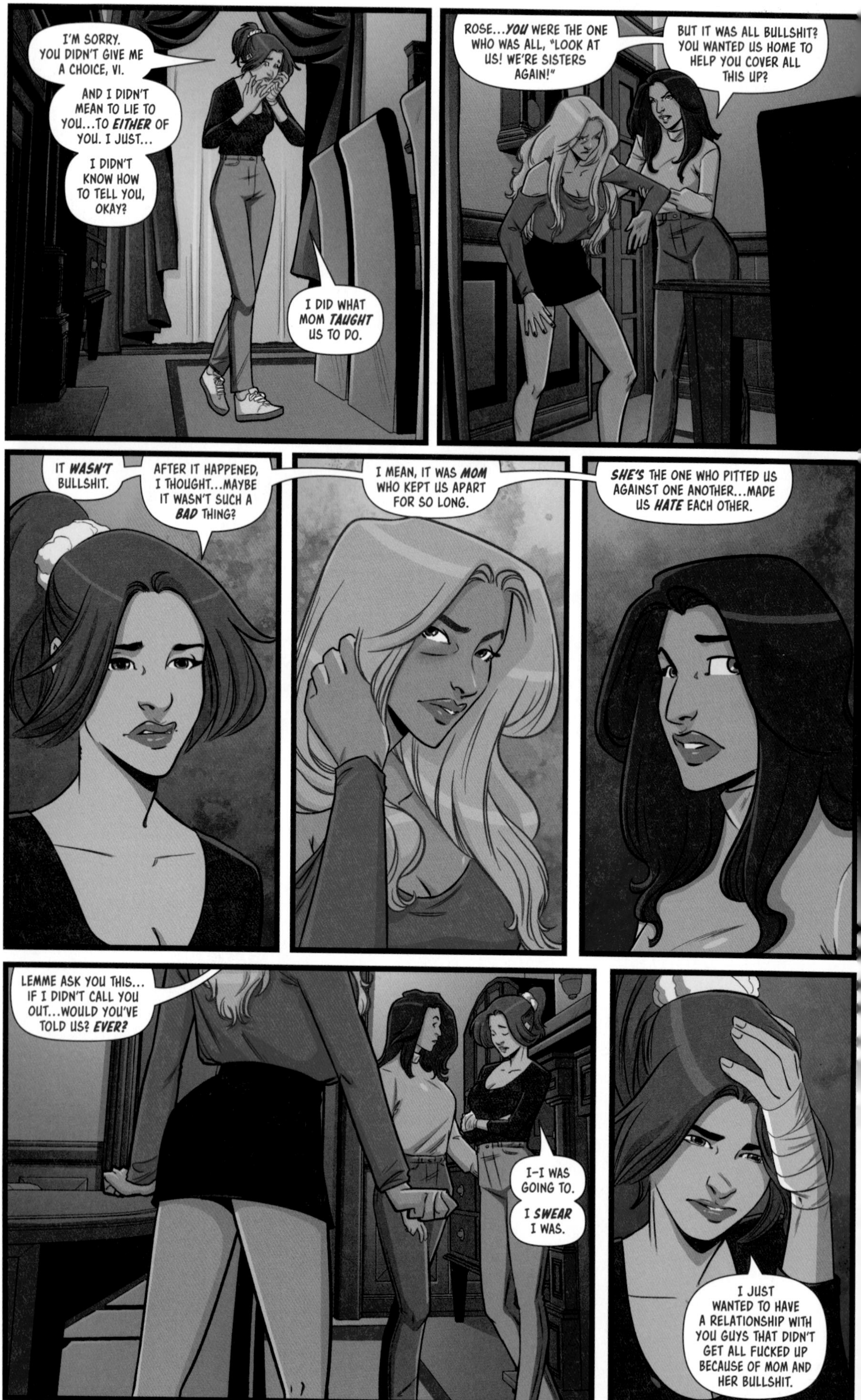
I'M SORRY. YOU DIDN'T GIVE ME A CHOICE, VI.
AND I DIDN'T MEAN TO LIE TO YOU...TO *EITHER* OF YOU. I JUST...
I DIDN'T KNOW HOW TO TELL YOU, OKAY?
I DID WHAT MOM *TAUGHT* US TO DO.
ROSE...*YOU* WERE THE ONE WHO WAS ALL, "LOOK AT US! WE'RE SISTERS AGAIN!"
BUT IT WAS ALL BULLSHIT? YOU WANTED US HOME TO HELP YOU COVER ALL THIS UP?
IT *WASN'T* BULLSHIT.
AFTER IT HAPPENED, I THOUGHT...MAYBE IT WASN'T SUCH A *BAD* THING?
I MEAN, IT WAS *MOM* WHO KEPT US APART FOR SO LONG.
SHE'S THE ONE WHO PITTED US AGAINST ONE ANOTHER...MADE US *HATE* EACH OTHER.
LEMME ASK YOU THIS... IF I DIDN'T CALL YOU OUT...WOULD YOU'VE TOLD US? *EVER?*
I-I WAS GOING TO.
I *SWEAR* I WAS.
I JUST WANTED TO HAVE A RELATIONSHIP WITH YOU GUYS THAT DIDN'T GET ALL FUCKED UP BECAUSE OF MOM AND HER BULLSHIT.

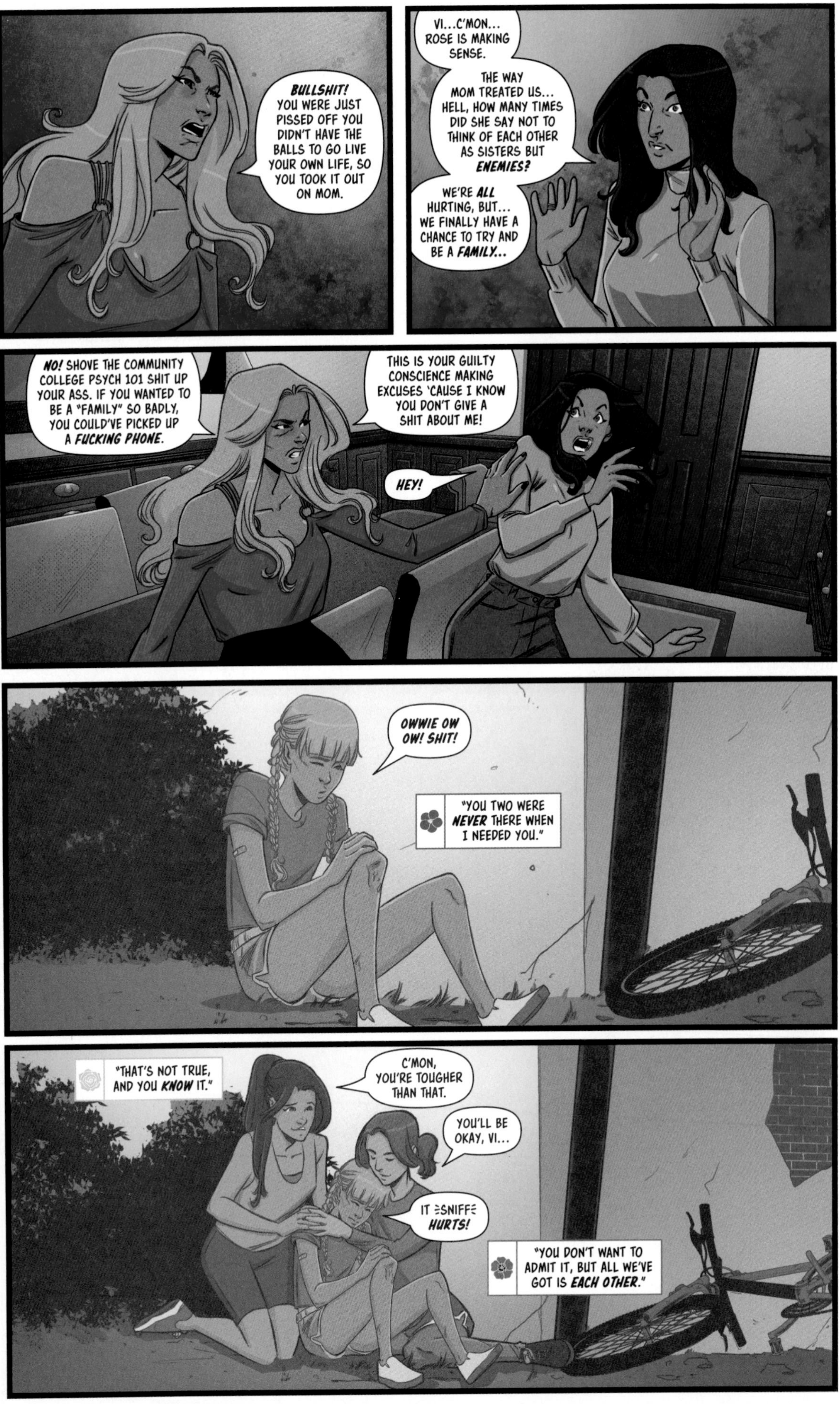
BULLSHIT! YOU WERE JUST PISSED OFF YOU DIDN'T HAVE THE BALLS TO GO LIVE YOUR OWN LIFE, SO YOU TOOK IT OUT ON MOM.
VI...C'MON... ROSE IS MAKING SENSE.
THE WAY MOM TREATED US... HELL, HOW MANY TIMES DID SHE SAY NOT TO THINK OF EACH OTHER AS SISTERS BUT ENEMIES?
WE'RE ALL HURTING, BUT... WE FINALLY HAVE A CHANCE TO TRY AND BE A FAMILY...
NO! SHOVE THE COMMUNITY COLLEGE PSYCH 101 SHIT UP YOUR ASS. IF YOU WANTED TO BE A "FAMILY" SO BADLY, YOU COULD'VE PICKED UP A FUCKING PHONE.
THIS IS YOUR GUILTY CONSCIENCE MAKING EXCUSES 'CAUSE I KNOW YOU DON'T GIVE A SHIT ABOUT ME!
HEY!
OWWIE OW OW! SHIT!
"YOU TWO WERE NEVER THERE WHEN I NEEDED YOU."
"THAT'S NOT TRUE, AND YOU KNOW IT."
C'MON, YOU'RE TOUGHER THAN THAT.
YOU'LL BE OKAY, VI...
IT *SNIFF* HURTS!
"YOU DON'T WANT TO ADMIT IT, BUT ALL WE'VE GOT IS EACH OTHER."

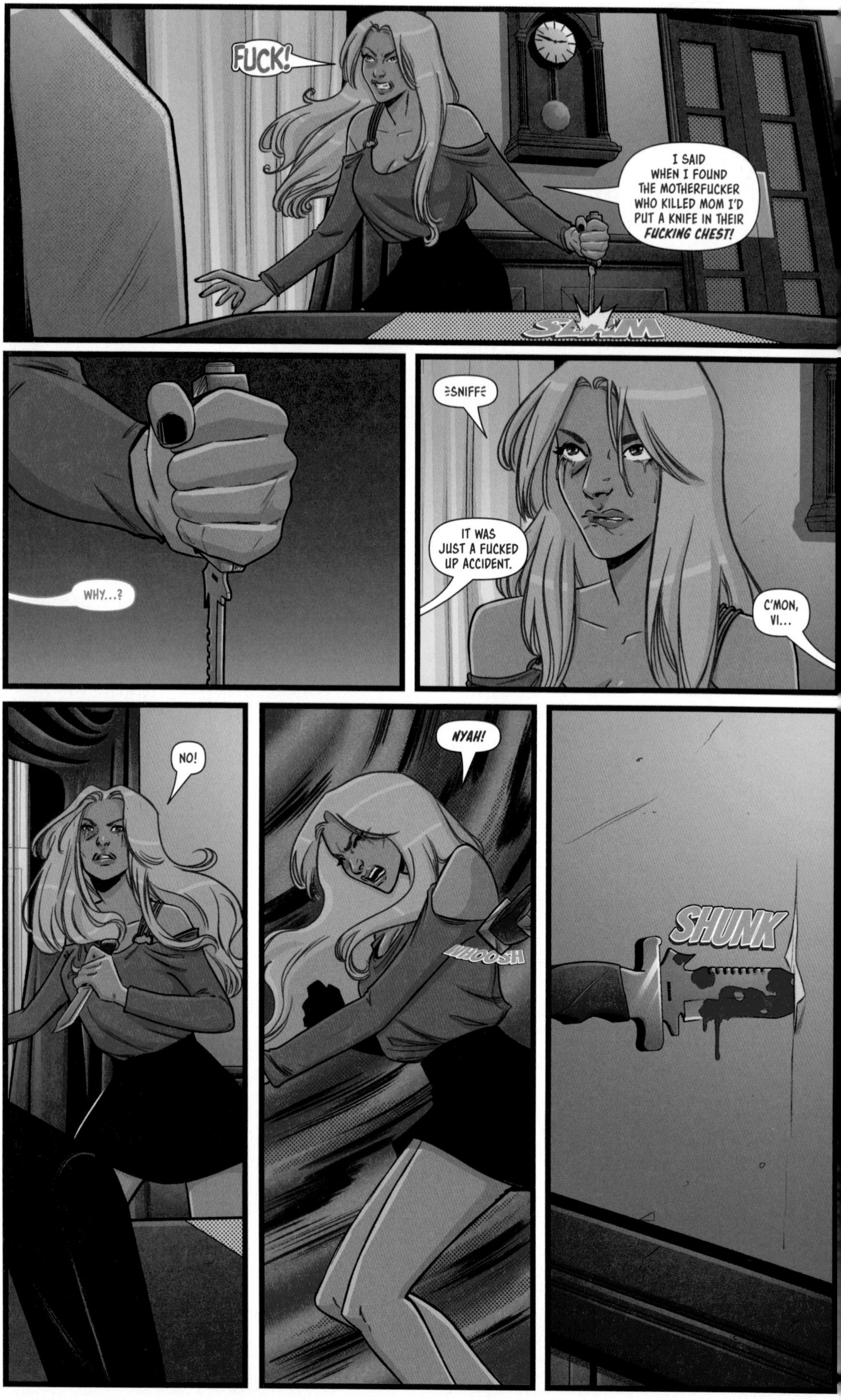
FUCK!
I SAID WHEN I FOUND THE MOTHERFUCKER WHO KILLED MOM I'D PUT A KNIFE IN THEIR FUCKING CHEST!
SLAM
WHY...?
SNIFF
IT WAS JUST A FUCKED UP ACCIDENT.
C'MON, VI...
NO!
NYAH!
WHOOSH
SHUNK

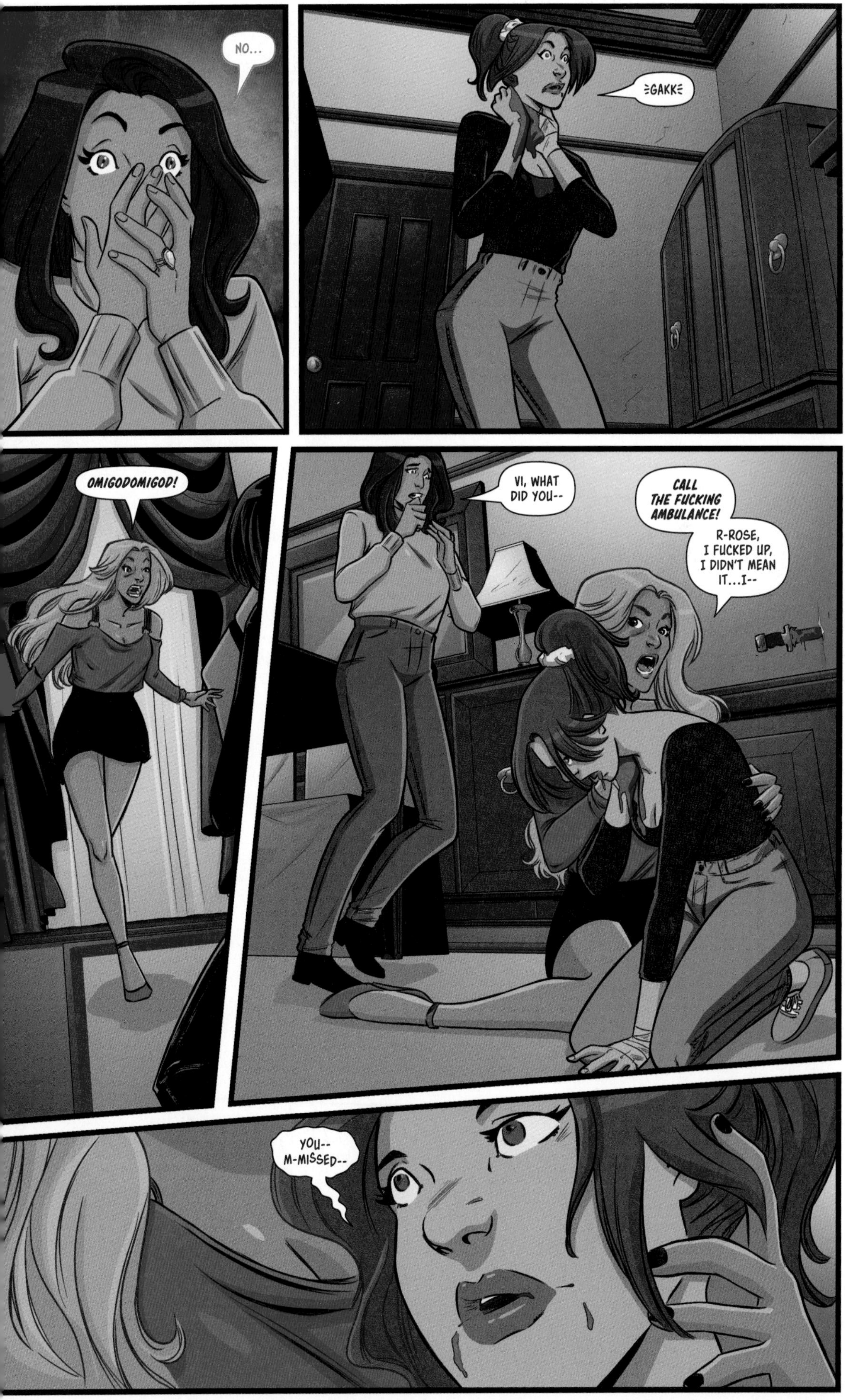
NO...
≡GAKK≡
OMIGODOMIGOD!
VI, WHAT DID YOU--
CALL THE FUCKING AMBULANCE!
R-ROSE, I FUCKED UP, I DIDN'T MEAN IT...I--
YOU-- M-MISSED--

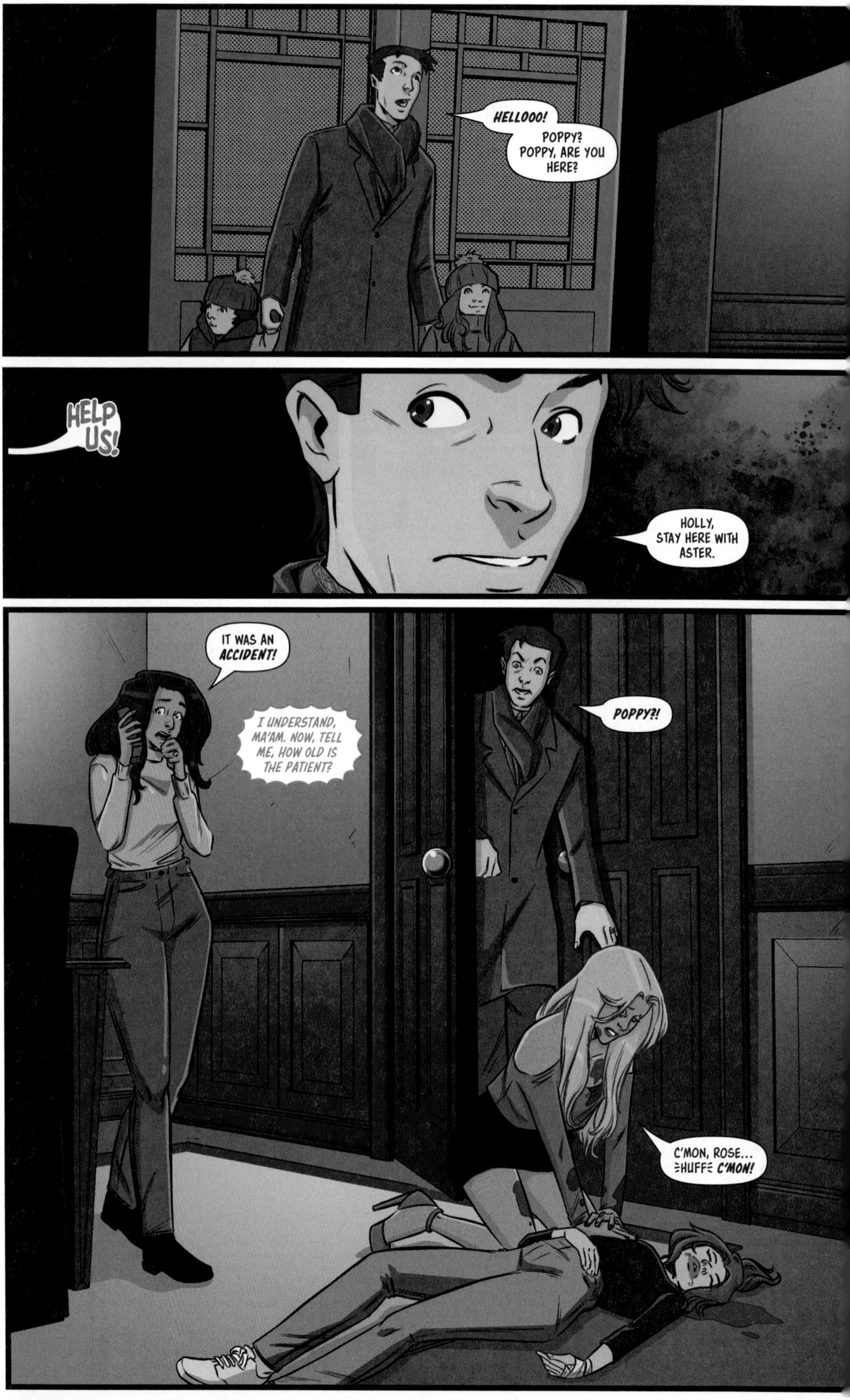
HELLOOO!
POPPY? POPPY, ARE YOU HERE?
HELP US!
HOLLY, STAY HERE WITH ASTER.
IT WAS AN ACCIDENT!
I UNDERSTAND, MA'AM. NOW, TELL ME, HOW OLD IS THE PATIENT?
POPPY?!
C'MON, ROSE... HUFF C'MON!

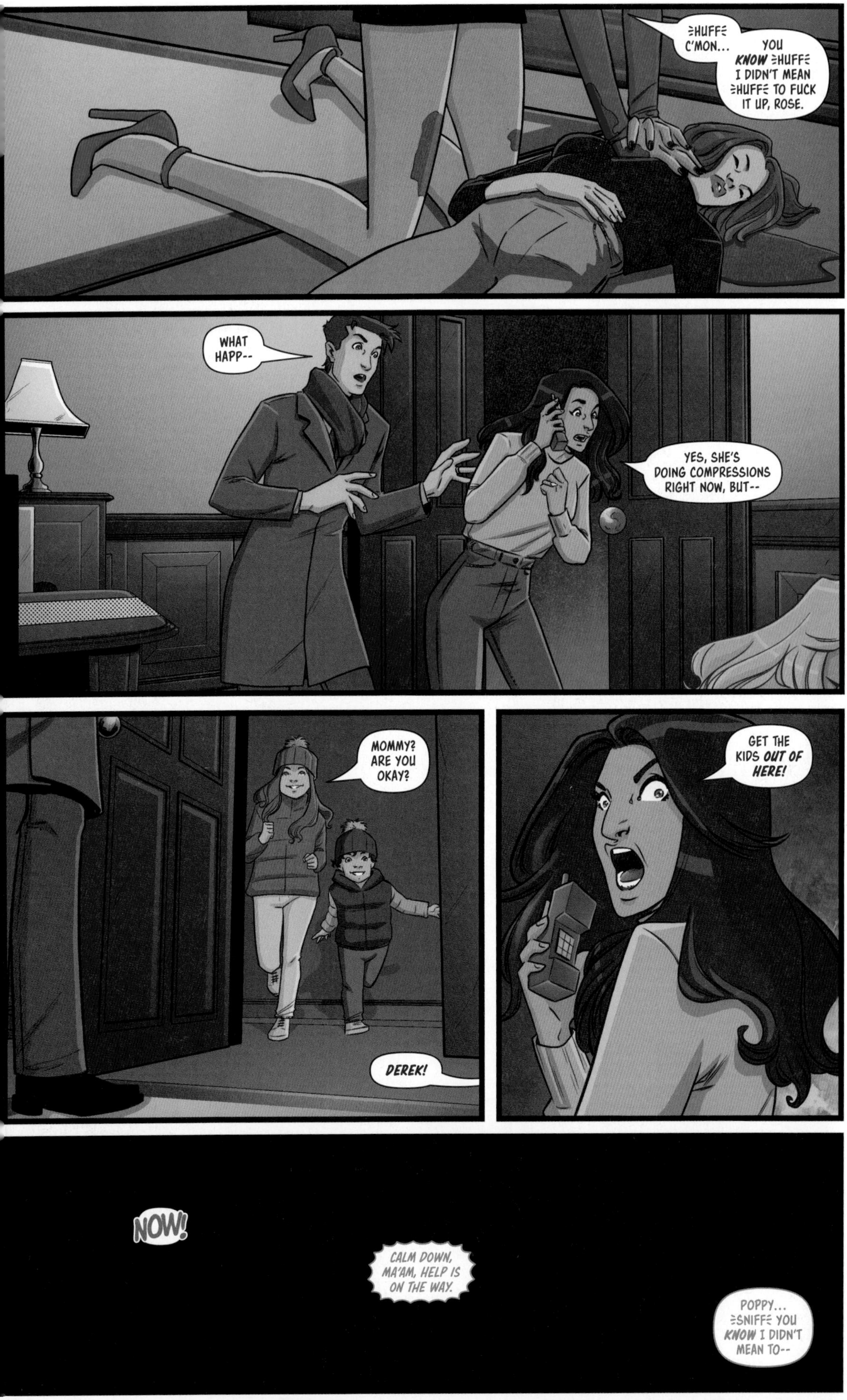

=HUFF= C'MON... YOU KNOW =HUFF= I DIDN'T MEAN =HUFF= TO FUCK IT UP, ROSE.
WHAT HAPP--
YES, SHE'S DOING COMPRESSIONS RIGHT NOW, BUT--
MOMMY? ARE YOU OKAY?
DEREK!
GET THE KIDS OUT OF HERE!
NOW!
CALM DOWN, MA'AM, HELP IS ON THE WAY.
POPPY... =SNIFF= YOU KNOW I DIDN'T MEAN TO--

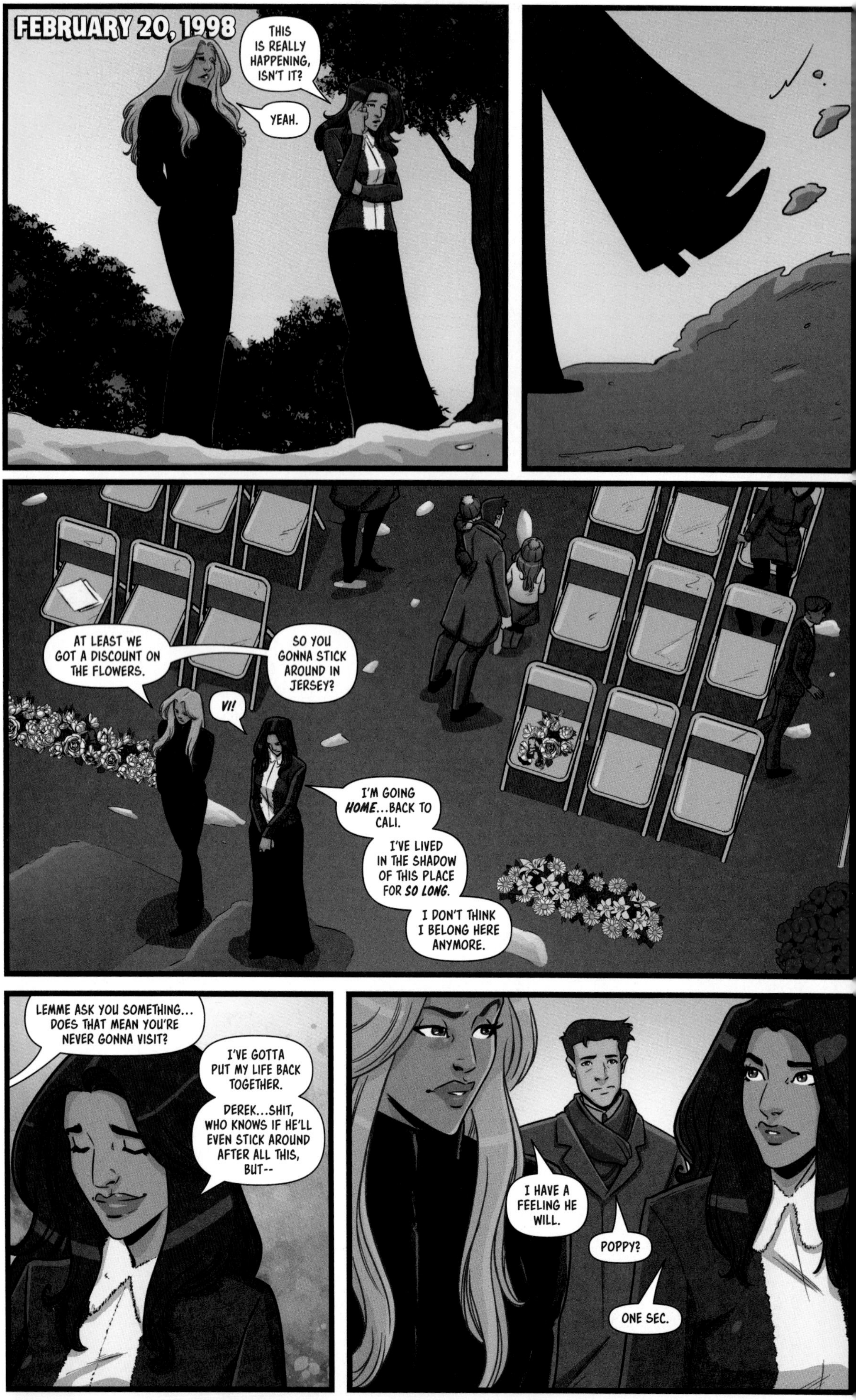
FEBRUARY 20, 1998
THIS IS REALLY HAPPENING, ISN'T IT?
YEAH.
AT LEAST WE GOT A DISCOUNT ON THE FLOWERS.
SO YOU GONNA STICK AROUND IN JERSEY?
VI!
I'M GOING HOME...BACK TO CALI.
I'VE LIVED IN THE SHADOW OF THIS PLACE FOR SO LONG.
I DON'T THINK I BELONG HERE ANYMORE.
LEMME ASK YOU SOMETHING... DOES THAT MEAN YOU'RE NEVER GONNA VISIT?
I'VE GOTTA PUT MY LIFE BACK TOGETHER.
DEREK...SHIT, WHO KNOWS IF HE'LL EVEN STICK AROUND AFTER ALL THIS, BUT--
I HAVE A FEELING HE WILL.
POPPY?
ONE SEC.

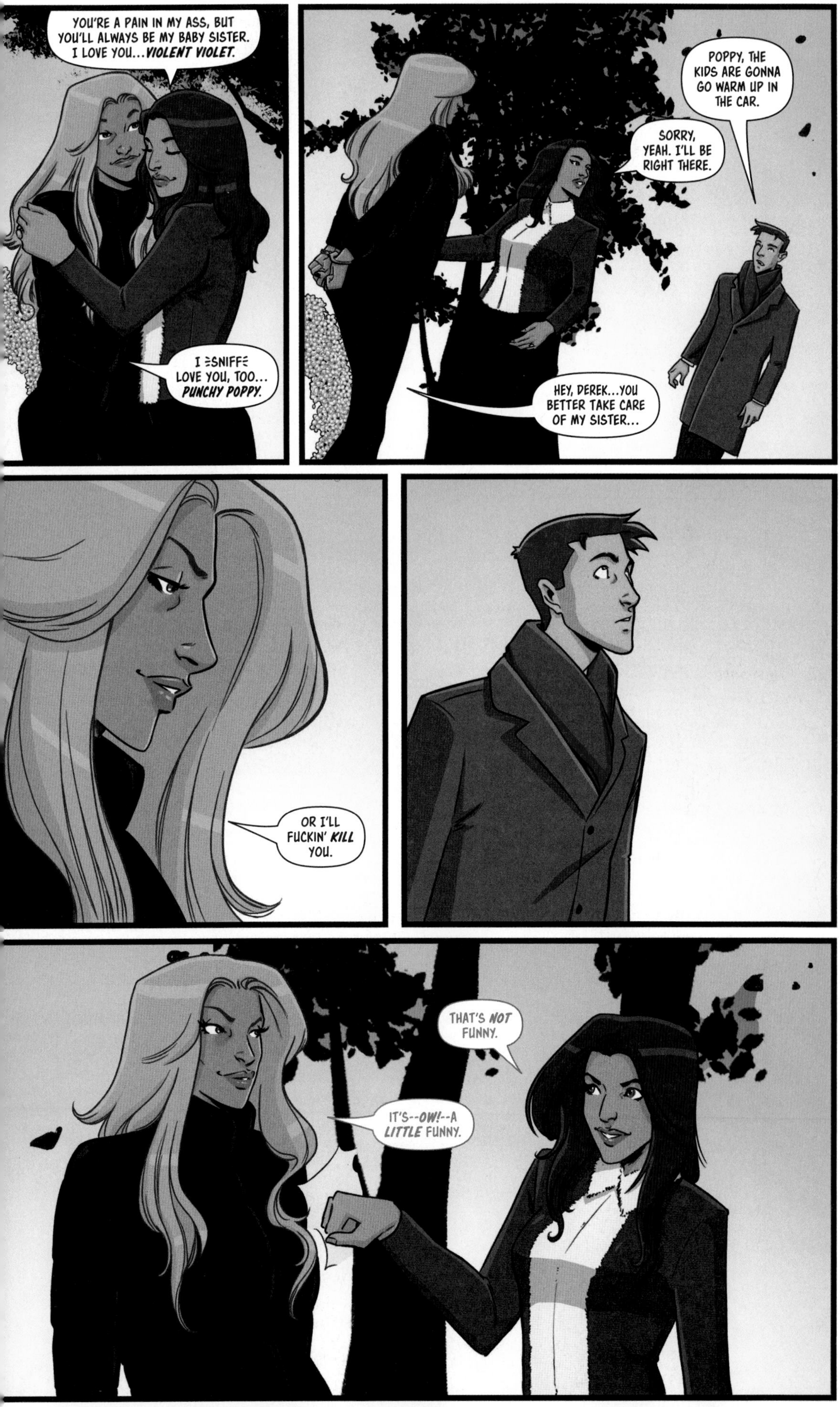
YOU'RE A PAIN IN MY ASS, BUT YOU'LL ALWAYS BE MY BABY SISTER. I LOVE YOU... VIOLENT VIOLET.
I =SNIFF= LOVE YOU, TOO... PUNCHY POPPY.
POPPY, THE KIDS ARE GONNA GO WARM UP IN THE CAR.
SORRY, YEAH. I'LL BE RIGHT THERE.
HEY, DEREK... YOU BETTER TAKE CARE OF MY SISTER...
OR I'LL FUCKIN' KILL YOU.
THAT'S NOT FUNNY.
IT'S--OW!--A LITTLE FUNNY.

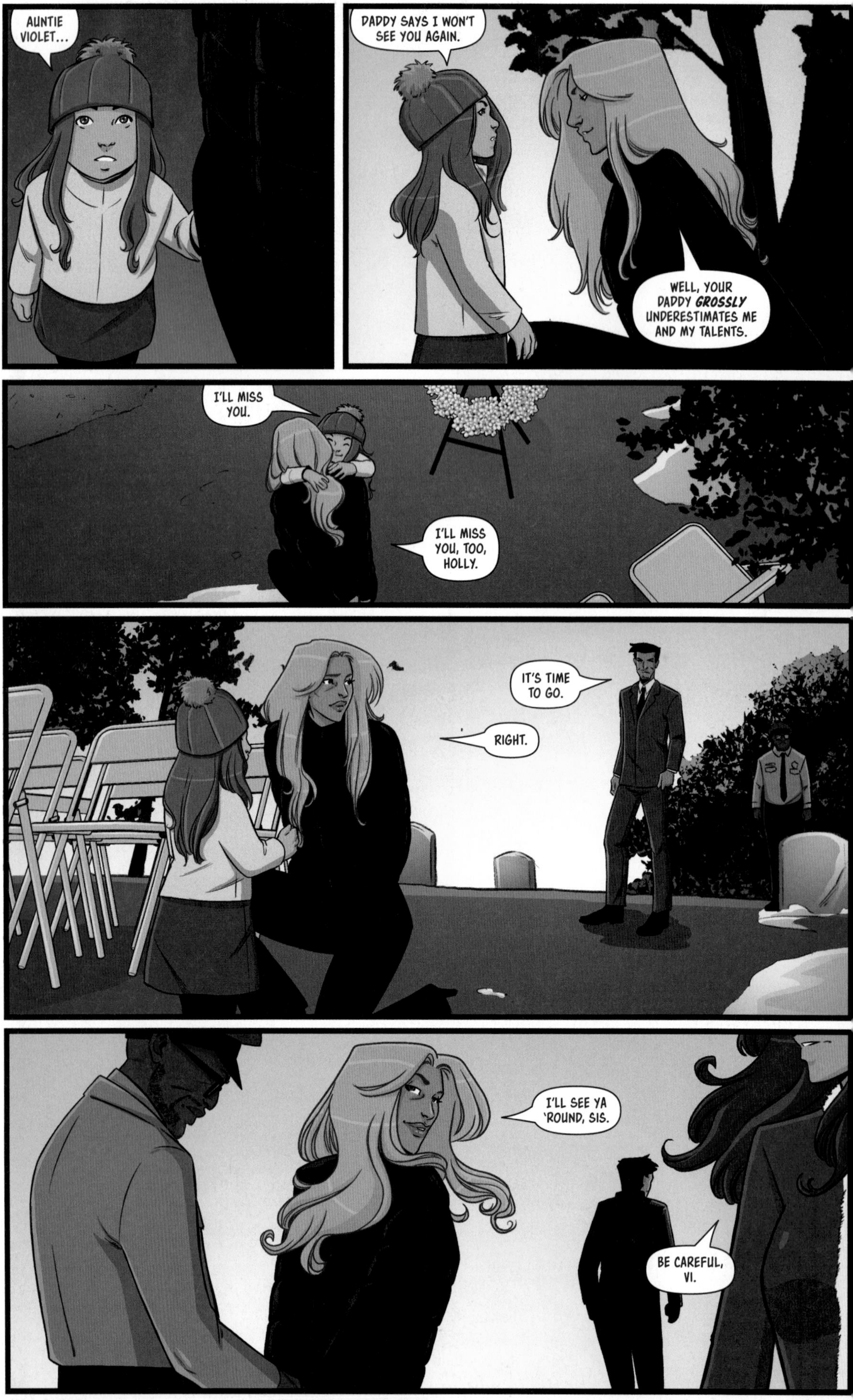
AUNTIE VIOLET...
DADDY SAYS I WON'T SEE YOU AGAIN.
WELL, YOUR DADDY GROSSLY UNDERESTIMATES ME AND MY TALENTS.
I'LL MISS YOU.
I'LL MISS YOU, TOO, HOLLY.
IT'S TIME TO GO.
RIGHT.
I'LL SEE YA 'ROUND, SIS.
BE CAREFUL, VI.

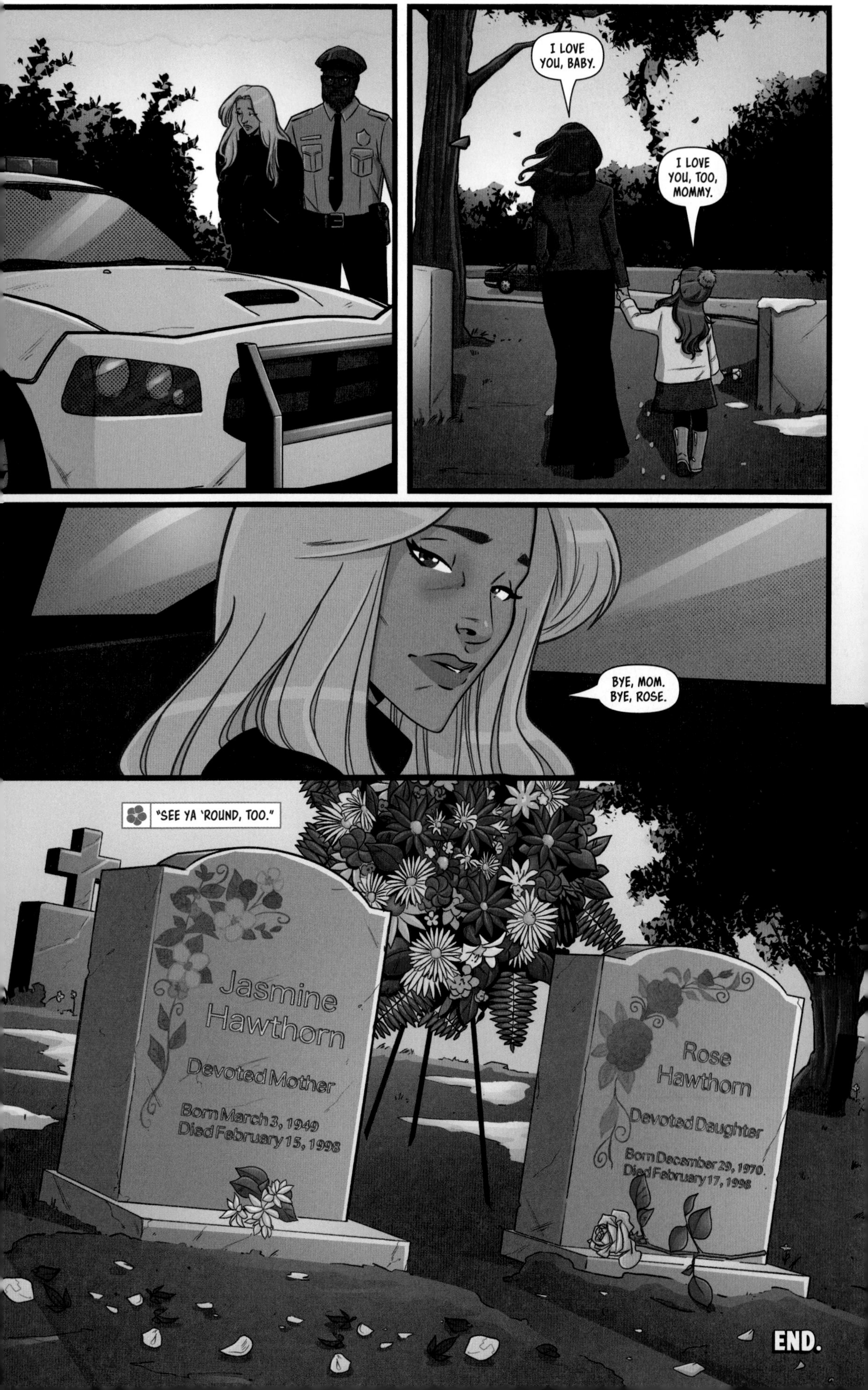
I LOVE YOU, BABY.
I LOVE YOU, TOO, MOMMY.
BYE, MOM. BYE, ROSE.
"SEE YA 'ROUND, TOO."
Jasmine Hawthorn
Devoted Mother
Born March 3, 1949
Died February 15, 1998
Rose Hawthorn
Devoted Daughter
Born December 29, 1970
Died February 17, 1998
END.

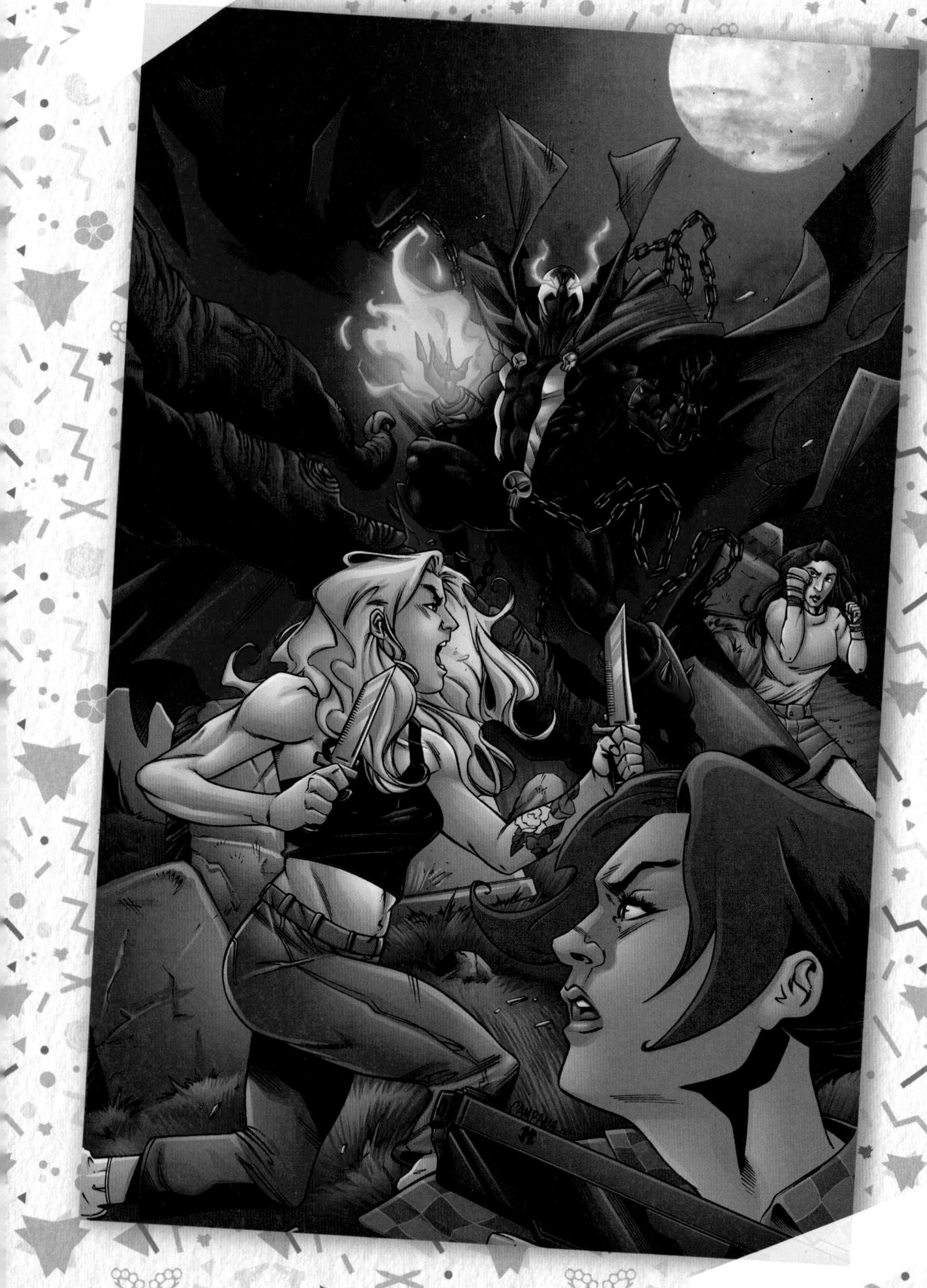

ISSUE #5 SPAWN VARIANT

CHRIS CAMPANA, JEREMY CLARK & TOM CHU